A
Finntown
of the
Heart

Patricia Johnson Eilola

NORTH STAR PRESS OF ST. CLOUD, INC.

Cover photo of Virginia, Minnesota, circa 1920s, showing an open pit mine in the background. (Courtesy of the Virginia Area Historical Society) The back cover shows a typical house in Kinney in which the Brosi family might have lived.

Printed in the United States of America by Versa Press, Inc., East Peoria, Illinois.

Published by   North Star Press of St. Cloud, Inc.
               P.O. Box 451
               St. Cloud, Minnesota 56302

Dedication

Bump, this one's for you . . .
with all my love and thanks
for patience and support
far beyond any call of duty
or any marriage vow.

Preface

My mother, Ilmi Marianna Brosi has, for most of her eighty-eight years, been far better known as Marion Brosi or as Mrs. Clifford Johnson to students who have loved her almost as much as we do. Her remembrances and her indomitable spirit constitute the base line of this story.

Uncle Charles really did live—and die—in Ely. His obituary appeared in the May 23, 1923, issue of the *Ely Miner*. But the story of his death and the disappearance of the money he had withdrawn for the downpayment on a farm in Zim, based on family legend, took on a life of their own in my imagination, as did the personalities of the people whose lives—or names—appeared in Mom's reminiscences.

Because the magnificent work done on the history of Ely and the Great Scott Township centennial book provided specific information and, therefore, I hope, an air of verisimilitude to the book, I drew upon the stories found in each text freely, interweaving the memories of those pioneers into the story as a whole. The specific settings for the chapters, however, and the characters who appear in this book, no matter their names, are wholly the products of the imagination of the writer. Even Ilmi Marianna Brosi, no matter her origin, took on her own identity, as did Alex Savolainen and the grandfather and John Porthan and Diodado Carmen Joseph Vanucci and all the others. Should anyone suppose to know anyone with the name or identity of a character in this novel, he or she must remember that this is a work of fiction, albeit historical fiction, so that, while some events, some people are part of my family's history, this story is not and should not be considered a parallel to real life even though, for me, the characters became as real as members of my own family. Like Ilmi Marianna, I grieve for the loss of Young Mr. Smith; I cherish the kindness of the gypsies, the Savolainens, the young John Porthan, and Jaacko.

The creative process is a strange one. It draws the writer into another world, one which is at least as real as this. Those who live in that world come alive of their own accord. When they do, they become friends, enemies, accomplices, protagonists, cherished or hated members of an extended family that never lived at all and yet will live forever . . . as long as there are books to write . . . and readers to enjoy them.

Prologue

I remember the exact moment—the time and the place—when I discovered the key to power—my own power.

As soon as I was old enough to talk, Ma made it clear that crying was not the key to getting what I wanted, not for me, anyway. When Lil cried, Ma picked her up and crooned and cuddled her. Crying worked for her, and eventually she turned into an expert at it. But when I cried, Ma slapped my face.

"Don't act like a baby, a great girl like you," she said—in Finnish—if my face even began to pucker in warning. "What do you want?"

If I pointed, she snapped, "Use your words. Communicate."

Unfortunately, I could not always find my words. I did not have very many of my own. Ma's words worked well enough when we lived in Port Arthur, Canada, with Aunt Betty, though if I tried Aunt Betty's words on for size, Ma slapped my face again. Every time.

The problem compounded itself when we got to the train station to buy three tickets for Ma and Lil and me to go from Port Arthur to Thief River Falls in Minnesota. Then Ma's words failed completely—failed me, even failed her. Neither the man at the ticket office nor the conductor on the train understood one word that came from her mouth. It was abundantly clear from the looks on their faces and the tones of their voices that to them she was talking jibberish.

It's only Finnish, I wanted to tell them. But I didn't know their words either.

Aunt Betty told Ma in Finn to *"Pane suus kiini."* I expected Ma to slap her face even though adults as a rule don't, of course, even when told most rudely to shut their mouths. But, holding her legendary temper in check—with a considerable effort, her lips compressed and cheeks red—Ma did as she had been told and kept still.

"Three ticket-ia," Aunt Betty indicated with word and gesture. The gesture helped. The words slipped away from me, for though they had the Finnish lilt, they had no Finnish substance. Pointing at Ma, then me, then Lil, she counted. Not *"yksi, kaksi, kolme"* but "one, two, three."

The ticket man frowned briefly, his face wrinkling, then nodded and, reaching under the counter, began to tear tickets from wide flat rolls. Watching him, I counted and repeated the words Aunt Betty had used—"one, two, three"—first mouthing them, then saying them out loud.

The ticket man cast me a sidewise look of approval: "Well, good. At least one of you can speak the King's English."

Hurrying away from the line that had formed behind us, Ma gave me the tickets to hold, admonishing me sternly—in Finnish, of course—not to lose them. She had her hands full with the carpetbags and Lil and the lunch Aunt Betty had fixed us and her own long skirts, which dragged in the dirt. Ma hated dirt.

Lil was crying as we stood on the platform, not so much because of the train, though it was enormous, the wheels alone taller than she, but because of the noise and the steam it belched from smoke stacks on top and from its undercarriage. I wrinkled my nose at the reek of coal and the heavy hot whorls of gray-white swirling around us. Our trunk had disappeared, but since neither Ma nor Aunt Betty remonstrated when it was loaded on a flat-bed wagon with a lot of other trunks and trundled down the wide wooden sidewalk stretching between the depot and the tracks, I forebore from crying or pointing.

Ma shushed Lil much less gently than usual as she continued her juggling act, trying to get everything on board and still hold onto Lil, who was by that time both screaming and struggling. I followed in Ma's wake, holding the tickets firmly and carefully in front of me like a beacon.

The conductor doffed his hat to Ma and offered her, not the arm that courtesy usually dictated, but an actual two-handed lift propelling Lil and her together up the two stairs from the platform to the clanking iron floor forming a juncture between our passenger car and the one behind. Slinging the carpet bags up behind her, he turned to me.

Slowly, standing erect and proud, I offered him the tickets, counting them as the ticket master had done: "One. Two. Three."

"Thank you, young lady," he responded with a nod and a smile, waving the tickets aside. "Have a good trip." Just as if I were a real lady, he put a hand under my elbow and assisted me, too, up the stairs.

It did not take much wit to grasp his general meaning or to understand that "*kiitos*" would not do as a response so I tried repeating his first words, articulating them as clearly as I could. "Th-tha-n-k you." I had some trouble with the first word, but the second formed itself easily, I thought rather smugly.

The attempt earned me a second smile and a gesture just between a full tip of the hat and a salute: his hand almost lifted the hat off his head. But not quite.

Obviously I wasn't quite the lady I wished myself to be.

Then I hustled after Ma, who by then had found two seats on the depot side of the train so we could wave good-bye to Aunt Betty. Shoving the carpetbags under the seats, she stood back waiting with tapping foot for me to slide into the seat by the window before settling herself into the aisle seat with a deep sigh and Lil on her lap.

Mostly on her lap. Lil's squirming had reached a proportion of movement equivalent to the decibels of her voice, and Ma was hard put to keep her there. Lil had just learned to walk—well, to toddle really—by herself. Rebelling at the enforced constraint, she was determined to be released to do her own thing.

It behooved me to sit still and hang onto the tickets.

A piece of *korppua* Aunt Betty had slathered with butter before packing it into the lunch basket helped with Lil—food always did— though Ma's sigh made it clear that she knew where the butter would end up. Not in Lil's mouth. She was no more neat than she was quiet.

Although I desperately wanted to kneel on the seat to see what was going on, I stayed put, twitching my dress to keep it from wrinkling.

The back door slammed shut, and I heard the conductor repeat the same phrase over and over again as he advanced up the aisle. Since we were sitting in the eighth row of seats from the back, I practiced the phrase, mouthing the words as best I could without sound until he reached us.

"Tickets, please." He reached out a hand.

"Tickets. One. Two. Three." I said the words loudly, reaching across Ma to hand them to him. Ma did not slap me for reaching.

Keeping his balance without visible effort though the train had begun jolting forward, he responded mechanically, "Thank you."

It didn't seem necessary, but I wanted the practice so I mimicked the sounds, emphasizing the "you."

Smiling briefly, he touched his hat and nodded at Ma before continuing up the aisle.

Ma drew a deep sigh of relief and told me in Finnish that we were finally on our way to Minnesota and to Pa.

Although I did not shake my head, for that would have been impolite and difficult to explain, in my heart I sensed that she was not altogether correct. We had begun one kind of journey, but another even more difficult one lay before us, for every time we opened our mouths, we confirmed the fact that we were not Canadians and certainly not Americans. We were Finns, traveling from Finntown in Port Arthur, Canada, to the home of Pa's relatives living just across the border in a Finnish community called Malcolm near Thief River Falls.

None of those words came clearly to my mind right then, of course. Even now, it is difficult to explain that second journey, which has had only a little to do with borders and trains and countries and much more to do with ourselves and others' perceptions of us. Dimly, deep inside, I knew it would be a difficult path to tread, a path with the signposts all written in the wrong language because—for all of my admittedly young life and for all of Ma's many more years—all of our thoughts and feelings had been formed into shape by our words, and our words and thoughts had all been in Finnish.

Dimly, deep inside of me, I had begun to understand that we could no longer rely on or trust in those words. They had lost their power, and in their lea we too drifted, helpless. As the train jerked and snorted and steamed and huffed slowly away from the depot, leaving behind Aunt Betty, waving her handkerchief and patting her eyes and waving some more, I realized I did not know the name of or the word for or the meaning of anything around me— except the words I knew in Finnish. The window out of which I looked, the seat where I sat, the signs on the walls, the conversations ebbing and swirling around us like the steam had meaning and identity for me only when they were articulated in Finnish, and the look on the ticket master's face had made it clear that we had been found wanting. In his eyes, we had been the less.

In my mind's eye I could see Pa waving good-bye to us as Aunt Betty just had but long ago, from high on the deck of the *S. S. America*, sailing from Port Arthur down Lake Superior to Duluth, Minnesota, where he planned to seek a job and find us a new home. Up and down the boat had moved, even though it had been lashed to the dock with ropes thicker than my arm. Around it, waves rose and fell. Huge as that boat seemed, they bobbed it up and down, pulling it sideways away from the dock. Or perhaps the boat was itself unwilling to stay in place, tied up, as was Lil right now. I remembered the ropes being pulled up and the *America* moving away. I had waved until I could not see Pa anymore. I had hoped he was there somewhere waving still at us, but I couldn't communicate the wish because of the distance between us, a distance that had widened with every day of the long long weeks and months since he left.

Now suddenly I was the one leaving, and my power to communicate was failing again, not just because of distance this time, but because of a total and abysmal lack of words.

Leaning back against the seat, adhering to that firm textured surface, I nonetheless felt totally adrift.

"Use your words," Ma always insisted. Suddenly I had none. Well, almost none. Six at the most. And Ma had none at all! We could not get far with "tickets, one, two, three" and "thank you." "Hopeless," I thought, trying to stop the tears that threatened to make themselves visible, "It's hopeless."

Reaching down to the basket to find another piece for Lil, Ma turned to ask me if I wanted some *korppua*, too. That did it. The tears spilled out. Of course, she had asked me in Finnish.

I answered. In Finnish. In despair.

We were going to the United States of America. To Minnesota, where people spoke an English even newer than the King's. How would we survive? How could we communicate when we knew no words?

Looking out the window, unseeing, I worried at those questions, picking them apart and putting them back together without finding any solution, eating my *korppua* and some *fiilia* from a white stoneware bowl that just that morning had sat in Aunt Betty's cupboard, taking my turn to walk Lil up and down the aisle, making myself smaller so the two of us could sit on the same seat, and crooning songs to her, in Finnish of course, until, as exhausted and frustrated as I but for a different reason, she finally fell asleep.

In the process of caring for Lil, I added a seventh word to my list. On the doorway in back of the passenger car I saw the letters "t-o-i-l-e-t." I could not decode the letters even had they been in Finnish since I had not yet learned to read, but when I opened the door, I understood clearly what that English word meant.

The conductor, walking by me, said clearly, slowly, and rather unnecessarily, as if I were hard of hearing and slow of wit, "That's the *toilet*."

I had no pencil to use to write the word down. No paper. Very little skill with either had they been at hand. So I committed the letters to memory, their shape and their obvious definition.

In retrospect, I think that may have been the moment, the time and the place, when I took hold of my destiny. I knew one English word. I knew its letters. I knew its meaning. It was a start, clarifying for me a direction, a goal. Even though I didn't know exactly where we would ultimately find a home, for we still did not even know how to find Pa, I had identified where *I* wanted to go: to the land of the literate. An English land.

We had heard nothing from Pa since he left us in Port Arthur. I liked to think that was because neither Ma nor I knew how to read and write. In reality, had he tried, he could have gotten word to us somehow. We did find out, indirectly and via the normal Finnish grapevine, that he and others with whom he had traveled down the shores of Lake Superior to the port of Duluth, had left that city, finding it inhospitable to those without either knowledge of the language or seafaring skills.

Unfortunately, Pa lacked any kind of useful skill: he did not know how to dovetail the corner of a log cabin or, for that matter, how to choose or cut the trees used to build a homestead house. He had never sown a seed, weeded a field, scythed or threshed grain, or taken care of farm animals.

Instead, before he left Finland, he had gone to school, learning to write a fine hand and read and write Finnish, Swedish, and a bit of Russian. Poetry rolled from his pen in metric measure, and he knew the names, the Latin ones and the Finnish ones, for all the plants and animals in the world, it seemed to me.

Much later when I was in high school, in a biographical sketch of the English writer and artist, William Blake, I recognized Pa. Ma and I could have echoed Mrs. Blake's description of her husband: "I have little of his company," she said. "He is always in Paradise."

Unlike Blake, Pa did not propound to see angels in trees or to have spoken to Jesus; unfortunately, also unlike Blake, he had no innate instinctive sense with which to gauge the basic moral standards of the people he met, being taken in as easily as a child by any smooth-talking visitor. But like Blake, Pa was full of dreams, and sometimes when he floated away into his secret world of thought and feeling, he seemed to be so at one with all things, with the universe, so to speak, that animals came to him without fear, chipmunks nibbling from his fingers, birds perching on his shoulders, deer pausing in their stately tread to meet the gaze of his blue eyes with their brown ones, melding into a silent understanding that cast out fear.

Would that he had the same affinity for Ma and Lil and me.

But, I sighed, as the train slowed down and drew to a halt at the small station in the small town, really more a village, called Thief River Falls, Minnesota, that was probably never to be.

It was Ma who had scraped together enough money with sewing and mending, cooking and baking to buy our tickets. She had decided we would probably best find Pa by contacting his family, and to them she had appealed—by word of mouth, of course.

The only ones to disembark, we clung closely to each other and our trunk, waiting, until a tall, stooped man with a dour face approached us and introduced himself as "Kalle Nestori Brosi." He did not offer to help Ma with Lil or the carpet bags, but he did signal to the trainman to load our trunk onto the back of an open car sitting alongside the platform. Lil and I were directed to the front seat across the gear shift from him; Ma, into the back. Ma's fastidious nose curled at the residual evidence of what had been carried in that car. All three of us clung to the tops of the side doors and Lil and I to each other as the wheels lurched in and out of deep ruts, for the roadway was less road than a fallow field that had been plowed with deep furrows in the prairie grass but never harrowed flat. The car engine snorted as badly as the train, its bald tires bouncing as the car bumped up and down.

Mr. Kalle Nestori Brosi never once turned his head to see how we were doing, which perhaps was just as well, for we were not doing well at all. Lil was too uncomfortable with motion-sickness even to cry. Eventually she threw up, but Ma had the presence of mind to grab her from me and hold her head over the side adding green to the brown of the earth and one more fetid smell to the side of the car. Worst of all, Mr. Kalle Nestori Brosi's contempt for Lil's weakness and his high-handed treatment of Ma and me showed in the set of his shoulders, the straightness of his back, the lifted eyebrows, the distant manner. Pa may have married Ma, his body said, but she was not worthy of the Ambrosius family. She was a peasant.

I knew Ma was smart, but not book-smart. She said it herself with cynical asperity—"I'm just a peasant. What do I know?"—whenever Pa and she butted heads, a common, daily, sometimes hourly occurrence.

Yet Ma made every speck of our clothes, crocheted and knitted caps and mittens, turned and restitched our dresses and coats, felted shoe-packs to line our rubber boots and serve as house slippers during the winter. Ma could make one small chicken last for a whole week of dinners; Ma, wherever we lived, planted a garden so we always had potatoes and rutabaga and carrots. Once she even managed to save a sickly cow from the butcher and nurture it back to health so we could have milk and butter and cream, enough to sell sometimes. There was nothing, in fact, that she could not do around the house and yard.

But I could see her swallowing hard as she clasped a wailing Lil hard against her and gazed back over the rutted path we had just traversed. It was easy to see where we had been, looking back. No matter how high I stretched to peer over the high hood and fenders in front of me, I only caught glimpses of where we were going.

That was probably also for the best. What we saw when the car stopped and we clambered out, shaking our skirts and unkinking knots from muscles that had been too long confined, was hardly prepossessing. "Ramshackle" would have been a good adjective had I known it or the word "adjective." The doors and small windows of the house were open. That meant flies. The barn had been built too close to the house and the manure pile allowed to rise between them. That meant smells. There was no door on the outhouse, also set too near the door. More smells. With no visible sign of a caged or fenced in area or a coop of any kind, chickens and geese apparently roamed at will in and out and around.

The inside of the Brosi cabin was even worse. The curtainless windows were too small and dirty to allow in much light. A clothes line had been strung all across the kitchen, and from it hung what looked like "Sunday shoes" and clothes, none of them clean.

No one smiled. No one greeted us. No one introduced us to Mr. Kalle Nestori Brosi's wife or to the four children sitting hunched over wooden bowls at a table covered with crumbs and food scraps.

Ma swallowed hard. Lil clung to her like a limpet. I went back outside, sat down on the trunk, and heaved a deep sigh. We were in for it now. I wondered how long Ma would hold her temper. I wondered how long it would take for her to build a chicken coop. I wondered how I would ever keep Lil out of the chicken poop. I wondered how Mr. Kalle Nestori Brosi and his wife and children could find room for us in what was obviously no more than a two-room cabin.

And what hope had we of escape? Ma couldn't write a letter to Pa even if she knew where he was, and we didn't. We had no way of making a living, the three of us, with Lil and me so little yet, though I was trying hard to grow, even drinking beet juice and taking cod liver oil, though I hated both.

And worst of all, because all we knew was Finnish, we were ineluctably tied to the Finnish-speaking community. Ma had no hope of getting work, even a job "in service" as a maid, when she had two children tagging along behind her and no command of the language of choice.

We were lost. Almost bereft of hope. I still had my dream and my direction, and with a sigh so deep that my rigid shoulders and back and lifted head gave me an extra inch in height, I vowed, "We will not . . . we will *not* . . . stay here. Somehow I will learn to read. Finnish first, if necessary. Somehow I will learn to speak English, a word at a time, if necessary. And I will keep adding words every chance I have so that some day I will be able to communicate not only with Pa but with . . . other people. I will go to school and get a good job that pays good money, and I will take care of Ma and Lil."

I already had a start: I knew six . . . no, seven . . . English words by heart, though I didn't know how to spell or how to write them all. I knew the meaning, the pronunciation, and the spelling of one solid English word.

Was it a sign of the future that the only word I knew was "toilet"? We certainly weren't going to find one at the Brosi house.

I quiver still when I think back over the ensuing months. We did not, in the final analysis, spend more than a few days with the Brosis, who, in spite of the squalor in which they lived, maintained their supercilious attitude toward us, seeing us as far below them in the Finnish social strata, which we were, of course. Ma's family did not even really have a family name. One of her brothers was named Jack Hietajarju Maki, another Jack Hill, a third John Wainio; her sisters Betty and Amalia had been named Hill before their marriages. But Ma's name on their wedding certificate was Maria Kustava Rajamaki. The Brosi family, on the other hand, could trace name and lineage to the year 1606 when, according to Pa,

Ambrusius, a merchant of Lybeck, Germany, traveled to Karijoki, Finland, to live. There he changed his name to "Brusi." Only one vowel separated Pa from a hierarchy of successful and well-educated landowners. Successful they may have been in Finland, well-educated they may still be, I thought, but kind and cleanly they were not.

Thankfully, other Finns in the neighborhood, especially the Ahola family, were both. Mr. and Mrs. Ahola moved us into an abandoned storage shed not far from their house, which we could use without rent, they said, though it needed a lot of fixing up. "Desolate" wasn't a harsh enough word to describe it at first, but eventually Ma had it shiny clean with fresh curtains made from flour sacks and enough furniture borrowed and trumped up out of orange crates and bits and pieces and ends of boards to make it livable.

Lizzie Ahola gave Lil and me a doll she had outgrown and showed us how to make shoes for her out of lady slippers, moccasin flowers.

And all the while, we waited for Mr. Kalle Nestori Brosi to get a letter from and a response to Pa.

When it finally came, telling us to go to Virginia by train, the summons arrived, typically, without money to pay for our tickets.

Despite his having overlooked that detail, however, in all other ways, the ride across northern Minnesota toward the Iron Range's Queen City was a voyage into many splendors of joy, for during the next few years, though they were not totally without heartache, we were a family. Pa worked to support us. Ma kept house. I kept a watchful eye on Lil, drank my cod liver oil, tried to stay healthy, counted the years, then the months, and finally the days until I could begin to go to school, and struggled daily to grope my way toward learning to read and write both Finnish and English.

To go to school, to learn, to get an education—that was the deepest desire of my soul. And finally, with illness and trauma and false starts behind us, at the two-room school in Kinney, Minnesota, my forward-looking thoughts began to turn into reality.

Yet, of all the ironies that fate can clothe in shadows, the greatest may have been that no matter how I tried—and I tried mightily—knowledge alone did not turn out to be the key to power. Nor did the words I strove so mightily to amass. Other forces wrought and tempered the direction of my dreams, few of them susceptible to either willful wiles or steadfast will. During the critical months of our sojourn in Kinney, I was to learn lessons other than those of spelling and penmanship and literature and vocabulary, some of them lessons I still struggle to master.

Reshaped by the auguries of the gypsies and the magic of my guardian angel, tested by untimely death and wrongful acts, wracked by the horrors of the pest house, my dreams and I found ourselves attacked by Apollyon and cast into John Bunyan's Valley of Humiliation just when it had seemed that, after a long and tortuous journey, we were approaching Palace Beautiful, when my dreams were as bright as the sun gods, I as lovely as lady moon.

Yet through it all, with few exceptions, I held fast to my key, sharpening it on Wilho Field's displeasure, enhancing it with constant application and Eino Salin's vocabulary notebook, and steadfastly refusing to forswear either its potential to effect change or the potency of its power.

Chapter One

"Wilho Field's Revenge"

The tin can in the vacant lot between Salin's grocery store and our rented house in Kinney pinged early that fine late-April morning. It was the first sign that disaster was not only impending but imminent.

All of us in the Good Gang (the Finn gang) knew better than to allow that can to ping. We had solemnly sworn as part of our secret pact that, when any member of our gang inserted a message, we would hold both the string hanger and the can itself until the two were still. We pinky-swore. Therefore, I knew at once when I heard a metallic sound that the can, allowed to sway free, had hit tin. A warning signal had sounded. An enemy was abroad.

I sprang out of bed. To the window I "flew like a flash, tore open the shutters (well . . . pushed back the curtains), and pulled up the sash." To the memorization—wrong season though it was—I added mental quotation marks, correctly placed after the period, as Miss Loney had indicated to the older kids just the day before. I had eavesdropped on their lesson as I usually did, those theories and practices being far more fascinating than the elementary doings of Nan and Sam in *The Rational Method of Reading*.

Miss Loney still did not know that she had not taught me to read. She had been so proud of having a first grader master both primer and first grade reader before Christmas time that I had not had the heart to tell her that, in truth, I had begun to decipher the written word two years earlier when we lived in Malcolm, just outside Thief River Falls, while awaiting the reunion with Pa.

Every day either Ma or I walked from the Aholas, where we were staying, to the Brosi household, not to visit but to see if they had received word from or about Pa. Like everything else in that house, the newspapers lay helter skelter all over the kitchen table, drooping over toward and sometimes covering the floor. They were Finnish newspapers, copies of the *Työmies*, published in Superior, Wisconsin. Recent issues remained at least partially intact, but the older ones gravitated toward the wood box or lay in a pile near the stove. I hounded Ma until she finally asked if we could borrow one or two of the old ones, and eventually a system developed whereby we were allowed to take the old ones at the bottoms of the piles as new ones were stacked on top.

Thereafter, every night before we went to bed and after chores were done and faces washed and pajamas donned, I patiently worked at decoding. It was easy to piece out the sounds of the letters on the masthead. Then I found words that included those letters, and pretty soon I was managing a pretty fair oral rendition of headlines for the edification and pleasure of elderly Gramma Ahola, who lived alone in a tiny house right next to her son and daughter-in-law, not far from us.

Her house had only two rooms—a fairly large kitchen with a huge black iron cookstove and a small bedroom with a white iron bed covered with a wedding-ring quilt Gramma Ahola had made by hand before her eyes weakened.

My favorite part of her house, however, was an alcove built just off the kitchen, abutting the bedroom wall. Into that small space, perhaps six feet long and not much wider, Grampa Ahola, before he died, had built cushioned sitting-benches and bookshelves that reached from the sitting-bench to the ceiling. Oh, how I loved to visit Gramma Ahola! She served me milk-coffee in a white stoneware mug, poured in a generous dollop of fresh sweet cream, allowed me to help myself to the sugar lumps, and perched herself on the chair opposite mine at the table, her hands crocheting doilies that her eyes would never see, until, my milk-coffee gone, I spread a newspaper out on the table, and we read as much as we could. When I hit a word I did not know, I spelled it aloud. She pronounced and explained it, and I made myself a list to study later. Gramma Ahola applauded my efforts wholeheartedly.

2

When, on one of the bookshelves, I found an old, well-worn *Aapinen*, a Finnish primer, she helped me with that, too. In no time at all, it seemed, I was reading.

One book on those bookshelves, however, was absolutely forbidden me. It was a diatribe against white slavery, which Ma grabbed when she heard me trying to piece it out. Making the switch from Finnish to English had not been nearly as challenging as our argument over that book.

At any rate, neither Ma nor Miss Loney knew that I had long since traversed the second, third and fourth grade readers, too, and was well on my way through Francis Hodgson Burnett's *The Secret Garden*, which Miss Loney was reading to the class during rest time after lunch and which I surreptitiously commandeered when I stayed after school, ostensibly to wash blackboards and clap erasers and straighten up the classroom while Miss Loney had a cup of coffee and talked to the janitor, Weino Salin.

Weino, the oldest of the Salin boys, had lost his job in the mines when he joined the International Workers of the World (I.W.W.) trying to start a union. So had Pa. At least neither of them had lost their lives like the man whose blood stained the front porch on North Side in Virginia, just blocks away from the apartment we were renting. Pa brought Lil and me to see that blood and told us all about unions and mining companies and scabs and spies and closed shops and the evils of capitalism.

The blood had been spilled for naught, however, for neither Pa nor Weino nor any of the strikers got their jobs back. Nor were any changes in policy enacted. All that did result from the attempt was that Pa and Weino and the others were blackballed: never again would they be hired by any Iron Range mining company. Their names, we were all informed, had been put on a list.

Luckily, Pa got a job with the maintenance crew working on the streetcar track that ran from Virginia to Hibbing, and we moved to Kinney, roughly halfway in between, to the ground floor apartment of a brown frame house with a maple tree and picket fence in front of a wide open porch.

Weino now spent afternoons and evenings sweeping and cleaning classrooms. We always greeted each other when we met because we shared some of the same agonies. No more Finnish looking than I, he too had thick black hair, green eyes, an aesthetic nose, and freckles.

When our neighbors came over for afternoon coffee, they always looked approvingly at Lil and said, "*Kaunis pikku tyttö*—Nice little girl," patting the soft airy blonde wisps of hair floating around her cherubic pink cheeks, pinching her plump arms, smiling approvingly into the sparkling blue eyes.

Of course, it took awhile for Ma's friends to grasp the reason why they sparkled: Lil was *not* nice. When we each got ice cream cones during the Fourth of July celebration in Virginia, she dropped hers on the ground when it was almost gone, and I had to give her mine because I was older. When she and the Moore boy, whose father owned one of the mines, got together—his mother often came over to ask Ma to alter or sew a dress—which was far too often as far as I was concerned, evil ensued. They pounded nails through boards and set them in the middle of the street with the sharp ends of the nails up. They built drawbridges over the ditches being dug for the new sewer lines and, of course, fell in. I got my hair pulled because I was older and should have been watching.

It was, therefore, in my best interest not to wake Lil when I heard the tin can ping but to slip out of bed as quietly as possible.

Sure enough, a shadow flashed around the back of Salins' house just as I reached the window. A shadow! Pauline had been thus imperiled during the last Saturday picture show in Boziches' garage. Since it had been my turn to pump the player piano, I had had a front view. Aware of the danger, I knew that I too must act, that steps must be taken, action stations made ready.

Thank goodness Ma had not brushed out my braids the night before. She and Pa had spent the evening at the Finnish Temperance Hall practicing with the City Choir for the Kinney Community Spring Program, to be performed at the hall on Friday of that week. Sitting on the wooden folding chairs that lined the sides of the dance floor below the stage, studying my lessons and sneaking vocabulary words from Weino Salin's younger brother Eino's notebook, I could hear Ma's lilting soprano and Pa's sonorous bass carrying the harmony. It had been extra late when we got home because Pa and the other men from the choir had repainted the canvas stage backdrop, making it into a starry night sky, and had built a dark blue screen for the ladder I was to climb during our class's part of the program.

I shuddered when I thought of that ladder. Thus far during rehearsals held in our own classroom, I had been required to climb only to the top of Miss Loney's desk and sit there, skirts decorously arranged around my knees, while the class formed a perfectly equidistant semicircle, made a half-turn in unison, and sang to me, "Lady Moon, Lady Moon, where are you going?"

From my vantage, high above, I looked down upon them, swung a sparkling crescent moon from side to side, and answered, "Over the sea . . . over the sea."

Miss Loney had made the crescent moon out of cardboard, but we didn't think anyone would guess that such mundane material underlay the coatings of white paint and glitter that turned it into lunar starlight. A kind of contradiction of terms, I was aware, but an appropriate one nonetheless.

On Friday during the program, my voice alone would respond to their "Lady Moon, Lady Moon, whom are you loving?"

"All who love me. . . . All who love me."

My costume had not been completed yet, but word had it that it was blue and sparkly. Everyone else was to wear clean white shirts or dresses. Miss Loney had requested neckties for the boys and black knickers and, if possible, white hose and shoes for the girls.

Only Eino Salin's sister Sara had white shoes, of course, since Salins owned a grocery store. The rest of us sighed over her patent leather Mary Janes and accepted our black lace-ups, polished brightly, thus even more noticeably dark. Sara Salin always sported the biggest bows on both dress and hair. Her dresses, ordered from the Chicago Mail Order Catalog, were made of the softest lawn rather than sturdy poplin; and if this one had real lace trim instead of hand-made tatting or crocheting, she'd let us know about it, that's for sure. Even the price.

Sara Salin and my sister Lil were friends. They deserved each other. But willynilly because both of them were Finnish, they were loosely considered a part of the Good Gang, held together by threads not only of nationality but of hatred for our supreme enemies, the Bad Gang, composed of a combination of Slovenians and Italians.

It must have been one of them invading our territory early this school morning, I hypothesized, pulling on the long black socks that Ma insisted I wear until the first of June. I pinned them to my garters, dashed into a shirt, slip, and school dress, and raced into the kitchen to dab my hands in the washbowl by the water pail, slosh my face, and dip myself a quick drink of cool water. Pa had pumped the pail full before he left for work. Although I skidded out the back door, I did not allow the screen door to slam behind me. I had had my hair pulled too many times for that mistake.

Ma was out in the back yard throwing feed into the chicken coop, but her back was turned, so I slipped by unnoticed and made it to the tin can tree unseen. I was first. Of course, I was usually first since the tree was closer to our side of the vacant lot than to the Salins' side. Taking the prescribed five quick steps to the right followed by six steps to the left, looking quickly in all directions—I was safe!—I hurried to dig the fingers of my right hand into the can while my left hand from long practice held string and can securely and returned both to stability before I allowed myself a glance at the paper.

Startled, I saw on the outside of the carefully folded epistle my own full name—Ilmi Marianna Brosi.

"Oh, dear," I said aloud, skulking down along the tree trunk to unwrap the message. It might be bad; it might be good. But the secrecy with which it had been delivered boded ill. Sure enough. "BEWARE!" was the terse warning inside.

Shuddering, I asked myself, "Beware of what?" and shivered with a combination of fear and delight. It was I, not Pauline, who was now in peril. I had no time to consider the possible dangers lurking around me, however, for Ma saw me and ordered me inside to eat my *puuroa*, butter and brown sugar melting into the hot creamy cereal. While I ate, she plastered my hair down, flattening the curls that always escaped the braids, even when she wound them so tightly my eyes slanted.

Then Lil had to be awakened, cranky as always, and dressed, unwilling as always, and fed without her spilling, impossible as always, and packed off to school, whining as always. There was simply no time between breakfast and chores and school to do more than mull over the danger. There was no time to act.

Of course, I kept still to Ma about the message. She had enough to worry about what with sewing to take in and all the cooking, cleaning, and baking to be done. It was Wednesday, baking day, and the yeast sponge was already bubbling and proofing in the big stoneware bowl. Sugar-glazed braids of sweet cardamom *pulla* would greet us when we got home from school.

Less welcome thoughts encroached as I pulled the flannel sheets and yarn-tied quilt straight, tucking them in neatly and closing our davenport bed up for the day. Lil was supposed to help, but of course she had to go to the outhouse when it was time for us to do any of our household jobs. And it took her twice as long as it should. Ma always told us to carry out the slops as we went and carry in some wood when we returned. Lil did carry slops out and wood in. Otherwise, she dawdled. And she always used twice the number of pages from the catalog for wiping that Ma said we should use. I knew she lollygagged on the low hole Pa had built just for her, looking at the catalog while I made up the bed or wiped the dishes or carefully dusted the window sills and tables.

Ma said it was important for me to learn to do things well. If I didn't do them well, I got my hair pulled.

But that morning, although technically speaking a bit of quilt still peeked from the edge of the davenport, she was too busy to notice, and I was too preoccupied to care. Other things took precedence.

Maintaining a firm grip on the back of Lil's dress, I considered the ramifications of the warning message all the way to school and carefully studied everyone who joined us on the trek along Kinney's narrow gravel main street past Salin's Grocery Store, past the butcher shop with its enticing mountain of sawdust in the back, past the hall, past Boziches' garage where we had watched Antonio Moreno unveil "The Veiled Mystery," where Pauline endured her on-going perils, and where we had fallen in love with Rudolph Valentino. Ann Zakula joined us, school books in hand. So did Wuokka Maki and Helmi Field. I looked each one straight in the eye. Hard. No one flinched or shied away. It was not one of them, I was sure.

After depositing Lil into the firm hands of the beautiful Miss Ethel Langford, who spent some time each morning with a small group of pre-first graders, trying to teach them English, I hurried past members of the Bad Gang who had congregated in the hall outside our classroom plotting dastardly deeds, I was sure, before entering the safe zone just inside the door. They had already that winter planted what was alleged to have been a bomb in the cave on the side of the ore dump, and they had almost succeeded in burying Eino Salin in the sawdust heap behind the butcher shop. But Miss Loney did not brook dissension in her classroom.

Then I saw him. Seated two rows nearer the window with the bigger kids was Wilho Field, Helmi's cousin. He looked at me. I looked at him. And I knew from whence the message had come.

At once I also knew why. When the Fields had come to visit after dinner last Sunday, while the grownups drank coffee and talked, Wilho, Lil, and I sat on the opened davenport and behaved ourselves. But when we got up to have our own milk-coffee and coffee-table treats, I had experienced a sudden untoward lapse in conduct. We had been directed to open the davenport because only then was there room for the three of us. We had been told to sit quietly and play or read. We had been reminded several times to behave ourselves. This time, Lil did. I didn't.

Of course, there were mitigating circumstances. Wilho Field, although still technically in the lower-grade room, was always above himself, even Ma admitted. He was an only child, much adored, much pampered, much spoiled. Truth be told, he had been raised to be above himself. The end result was that he had become an obnoxious, authoritative, aggravating boor who lacked one single redeeming feature. Although he was a Finn, he had never been admitted into the Good Gang. Even other Finns couldn't stand him. I couldn't stand him.

First, by sheer luck alone, he had won the vocabulary contest at the Kinney School, beating even Eino Salin when called upon to provide a word that matched a given definition. It was his name, Wilho Field, not Eino's . . . or mine . . . that had appeared in the latest issue of *The School Chronicle*. Never again would that happen. Having gained access to Eino Salin's secret vocabulary notebook, which I copied surreptitiously whenever opportunity presented itself, I had privately and publically vowed to beat both Eino and Wilho next year.

To make matters worse, it was Wilho who had recently won the area spelling bee at the Buhl School and had thus been awarded an enormous box of chocolates wrapped in purple ribbon as the prize. I would have shared the chocolates with my classmates instead of eating them all myself. I would have pinned the purple ribbon to the bulletin board for everyone to see instead of taking it home. But when the teacher from the Buhl School had said "pigeon," I had added a "d." Wilho Field had dropped the "d" and won the prize.

He was insufferable.

Suddenly, just as we were about to rise from our places on the davenport, my soul rebelled. I lifted Lil off and clambered off myself. Before Wilho Field could move, I lifted the bar and closed the davenport. On Wilho Field.

Of course, he screamed. Of course, his mother came running. Of course, I had my hair pulled and apologized profusely. But it had been worth it to see him red-faced and terrified, enclosed in the davenport like a coffin, immobilized and, for once, quiet.

When I saw my name on the outside of that message in the tin can, full name spelled correctly, I should have known. Thus, I was certain of whom. All that remained a mystery was what. What could he do that I should be aware?

The question perplexed me for the rest of the week, even to the point of my making errors with sums when it was my turn at the blackboard, even to the point of missing eight-times-six when we recited the multiplication table, though everyone in the room knew I was the only one adept even with the nines.

Wednesday morning slipped innocently by. So did Wednesday afternoon and Wednesday night with sauna at Salmis', where we paid twenty-five cents to use their steam and dressing rooms.

Thursday came and went in a whirl of practicing. Miss Loney came to our house after school to set my hair in rag curls and deliver the blue crepe paper dress I was to wear in the program. It was beautiful.

Friday morning dawned while it was still dark, for in the middle of the night we heard a knock on the door, and there, his arms full of presents, stood Uncle Charles, come all the way from Ely for the show.

Every time he visited us, the only *suku laisia*—relatives—he cared about in America, he brought a gift. That morning, he outdid himself. Ma turned as pink as the flowers when she opened a matched set of gold-trimmed pitcher and glasses with gilt-edged moss roses. Surprises for Lil and me were hidden until after the program.

Far too excited to go back to bed, we planned the day. For once, Ma said she would worry about Lil so I could get to school early and have my curls brushed out before the other kids came. Pa left for work extra early so he could leave a little early and change before the program. Uncle Charles divulged his secret. He was going to spend the morning checking out some land that was for sale in Zim. But, to satisfy my anxious gaze, he said he would be back for sure by afternoon.

And then it was afternoon. Curls brushed, I stood behind the painted backdrop while the upper graders sang and recited memory work. I did not sit down for fear of crumpling my crepe paper dress.

When the stage door opened for the upper graders to file back down into their rows of seats in front, I peeked at the audience. Ma and Pa and Lil and Uncle Charles had taken the side seats closest to the stage. Uncle Charles waved to me and pointed to his coat pocket, bulging with the shapes of two small boxes.

In between acts, Eino Salin pulled the rope to close the curtains. While he concentrated on his job, I captured five more words from his vocabulary notebook.

I couldn't see my class, but I could hear the rustle of Miss Loney's silk dress as she stood up and the creak of chairs as my own class rose in unison and marched up the stairs and onto the stage. Eino had moved the ladder, wound on top with dark blue crepe paper, onto stage center, ready for me to climb at Miss Loney's signal.

I nibbled my nails behind the backdrop.

9

Miss Loney at the piano began the introduction to "Lady Moon." I moved slowly across the front of the class toward the ladder, holding the crescent moon swaying in front of me. Carefully, moon above my head, I stepped onto the first rung of the ladder and groped my way up, one rung at a time.

"Lady Moon, Lady Moon, where are you going?" the class sang.

Nearing the top rung, I swayed and opened my mouth to utter the prescribed response. "Over..." was all that I managed. That's where the ladder went. When my weight hit the last rung, the whole thing collapsed.

This time I screamed, and Wilho Field laughed.

It was a public debacle.

Oh, I was rescued intact, and eventually the song continued and concluded, albeit without the ladder. Wilho Field was well and truly disciplined not only by Miss Loney and by every member of the Good Gang but even by the members of the Bad Gang, who ostracized him so severely that his parents eventually sent him to school in Buhl.

Good riddance, I thought when I heard about it later that summer.

Uncle Charles gave us the packages. Lil and I both got watches. Mine was a lapel watch that hung from my shoulder with a solid gold ribbon clasp. Ma confiscated Lil's until she was older and responsible.

After the program, Weino Salin asked me to dance and taught me the schottische.

"All's well that ends well," said Ma.

But it was far from the end. I knew that Wilho Field had not been the only one who had been above himself. I, too, had gotten my comeuppance, and I had well and truly deserved it. "Pride goeth before the fall" says an old adage. Mine did not leave until long, long after. I had a lot to learn, not the half of it about vocabulary.

Chapter Two

"Uncle Charles Brosi's Promise"

The previous afternoon while we had been preparing for the program, Uncle Charles had, in fact, gone to Zim and had found what he told us before we went to bed was the perfect location for our farm. Thus, early the next morning after breakfast and chores, we set out, all of us, our whole family—Pa and Ma, Uncle Charles, Lil and I—on an adventure to survey the land.

Ma packed a picnic lunch of venison sausage and homemade bread with jars of homemade beer, *kalja,* for the men, buttermilk for her, and two precious bottles of cream soda for Lil and me, bought by Uncle Charles from Salins' store at the same time as he hired a buggy and horses from Nylund's Livery Stable. Even Uncle Charles could not afford a car.

It was hot for May, a fact which, like most others, prompted me into creativity, with words of course, as always. Miss Loney always assigned our class vocabulary sentences to write, one for each new word. But the older kids like Eino Salin got to write whole paragraphs, stories even sometimes, into which they worked their words. I did the same thing in secret all the time, especially when I was making beds or doing dishes. My mind didn't have to worry about what my hands were doing: Ma had trained them well. Thus, that morning, glancing out the window now and again as I did my morning jobs, I delved into Eino Salin's most recent list and wrote, in my head, of course, "Shy Minnesota spring, reticent in April

11

when showers fall more often as snow than rain, has suddenly flowered into sunbursts of buttercups and nascent green tendrils, promises of leaves. Although too often the deluges of June burgeon into gusts of mosquitoes, at her best May floats sylphlike between the silvery crystal of winter and a languorous, full-bosomed earthy summer." The last phrases weren't Eino's. I lifted them intact, transferring the Finnish into English equivalents, from what I could remember of the Aholas' forbidden book. They worked in well, I thought.

Finally, chores completed, we started out, dressed in our best—Pa and Uncle Charles in suits, white shirts, suspenders, ties, and hats; Ma and I in our new lawn summer whites with cutwork collars, tatted waists, and long full skirts. Lil's dress, though designed like mine, had been made of heavier poplin, sturdy enough to withstand her escapades.

That morning, for once, Ma had not rebraided our night-loosened hair. Some residual curl made mine fall in what I hoped looked like thick, black, heavy natural waves, held back from my face with a big silk bow. Lil's feathery wisps had braid-ridges, too, so she felt elegant insofar as she understood the word.

We set off in great style in the coolness of the morning. Uncle Charles drove the team with Pa beside him on the front seat. Ma and I were perched behind, Lil wedged between us. Early though it was, enough people were out and about for me to wave and make sure it was noted that we were all dressed up and traveling in a hired buggy. Pa tipped his hat to Mr. Salin, who was sweeping the boardwalk in front of his store.

In the back of the Spina Meat Market, the huge pile of sawdust steamed in the sun. Ma had warned Lil and me never ever to play there for fear that the pile would slide and suffocate us as it almost had Eino Salin. But I really hadn't needed the warning. I never considered going near that pile even though for most of the town kids it served as the site for King of the Mountain and Castles. So pleasurable did the boys find those games that lines of demarcation had finally been drawn between the heights attained by the Good Gang, Eino Salin at the head, and those claimed by the Bad Gang, headed by Diodado Carmen Joseph Vanucci, known to us as Kabe, though his mother used his full name when she called him to dinner. So staunchly did the foes defend their regions that the fetid sawdust was additionally stained with their dried blood. But after the close call when Eino Salin was actually buried for a time, a truce was agreed upon, and a buffer zone of no man's land decreed and enforced.

I had on occasion filched small pailfuls of sawdust, sniffing the grainy chips to make sure they were fresh and using them to make bread and cakes for my doll Susie. But never ever did I participate either in the battles or in the festivities following victorious assaults. I did not want ringworm. Roaming cats liked and used that sawdust pile, too, and Ma did not need to warn me about the dangers of contagion. When we lived in Virginia, Dr. Good had dosed Sylvia, one of the Wirtanen kids, for ringworm. The rest of us had seen and heard not only her miserable purging but the dire warnings of the two Maijas.

One Maija was Ma, Mary Brosi; the other, her best friend Mary Wirtanen. The two came to be known as the Maijas of Virginia's North Side. Heeding my teacher's insistence that we "speak English," however, I always tried to call each of them "Mary."

I remember the day we first met Mary Wirtanen. We had arrived in Virginia after our long journey by train from Malcolm across the northern reaches of Minnesota to the eastern end of the Mesabi Iron Range. Pa had gotten a job there in an open pit mine when first-hand experience confirmed that there was no gold lying on the streets waiting to be picked.

The mining companies owned the grocery stores and a good many of the rented houses, so, by the time our monthly bills were paid, there was precious little money left and none of it gold. But the promise and the dream had glittered, luring Pa out of the inner world of words and music where he usually lived with his pencil and his fiddle, down the shore of Lake Superior, through a brief sojourn in Duluth, and finally to Virginia. Once he found out we were in Minnesota already, he sent for us to join him—directions mailed without tickets or ticket money, of course.

Unfortunately, the job in the mines didn't last much longer than jobs had in Port Arthur. Ma told me that she had known from the beginning that moving from Canada to Minnesota was not really the answer. Pa took his self along wherever he went, and the Pa who hid behind the door at Maija Wirtanen's house in Virginia, intending to surprise us, still carried that fiddle and the songs in his head. When he popped out from behind Maija Wirtanen's front door, Ma slapped his face instead of giving him a hug.

Although it was wonderful beyond words to see him, I knew he deserved the slap. He should not have left us behind when he boarded the steamer packet *America* and entered the United States illegally. An alien rather than a citizen, he had never gotten naturalization papers, which didn't mean a lot in those days but did mean a whole lot later.

13

The truth was that he always felt himself to be an alien, different from, separate from others, even in Kinney, where we had thought him content. Perhaps only at Mesaba Park, where in later years he shared his caretaker's cabin with his dog Baby and the chipmunks who ate from his hand, was he truly happy.

After Ma slapped him, that over with, she set herself to checking out the apartment he had rented for us from Maija Wirtanen, who got a cut rate on rent in return for serving as caretaker and broker.

"It's dirty," Ma told Maija Wirtanen with asperity, sniffing corners and closets permeated with a noxious combination of urine and cabbage.

"*Joo*," agreed Maija Wirtanen, taking Ma's measure and finding in her a kindred spirit, "but *kyllä kusi kuivaa ja paska muuten murenee.*"—"The urine will dry, and the feces will sweep out."

They did, too, under Ma's relentless scrubbing. I lent a hand. Lil was passed along to the care of the other Maija's oldest child, Sylvia, and among us—the two Maijas and me—we won that battle.

Women's battles, it seemed, were always hard-fought. Some were lost. Thus it was with Mr. Wirtanen, who also had his own priorities. Maija Wirtanen, too angry for tears, told Ma that, for weeks that summer, he had gotten up early, dressed for his shift in the mine and left for work with Pa, carrying the lunch pail she had fixed. But at the end of the pay period, no money came in. His Maija panicked when the rent came due and the grocery store refused more credit. Sylvia was barely five then, Art three, Roini not born. One morning his Maija followed him as he trekked off—not to his job in the mine but to a garage two blocks away where he spent the entire day. Not until the shift changed did he head back again, pockets empty, for his gambling luck continued bad. Had we lived two blocks away instead of next door, we still would have heard the battle that ensued. Eventually Maija Wirtanen followed him in search of greener pastures, heading toward Duluth about the same time as we left for Kinney.

But none of hers or Ma's tribulations mattered that morning as Uncle Charles headed the rented buggy toward the end of Main Street. That was all behind us now, I thought with heartfelt relief. Life had changed with the advent of Uncle Charles.

At the end of Main Street, where the road took a sharp right turn toward the streetcar tracks, chicken wire fencing lined the road delineating a second danger zone, Kinney's forbidden ground, far more dangerous than the sawdust heap. Leaning forward, I clasped the back of the front seat with both hands, fighting my terror. On the other side of that chicken wire fence lay the vast abyss, the Cavour Open Pit iron ore mine, already deep enough to touch China. If we did not make the turn, I believed, if even Uncle Charles, invincible though he was, could not control the horses, we would run straight at, into, and over the chicken wire fence. On the other side we would plunge down down down into the bottomless pit.

The Cavour Mining Company, like the dozens of others that pock-marked the east range, had begun operations not long after the Merritt brothers' discovery that Minnesota's richness lay not in veins of gold or silver, but in the ochre soil that covered glacial granite. Unlike the areas around the small towns of Tower and Soudan, north of Kinney, where the ore lay deep underground, on the east range, the Mesabi Range, it was threaded by the root systems of towering pines. At first, miners had but to skim away the surface cream of forest growth, dip into the substrata, and pick the ore away. Then off it went, red as the dried blood on the sawdust pile, to parts unknown.

Left behind were the residue on the clothing of the miners, the pits that deepened day by day, year by year, as the miners pursued veins of ore deeper and deeper into the earth, and, nearby, the slab-sided flat-topped mountains of surface dirt, stark and bald, the dumps where the tailings were carried and left.

Even then I was not sure which was the worse horror—those dumps that rose day by day, cancerous growths bereft of grass or trees, or the broad deep holes in the earth with their sharply ridged edges and sides leading to a level of hell descried even by fire. Raw and ragged as a knife slash, the raped earth bled ore, Pa said. It was not white slavery, I gathered from Pa's angry outbursts whenever he considered the dumps, but it must have been something very like it.

When the eighth graders in the room across the hall recited their memorized passages from John Milton's literary epic *Paradise Lost* in the school yard at recess time and on the way to and from school, I listened and absorbed, and my soul touched Milton's. He too must have felt the whole of it, a pun I relished in private, his hell too a place where darkness was visible, where neither sun nor rest nor sleep could dwell.

I could hear our earth scream, too.

Never did I breach that chicken wire fence although I knew that deep in the night, the boys dared each other to walk along the very verge of the crumbling edge of the pit. Even on that bright morning, safe behind

Pa in a buggy driven by the omnipotent Uncle Charles, buffered on the danger side by Ma, an intransigent protectress, I shuddered.

I was not sorry at the prospect of leaving Kinney behind forever, though we had been happy there. We were moving to a paradise where we could live together as a family, where the trees and the earth remained equally undefiled.

I did not even mind the thought of watching Lil.

To my heartfelt relief, we traversed the turn safely and turned up what is now Highway No. 7, unnamed then, but clearly the pathway toward Zim, our promised land.

For as long as we lived there, our place in Zim was to be our "Happy Corner," but there, too, we had to make our own happiness, and it was not wrought in the form we had expected.

But all of that lay as far ahead as Zim seemed that morning as we passed the stairway up to the streetcar station on its raised platform alongside the trestle and thence set out on the road without a name, the road that would lead us, I was sure, to the future.

The horses pranced, and Uncle Charles talked to Pa about the money he had hidden safely away in the bank in Ely and about how wonderful it would be for us to live together on the farm in Zim, about how good it felt to have us, his family, all around him and how much easier it would be to wrest a farm from the wilderness with two men to do it and how thankful he was that Pa had found a good woman like Ma, who was not only beautiful but kind and clever and hard-working. Ma blushed. And about how lucky he felt, finally to have nieces to sit on his knees, nieces just the right size for him.

He meant every word. We knew he was as truly grateful to have found us as we were to have found him.

It had all happened so strangely. For all that Pa lived more in his own world than in ours, he did periodically communicate to our world via submissions to Finnish newspapers. Uncle Charles had read a poem published in the *Työmies* just months before, signed with Pa's full name, Knute Pietari Brosi. Hopeful that this Knute Brosi might be the brother he had thought lost forever when they had left Finland at different times with different destinations, members of a family rent by internal rifts, the nature of which I could easily guess, having met Kalle Nestori Brosi. At any rate, Uncle Charles had written to the editor of the newspaper, requesting that the enclosed letter be addressed and mailed to Pa. After that, letters had flown back and forth between Kinney and Ely with visits to Kinney whenever Uncle Charles could manage. Out of those visits and the long nights of talk, the dream had been born of a farm where we would live and be happy forever.

Uncle Charles and Pa talked sporadically in the front seat. Warmed by the sun and lulled by the jogging motion of the buggy, still tired from last night's program and dance, Lil quit squirming and went to sleep, her head in Ma's lap, her shoes, of course, making dirty marks on mine. Ma and I sat quietly, partly to keep Lil from waking, partly to savor the moment.

It is good to travel with hope, Ma always said. That day both travel and hope came easily.

Once when Lil stirred, Ma began to hum the melody of a new song she and Pa were learning. Pa has bought the sheet music from a store in Virginia partly because, except for the whiteness of his hair and the length of his moustache, the man on the cover, the *"Vanha Mustalainen"*—"The Old Gypsy"—caressing his fiddle so lovingly with his bow, could have been Pa himself. Published in Budapest, Leipzig, and Helsinki, in both German and Finnish, this piece by Ernst Kondor was Finnish to the core in its meditative melody and minor key.

"Helmassa metsän mustalais vanhus veittävi päivänsä köyhänä vaan," Ma began adding words to the tune. Pa and Uncle Charles contributed their bass and tenor tones, diminuendo, to the waltz tempo of the refrain: *"Tänne mun viuluni tuokaa, kevät mun rinnassa soil, Kaupunkiin tahdon mä käydä, tänne en jäädä voi! Vielä me tahtoisin koettaa tunteeni tulkita nuo, soittoni kaikki on mulle, yksin se rauhan suo, kuolohonkin lohtua luo!"*

I knew I should be translating the descriptions of the life of the gypsy, wandering through towns and villages, into English, as prescribed by the Kinney School's "Speak English" campaign. But when I took over the soprano part and Ma tried a kind of muted alto, I could not think in English. The beauty of the music was intrinsically Finnish, and it made me proud to be, too. So we sang away the miles until the double track of gravel ruts began to curve into semicircles to ease the horses' load as we wove up and around a hill.

Then Uncle Charles went so still that I knew we were nearing the place. I hung on tightly, excited, though the slope was gentle, its verge roundly softened with birch and poplar trees, not precipitous in its rise, but gentle as the earth mother.

"Cover your eyes, girls," Uncle Charles told Ma and me. "No peeking till I tell you." We did. And we didn't.

As we reached the top of the hill, he tugged on the reins and stomped the brake though we had been traveling so slowly that the horses pretty much stopped of their own accord. Pointing with the whip, he said quietly, "There it is."

Pa looked without a word. Ma craned her neck over Uncle Charles' shoulder. Lil woke up with a bounce, and I stood up. Below us lay the land.

"This will be ours as soon as I can get the money out of the bank," Uncle Charles said in his gentle voice, which nevertheless seemed strong, "if," he amended, looking at Pa and then back at us, "if you like it, too."

The road held it all in an embrace—a green lagoon with flowing waves of trees, some still wearing winter's spume of dark, dull gray, others already awash in spring.

I had no words. Nor, it seemed, did Ma or Pa. It was all our hopes made manifest.

Little did we anticipate then that our pathway to the farm called Happy Corner was destined to follow a route far more twisted than that roadway, through dark days of sickness and quarantine, where one of us far too soon crossed not just the river that flowed so gently at the bottom of the hill but another river called Death. For all its verdant richness, the roadway we followed did not lead to the Palace Beautiful of our dreams.

But, oh, how beautiful it was that morning! Dressed in buttercups, the margins of the meadow danced around us. Uncle Charles lifted us down, and Lil and I, atune for once, ran and danced and picked buttercups and sat among them, winding chains and crowns and bracelets.

Ma floated around the clearing, stepping out measures for the house: here the living room on the cool shady side, there the kitchen table to catch the sunrise, here the kitchen itself protected from the afternoon sun on the north side where the wood stove would fight the winds of winter, there the bedrooms—one for Ma and Pa, one for Uncle Charles, here a ladder leading to the loft where foodstuffs could be stored and Lil and I would sleep.

Uncle Charles marked her steps, made pencil sketches and notes, tried water witching with a willow stick, and built a cairn of rocks marking the spot for a well.

Where the meadow turned to marshland dotted by stands of pine trees so high and thick they laced the sun away, I found moccasin flowers, ladyslippers just the right size for doll shoes. Along a mossy slope, I stretched myself full length in a patch of fragrant arbutus, pink and lavender and white, so sweet I lay careless of my frock, breathing deeply, losing the scent, then waiting patiently until I could make myself one again with their heady fragrance. I picked handfuls of them for Uncle Charles, who made a birchbark basket to hold them, and for Ma, who showed me where they should go, in the center of the rock where our kitchen table sat.

Lil climbed into the comforting lap of a maple tree, and I joined her, willing to battle the pirates preying upon her treasure trove. Ma did not demur even when Lil lost her balance and fell. She did not cry out until her dress caught on a branch and she swung from it, pinioned. But the poplin held, and she flew unimpeded until Uncle Charles ran to rescue her. Ma did not even bother to chastise her, only followed along, brushing her clean of twigs and smiling. That day I did not get my hair pulled for not watching.

Pa made some half-hearted stabs at fishing for brook trout, surprising even himself when he caught enough for us to roast over an open fire for lunch. Mostly he sat with his ubiquitous fiddle on a rock midway between the river and the trees, making up a song that blended bubbling, warbling river staccatos with the swishing, murmurous tenor of the trees.

We glutted ourselves on the brook trout, charred black on the outside, moist inside, leaving a heap of heads and bones for the crows' lunch.

Not until even Pa recalled himself to reality did we pack up to leave, and even then Ma moved without her usual briskness, looking around bemused for more than one last time. We stayed until it was almost too dark to see our way home, but Mr. Nylund's horses knew the way back. Replete with meadow grass, they plodded homeward placidly.

I don't remember much of that ride. Lil slept, full of food and play. I leaned back and watched the stars, and Ma sang softly, finding words for Pa's fiddle's melody. On that one night, they were in tune. Finally, I too slept, sprawled across the front seat and Uncle Charles and Pa. I hardly remember being lifted from the buggy and tucked into bed with Lil curled beside me, her hair soft as dandelion fuzz.

Not until next morning when I woke up under the quilt on the davenport in our house in Kinney did I return to reality and then only marginally. Uncle Charles had left. But Ma was singing still, and this time it was Pa who was feeding the chickens while she sat on the stump, her busy hands quiet, resting in her lap.

Hope held us all in thrall.

Chapter Three

"Miss Loney's Speak English Campaign"

But when I went back to school and to my study of vocabulary the following Monday, hopes for the future were deferred for a time, while my class confronted the needs of the present.

"Mothers' Day is approaching as are the end-of-the-school-year exercises," Miss Loney reminded us, "and this class has been chosen to write and enact an original Mothers' Day play."

She made it sound as if it were a signal honor, and murmurs of pleasure rose accordingly.

"Now," she continued briskly, "we need a chairman for the play committee. Are there any volunteers?"

Wilho Field raised his hand immediately. He was the only one.

I hesitated. Perhaps we would not be in Kinney long enough for me even to participate in the Mothers' Day Program. Perhaps the school year would end for me before the end-of-the-school-year exercises. But the irritatingly self-important and complacent expression on Wilho Field's face moved me to action, and I raised my hand, too, anticipating a fight and estimating the number of votes I would get should our names be written on the board and the class be asked to decide between us.

Unfortunately, Miss Loney, taking the path of least resistance and indicating that there was more than enough work for two, assigned total responsibility for the writing, the casting, the staging, the costuming, the directing, and the performing of the Mothers' Day play to the two of us together. Joint chairmen, she called us.

Just like Siamese twins, I thought wryly, and blanched at the thought. But I held back the groan that Miss Loney might consider rude.

Wilho Field looked at me and made a face—carefully when Miss Loney's back was turned.

Until that day I had considered Miss Loney a paragon among women and had striven to gain her approval. But that Monday things between us began to go awry. First, she yoked me to Wilho Field. Secondly, when the rest of the class was dismissed at the end of the day, she asked me to stay.

"Not to wash the blackboards and clap erasers," she explained, uncharacteristically discomfited, "but to discuss a serious concern."

As the rest of the class filed out, I sat straight-backed in my seat, holding my breath, and trying hard to remember what I could have done that had caused me—me!—to be kept after school. Being requested to stay felt very different from asking permission to stay.

When the room was empty, Miss Loney, too, sat down, picked up a red pencil as if to begin grading assignments, then studied it as if she had never seen one before and said, more to the pencil than to me, "Ilmi Marianna . . . ." The word drew itself into a long pause.

I waited.

She forged ahead, still looking at the pencil. "Ilmi Marianna, I foresee that you . . ." looking up at me finally, she continued, "that you will someday take your place among the movers and shakers of tomorrow's world."

That sounded more like a compliment than a reprimand, and I relaxed a little.

"With that in mind," she hurried on, "it seems to be exceedingly important that your identity be presented from the beginning in the most modern, up-to-date, psychologically advantageous form."

"Oh, dear," I thought, clasping my hands together to keep them from shaking, wondering what she meant.

"Oh, dear," she sighed, "let me see now. How can we approach this?"

Unable to sit still, I stood up, marched to the front of her desk, took a deep breath, clasped my hands behind my back, and steadied myself.

Finally, she looked at me. "You are very aware, Ilmi Marianna, of the 'Speak English' campaign?"

I nodded. I had supported that campaign whole-heartedly ever since I got to the Kinney School, except for a lapse or two, I had to admit, when it came to Finnish songs, which often lost something in translation. "Could she know that?" I wondered, feeling guilty.

Having begun, however, she continued on a pace disregarding my lack of response. "The Mothers' Day program and the end-of-the-year exercises will be attended not only by parents and friends and by the members of the Kinney School Board . . ."

I knew whom that meant: Mr. Salin, owner of the grocery store; Mr. Spina of the meat market; and Mary Peterson, who maintained a commercial establishment that provided refreshment for gentlemen. Not *kalja*. Strong beer. Sometimes spirits. Although Mary's Bar was, in general, considered a reputable business enterprise, Pa did not find the society that frequented her establishment compatible: they did not share either his dreams or his interests.

". . . and, in addition, George Bakalyer, the assistant superintendent of schools for the entire St. Louis County School System, will be attending both performances to hand out awards and offer a few words. It is he who hires teachers out of normal school to serve the smaller one-room country schools."

This time when she paused, her eyes gleamed, her gaze met mine, unflinching. "It is he who could possibly offer you your first job."

I gaped, my jaw and my grip on reality slackening alike. We were traveling into another realm of hope.

"Should he be impressed with you even now when you are only an elementary school student, he will remember. And some day," she leaned toward me intently, "that memory may stand you in very good stead. Therefore, it behooves us to present you to him from the very beginning in the most auspicious possible light. Do you understand?"

I nodded, enthusiastic though still somewhat bewildered. "But how am I to do that?" I knew that I was hardly prepossessing: I did not have either blonde hair or blue eyes. My complexion tended toward creamy olive rather than pink. I was way too skinny, my hair way too thick. And that was not even to mention the freckles. Yet Miss Loney had chosen me to be Lady Moon; it was she who had set my hair in rag curls. Clearly, the way I looked had not seemed problematical to her. Then what was the problem?

Sometimes directness is the only route to revelation so I was direct. "What about me needs to be changed, Miss Loney?" I asked, gripping my hands together until they hurt.

Standing up, she turned, picked up an eraser, began to wipe the board, paused, and then without looking back at me blurted out, "I am sorry, Ilmi Marianna, it is . . . your name."

"My name?" I was dumfounded.

"Your name," she repeated, more firmly, this time eye to eye. "Your name is Finnish. *Ilmi* is a Finnish name. And *Marianna* . . . well . . . it could be Finnish. It could be Italian. But it is certainly not English. To have your name as director of the play on the program as . . . ," she shuddered, ". . . *Ilmi Marianna* . . . is to controvert the very basic presumption of the Speak English campaign. Besides," she set her jaw, "the name is ugly."

I shrugged my shoulders and agreed. It was. But so was I.

Moving down, Miss Loney perched on the edge of the dais where her desk sat and motioned for me to join her.

"I have been thinking about this for many, many days," Miss Loney admitted, "and I do have a suggestion."

I raised my eyebrows slightly, shook my head in frustration, and shrugged again. Any idea was better than the vacuum in my mind.

"We change your name." She leaned back and awaited reaction.

I smiled, the solution waving before me like a flag, rising like a rocket, exploding into my psyche like Fourth of July fireworks. How devastatingly simple! We would simply change my name. Limp, I leaned back and asked, "To what?"

"What do you suggest?" she asked, clearly relieved by my response.

"Well," I said, drawing the single syllable out and up into an exclamation. Clearly, there was no way of improving *Ilmi*. "*Ilmi* has to go."

She nodded.

"And *Marianna*? Make that my first name?"

"Perhaps some variation of *Marianna*," she offered. "Mary?"

"No." I was firm. "There are already too many Marys around, and everyone who's Finnish will call me Maija just as they do Ma." It would make no difference though it would look better on the program.

Silence ensued.

Then I looked up quickly, an idea having taken shape. "Miss Loney," I suggested, my voice tentative but hopeful, "let's look in the dictionary." The dictionary, so full of rich, new words, was to me as sacred as the Bible.

We did. There, above the word Mary, both of us in one flash saw the answer: Marian. Like Robin Hood's maid. "Marian," we breathed. It sang. Even Marian Brosi was not totally lacking in poetic rhythm.

23

"Marian," she nodded, and we beamed at one another.

Two problems remained. Respectively, Mary Gustava, also spelled Kustava, Brosi and Knute Pietari Brosi. What would my parents think of such a change?

We decided to broach the subject together after school the following afternoon, which would give us twenty-four hours to figure out the approach most likely to achieve success. In a spirit of hope—there it was again—we said, "Adieu."

I had learned early on that the time to raise topics that could result in controversy was not during the dinner hour. Children then were to be seen and not heard while Ma and Pa concentrated in theory on making adult conversation and in practice on getting more food into Lil's mouth than she got on her clothes and the floor.

I waited with bated breath and barely contained patience until the optimum time for talk—the quiet time when Ma and I did the dishes.

To my unutterable relief, Ma raised absolutely no objection to my tentative overture: "Ma, I think we should do something nice for Miss Loney because she's been so nice to me. Maybe invite her for dinner? Or for afternoon coffee?"

Ma's afternoon coffee table was justly renowned. Of course, all Finnish ladies knew how to set an elegant table for company with a china coffee cup, saucer, bread-and-butter plate, and tiny coffee spoon, an embroidered napkin for each guest, a bowl of sugar lumps, a pitcher of thick cream, and a pretty vase of flowers centered on a linen cloth. Everyone knew a coffee table for guests must include seven baked items: a pound cake, a frosted cake, four kinds of cookies, and *pulla*, a braided cardamom bread with fat sugar on top.

But Ma prepared the prescribed menu with sumptuous abandon. Her *pulla* was lavishly proportioned of one egg to one cup of rich milk or cream to eight tablespoons—a full half cup—of butter. Because she didn't skimp on the yeast, her *pulla* was light as dandelion fluff. Because she was sparing with the flour, adding it slowly a bit at a time while she kneaded the sticky dough, her *pulla* remained soft.

My contribution was to break open the woody shells of cardamom, to pick the small black kernels out with care so as to keep the ground mixture free of shells, to wrap the kernels carefully in a corner of white dish cloth, and to pound them with Pa's hammer until they were ground to Ma's satisfaction, not so small that they lost their flavor nor so large that the flavor was too strong.

24

As soon as Ma was able to handle the dough with buttered hands, she turned it into a huge stoneware bowl and set it to rise until it had doubled.

After an hour or two, Lil stuck two fingers into the dough. If it had risen high enough, the finger indentations remained. That had been my job, too, when I was little. Now that I was bigger, after I washed my hands and dried them carefully, Ma trusted me to punch the dough down to its original size and turn it over carefully for a second rise.

At that point, Ma popped a round glob of dough into each of our mouths as a special treat. We could easily have eaten the whole bowl.

The next steps required perfect timing. Ma checked the dough every fifteen minutes or so as it rose again, almost doubling this time. Then she turned the contents out onto the kitchen table to rest, covered it with a dishtowel as tenderly as she covered us at naptime, waited again, then formed the dough into thin round strands, three to a loaf, braiding them from the middle to the end on one side then flipping the dough over to braid the other side middle to end.

That flipping step was the reason her braided *pulla* looked beautiful and even. It was one of her secrets. We never told.

Lastly, and these were critical steps, too, she allowed the braided loaves to rise again in the pans, sprinkled the tops with egg white and sugar, and baked them, watching them like a hawk. To bake them one minute too long would dry them out, she explained to us as we waited, impatient for our first taste; to bake them one minute too little would leave the centers doughy. We grimaced. We had tasted doughy *pulla*, we had tasted dry *pulla*, and we had tasted Ma's *pulla*.

Sometimes when a freshly baked braided loaf had its final coating of sugar, Ma allowed us to pull it apart and eat as much as we wanted. But that only happened when the loaf was an especially small one made of leftover dough. Usually she required us to wait patiently until coffee time when she cut each of us a slice. Lil slathered hers with butter, but I ate my fresh pieces plain. Second-day *pulla* needed butter; first-day *pulla* stood on its own, the epitome of all that was special about Finnish cooking.

We were not sure whether Miss Loney understood or appreciated the ceremony that accompanied the coffee table treats. It was a tradition. With the first cup of coffee, guests always took a slice of *pulla*; with the second, the unfrosted cake; with the third, a bit of decorated cake; with the fourth, a choice of cookies. With the last, they sipped coffee through a sugar lump, and during rests in between, they carried on conversations.

The following afternoon at Ma's request—an invitation was sent along with me right away in the morning—Miss Loney did come over for afternoon coffee, and Ma had outdone herself. The cookie plate held gingersnaps, prune tarts, egg rings, and tiny chocolate meringues. The *pulla* was fresh; the pound cake, rich with butter; the chocolate cake, frosted with fudge.

But both Miss Loney and I were too nervous to do it justice. We should, we agreed afterward, have broached our subject first rather than waiting so that we could have enjoyed the feast. As it was, to me at least, everything tasted as grainy and flat as lumps of dirt. Not until the discussion was over could we rather rapidly repeat the whole sequence, gobbling more than was really polite, even Miss Loney, for Ma's treats were simply not to be missed.

Thank goodness, Ma was pleased rather than put out. To have guests eat well constituted the ultimate compliment to her baking.

Incredibly, our worries had been for naught. Ma raised not one single objection to Miss Loney's tactful suggestion that for school programs and perhaps for the future it might be well to anglicize my name.

But there was still Pa to consider, and he didn't get home until Miss Loney was long gone and supper ready to be served.

By then the *pulla* and cakes and cookies had formed mud balls in my tummy, and it was I, not Lil, who spent clean-up time in the outhouse.

As soon as I returned to clear the table and stack the dishes while we waited for the water to boil, Ma repeated Miss Loney's suggestion to Pa.

Pa sat silently, considering.

I sat frozen.

Instead of answering with a *joo eli ei*, a yes or a no, he got up from the table and disappeared into the small parlor where he kept his fiddle and where Ma had placed the red velvet couch Pa stole from a whorehouse (I was not supposed to know that word) in Port Arthur and where a crocheted *tuuk-ki* covered every inch of the round oak table in the middle of the room. He came back with the big book that sat in the center of that table, a book I had never been allowed to touch, for its pages were very fragile.

Picking me up to sit on his lap (me, not Lil), he opened the book and showed me what he called a "family tree," a tracing of his family's lineage back to his ma and pa and his grampa and gramma and their ma and pa and so on to a time before time began, when Ambrusius, a merchant of Lybeck, Germany, traveled to Karijoki, Finland, in the year 1606 and changed his name to "Brusi."

Brusi's son Matias was born in 1630, Matias' son Henrik in 1670, Henrik's son Goran (Yrjo) in 1713, Goran's son Anders in 1758, and so on through Malachias Brusi and Valachias Brusi until Valachias Brusi's daughter Gret Lisa wed Joseph Nestor Hogblom of Teuva. Their son Nestor was known as Hogblom when he married his second wife, but at some time during the following years he changed his name to Prosinen and then to Brosi, which the family used to this day, sometimes with the addition of an "e" at the end, sometimes not.

Thus, Pa made clear, name changes in his illustrious family history were not without precedent. Were we ever to return to Finland, he continued, musing about all of this, he wanted me to return to being "Ilmi Marianna." But so long as we stayed in America, he was not averse to being as American as possible. In fact, he himself was considering revising his name from "Knute Pietari" to "Knute Peter" in honor of our new country.

The prospect of change had taken on a magical element for me, as if in becoming "Marion," I could shed an old-country skin and don one that was new and fresh and untried and beautiful and full of hope for a similar future. I was certain that a *"ruusu"* or *"ruusunnuppu"* could never smell nearly as sweet as a rose.

And so it came to pass that the first steps were taken in my transmogrification from the Finnish "Ilmi Marianna" to the truly American "Marion." Pa liked the name better spelled with an "o" perhaps because he did not have a son, and I was the elder. We threw "Ilmi" into the middle, but Ma suggested we change its spelling, too, to "Elmi," just to be creative and make it look a bit less Finnish.

But my name was not the only issue Miss Loney wished to address with me. The next night I was kept after school again, and that time the news was dire.

Chapter Four

"Wilho Field's Downfall"

Limp with relief at having the business of my new name settled, I slept well, too well, and awoke to a day that screamed disaster from beginning to end because Ma had done the unthinkable: she too had overslept. Thus Pa was late for work. I was late for school. And the crunch of time caught Lil in a vise that was even worse.

Every morning of her life, Lil experienced the same wrenching readjustment to life's normal daily functions, which to her included every facet of living. In the world according to Lil, slumbrous mornings began in a leisurely manner with ample time to luxuriate in bed, stretching and yawning, alternating between sleep and wakefulness. Breakfast varied according to the whim of the moment—thin Finnish pancakes with sausage or bacon, perhaps, or hot *puuroa* laced with butter and brown sugar. It was to appear with a kind of sleight of hand, as it were, at the moment when she was well and truly hungry, not a moment before. Such mundane concerns as uncombed hair, an unwashed face, ill-matched, wrinkled, or even worse, actually soiled clothing, all anathemas to Ma, left her totally unmoved until such time as she was ready to rectify the oversight. Usually by then, the time needed had elapsed.

When the world refused to bend to her wishes, as unfortunately was often the case, especially on weekdays, Lil screamed.

Screaming, it has been recorded and never denied, was one of her better things, the one accomplishment, perhaps even more than procrastinating, at which she truly excelled. Shrill, eerie, ear-splitting treble crescendos ran up and down the scale until they settled into a steady wail that permeated virtually all of Kinney, certainly at the very least the Salins' house and store, there at full volume.

"Can you not keep that child quiet?" Mrs. Salin asked Ma one particularly harried day.

"No," Ma forced herself to admit, shame-faced.

Undeterred by threat of spanking or by its actuality, once crossed, Lil screamed until she reached that equally disturbing state in which breaths became gasping stutters and the rigidity of her fury lapsed into a languid torpor, much like death, creating as much disturbance as had the earlier noise.

That morning all was lost before the day had even begun. Ma finally gave up completely on Lil, got me ready, and sent me along to school in such haste that I was not sure until I checked just before entering the building whether I was, in fact, decently clothed.

Thus I presented myself at the door of Miss Loney's classroom, out of breath from the run and mortified at the prospect of having to walk in late in front of everyone. Even my hair was disheveled in spite of Ma's brushing, which had slashed through the night's snarls with reckless and, it seemed to me, cruel abandon.

Had they been kind, the members of the Good Gang might have mitigated my anguish by a smile or a glance of commiseration. But I had earned too many stars, flaunted too many hundreds, recited times tables with ease too flagrantly. With a sinking awareness that every single child in that room, particularly Wilho Field and Sara Salin, relished my fall from favor, I slipped in through a barely opened door, slid into my seat with an abject "I'm sorry, Miss Loney," and folded my hands in my lap, awaiting judgment.

It came, but not in the form I had expected. It came in the guise of help, a hideous masquerade.

"Well," Miss Loney began breathily, as if she too had hurried, looking first at the clock and then at me with an arched eyebrow, "the class all present, let us begin with the plans for the Mothers' Day program."

I cringed. During the previous evening's concentration on my name change, I had forgotten about the Mothers' Day program. To tardiness was thus added irresponsibility.

Moreover a small part of me rebelled at what I considered an excessive amount of disfavor. The look was adequate; the eyebrow, excessive. I had not been *that* late. All I had missed were the bell and the march into the school building.

Miss Beck, the principal and teacher of the upper grade room, signaled the beginning of each school day by appearing at the top of the front entrance stairs, six-inch school bell in hand, Miss Loney at her side. By the time the clangor ceased, the entire student body had lined up in single file by grade with only a bit of jostling for position. Everyone wanted to be first, especially everyone in our room, because Miss Loney conferred upon that first one a special smile as we filed past her into the building. When the last one in our room had passed by, she too fell into line. With serious faces and in utter silence, we marched ahead of her into our classroom.

Whoever was first got to open the door and hold it open even for Miss Loney. Everyone else proceeded to the cloakroom to hang up outerwear, place rubber boots neatly together, and don clean shoes when necessary, remaining through all of this as quiet as could be so as to impress Miss Loney. Hurrying to our assigned seats, we stood at attention until the door monitor too was in his or her place and Miss Loney at her desk.

Most mornings then followed a prescribed sequence. We said, "Good morning, Miss Loney," in unison. We recited the Pledge of Allegiance, hands on hearts, eyes on the flag. We sang a fervent if somewhat flat rendition of "My country 'tis ka rein, sweet land of leipurein, to thee we sing."

That the words made no sense at all was immaterial. We meant them with all our hearts. It was much the same for kids who went to Sunday School. I heard them singing "Sadly, the Cross-Eyed Bear." Neither of the lyrics made sense to us, but there were many seeming non-sequitars in the Speak English campaign, all to be born with fortitude if not understanding. Later, when it was all explained, it was too late. Though we blushed with embarrassment, we never were able to sing the words differently.

Once in a while, however, because we all liked Miss Loney so much, one of us altered the regular pattern and began the song, "Good morning to you, good morning to you! We're all in our places with bright sunny faces, and this is the way to start a new day!"

Miss Loney's smile on those days was even more radiant.

Unlike other teachers, she rarely pulled the shades on the long, high multi-paned windows in our classroom, either the top shades, which rolled up from the center, or the bottom ones, which rolled down. The sun beams were as welcome as we in that classroom, and they danced with the dust motes much as we waltzed through the days to the rhythm of Miss Loney's schedule, carefully posted by the door for inspection by the principal, members of the school board, or St. Louis County supervisors. At 9:12 our class was engrossed in the Palmer Method of penmanship. At 10:09 on the dot, we were completing our spelling lessons. At 11:13 half of us were sure to be copying arithmetic problems on scratch paper while the other half did sums and subtractions on the black chalkboard to be checked orally for the edification of all. Making sure that all of the four grades in our room finished all of our prescribed lessons required such intricate interweaving, such skillful footwork, that only artistry like Miss Loney's could make the pattern of the day fulfilling rather than simply full. "There is not a moment to be lost," she warned us when we faltered.

That day Miss Loney rushed through opening exercises so that we could fit in a quick discussion of plans for the Mothers' Day program.

It was then that Wilho Field struck, his rapier well disguised as helpful concern for my predicament. He knew very well that I had nothing prepared. Not only had I been tardy in body, I had been derelict in spirit: my homework still lay near my school bag on the kitchen table. I had walked in with empty hands.

Wilho Field raised his.

When Miss Loney recognized him with a polite "Yes, Wilho?" he stood up, sheaf of paper in hand, and adopting a sickeningly understanding tone, said, "I was afraid that Ilmi Marianna might not have time to do her share of the work last night . . ."

The rapier point slithered in and out.

". . . so I wrote a Mothers' Day skit." He held out the neatly folded packet.

Miss Loney glanced at me, recognized my distress and sighed, but accepted both the papers and the inevitable.

"Please describe your plan to the class," she told Wilho in a voice that never failed to be pleasant.

"Yes, Ma'am," he replied with a barely concealed smirk, marching toward the front of the room, taking a stance with his hands clasped behind him, his legs wide apart, and his eyes on me triumphantly. "First, I wrote a poem that addresses the question of how we should treat our mothers. Would you like to hear it?" he asked, a rhetorical question if I had ever heard one. Without waiting for an answer, he continued, "It goes like this" and recited, from memory yet:

"I love you, Mother," said little John;
Then forgetting his work, his cap went on,
And he was off to the garden swing,
Leaving his mother the wood to bring.

"I love you, Mother," said little Nell,
"I love you more than tongue can tell";
Then she teased and pouted full half the day
Till her mother rejoiced when she went to play.

"I love you, Mother," said little Fan;
"Today I'll help you all I can!"
Then to the cradle she did softly creep
And rocked the baby till it fell asleep.

Then stepping softly, she took the broom
And swept the floor and dusted the room.
Busy and happy all day was she,
Helpful and cheerful as child could be.

"I love you, Mother," again they said,
Three little children going to bed.
How do you think that Mother guessed
Which of them really loved her best?

"To illustrate this poem," he continued, "we will set up a series of four shadow tableaux, one for each scene. The mother, sitting silhouetted in a rocker, will be the central figure behind the sheet with a strong light to make her shadow clear. Students will play the parts of John, Nell, and Fan. I, of course, will serve as narrator, reciting the poem once before, once during, and once after the tableaux.

"To complete the program, each pupil in turn will introduce his— or her—mother, who will stand while the pupil recites a short poem of his —or her—own composition, making it clear what he—or she—would do to prove his—or her—love for mother."

The way his voice dipped when he added the "or she" and "or her" set my blood aboil.

"For example," he continued in that sickeningly didactic voice,

"Oh, Mother, dear, I love you best,
And so that you may have some rest,

32

My task will be to wash each dish
And dry it if that be your wish.
For everything you always do—
My heartfelt thanks. I honor you."

At that he clamped his heels together and stood at attention, await-ing comment.

Miss Loney nodded and smiled. In spite of a general displeasure with Wilho Field, the class applauded. His plan was unanimously accepted.

Thus, "Will Field"—for so he called himself when brought to the fore—would appear on the program. We had worried for naught about "Ilmi Marianna." During his recitation, I had become a cipher. Score two for Wilho Field, I thought, clapping without enthusiasm. It was an excellent plan. The poem especially was a masterpiece, worthy of publication.

Mortified, I had lost face twice, and the day had hardly begun.

Add to that a foolish error in spelling, an inability to verbalize the difference between past and present perfect tenses, the subtraction of one hundred and twenty-two from four hundred and four given at two hundred and seventy-two (on the blackboard, to Wilho Field's great delight), and my pronunciation of the "p" in pneumonia in our vocabulary assignment, and I was clearly in deficit.

Moreover, for lunch Ma served liver and beet greens because Dr. Good had said I still needed iron. The liver and beet greens stayed down until I was past Salins'. That was the only bright spot in a day of what seemed to hold uniform despair.

Finally, just before the dismissal bell, Sara Salin passed me a note that invited Lil but not me to her birthday party. Feeling like a complete and utter failure, I tried to slink past Miss Loney as we all filed out, bare-ly mumbling my "Good-bye, Miss Loney."

"Good-bye," she said, smiling, to everyone else. But she motioned me to stop.

When everyone else had filed by and the upper grade room too had been dismissed, like Ma Miss Loney did the undoable. Reaching out her hand, she led me down the hallway, through the library, and into the teacherage, the living room of which abutted one library wall.

I followed her, my mouth open, astonished. The door through which we passed, though it looked like every other school door, was not. It was the portal to an inner world utterly forbidden to students, as isolated from our world as the cells of a nunnery where proselytes abjure all earthly contact. None of us had ever passed through that door. We knew that the teachers who did must live in rooms like ours at home. They must have bedrooms since like ordinary mortals they must sleep, a kitchen since they too must eat, and a living area where presumably they carried on conversations, where they performed such sanctified tasks as the correcting of papers, the awarding of grades, the planning of lessons.

What a surprise it was to see that the living room into which we walked had curtains made of lace, like ours, a davenport that looked as if it opened like ours, two big chairs that looked well used like ours, and a table on which lay a deck of playing cards! I marveled.

Miss Loney motioned for me to sit down near the the table and asked, just as if I were a grown-up, "Would you like a cup of tea?"

Perching on the very verge of the chair, feet together, back straight, hands folded, I answered primly, articulating with care, "Yes, please, Miss Loney." Amy March seeking to impress Aunt March could have done no better.

Ma had lectured me about curiosity too many times for the lesson not to have taken hold. Thus I carefully refrained from looking about me and kept my eyes fixed on the reproduction of Gilbert Stuart's painting of George Washington, which was hanging on the opposite wall. Someone had taped a festoon of buttercups onto his powdered wig and had given him a black crayon handle-bar moustache. Shocked, wondering which upper grade boy might have gained access to the room, I hoped it had not been Eino. The artwork looked more creatively Italian than carefully Finn. Perhaps it had been Kabe.

Miss Loney wore an abstract look when she reentered with a tray of tea—pot, cups, saucers on a linen cloth. I averted my eyes from George, praying she would not see his embellishments, and awaited developments, struggling to find words to articulate a very real apology for my negligence.

Surprisingly, Miss Loney seemed as ill at ease as I. Perhaps she was regretting the impulse that had prompted her to invite me here, I thought.

Moving the cards, she sat down herself, poured the tea, and offered me a cookie, which I ate as gracefully as I could. It was hard and crumbly, probably a gift from Mrs. Salin, who was always generous with left-over bakery, and the store had a lot of left-over bakery. Mrs. Salin was a mediocre cook.

Then Miss Loney sighed, gave herself what looked like a mental shake, and began. It seemed to be a case of first things first, and I could almost see her ticking items off of a list. "After today, are you to continue to be 'Ilmi,' or may I begin to call you 'Marian'?"

I smiled. "Pa didn't object at all. I am to become 'Marion' with an 'o' whenever the change can most easily be made, in school at least."

Her rigid posture softened imperceptibly then stiffened again. "Had you given any thought to the Mothers' Day program?"

Slumping to make myself smaller, I answered miserably, "No." It was not quite the truth. I had not given thought to the program the night before; I had thought of little else all day. But Ma did not brook excuses, and to be honest I had none to offer.

Patting her lips with the soft linen napkin, she surprised me. "Will you do so, please, tonight?"

"But why?" The words snapped out sharply before I could close my lips on them.

She bit her lip, looked hard at George Washington without, surprisingly, any reaction at all, then pinioned me to the chair with the same look, accentuated. "I have always had great faith in you, Marion." Smiling briefly, she accented the name, as pleased as I with the sound, then paid me a compliment so unexpected that it brought tears to my eyes. "Faith and trust," she told George and me, "are elements of any friendship. I believe that we share those qualities, for though our ages and backgrounds are very different, I have long felt us to be kindred spirits."

Fervent blinking held back my response, aided by an inclination of my head that could be taken for a nod. I had read *Anne of Green Gables* at least four times, mostly at night when I was supposed to be asleep. Ma often wondered why the kerosene lamp on the kitchen table needed filling more than any other lamp in the house. Since it was my charge on Saturdays to wash the lamp chimney, fill the base with kerosene, and trim the wick, she had no idea how much it always needed filling. Thus I understood "kindred spirit." It was the penultimate compliment, one I felt I did not deserve.

The tears threatened to spill over because she had used the present perfect tense of the verb indicating a past action that was to continue.

Then she threw me a curve as sharp as any Kabe ever pitched during summertime ball games: "How old are you, Marion?"

I was aghast. Because I had always been skinny and small and because no records had followed us from Canada to Minnesota, no one

35

other than Ma and Pa knew my exact age. Ma had fudged about it when I started school in Kinney.

"It's just a small white lie," she had explained to me, "because I do not want you to be any more uncomfortable in school than is needful."

When I was six and seven years old and should have begun first grade, we had moved twice—from Canada to Malcolm and from there to Virginia. Ma did not enroll me in school in Malcolm because we never intended to be there more than a month or so. She had enrolled me in school in Virginia, but for some reason I had taken poorly there. Dr. Good had prescribed liver and beet greens because I was "anemic" and told Ma very firmly that I needed rest and fresh air and good healthy food—lots of milk and cream and red meat—far more than I needed an education. In fact, were we not to heed his warnings, he further indicated with a significant look, any education might well be wasted.

So I spent time that I should have spent in school taking naps and watching Lil and listening to Ma and Pa fight and trying not to throw up the liver and beet greens. Dr. Good also prescribed cod liver oil, a teaspoon morning and evening. It smelled as bad as it sounded and slithered down my throat like the rotten fish it was made from. I held my nose and gagged. Nothing eradicated either the aftertaste or the lingering reek of rancid oil left too long in the sun.

"Phew," Lil said when she got near me.

At any rate, the year before, when we moved to Kinney and life finally stabilized, I entered first grade ostensibly as a six-year old. I had really been ten. On March 19 of second grade, though I was no bigger than the other seven-and-eight-year olds, I had actually turned eleven.

Gulping, I considered a lie. But lie to Miss Loney? It was the equivalent of breaking the Ten Commandments. From my slump, I constricted my being still smaller, pulling my knees up under my skirt onto the chair, holding them with my arms, and burying my face in my skirt. To my heels I whispered, "I am eleven years old. Eleven years and almost two months."

Miss Loney embraced the ball of misery that was I and whispered very gently, "I'm glad." She did not seem surprised. "It makes this a bit easier."

Somehow I uncoiled, and we moved onto the couch where we sat together, Miss Loney patting my hand. "I can now treat you like the almost grownup that you are." Reaching over to refill my cup of tea, she added three sugar lumps, handed me the cup, asked me to wait a moment, please, and hurried out the door into the library.

A minute later she was back, a book in hand, one so new that it had not yet been catalogued. Both the pocket card and the Dewey Decimal System code number on the back were missing.

Showing me the title, *Holydays and Highdays: Our Holidays in Poetry,* she opened the book and handed it to me.

I read the title of the poem on page 126: "Which Loved Her Best?" and the author's name, "Joy" Allison, before scanning the opening lines:

"I love you, Mother," said little John.
Then forgetting his work, his cap went on,
And he was off to the garden swing,
Leaving his mother the wood to bring.

I looked up, aghast, my eyes meeting Miss Loney's in disbelief. The following four stanzas sounded equally familiar. Letting the book drop onto my lap, I shook my head, appalled to the depths of my soul by Wilho Field's perfidy. He had plagiarized, blatantly copied and plagiarized, passing the poem off as his when in truth it had been written by someone else.

In Miss Loney's eyes, and in mine, such an act of violation was truly heinous. Oh, I stole words all the time from Eino Salin's vocabulary notebook, but I knew the difference between taking single isolated words or phrases to improve my vocabulary and copying whole paragraphs . . . or poems . . . created by someone else. To steal another's child, even a child of the mind, was the kind of mortal sin only outcasts like the gypsies would commit or condone. To take unto oneself the combinations of words created by others in my mind ranked right up there with white slavery and ore dumps as a violation of all that was good and true, a sullying of the soul of nature and right. By wrongfully attributing another's creation to himself, Wilho Field had finally and truly set himself beyond the pale. There was no hope for him.

My eyes met Miss Loney's, and she nodded. "We have two choices. We can divulge the truth, or we can give Wilho Field an opportunity to withdraw gracefully and leave it to the principal, Miss Beck, to exact retribution. But we need a Mothers' Day skit right away." She paused, waiting for my response.

I paused, weighing my response. On one hand, the desire for revenge and the thought of Wilho Field's being abased, publically chastened, beckoned a sylph-like hand, a siren song as alluring as Circe. But the memory of my own day-long acquaintance with humility had had an effect, as had Miss Loney's testament of faith and trust.

"I shall write a new skit tonight," I promised, as if it were a vow. "And I shall leave this all to you and Miss Beck and Wilho." Almost against my will, my heart went out to him. I knew well to what devious depths a desire to excel can lead. No spelunker could explore a deeper or more dangerous cave. Standing up quickly, I moved toward the door before my other self could take hold, my lesser self, the part of me that heard the siren willynilly.

"About your age," Miss Loney added before I disappeared, "let's talk about that tomorrow."

In later years I regretted with all my heart that Margaret Mitchell died too soon to indicate to her readers whether the really important things in life like forgiveness and love always disappear, gone with the wind. Time was to teach me, however, that whatever the future, Scarlet O'Hara was right about one thing—tomorrow always is another day, to be faced with equal parts of hope and trepidation.

Chapter Five

"Mother's Day Plans and Mothers' Day Reality"

Some people can tell a lie with impunity. No one sees through it, and they never reveal it themselves with blushes or guilty looks. They never forget to follow the big lie with little lies. Not I. I turn red or look away or blurt out the truth or forget what I said in the first place so the little lies reveal the big one. Or I get caught on the consequences.

It should have been no surprise, therefore, that the lie I told Miss Loney—tiny though it was—set into motion a series of actions that resulted in consequences so serious they changed my life forever: that one small white lie and my pervasive sin. Pride.

Had I thought about the Mothers' Day program? Miss Loney had asked. I had answered, "No."

What a farce! In truth, I had thought about the Mothers' Day program and very little else with great chagrin ever since I had heard Wilho Field's presentation. All during the ensuing school day I had been haunted by the awareness that I could never have written a poem even half so creative as the one I had believed original to Wilho Field, nor could I have thought either of personalizing the children's messages to their mothers, thus giving everyone a position of importance, or of setting up tableaux.

Finding out the truth about the poem did not eliminate either those feelings of inadequacy or, as I walked home considering Miss Loney's request, an overwhelming sense of downright panic. I could adapt Wilho

39

Field's plan by finding another poem or citing the real author of that one; I could use the rest of his ideas. But pride demanded that I write my own program, one for Miss Loney to perceive as equally creative and wholly original.

Thus, when she had asked me if I had thought of the program, I had shrunk inside of myself for two reasons—first, for forgetting to do so the night before; second, for doing nothing else since early morning—with absolutely nothing to show for it.

Even had I responded honestly, perhaps the future would have taken a similar turn. But perhaps not. Other influences than those within me were at work, too, forces beyond my power to understand, turning the wheels of fate willynilly.

Nonetheless, looking back, to some degree I still blame myself.

That night throughout my dilatory walk home, for I dawdled as much as I could, I desperately sought revelation; throughout the preparations for dinner—setting the table, stirring the gravy, mashing potatoes, cleaning up Lil from her overly enthusiastic digging trenches in the vacant lot—through it all my mind worked. To no avail.

At length, mashed potatoes and venison roast with rutabagas on the side having been eaten, Lil's spot at the table having been cleaned up and she excused, I broached the subject to Ma and Pa, who were drinking a last cup of coffee. In balance, perhaps they could provide me with a workable plan or, at least, a beginning, an idea, a concept. Pa prided himself on his felicity with language, on his ability to find in song and poem words for those deep feelings often thought "but ne'er so well expressed." Ma was equally adept with finding a practical down-to-earth solution to any problem.

When I asked Pa for help, however, he gave Ma a speaking glance and said, "I have had little experience with mothers, other than my own, and that a long while ago. Those experiences lend themselves to prose rather than poetry."

Obviously things between them had returned to normal.

Ma got up with a flounce to begin filling the dishpan with hot water from the wood stove boiler. I carried the dirty dishes to the enamel-topped side table and wiped the slops into the pig pail to be delivered to Mr. Spina, who was raising a pig for us. We had promised to help, come fall, with the butchering and the rendering of lard. He had promised to smoke the hams and bacon.

Ma always insisted on washing dishes herself—she had what she called *"sepan kourat,"* hands that could withstand the hottest water—and rinsing them too with boiling water kept steaming in the copper tea kettle that moved back and forth from the back burner to the front burner all day, kept warm and ready.

To me were left the menial tasks—wiping the table, sweeping the floor, covering the perishables and lowering them via a pail into the well, moving all other leftovers onto a shelf in the pantry, wiping the pots, pans, dishes, silverware, and glassware dry once Ma removed them from the rinsing pan. Lastly, I put them all away into their designated places.

The whole routine was so familiar that we went through it automatically and, in fact, rather enjoyed it, for it was the one time during the whole day when Ma and I had a chance to talk privately. Usually then I practiced my new words on her, and she listened and repeated them, enthralled. But that night instead I repeated my request for help.

"What do mothers want to see their children do?" I asked, careful, while I lifted the clean plates into the cupboard, to put the dish towel down and not throw it over my shoulder.

Looking out the window at Lil, who was dancing to the tune of Pa's fiddle in the back yard, Ma shook her head. Pa should have been carrying wood into the wood box. Lil should have been saying her numbers and letters in English.

"I mean for the Mothers' Day program," I amended, well aware that efforts to change either Pa or Lil had proved futile and that Ma was too tired to push any more.

She didn't respond right away. Then, rather abstractly as if in deep thought, leaving the last pan to soak, she poured each of us a cup of coffee, waved me toward the sugar lumps and fresh, sweet cream, and sat down herself, elbows resting on the oilcloth tablecloth in spite of her usual dictum against such sloth.

She was really tired that night, I realized and vowed to listen and do everything she wanted.

"What means the most to me," she began slowly, "not only on Mothers' Day but on every day of the year, is what you and Lil do for me yourselves." Pausing, she looked at me with the love she was loathe to speak shining in her eyes. "I love hearing the new words and the stories you make up using them. I love having you be helpful and thoughtful to me and Pa, and . . . ," she grimaced a bit, aware of the difficulty, "and Lil."

She stopped to sip her coffee, and I waited. Words, which were sacred to me, came hard for her. We were not an open or an expressive family given to grandiose gestures of emotion, unlike the Vanuccis, our neighbors down the block, who fought vociferously at least once a week. Mrs. Vanucci had been known to dump an entire pot of spaghetti over Mr. Vanucci's head, and the Vanucci children had been raised to accept and expect cuffs on the head and spanks on the rear and loud and furious reprimands. Yet they were a happy family, for in equal and fervent ways were affection, love, and tenderness shown. Mrs. Vanucci even kissed me and hugged me close to her ample, warm, tomato-saucy bosom. The Vanucci children were as likely to hug as to punch each other. When Eino Salin attacked Kabe Vanucci's younger brother Alcide, Kabe beat him to a pulp. In fact, Eino's fight with Alcide had been the precipitating factor in Eino's being buried in the sawdust pile. The Vanuccis loved and hated with equal passion.

We, on the other hand, lived a life of icy restraint. Ma and Pa rarely raised their voices to us or, though they disagreed about everything, to each other. Yet loathe as they were to show anger openly, so loathe were they to love openly, either each other or us. Rarely were we hugged, even more rarely kissed, rarely praised except by Uncle Charles, who in his initial delight at having found us had forsworn his Finnish imperturbability and never sought its return.

Thus, for Ma actually to sit down and say openly to me what she felt and wanted and appreciated and sought constituted a revelation, one I took to heart. Setting my coffee cup aside, I dug into my school box for a pencil and foolscap paper and settled myself at the table to try to make Mothers' Day give to Ma what she so richly deserved.

It took the whole evening and a large part of a restless night, and in the end I did wind up stealing somewhat from Wilho Field. But finally, inspired by Miss Loney's interest in and encouragement of "group process" and "cooperative learning," I arrived at the suggestion that I presented to Miss Loney in writing as I passed her at the entrance to our classroom before opening exercises the following day.

Her quick perusal and resultant smile indicated that she liked it very much.

Each family, I suggested, will present its own Mothers' Day message. One child will usher Mother onto the stage onto a throne, a concession to Wilho's rocking chair. A second will show her a scroll. A third, if there were a third, or the other, will read to Mother and to the audience the words on the scroll.

Each scroll must include the following:

—information about Mother such as her full name and birthplace, dates of her birth and marriage, the names and ages of all of her children;

—a description of the way Mother spends her days, the kinds of work she does;

—one task the child promises to learn to do, one that Mother might prefer to delegate.

Each scroll must be written in a perfect Palmer Method hand and signed by each child, and each child must vow to keep his or her word.

In token of this commitment, each family must prepare a circle of clay into which they press hands, names, dates, and symbols of the vow. Like Moses' clay tablets, these are to be hung as household commandments.

Miss Loney liked the idea so much that she passed it along to Miss Beck, who adopted it for the entire Kinney School Mothers' Day Program.

I was not sure where Fate stood in relation to my presence at the Mothers' Day program. I wanted to see my name as chairman; I wanted to usher Ma to the throne. But with equal fervor I wanted Uncle Charles to come and us to move to Zim.

Even more equivocal was my response to Miss Loney's own plan for my future, described to all of us, Ma and Pa and Lil and me, that very weekend when she surprised us with an evening visit.

"I have been very impressed by your daughter's work this year," Miss Loney began, having smilingly refused Ma's offer of coffee with a quick, "Thank you, but I am here on business tonight."

"I have been so impressed by her diligence, her will to succeed, her creativity, " she continued, looking squarely at Ma and Pa, hoping they would understand these concepts for which she had no Finnish words, "that, pending the results of this month's work," she paused and gathered herself together, "I am considering triple promoting Ilmi Marianna." She corrected herself, "Marion. To the upper grade room and to fifth grade. Of course, such an action would be governed by her scores on the end-of-the-year tests. So, in the meantime, I have come here to ask you to encourage her to study—to give her time to study—even more intensively than usual.

"I have brought several textbooks that contain concepts covered by the third and fourth grade classes, most of them lessons Marion may well be familiar with already since recitation and discussion have occurred within her hearing all year."

It was true. I always eavesdropped on the third and fourth graders' lessons, trying their maths, spelling their words, doing as many of their assignments as I could, sometimes during the day in school, sometimes at home, for Ma and Pa did not know the difference.

"I have also prepared a schedule which she should follow for the next several weeks. At the end of that time either the principal herself or I will administer two extra examinations, one oral and one written." The books that she took out of a school bag were piled neatly before me.

"As you know," she told the four of us sitting at attention, even Lil, "report cards include a special provision. On the back page is a blank for the name of the student then the words 'is hereby assigned to' followed again by a blank 'grade for the next school year.' Should a student do poorly, he or she could be dropped back a grade."

Every one of us was aware of the danger of that indignity.

"Should the student not fulfill the class objectives, he or she could be retained."

It had almost happened to Sara Salin the year before. She cared much more for her bows and beaus than for her schoolwork.

"Most students are, as you know," she continued, "simply promoted to the next grade level."

We nodded. Thus it had been in Finland, too.

"It is possible, however . . ." she smiled.

We held our breaths.

". . . that should a student show signs of unusual promise and aptitude, he or she could be double-promoted, from first to third grade, perhaps, or from second to fourth. It is up to the discretion of the teacher." Her smile broadened, and she reached out to pat my hand supportively. "I want Ilmi . . . Marion . . . to move ahead enough for her not only to catch up with what is really her class but to find herself in an environment that offers both challenge and promise. Now."

She leaned back, relieved to have it said, awaiting response.

Ma and Pa looked pleased; I, aghast.

On one hand, such a possibility constituted a reward beyond any I had ever considered during long nights of dreaming about the future. Even double promotion was granted only to truly exemplary students. To be triple promoted! It outweighed any honors won in spelling or vocabulary matches.

But such a leap would also catapult me from the safety and security of Miss Loney's room into the rarified atmosphere of the upper grade room. I could easily anticipate the reactions. From the big kids, an adamant refusal to admit me into their circle; from my peers, equal ostracism. All of them, unified in their hatred of what they called a "brownnose," a Pickthank, whose advancement was based not upon merit but upon kowtowing to the teacher, would label me not as an exemplary student but as the lowest of the low, the teacher's pet. They would consider my actions and my promotion unconscionable.

Where, thus, had effort—and pride—brought me? Into possible isolation, once more. Until I had met Miss Loney, I had never felt as if I fitted in anywhere—not into this new country with its bewildering though richly beautiful language; not really into the Good Gang, who accepted me provisionally but whose feats of daring-do actually frightened me; certainly not into the circle of Finnish family and friends, for I wanted with all of my heart to move out of their narrow boundaries into the great world, the English-speaking world, where my words could earn me position and power.

One small lie and my own pride had put the touchstone into place —I was sure that my work on the Mothers' Day program had contributed in a significant way to the development of Miss Loney's own plans—and an archway to the future stood open before me. I was to be pushed through . . . cast out . . . up, it is true. But also out.

Yet Ma and Pa were shaking Miss Loney's hands with enthusiasm. Miss Loney turned to me, expecting gratitude. All I could offer was despair. Life had begun to move too quickly. For all her faults, I knew "Ilmi Marianna." I was unfamiliar with this new "Marion," with what she was doing, with where she was going. Although Miss Loney definitely had her hand on the whip or her foot on the accelerator, whatever the vehicle that was forging ahead, it was I who clung to the passenger seat, hanging on for dear life.

For that moment, more than anything in the world I wanted not success but escape.

"Oh, Uncle Charles," I thought, "please come back and save me. Please!"

When Uncle Charles returned and we moved to Zim, it would all become moot. I could start again there and keep my pride in check even though even there I would be hard put not to try my hardest all the time in school.

Before I had gone to sleep at the end of each of the seven days which had passed since Uncle Charles left, I had asked Ma, "Will Uncle Charles be back tomorrow?"

Every night before she had turned down the kerosene lamp, she had said, "Perhaps tomorrow. But remember, he has a lot to do first."

I knew she was right. Before he left he had explained clearly that he must resign from his job for the Oliver Iron Mining Company, work out any last days while a replacement was found and trained so he would get a good recommendation, withdraw the funds necessary to buy the farm, and pack the few things he wanted to bring from his room at the boarding house. He asked us to trust him to expedite the process. Knowing that being with us was what he wanted above all other things, we did.

Just as Ma always told Lil it was her job to go to sleep when she wanted to play all night, Ma had to remind me that it was our job to wait patiently.

I tried. I truly tried. But every one of those seven days had seemed to last longer than the day before, and I was sure that a whole month had squeezed itself into that first week.

Still, Uncle Charles did not come.

I temporized with Miss Loney, thanking her with real appreciation for her concern and interest and promising to think very hard about her suggestion. So sensitive was she to my feelings, so kind, that she did not remark upon my hesitation but simply took my hands in hers and smiled and told me gently, "It is the teacher's place to open doors for her students; it is theirs to choose which to enter."

Standing gracefully at the door in her peach georgette dress with its gold-trimmed cape-like collar, she pressed my hands, nodded good-bye to Ma and Pa and Lil, and slipped out the door. I wanted to follow her, to hug her and cry, to explain how I felt and why this was all so difficult. But for once I who could not find the words.

Surprisingly, Pa and Ma forbore from comment, Ma limiting herself to a single line, offered obliquely while I bathed in the wash tub in front of the wood stove on Sunday night and she poured a vinegar rinse on my hair. "In the last analysis," she told my back, using the dipper to swish off some soap, "it is your decision."

After school on Monday, glancing at the pile of books but bypassing them still, I paced the floor and finally, desperately needing distraction, set myself to beginning Lil's and my Mothers' Day scroll. "Just in case we are still here for Mothers' Day," I thought, trying to squelch the niggling desire to have our small part of the program be the best. The truth of the matter was that, whether or not it was part of the program, Ma deserved to have her efforts recognized and my commitments solidified.

Most of the scroll virtually wrote itself. I knew exactly how Ma spent her days.

On Mondays she washed clothes, a necessary evil which steamed up all the windows and made a mess of the kitchen. Sometimes Pa remembered to fill the wash tubs on Sunday night, but usually Ma hauled water from the back yard pump herself, pailful by pailful into the wash tubs on the stove. By morning, the water was hot, and between us she and I lifted the tubs down onto the stand she had built herself from waste lumber. By the time Lil got up, white things were already soaking in a solution of water and lye. By then, too, the kitchen floor was covered by carefully sorted mounds of clothing—the more fragile whites, the towels, the colored clothes, the work clothes, the rugs.

Ma did not often win the Monday morning contest. She was rarely the first on our block to hang clothes out on the lines or the first to have the lines filled. But careful scrubbing, bleaching, and a last bluing rinse made our whites radiant, and great care with sorting and water temperature ensured that our colored clothes maintained their individual identities and never ran.

Even Pa's work clothes and our rag throw rugs came through the last rinse immaculately clean and almost as flat as if they had been ironed. Ma never just threw a corner into the wringer, allowing the clothes to be pulled helter skelter. She lifted them out of the water and folded them before inserting them into the wringer, which I turned with equal care when I was home. That extra step was worth the time and effort, she assured me, because it made ironing much easier.

By the time our school day was over on Monday, she had emptied the wash waters, scrubbed both the kitchen floor and the outhouse, and wiped down the windows, sparkling steam cleaned. I took the clothes down from the lines, folded the ironing carefully into baskets, and put everything else away neatly.

On Tuesday mornings, I got up extra early, though still not as early as Ma, to do my share of the flat ironing. On Monday night, Ma had sprinkled the starched clothes and rolled them tightly into balls. As soon as she arose on Tuesday, she set the flatirons onto the stove to heat and put a fresh white cover on the wooden ironing board. Ma never allowed me to attach the handle to the iron. She did that, making sure the clamp was tight before lifting the hot base off the stove. Then it was my turn. I ironed seven dishtowels; four pillowcases with crocheted filagree edges; two clean sheets, the bottom ones from each bed, top ones having been moved down; at least twenty-eight handkerchiefs, for we were expected to take a clean one each morning; and any doilies or antimacassars from the backs of the davenport and armchairs, crocheted in patterns of roses and pineapples and stiffly starched. Ma did the linen napkins and the tablecloth she had brought from Finland, Pa's work clothes and dress shirt, our school and play clothes, and her good dress and house dresses and aprons. She even ironed our underwear and stockings.

Wednesday mornings when we ate fresh doughnuts or coffee cake hot out of the oven were undoubtedly my favorites. The yeast bread and biscuit doughs were rising too by breakfast, and we came home to coffee, company, and treats.

Although lots of mothers left cleaning for the end of the week, Ma liked to do our house on Thursday. When we got home after school, it gleamed from top to bottom with the windows re-washed, the floors scrubbed, fresh rugs laid down, stove blacked, the stoop and board sidewalk swept. Our neighbors teased Ma that she even scrubbed out the chicken coop.

Of course, Ma's week did not end on Friday, when she mended and did her handsewing. On Saturdays and Sundays she still prepared meals and did yard work and fed the chickens. And ever and always when she had a spare minute, she worked at making and remaking, turning and stitching, designing and cutting and piecing out clothing for women not as adept as she with needle and thread. Ma never sat still, rarely sat at all except for the times when she sewed or did handwork. In our household, she was the worker bee, not the queen.

Except that she seemed like a queen to me. It never occurred to me that she was also human.

Recording her daily schedule, I starred the parts of it for which I was also responsible. Ma never had to ask me to do my regular daily tasks. I knew what was expected of me, and I learned early on that life was a lot more pleasant if I completed them willingly and diligently. But I despised scrubbing the outhouse. I even hated using it—the fetid smell, the ugly lime bag, even the old mail order catalogs with their paper pages that we crumpled in a futile attempt to soften them.

Moreover, try as I might, I could not get the hang of either cooking or baking. Even Mr. Spina's pigs refused my dinner rolls, and my cooked cereal lumped. My pie crusts either fell apart or formed themselves into gluey paste, and my cookies burned and stuck to the pan. Worst of all, every cake I ever attempted fell in the middle. Shaking her head, Ma bemoaned the sad waste of ingredients. She strongly suspected that the base of the problem was a want of effort, and I strongly suspected that she was right.

Thus, I vowed not perhaps to like baking and cooking, which might be beyond me, but to learn to do both, one step at a time.

On my scroll, I even wrote out steps which would lead to my taking those daily tasks off of her hands.

For the fact of the matter was that, skilled as Ma was with ordinary household jobs, her real joy lay in the creative ones—stitching dresses from her own designs, working scraps of wood into usable articles. As a special Christmas gift, she once made Lil a table, chair, and cupboard just her size. I got my very own vanity, made of orange crates covered with stiffly starched and gathered pink gingham skirting.

When I was ready to do the good copy of the scroll in my best Palmer Method hand using ink and good paper, I needed only the details of Ma's full name and birthplace in Finland. I could have asked Ma. I knew Lil and I were not to touch the big book in the parlor. But, I rationalized, since I might, after all, be going into the upper grade room, I was, so to speak, on the stoop of adulthood. So that morning while Ma took Lil with her to the meat market to bring a pail of slops and choose a roast for dinner, in my arrogance, I took it upon myself to open the door to the sanctum sanctorum. Tiptoeing to the big book, a combination Bible and family record, I opened its pages carefully and traced the long series of entries to its most recent additions.

There.

May 16, 1910. Knute Pietari Brosi of Salonkylassa, Karijoki, Finland, b. June 19, 1884, m. Maria Gustava Maki (Rajamaki) of Teuva, Vaasanlaani, Finland, b. May 18, 1885. Daughter Ilmi Marianna b. March 19, 1910. Port Arthur, Canada. Daughter Lillian Linda Lydia, b. March 4, 1914. Port Arthur, Canada.

Copying it all quickly, without really reading the words, I folded the paper, closed the book, tiptoed back out of the parlor, relieved not to have been found out, closed the door behind me, and stopped.

Opening the paper, I looked at two of the dates again.

March 19, 1910. On that day I was born.

May 16, 1910. On that day Ma and Pa were married.

That, I realized with a stab of pain, was the real reason no one was to know how old I was. I was almost two months too old.

I blanched and shook, crumpling the paper as I ran across the kitchen, out the door, and across the back yard into the vacant lot until I was hidden by trees. There I threw up until I couldn't throw up any more before I unfolded the crumpled paper to look at the dates again.

At almost that same moment, I heard Ma scream.

At almost that same moment, the days of my childhood ended.

Chapter Six

"The Fires of Summer"

Ma screamed. Yet, horrified as I was by the sound, I stood transfixed, unable to run to her aid. Evil echoed around me, and in its rever-
berations I heard again another scream, Ma's that time too.

I wanted to forget. But I remembered.

So did Ma, I was sure, though neither of us had ever spoken again
of what we had seen that day. We did not tell anyone—not Pa, not Ma's
friend Maija Wirtanen, not my friend Amalia, certainly not Dr. Good or
That Child's mother. By pretending it had never happened, we had
hoped to erase reality. Only in flashes had the memories returned—in
dark dreams, in silent screams, in moments when we faced each other
with an unarticulated yet wholly communicated shared horror. We had
come face to face with evil and ugliness that day and with man's inhumanity to man. To make matters worse, the inhumanity had been committed upon a child by children who gave evil bodily form, substance,
and voice.

But the walls of silence we had erected as a bulwark against remembering were neither high enough nor strong enough to withstand the memories, which returned full force when I heard Ma scream. The experience
had been one reason we had both been happy to leave Virginia. We had
hoped to leave the memories there, too, in that house on North Side where
we lived after we came from Malcolm.

51

Pa had not been able to find a place to rent in Finntown, which wove through the lower part of North Side along the eastern edge of Bailey's Lake, where company rental houses encircled the Finnish Temperance Hall. So he had compromised by taking one on its boundary, the one managed by Maija Wirtanen, the one Ma cleaned up just as Maija had said she could. But it never felt quite as safe as it was clean, for it lay at the foot of Seventh Street North about four blocks from the Jefferson School on the verge of "Italia vitsi."

Italian families lived in that area between the western and northern shores of Bailey's Lake and the iron ore dumps and swampland, though the woodland between was relatively open territory. The Finn kids, carefully skirting the huge backyard gardens and the Italian and Slovenian homes that smelled of wine and cabbage, ventured there sometimes, but mostly, Finns stayed within Finntown, its boundaries established by custom, by a language, heritage, and religion held in common.

Neither Ma nor Pa fit in well in the latter respect, Pa preferring the pathless woods and lonely shore to any church, Ma more concerned about our family circle, including friends like the Wirtanens, than she was with religion.

Nevertheless, whenever the Reverend Risto Lappala spoke at the Finnish Temperance Hall, Ma went and took me, too. Had we stayed in Virginia, she would have joined the fledgling congregation of his new First Unitarian Church rather than the Finnish Evangelical Lutheran Church to which most everyone else belonged. Ma had little faith in evangelism, which she said was often a mask, and she laughed when she told Pa about the most Reverend Victor Kuusisto's summer confirmation class. Scandalous rumors spread about Maxine Ketola's playing the flea hop on the organ while the big kids danced in the church aisles and Bill Huhtala stood at the door on guard pending the Reverend Mr. Kuusisto's return from lunch at the parsonage. "Huhtala" and "Ketola" were important names in Virginia. Mr. Huhtala was an attorney; Mr. Ketola, owner of a large department store on Chestnut Street. But Ma, unimpressed by proximity to what she called the "kerma kerros," the cream of Finnish society, kept me home when the other kids went to Sunday School.

I was happy to stay at home, waiting for Amalia Barone, my best friend, to come home from Sunday mass. In spite of the fact that Amalia spoke only Italian and I only Finnish, from the beginning we had communicated effortlessly in part perhaps because playtimes involved less conversation than they did activity. In between dosings of cod liver oil, beet greens, and liver, when the weather was neither too cold nor too hot for me to be allowed outside to play, Amalia and I met under the third elm tree from the corner, not much more than a seedling, with our dolls, mine a rag body with yarn hair and embroidered eyes, eyelashes, lips, and nose.

I took good care of my Susie Doll, keeping her well out of Lil's reach. Lil, obsessed with funerals, buried all of her dolls with due ceremony including a cortege of sobbing neighborhood kids, a wagon draped in black, and appropriate music played by musicians wearing black armbands, playing sticks, rocks in a can, and a drum made of an empty oatmeal box.

Amalia and I preferred to be mommies, making meals from mud and moss and serving them to our hungry children, including Lil, who was always willing. We borrowed scissors, thread, and needles and stitched whole wardrobes not only for our doll families but for the kittens who lived in the Barones' barn. We laid out rooms and made furniture from birch logs and stumps and rocks.

Once in a great while, we followed the big kids to the ore dump, climbing to the top in winter to speed down on sleds, in summer to look for berries. But usually not. The big kids, those who went to school, including Amalia's brothers and sisters, tended to scoff at us, calling us "babies," so we mostly kept to ourselves, searching for pirates from the mast of our tree-house-ship, traveling to faraway lands in the buggy the Barones used on Sundays for the two-block ride to the Sacred Heart Catholic Church.

Very little was forbidden Amalia and me during the last summer that we lived in Virginia. I was considered "not well" and for large parts of the day was free from either housework or Lil-care. Since Amalia was one of the younger members of a family of sixteen, she too was often exempt from household jobs. There were plenty of other hands.

But Amalia and I were bound by one absolute constraint: we were not allowed to play with That Child, a little girl our age who lived on the North Side's three hundred block, not many streets away. The first time we saw That Child watching us play and invited her to join us, Mrs. Barone called Amalia in, spanked her soundly, and forbade her ever to speak to That Child again. Of course, the warning was given in Italian and I understood none of the particulars, but I did grasp the message: That Child was what I later called an anathema to Mrs. Barone.

Smaller than Amalia, even smaller than I, but not that much smaller, for I was a shrimp so the big kids said, she was, even worse, a half-breed, neither Finnish nor Italian but both. That I gathered from the names the big kids called her. To the Ketolas and Huhtalas and their friends, she was a "Wop" or a "Dago"; to the Barones and their gang, she was a "dumb Finn." But the commonest epithet, yelled loudly whenever any of them saw her outside, was "Bastard!"

Most of the time she stayed out of sight, winding her way along the periphery of our mixed neighborhood, climbing trees, sneaking carrots from back yard gardens or eggs from henhouses, always forlorn, her hair snarled, her dresses sizes too small and dirty. Ma always said it didn't cost a thing but elbow grease to stay clean. Her ma obviously didn't even have that.

Although I did not quite understand how it could be, I knew That Child did not have a father. I knew her mother Worked the Trade. Her mother had been Taken by a White Slaver, whispers repeated, and had gotten involved with a Married Man, and "That was all she wrote," the grownups said.

We could not help but overhear what we couldn't understand, especially the words said with capital letters, for we listened twice as hard when the grownups whispered. Moreover, houses were too small for secrecy, and the big kids repeated everything they heard, and they heard a lot, especially that summer, the summer before the strike and the shooting, before Pa lost his job in the mines, before our move to Kinney, where life took a very different turn, a highly desirable turn for me.

That summer no one bothered to keep doors or windows closed, except Ma, for the weather was boiling, the temperature hovering in the nineties day after day all through July and August with very little rain.

Across northern Minnesota that summer, forest fires broke out, threatening even the towns, overrunning countless farms. Children no older than Lil and Amalia and I stood atop the barns and homes and outbuildings dipping burlap sacks into pails of water, trying to put out the sparks. Their pas cut fire lines and dug ditches and built backfires. Their mas prayed and refilled pails and cut brush and prayed some more.

Along the shores of Lake Superior, Pa read aloud from the *Range Facts*, women buried furniture, silverware, dishes, even clothing, in the sand of the beaches to protect them from the holocaust. One story circulated of a mother and father devastated not merely by the loss of their belongings but by the deaths of their five children who, ensconced in a root cellar to keep them safe, suffocated from the smoke.

Later that fall, huge fires scorched a hundred-mile-long path from Hinckley north into the outskirts of the city of Duluth at the tip of Lake Superior, into parts of Duluth itself, in fact.

Virginia was never threatened by fire in that sense, but the summer's heat wreaked another kind of devastation upon communities like ours. As lawns dried to a brittle brown, as wells dried up, as rain clouds rumbled then skipped by us, even Amalia and Lil and I were aware that our community of souls was seething.

Once in July when we did have a thunderstorm, the clouds roiled gray and black and purple, but though they lowered themselves upon us, the torrents fell and flowed too swiftly for the parched earth to absorb, and waves of topsoil and gravel washed down the hills and ran off into the swamps and lakes, raising those water levels for a time before evaporating into an airless sky.

At any rate, that August morning, the Italian and Finnish communities in Virginia alike awoke, if they had been able to sleep at all, to a heat so intense that any kind of movement actually hurt. Most of the men, including Pa, went to work as usual because it was not much worse in the mines than it was in town. Moreover, once in a great while on a very hot day, the foremen let the men buy beer to wash down the contents of their lunchpails. From a company-owned bar, of course.

Ma knew that and disapproved in principle even though Pa and Uncle Charles, members of the Vesi Temperance Society, largely abstained, but the air was too heavy to hold up an argument, and even breathing took effort. Ma opened the windows at night as soon as it got dark but closed them again early, as soon as the faint nighttime breeze died, pulling room-darkening shades against the sun. To me, the feeling of being enclosed made the heat even worse, but she adhered stringently to the delusion that when the sun was kept out, the house retained the relative coolness of night. So I stayed out, too.

The morning of the day we tried hard to forget, Ma insisted as always that I don the child's version of her daily ensemble, which included corset, long cotton stockings, underpetticoats, a chemise, a waist, a skirt, and an apron, that every good woman must wear, though she gave in on the stays, stockings, and shoes for me, since that saved on laundry, clothing bills, and arguments.

It was too hot that day to work; it was too hot to play. Most everyone lay in whatever shade they could find. I made up stories to try to keep Lil occupied, but she was fractious nonetheless. Neighborhood women fanned themselves and talked desultorily and rocked in rocking chairs on the porch and watched the little kids and rocked some more.

The big kids fretted and moaned and felt sorry for themselves and whined. They wanted to go swimming. They wanted ices. They wanted to go to the park. They wanted to jump into the fountain. They wanted to ride their bikes to Sand Lake. They wanted everything their mothers refused them. Like the thunderclouds, they roiled, and the heat pressed them down.

That is no excuse, of course. But it was the truth.

They needed an outlet. They needed action. They needed a victim. They saw That Child.

Because her mother entertained a steady stream of "uncles," she was expected to remain outside. Sometimes when she slunk by, Ma slipped her a slice of fresh bread or biscuit and a bit of salt fish so she often passed our house, never asking, but always looking hopeful. That afternoon I saw her sidle by, but I was too hot to care, and Ma had gone inside to put Lil down for a nap.

The big kids, energy unabated, requests denied, were roaming free. I saw the big boys pushing bikes, the big girls following at a distance. Usually they had jobs assigned in the yard and the garden for the boys, in the house for the girls. But that day, even chores floated away on waves of heat.

Down the block the Finnish contingent saw That Child and started to chant "Little Dago bastard, dirty little Wop, find a puddle and flop, flop, flop!" From up the street, the Italians and Slovenians chimed in "Dirty little Finn, you smell like shit. Go and jump in the pit, pit, pit!"

Restless and uncomfortable, I stood up from the porch floor where I had been feeding Susie Dolly preparatory to putting her down for a nap. I did not know where to go or what to do to stop them. I put my hands over my ears.

Obviously That Child did not know what to do either. She crossed our front lawn, looking back as the big kids followed her. Then, perhaps in panic, she made a very unwise decision. She started to run, heading up through "Italia vitsi" toward the woods, dump, and swamp.

Hearing the furor, for the big kids followed in a pack, baying, Ma hurried to the screen door.

"Should we go help?" I asked.

Lil, sneaking behind Ma, picked up the refrain, "Dirty little Dago . . ."

Ma grabbed her, walloped her on the rear, told her to stay inside and go to sleep, closed the screen door firmly behind her, and hooked it from the outside. "Yes," she nodded. "Go ahead. I'll follow."

As vigilantes, we were a sad pair. In truth, I don't know that either of us had thought through what we would do were we to catch up with the big kids. But Ma had the power of an indomitable will, and we held a moral advantage that could not help but give us strength.

Without stays and the encumbrances of a petticoat or long skirt, I raced ahead. Instead of yelling for me to wait, Ma urged me on in the general direction of the chant. "Hurry!" she panted, not as far behind as I had expected.

I did. But I was not fast enough.

By the time I reached the wood lots, thickly green, both That Child and the mob of big kids were out of sight, though I could hear remnants of the chant off toward the dump. Heading in that direction, I tripped on a root and fell headlong, lying prone for a minute, the breath knocked out of me.

Even in the lea of the pine trees, the heat bore down like a boulder on my back, and I lay there prickling from the needles and a formless fear. By the time Ma picked me up and we ran on, finally reaching the dump, the big kids had disappeared.

Ma and I clambered up the side of the dump, pulling on branches and bushes, but when we reached the top, it was empty, like a vacuum, as if sound and air had been withdrawn. My head pounded with every heartbeat, and Ma gasped, and I heard my heart beat and Ma gasp but nothing else.

Crossing the flat treeless plateau, we held onto each other, waiting for our bodies to quiet, listening still, but hearing nothing. Only when we reached the sharp ridge marking a precipitous drop on the north and looked down on the swamp far below us, did we see . . . something. Tied to one of the dead tree trunks that protruded from the surface scum like the tines of an Iron Maiden or the points on a bed of nails, it was shaped like a child, but not a child, writhing, brown.

Slipping and sliding down, we cried out that we were coming.

The form did not make a sound. When we got closer, we could see why. A gag, a rag of some sort, had been tied around her mouth. But clearly, it was That Child, clothed with swamp mud, and . . . ("Oh, God," Ma whispered) . . . with bloodsuckers.

Hung like strips of reddish-brown liver from her arms, her legs, her stomach and chest, her neck and face and scalp, they adhered. Only her eyes had been spared, but they were closed. She hung suspended there, limp, like the figure of Christ on the crucifix behind the altar in Amalia's church.

That was the first time I ever heard Ma scream. She screamed imprecations and cried and screamed again.

The eyes opened, focused on something far, far away in the distance, swam somewhere past oblivion, and closed again.

"How could they? Horrible . . . horrible . . . evil . . . cruel . . . ," Ma's words punctuated our movements.

I gagged and held my mouth tightly closed, the bile of vomit contained, for I could not then allow myself to think of myself or of what we were doing. Somehow we tore at and untied the rag bonds. Somehow we got That Child down. Somehow we picked and pulled and yanked off the loathsome leeches, blood oozing from round red spots on her skin. Wiping off the worst of the swamp muck with Ma's apron, we wrapped That Child in Ma's pulled-off petticoats and carried her home.

She lived with us for several weeks, sleeping between Lil and me, eating Ma's good food voraciously, taking as much steam as we did whenever we could afford a sauna, but never talking, never talking at all.

When her ma came to take her home, driven the few blocks in Mr. Ala's huge black hearse, That Child clung to Ma with the strength of a larger leech, her eyes wild and beseeching.

Ma held her until her ma shrugged and went away.

Eventually Dr. Good found a place for her in a hospital that he assured us knew how to care for such children. Ma and I knew that she did not want to go. But even when Dr. Good finally came to lead her away, she did not say a word.

I cried. Ma cried. Lil cried without having a tantrum. But That Child just walked away, holding Dr. Good's hand, lost in a world she could not comprehend, lost even to herself.

I had not been able to forget her, no matter how I tried, and I had tried hard.

Nor had I forgotten Ma's scream.

It had been a relief to move to Kinney. I had not even minded leaving Amalia Barone behind.

Nothing had happened to the big kids, of course, but they knew we knew. It had felt good to leave.

I had not heard Ma scream for two years, but when the sounds she made overpowered even my retching gasps, I knew something must be very wrong. Part of me remembered That Child and all of that horrible evil time in a flashback that lasted seconds too long. Another part of me was pinioned still in my own present horror. That part wanted to scream right back, "Ma, help me! ME!" I did not want to be the responsible older child. I did not want to take care of Lil or anyone else, even Ma. I wanted someone else to take care of me.

Of course, Ma might have a plausible explanation for the discrepancy between hers and Pa's wedding date and my birth date as they were recorded in the family history book—an error in transcribing, perhaps. Whoever recorded those dates might simply have written down the wrong numerals. Heaven knows, even though I had mastered the times nines, I had often made mistakes in sums because I had written down an incorrect base for computation, miscopying the numbers from the problems on the board. Errors happen. But clearly, other things equally ugly also happen, and the other possible explanation was one I could not bear to face. Inside I was screaming, too, silent screams as anguished as Ma's. Was I, too, an anathema? Was I like That Child?

Was I to become That Child's voice?

Chapter Seven

"Pa: "Ja niin minä 'kwittasin'"

Pa rarely drank. In that way, at least, as a husband and father he was vastly superior to Mr. Barone, who, though he usually arrived at home sober, rarely stayed that way past the dinner hour since his homemade wine was notoriously potent. Mr. Spina rarely went home for dinner at all, preferring to join Mr. Salin at Mary's Bar. We often heard him long after our dishes were done, sometimes singing, sometimes crying, stumbling up the outside steps leading to their apartment above the store.

But Mr. Barone, Mr. Spina, and Mr. Salin redeemed themselves every payday, at least in Ma's eyes. They brought home their paychecks and set aside money for household expenses with self-righteous regularity.

Pa did not.

Periodically during the years we spent in Canada, he appeared during the middle of a work day. Ma asked, *"Mikäs nyt on tapahtunut?"* — "What has happened now?"

Pa answered in Finnglish, *"Minä suutuin* (I got mad) *ja sanoin* (and I said) *'paasille'* (to my boss) 'Kiss my ass,' *ja niin minä 'kuittasin.'"* (Then I quit.)

The move to Kinney had been made necessary, Ma understood, by the strike and the job loss that had ensued. Once moved, however, Pa had promised not to quit another job but to work until we saved enough money to buy a farm, an unlikely eventuality until Uncle Charles appeared. Without Uncle Charles, we were sure to stay in Kinney forever, I thought, for Ma and Pa struggled to make enough money just to support us. Rarely was there surplus.

We had settled more firmly into the world of Kinney than Ma had ever allowed herself and us before, and we had been happy. Well, happier.

I should have known it could not last.

Moreover, as I ran from the vacant lot toward the front of our house and Ma, I realized that her scream had not sounded quite the same as the one that I remembered from that year in Virginia. This scream seemed to be generated less by horror than by anger.

I was right. Coming out of the butcher shop, mid-morning, Ma had seen Pa heading home. She had asked him the usual question and gotten the same old answer: he had quit his job again.

Rarely did Ma allow herself to lose her temper in any physical way. For her, the world ended in ice rather than fire. But her scream went on and on and on like an air raid siren before an attack, like a mine whistle after an explosion, like the warning signs that a dam was breaking, a volcano erupting, a tornado approaching. As I ran toward that scream, I glimpsed her marching into the house, Lil flying behind her like a kite. By the time I reached the front door, anger had escalated to pure, unalloyed fury. Out from its centrifuge flew a frying pan, the rolling pin, a kitchen chair, the contents of a bag of groceries, and the rest of my peace of mind. The illusions I had fostered—that we were not only a family but a happy one, that Pa worked to support us, that he protected us and kept us safe and secure—shattered with the broken dishes that flew by me next. Lil sobbed and cutlery crashed and Ma's sharp soprano hit notes the Kinney Choir had never attempted.

Mrs. Salin came out onto the front stoop of the store and looked toward our place with Eino and Sara behind her, gawking.

Pa just stood, looking as if he weren't there. Very soon afterward he wasn't.

Before he went out the door, he told me abstractly, "There is wood at the Andersons." But he did not meet my eyes. He did not say anything to Ma, just added in a general way that he was going to see if the lumber companies up north were hiring. He did not touch Lil, not even the usual pat on the head that acted in lieu of a kiss.

Then he was gone, and the house enclosed us in silence.

Ma stood still, holding onto the back of a chair until her breathing slowed. Then, always practical, she checked two spots right away—the flour bin, which served as our private bank, repository for all available coins and cash, and the wood box. Both were empty. Worse still, the woodpile outside had been depleted during the week of rehearsals and the spring performance and the trip to Zim and the visits from Miss Loney, with barely enough left to fill the woodbox for the next day's needs. No more.

Ma sighed. "Thank goodness it's May," she said, more to herself than to us. "But we still need wood to keep the kitchen stove going. And we will have to pile the wood from Andersons or it will not be dry by fall."

Shaking and gulping back tears, Lil crept over to me and crawled into my lap, though she barely fit there anymore. She had been too young to remember how often fights of this magnitude had occurred in Canada, and the ones they had had in Virginia had never escalated to these heights. I tickled her arms and rubbed her back and tried to soothe her, but I was still trembling myself—aftereffects of an almost lethal dose of reality.

Since Ma's favorite solution to problems of any kind was work, it was not surprising that, making little sweeping motions, she said briskly, "First things first," and "there's no time like the present," and ordered us off to Andersons with a wheelbarrow. "Lil can load the smaller pieces; you, the larger ones, Ilmi Marianna. Off you go now. Hurry. The sooner we start, the sooner we'll be through."

Bewildered and frightened, Lil clung to my hand, and, for once, I did not push her away. I too needed comforting. But since I was older and, therefore, responsible, I kept my back straight and my chin high, just in case the Salins were still watching, and told Lil stoutly, "When the heart aches, it helps to keep the hands busy."

We had no trouble there. Oh, there was wood set aside for us at the Andersons just as Pa had said. But I wanted to cry all over again when I saw the wet, criss-cross trunks of popple trees, felled and branched but neither chopped nor split, lying helter-skelter in the wood lot on the road to Lake Leander.

I shook my head and set the wheelbarrow aside to be picked up later. Taking a deep breath, I grabbed one end of one of the smaller tree trunks, lifted it up under my arm, and began the laborious process of dragging it home. When I told Lil to do the same thing with one of the medium-sized branches, she demurred, pouting and stomping her foot and looking around for a spot soft enough to throw herself onto the ground for a snit. But I was having none of that, and eventually she gave in enough to take a small branch in either hand and follow me out of the woods and across the field onto the narrow gravel road that led toward home.

I repeated that trek at least ten times that day until my hands were so raw and my back so sore I could not manage one more tree, no matter how hard I tried. Ma and I, utterly dismayed, studied what I had managed to haul. Every tree needed to be sawed into blocks, split into smaller pieces, and dried before fall and winter.

It seemed hopeless. Ma knew how to saw wood, and she was able to handle an ax. But this job assumed gargantuan proportions far beyond her strength, requiring a time commitment virtually precluding all other work.

"What do we do?" I asked, bewildered by the whole prospect. When Ma had faced such problems before, I had been too little to appreciate their magnitude. Now I was big enough to understand the difficulties entailed in the attempt to maintain a household with no man to help with the work.

"We start," Ma answered firmly. "First we eat, and then we start the sawing."

That is exactly what we did. We ate a supper of leftover biscuits and gravy, cleaned up the dishes, banked the fire in the wood stove, tucked Lil into bed—on subsequent nights made sure she was safely settled—and went outside to work until it was too dark to see, with me on one end of the crosscut saw, Ma on the other.

The night brought little respite. Though I slept like the dead, every muscle in my body ached, and my hands, refusing to open or close, stayed frozen in claws the shape of the saw handle.

And so the days went. As the woodpiles grew, Ma's anger diminished, banked well against Pa's return, and I bleakly accepted her overwhelming need for me to be of help. There was no time to attend school and precious little even to study. We sawed and split and piled and sawed and split and piled.

Mr. Salin wandered by one evening to ask if he could help.

Ma set her jaw and refused with thanks.

Mr. Spina happened by mid-afternoon to see how we were getting on.

Ma said, "Fine," brusquely and kept on working.

Both of them had seemed far too friendly. Clearly, word had spread about Pa's defection.

Pa's boss on the streetcar line, August Inflese himself, appeared at our back door another morning, hat in hand, apologetic. Pa could be a good worker when he wanted, Mr. Inflese told us, and there was some money due him.

Ma's pride wanted to refuse it, but pragmatism prevailed. Back and head broom-handle straight, she nodded her chin in an almost imperceptible gesture of appreciation and accepted the envelope. Mr. Inflese suggested that if we needed a man to help out with this kind of heavy work, he was willing to come for a few hours in the evening. Perhaps Ma could make dinner for him in exchange for his assistance.

Ma's back went even more rigid, and her chin formed a firm line.

Mr. Inflese's shoulders drooped, his moustache quivered, he wiped the sweat from his forehead, and he too disappeared.

But he must have shared some version of our story with the denizens of the Roosevelt Bar in Virginia, which occupied the corner of Chestnut Street and Second Avenue South, a block away from the Ala Mortuary. Soon Mr. Ala himself appeared, driving his long, black hearse up the road past the school and the meat market and the grocery store, stopping right in front of our house with only a couple of backfiring noises to accent the gradual cessation of sound. Disengaging himself from behind the wheel, he approached us, brushing dust from his black suit, doffing his hat.

Oh, we recognized Mr. Ala. After Maija Wirtanen's husband had left for Duluth, assisted on his way by her sharp tongue, before he got a job there on the docks and she and the kids followed him, Mr. Ala had been most kind to Maija, driving her and the children to Sand Lake one hot summer day and offering her his arm after church.

Everyone was aware that there was a Mrs. Ala, but she rarely emerged from the confines of the mortuary building, preferring to practice the organ, which she played for funerals, and to write poetry, which she often read aloud during programs at the Finnish Temperance Hall. Mrs. Ala's father had operated the mortuary originally. Mr. Ala had married both Mrs. Ala and her business interests when he moved to Virginia about the same time as the Ketolas and the Huhtalas.

They had all prospered, but none so visibly as Mr. Ala. Granted, he and his wife continued to live above the mortuary, but they had replaced the original double-hung windows with new ones made of stained glass and hung velvet curtains that matched the new oriental rug. Mrs. Ala played an Acme Queen Parlor Organ that anyone who looked into the Sears and Roebuck Catalog could see cost $27.45.

Periodically and ostentatiously, Mr. Ala checked the time on his 14-karat solid gold jeweled Elgin watch, engraved with the head of a stag, and adjusted a matching fob that reached from waist-pocket to waist-pocket across a midriff that could only be described as "portly." The ladies of Finntown agreed he was a "fine figure of a man."

Mrs. Ala did not notice. Mostly, except for the times when they performed funeral rituals, she pretended he was not there.

Usually, like Pa, he wasn't.

That Child's mother was another reason why, it had been duly noted.

Now, most everyone agreed that Ma was a fine figure of a woman, too. She had the high cheekbones and creamy complexion, the auburn-tinged brown hair and green eyes more common to the Irish than to Finns. Long enough to sit on when she let it down, her hair coiled in luxurious rolls, too full to need a "rat," the ball of natural hair most women used to give theirs an illusion of fullness. And although she had borne two children, she held herself beautifully, pliant and willowy as a young birch, Pa noted in one of his poems.

Moreover, because she had been in service before Pa and she were married, upstairs maid at a mansion so large it had been given its own proper name, she was as refined as any of the *"kerma kerros,"* more so in fact because it was not an assumed refinement. She did not have to crook her little finger as she held a tea cup. She was a lady, through and through.

Mr. Ala appreciated ladies. After all, he had married one. And he made his appreciation felt in many ways, going so far as to give discounts on the memorial markers to widows who bought directly from him instead of ordering them from the catalog.

When the influenza epidemic struck during the year of the fires, he made it clear that the widowed ladies who bought from him did not have to pay the cost of freight which, since we lived east of the Mississippi River, came to twenty-five to fifty cents per hundred pounds. That was significant when the tombstones chosen by the truly sorrowing weighed nearly a ton.

Maija Wirtanen had considered it in her best interest to cultivate Mr. Ala's acquaintance. Sylvia and Art had approved—they liked riding in his big car. Ma had not. It was the only chink in the solid marble of their relationship.

"Good evening, Mrs. Brosi," Mr. Ala said, pulling a bouquet of gladiolus from behind his back, both he and the flowers bowing in a forward gesture of offertory. The flowers looked as if they had been taken from a funeral spray.

Grateful for the rest, I collapsed on the stump Ma had set up for us to use as a chopping block. Lil, of course, grabbed the flowers with both hands and set off to plant them in the vacant lot. Her rolling gait contributed to the image she retained through the toddler stage and well into those early days of her girlhood—that of a chubby, pink Finnish baby.

Ma opened her mouth as if to take exception then closed it again rather wearily and, sitting down on a stump herself, offered one to Mr. Ala with a graceful gesture. She did not invite him inside or offer him coffee. That should have told him something.

If it did, he was not listening.

Of course, he preferred talking to listening anyway so talk he did, on and on and on about nothing in particular except the hope "that this summer there will be enough rain" and the fact that "Mothers' Day is approaching." He updated us on the latest deaths and discussed at length the long-range benefits of platonic relationships.

He offered to take us all for a ride. Lil jumped up and down. Ma refused. Lil yelled.

He offered to help with the sawing and chopping. Ma looked pointedly at his white dress shirt with its celluloid collar and his dark suit and dress shoes.

Finally, he made his move. He was, he said, planning to open a new *"poikatallo,"* a boarding house, in Virginia's Finntown down toward the hall from Jukola's and needed someone to manage it and do the cooking. Leaning forward, looking hopeful, he offered the job to Ma.

That time he did get her attention. Looking abstractedly first at the woodpile then at the miniscule amount we had been able to saw, chop, and pile, at the amount we had left to saw, chop, and pile, and finally at the house where we had been so happy, she clearly considered the offer.

I shook my head, remembering Uncle Charles and trusting in his faithfulness even though we could not trust Pa's. Without even looking at me, Ma shook hers too.

"Thank you for thinking of me," she said. *"Kiitos.* But Mr. Brosi's brother Charles will be coming for us soon. He's in the process of buying a farm in Zim. As soon as he can close out his business in Ely, we shall all be moving."

"Mr. Brosi, too?" Mr. Ala asked pointedly.

Ma sighed. "Knute, too."

My mind added, *Maybe.*

"Well," Mr. Ala temporized, "if you should change your mind or if something should happen in the meantime to prevent Charles from buying the farm, please remember that you can count on me. For anything."

The look he gave Ma made me want to kick his shins. But Ma forestalled me with a quick placating gesture. There was no real cause for us to be rude to Mr. Ala. He had ridden the fence admirably, making no untoward remarks, yet making the position of the stile very clear.

When he finally gave up and drove away, Ma mused, "If I knew where to address the letter, I would write to Uncle Charles and ask him to hurry things along."

I was certain he was already doing just that. I too trusted him implicitly. Because of that trust, thinking hard as I had pulled and carried and sawed and chopped and piled, I had vowed to lay the problem of my birth date before him when he came instead of bothering Ma about it. The burdens she was bearing demanded immediate attention. The burden I was bearing had lain hidden for years. It could wait a bit longer.

That day I gave thanks because Ma had made it very clear once again that whatever the truth of the matter, she bore absolutely no resemblance to That Child's mother.

Thus, I made it my task to concentrate on "now," doing as much as I could to help Ma during the day, taking the household chores and Lil off her hands so that, as soon as we had the wood piled, she could sew.

Studying continued to be left for evenings. Miss Loney helped all she could, keeping me abreast of the new assignments every day after school when she picked up my completed work, taking it with her to the teacherage to correct. In a way it was almost better than actually going to school. When Miss Loney came, I had her all to myself for the half an hour or so during which we did lessons and talked about life and books and the future. She helped me to believe in myself, for a while at least, confirming that plans for my future were set in abeyance, delayed, not destroyed.

Ma and I mulled over the possibility of double or triple promotion and, as life returned to a semblance of normalcy, I began to work extra hard to that end. The sooner I graduated, the sooner I could be of real help to Ma.

Eino Salin came over too, as often as he could, to share the contents of his vocabulary notebook. I tried out the new words on Ma as we worked, and she listened to my recitations and my times tables. We tried to talk more English than Finn, and Ma became more proficient every day.

Thus, the time slipped by, albeit slowly, heavily laden, as we waited for Uncle Charles to return, funds at the ready, to recharge our dreams.

Of course, we did not hear a thing from Pa. This time when he left, he had taken his fiddle. Somewhat bitterly, I remembered the time he had come back home much sooner than we had expected. That time, he had forgotten it.

Chapter Eight

"Eino, Kabe, and Fatso: An Unholy Alliance"

However, although we tried hard to hold on to some kind of normalcy in our daily lives, and by and large succeeded, at least on the surface, within us, the following weeks were imbued with a growing sense of despair, a kind of muted but pervasive agony.

The joy we had experienced during that day of hope when, Uncle Charles with us, we had traveled to Zim and laid out our plan for paradise only accentuated the present pain. It was as if, like the archangel Satan, we had fallen from heaven and awakened in hell. For weeks that winter I had listened to the upper graders reciting their memorization from John Milton's literary epic *Paradise Lost*. Eino Salin's notebooks had been rich with new words as his class struggled to understand the plight of Satan and the fallen angels, who, having warred against God in heaven, had been exiled to hell, a place without light, a fiery dungeon where they could never again know peace or hope but only torture without end. During those long days and nights I realized that such was also the case with us. We too had hit bottom.

During the day Ma and I addressed ourselves to survival. Ma had done it before during their married life whenever Pa, having decided that family life or work or both were too much for him, escaped into his own world, wherever that might be, usually away from us. But it was a relatively new experience for me. Oh, I had been peripherally aware of Pa's lack of family feeling all my life and had experienced the consequences of his leaving us in Canada and failing to contact us during the months in Malcolm, but I had not known what it meant for Ma to be alone until those days in May. Moreover, I was not only then enduring and sharing Ma's labors, but experiencing a roughly equivalent additional heartache, albeit for a different cause.

Every day I considered asking Ma about that discrepancy in dates. But every day I realized that even more than I, Ma was struggling. Perhaps she had let down her guard during those happy days in Kinney and come to trust Pa and his promises too fully. I think the hope had survived, well watered by dreams, that Pa had, in fact, changed and that there could be an accommodation between the dreamer who created beauty with his pen and his fiddle and the husband and father who provided for his wife and children. Who loved them.

The depths to which Ma fell in those weeks after Pa's leaving defied my ability to describe. But I was aware that she, even more than I, was living in a vast abyss more terrifying than the depths of the pits in the iron mines. She ate very little. She slept even less. I often caught her standing during the day with her hands pressed to her tummy, a look in her eyes so distant that I almost feared to bring her back, though I wanted to desperately, by word or gesture. I had no word to match what Ma was experiencing. I simply knew that it frightened me and, because I loved her, I had to accept the fact that though her body was with us, her mind was not.

There was no question of my going back to school. Ma couldn't spare me. Thus, I continued to address myself to becoming her assistant in every possible way so that Ma could make some money, doing everything she could to enlarge her sewing business.

Luckily, Mrs. Moore, the wife of the mine owner, had worn one of the dresses Ma made for her to a Penguin Club dance in Virginia. Shortly after that dance, a new customer drove up, chauffeured by her husband.

Everything about them spoke of their ability to indulge any whim. His pince nez and watch fob, gold watch and cufflinks, beaver fur felt hat and Chesterfield topcoat, their five-passenger Buick touring car with its elegant leather gypsy-style back curtain and solid silver beautygrams, two plates with initials, one on each side of the car, could be ordered from the Sears, Roebuck Catalogue. I knew because I had studied every page. But at prices ordinary people like us could never afford.

Lil and I had run to the window when we heard the car approach, but Ma's stern glance warned us away, and we sat down hurriedly to make our good manners make up for our poverty.

The pair presented themselves at the door courteously. "Good morning," the gentleman began in a cultured voice—Finnish but not the dialectical Finnish we usually heard. His tones were clipped, educated, like Pa's when he was of a mind to show off. "I am Alex Savolainen. May I introduce my wife, Anna? You have been highly recommended by Mrs. Moore as a dressmaker of considerable skill."

Ma smiled and motioned them in with another warning glance at us. We all three recognized the names immediately. One of the most successful of the area's Finnish businessmen, Mr. Savolainen owned a jewelry shop in Virginia with branches in Duluth and Ely. According to the society page of the *Range Facts*, he had met his wife during a buying trip out East and married her there. She had brought to Virginia a Boston-accented Finnish voice and manner and a whole-hearted desire to improve the community, but, it was rumored with great disappointment, no style at all. "She may be rich," Maija Wirtanen had commented with very little envy, "but you'd sure never know it by looking at her."

Maija had certainly been right, I thought, looking from Ma to Mrs. Savolainen. Our hard outside work and limited diet had turned Ma from slender to sylph-like, the weight of it resting on her shoulders when she sat. But she welcomed the Savolainens that morning with her head high, elegant in cotton house dress and apron, her eyes darkly green, her creamy complexion just a tad freckled, her auburn hair gilded by the sun.

Taking hats and coats, Ma offered coffee and indicated with a quick motion that Lil and I were to serve.

Lil curtsied with barely any prompting, and I took upon myself the role of servant girl, arranging a freshly starched cloth on the table and setting out cups and saucers, sugar bowl and creamer, and a fairly respectable array of baked goods, far short of Ma's usual splendid coffee table plenitude but adequate under the circumstances.

Ma, pencil in hand, copied down the orders, instructions, and desires of Mrs. Anna Savolainen, who ordered one dress suitable for the *Juhannus* Midsummer Celebration scheduled for the Finnish Temperance Hall in Virginia in June, one tea dress for an up-coming Penguin Club dance, and one traveling suit, for she intended to visit her family in Boston that summer.

Plump and short as she was, Mrs. Savolainen seemed equally warm and kind, offering—if Ma specified color and fabric—to purchase the material for the outfits herself and to return for fittings at Ma's convenience. I held back my deep sigh of relief until I got into the pantry, but

Mrs. Savolainen's manner prompted me to spread thin slices of fresh bread with the last of our homemade raspberry jam as well as butter and to cut the leftovers of Mrs. Leinonen's rhubarb-custard pie, payment for mending of socks, into three pieces rather than five.

While Mrs. Savolainen and Ma talked and Ma took measurements, Mr. Savolainen waited patiently, drinking coffee and watching Ma. She could not possibly have remained unaware of his gaze, but, except for a slight flush, she evinced no sign either of shyness or disquietude. At first I was discomfited by its steadiness as intent as Mr. Ala's had been, yet different in some essential way. At any rate, gradually I began to relax with him. Ma did too. When Lil began to relax, I was careful to send her out to play. These gentlepeople deserved our very best manners.

But their visits were only momentary lapses, flashes of light in the dark pattern of days to which we returned as soon as they left. Although around us the soft cocoons of pussy willows had broken into green tendrils and the shaded areas of the vacant lot had turned pink with fragrant arbutus, a bleak winter locked our hearts in gray.

Ma had always been the first one up in the morning. Those days I wondered if she ever went to bed. Breakfast no longer included a choice —bacon or sausage? pancakes, eggs or oatmeal? toasted bread or butter-slathered *pulla*? Instead we sat down to weak coffee—a cup for me, a cup for Lil, a cup for Ma—and thin, sugarless, butterless gruel—a bowl for me, a bowl for Lil, no bowl for Ma.

After breakfast we did the daily chores, but we did not shop on Friday because we had no money to spend. Although the families who knew us were unfailingly kind and helped in every way they could, money was not readily available to any of them. Whenever the ladies were able, they hired Ma to do sewing and mending, but most often her efforts were repaid not in cash but in barter—a dozen eggs perhaps or a free sauna or a chicken or potatoes, and that did help, although our meals tended to be monochromatic. When we got eggs, we ate fried eggs for breakfast and boiled eggs for lunch and scrambled eggs for supper. When Ma was repaid with potatoes, she baked them and fried them and boiled them into soup.

Still, we had monthly rent due on the house. The bills at Salins' grocery and Spinas' butcher shop had not been paid before Pa left. We had no slops for the pig, and our supplies of staple items such as soap and lye, flour and sugar, apples and crackers, and kerosene for lamps, purchased in bulk before winter set in, were running at a springtime low. Consequently though on Monday we washed, we were sparing with soap. On Tuesday we ironed but used very little starch. On Wednesday we baked *rieska*, a flat bread with only a bit of yeast and no eggs. All entertaining was curtailed, and Thursday's cleaning, though careful and thorough, was quick.

Morning work completed as quickly as possible, Ma sat down to her sewing. I went out to the woodpile with Lil and worked until the school day was over and Miss Loney stopped to collect the lessons she had left the night before and to update me on the new ones. Refusing even coffee, she rarely stayed more than a half an hour, but that time was the highlight of my day.

Except for Ma's clients, we kept to ourselves. With very little hinting, Lil managed a severe headache the day of Sara Salin's birthday party, for Ma had no time to make an outfit for Sara's doll as she was wont to do for birthday or name-day celebrations. I was too tired after supper to play pom-pom-pullaway or tag or hide-and-go-seek with the neighborhood kids, and anyway I had to clean up the kitchen and Lil for one last time and get her into bed so I could settle myself next to Ma at the kitchen table to work at my lessons until my eyes could stay open no more and Ma urged me to bed.

If I awoke during the night, Ma was still at the table, her face haloed by the kerosene light or by candlelight as the kerosene supply ebbed, and often instead of sewing, she held a pencil, making marks on foolscap that were clearly numerical. It did not take red ink for me to decipher the minus signs and subtractions on the papers she tried to hide: we were not making the grade financially. To fail that grade, I knew, could mean in the worst case to lose each other should Ma have to hire out and find a place to leave us.

It is no wonder I had no heart for play. The Good Gang gradually ceased leaving messages for me in the tin can, gradually stopped coming over. The Bad Gang seemed to understand that I could bear no more and ceased teasing when they saw me outside, hard at work.

It was even hard to muster up the energy to try out new words, and Eino Salin's visits too ebbed in the rising tide of my exhaustion. It was a great surprise, therefore, to find him at the back door one Saturday morning a few weeks later. "Good morning, Mrs. Brosi," he said politely to Ma, just barely stepping into the kitchen when she answered his knock. "May Ilmi Marianna please come with me to Boziches' garage for the moving picture showing this morning? It is her turn to pump the player piano."

It was not. Coveted turns at the player piano were assigned with great care to effect absolute equality because they meant free admission to the day's film. I had had my turn just before the Community Spring program. But when I started to demur and shake my head, Eino's eyes met mine so fiercely that my mouth closed with a snap and my head froze and Ma, unbeknownst, sighed and nodded.

"Yes. It would be good. Ilmi," she turned to me. The name 'Marion' had not taken hold. "You deserve a morning off. Go with Eino. Lil can play inside for an hour." Lil opened her mouth to howl, but Ma picked her up and cuddled her against her shoulder, and the unexpected pleasure of the caress lessened the volume of the howl.

"Go." Ma reached out to smooth my hair, tweaked the ribbons straight, gave me a pat that was also almost a caress, and pushed me toward Eino, who grabbed my hand and yanked me after him so quickly I almost fell down the back stairs.

"Hurry up." His tone allowed no dallying, and I obeyed even though I hated to take orders from him or from any of the boys. "We are having a meeting."

Then I understood. Moving my legs as fast as I could, I tried to keep up with his long strides. Since Eino never called a meeting of the Good Gang unless it was important, we obeyed his rare commands without question and went, no matter the time or place. During the last two meetings, we had been in desperate circumstances. First, the boys had found what could well have been dynamite near our cave. It had been rumored that the Bad Gang had managed to get through the chicken wire fence around the mining company's storage depot and had stolen a stick. At that meeting Eino warned us away from the cave and retaliated, catching the members of the Bad Gang one by one alone and beating them into submission.

Of course, Kabe Vanucci later almost succeeded in burying Eino in the sawdust pile, an episode that led to a second emergency meeting and eventually to the development of rules governing its possession.

A truce had been called during the preparations first for the spring program and then for Mothers' Day. We knew it would not last past the end of school.

"What's wrong?" I asked Eino, trailing in his wake.

"What's wrong? You know what's wrong," he threw over his shoulder as we neared Boziches' garage.

When Eino and I were together, we never lapsed into Finn, as tended to happen with some of the other kids. Not only did we honor English, we tried to enunciate clearly in order to eliminate even the brogue, the Finnish lilt that lurked insidiously on the fringes of words, the borders of sentences.

"How should *I* know what's wrong?" I panted, confused. "*You* called the meeting."

"Meeting then movie. That way no one will know." Opening the side door to the garage cum stable, he pushed me in. I stood still at first, blinded by the switch from bright sunlight to relative darkness. Then, as my eyes adjusted, I turned to run, getting as far as Eino, who was stolidly blocking the doorway behind me. Boziches' garage was full not only with the members of our Good Gang but with all of the kids from the Bad Gang, too, segregated of course on a separate side but sitting quietly behind and around Kabe.

Why was the Bad Gang there? We never met in unison. We had not watched a movie together for months. During the heaviest hostilities, Mr. Bozich had decided that, circumstances being what they were, it might be in his best interest to initiate two showings of the picture of the week, one for each gang.

For a minute, visions of That Child pinioned to the tree post, bloodsuckers writhing, swam around me. How had the gangs found out about me? My heart pounded so hard that I almost fainted.

Eino grabbed my arms, looking perplexed and unsure, for a second not at all like himself.

I understood. He did not know how to tell me that I was an outcast. Or, an even worse alternative, he had joined the Bad Gang in league against me.

Running had not helped That Child. It was clearly forbidden me. There were only two alternatives left. I could collapse in a heap and cry like a coward. Or I could confront them all with courage. Some of Ma's starch seeped into my spine, and I turned, spread my legs into a dominant stance, directed my gaze to Kabe, and managed an almost firm voice. "Tell me what's going on."

Eino shoved me toward a chair set between the two gangs and sat down himself in the center of the Good Gang.

Everyone from our room was there, except Wilho Field, of course, as were most of the kids from the upper grade room. Every single one of them was looking at me.

"Your Pa left." Kabe stated the obvious.

Since I was hardly to blame for that, I nodded, mystified.

"Your Ma's workin' hard t'make ends meet." Fatso Spina picked up the refrain.

I raised my chin and nodded again.

"She hasn't paid my pa," he continued.

Eino added, "Or mine."

I made myself taller in the chair. There was no denying any of it.

"You need help." This from Kabe.

I tried to shake my head, but it refused to move. I crumpled a bit.

For a pack, the kids were not baying at all. In fact, as I looked around from under my eyelashes, it seemed that they were looking first at whoever spoke and then back at me with . . . not with anger . . . with . . . pity? Back up went my spine.

"We've got an idea." For all that Fatso Spina never got any grade higher than seventy percent—barely passing—we all knew that he knew the answers. Perhaps because he had been teased so mercilessly about his weight ever since he was born, he refused to chance any more teasing. But whenever a problem called for a solution, Fatso had an idea. If Eino was the don of our Finnish Mafia, Fatso was his consigniore. He had mediated the sawdust battle and arbitrated an acceptable solution. When he spoke, everyone listened, Good Gang and Bad Gang alike. He spoke firmly now. "We've been savin' everything we could pick from the boardwalk."

The boardwalk offered notoriously fine pickings especially early the morning after payday when denizens of Mary's Bar, lurching and stumbling their way home, dropped loose change between the boards. Both gangs had long since availed themselves of this source of funds, alternating weeks, Fatso had decreed.

By mutual consent, thanks to Fatso again, all monies so gained by the Good Gang were claimed by the club membership in toto, none held for individual use. One contingent of our membership was intent upon an open and honest purchase of dynamite in lieu of theft.

Had they raised enough money? I wondered. Were they going to use it on me? Fatso held out two grimy pouches and dropped the act of illiteracy. "We want you to have it."

I almost fainted again. I opened my mouth, but no words came out. As the tears welled up and threatened to overflow, I stared fixedly at the pouches. One, tied and knotted, was made of a once-red bandanna like the kind Italian men wore around their necks to work. The other, a long, thin, leather pocketbook that clasped on one end, I had seen for sale at Salins'. "I can't . . ." I faltered, struggling to get the words out without releasing the sobs, " . . . can't . . ." That was as far as I could get.

Eino and Kabe took charge. "Yes, you can and you will. Here." Eino grabbed the pouch from Fatso and, untangling my hands from their death-clasp in my lap, pushed the pocketbook against one palm until my hand closed around it. Kabe grabbed my other hand and did the same.

Fatso went to the player piano. Someone started the projector. Both gangs turned their chairs to the screen and pretended I wasn't there.

Eino whispered in my ear, "It should be enough to get you to wherever your pa is. Or your Uncle Charles. And you can borrow my vocabulary notebook and copy it on your way." He patted my shoulder awkwardly.

Kabe inched over, a tangled mass of black curly hair almost masking his enormous brown eyes, his gaze vacillating between my nose and the floor. His right toe made long lines in the dirt floor, which he studied intently, his hands jammed into his overall pockets. But I heard the words that mumbled up, his heart to mine. "You done all th' work on th' Mothers' Day program, an' you din't even get t' be innit. "It ain't fair. An' . . . we're . . . sorry 'bout the ladd'r fallin' 'n' all. An' Miz Loney, she misses you somethin' awf'l in school. An' . . ." I could not believe I was hearing correctly, but the words sounded suspiciously like ". . . so . . . do . . . all a' us guys." His concern for grammar had decreased in inverse proportion to his sincerity. Then he, too, evaporated, and I was left alone clutching the kerchief and the pocketbook.

I tried to stammer out some kind of thanks, but the words were blurred by the music from the player piano and by my lack of control over my voice. Like a mouse stunned not by a cat's blow but by its purr, I crept out the door and down the street and into the vacant lot and back, far back into its innermost recesses, under the thick, heavy branches of a balsam tree, where I sat with my apron across my knees, emptied the pouches into my lap, and counted up their contents. The leather pocketbook yielded $2.87. The red kerchief, $3.14. I did not need a pencil and paper to arrive at the sum. Between them, the gangs had contributed $5.01 toward my family's survival.

Sniffling, I wiped my nose carefully on the clean handkerchief Ma always tucked into my pocket and thought hard.

For all of Eino's good intentions, there was no sense to using the money to try to find Pa. It did my pride some good to realize that not even the Salins were fully aware of how lacking in responsibility he was.

Sighing, for a part of me dreaded the pain I knew this would inflict upon Ma—she would never agree to the plan—I knew we really had only one hope. Help lay in one direction in the form of one person.

North to Ely. To Uncle Charles.

Ma could not go. Were she to lose the Savolainens' good faith, we would be hurt beyond measure, and there was Lil to worry about.

It would have to be I. Since I now had money, I thought with rising excitement, I could take a street car to Virginia. That would cost a nickel. From there, I could take the D&IR, the Duluth and Iron Range Railroad, to Ely. If $4.96 covered the cost of a ticket, and I was absolutely sure it would, though perhaps only a one-way ticket, I could get there in less than a day. Ma would barely have time to miss me before Uncle Charles wired her back news of my arrival and our rapid departure for home. Help could arrive within days.

Of course, once in Ely, I would have to find Uncle Charles. But, I clenched my jaw, I would do that if I had to walk up and down the streets of that town and knock on every single door.

I thought about what to tell Ma. To prevent her from worrying, it might have to be a lie, but a forgivable one, I was sure, given the circumstances. Remembering Eino Salin's notebook, I appended the word "venial—that which can be forgiven. Pardonable." If I had to, I would tell a "venial" lie.

Excitement washed over me like a tidal wave, leaving me shaking. To me had been given the opportunity to make all well, to save our family from destruction. It was *The Secret Garden* and *Anne of Green Gables* and *Little Women* rolled into one. And I had not had to sell my hair!

It was such stuff as dreams are made of.

Little did I realize then that of such heady draughts are nightmares also formed.

Chapter Nine

"Alternatives"

All through that long afternoon, I weighed alternatives with such fervor that it should have been no surprise to find that I couldn't let go of them when I got to bed. The afternoon led into an even longer night.

I did fall asleep right away, exhausted by emotion, but awoke perhaps an hour later, drifting on the edge of a dream and a conversation with Miss Loney. It had been so real I could hardly believe I was lying in bed, not sitting at the kitchen table trying to understand the difference between restrictive and nonrestrictive adjective clauses.

In the dream, working to diagram a complex sentence, I had broached the subject: "Miss Loney, may I ask you a question, adult to adult?" I had spoken very quietly so that Ma, bustling in and out with armfuls of tea dress, could not hear.

"Of course, Marion." Even in dreams, she was the only one to use that name.

"May I please ride with you to Virginia?" I almost fudged and said that Ma had an errand for me, thought better of it, and stuck to the truth. "I need to go to Ely to find Uncle Charles. If I tell Ma, she'll make me stay home, and if I stay home . . . I don't know what will happen to us."

Miss Loney nodded. Since she was a daily visitor, always during the time when Ma was preparing what passed for supper, she was probably the only one in Kinney who knew how truly dire our straits had become.

"Do you have enough money?" she asked, surprisingly practical.

"Yes, I do. Thanks to . . ."—It occurred to me that the gangs might not appreciate having their secret source of funds divulged. —". . . to some friends."

Too sensitive to pursue an area I had skirted so carefully, she simply nodded again and said, "Yes. You may ride with us this Friday night. I'll call to make sure that Bill is coming."

The dream collapsed right there.

Set on the scale against our pantry, Friday did not balance out. How odd, I thought, that something so empty can weigh so much. The week before, Ma had set me to giving it a good spring cleaning. Usually that was a labor-intensive task requiring much rearranging and moving of stores before it was possible to scrub down the walls and shelves and floor. But I had completed the whole job in one morning. By myself I had carried outside the metal bins that could hold one hundred pounds of flour and sugar, emptied the little that was left into smaller containers, washed them, and left them to dry in the sun. The jars still lining the shelves had already been scrubbed clean of blueberry and raspberry and strawberry sauces and preserves and the rich autumn stock of canned whitefish and venison. The box of apples was empty. So was the cracker barrel. Basically, so were all the rest of the storage containers.

Oh, yes, some eggs still cooled in the wellbox with cans of milk that had not soured. A bit of buttermilk, too. But precious little else.

Friday could not come soon enough even in a dream.

Punching the pillow and squirming to escape from the furnace that was Lil into a cooler spot, I weighed another alternative. I could just tell Ma the truth. "Ma, I am going to go to Ely to find Uncle Charles and tell him we need him right now. We'll come back together just as soon as we can. See, I have enough money."

"*You're* leaving to go to Ely. Not on your life, girl. I'm the one who needs to get away. You stay here and take care of Lil, and I'll wash my hair and change my clothes and take the streetcar and the train and go to Ely myself. I'll use that money to stay in a hotel and eat in a restaurant. As far as Mrs. Savolainen is concerned, you can tell her to kiss my ass. I quit."

I woke up from that one, horrified, seeing Ma's face superimposed on Pa's. It had been his voice that I heard.

There had been some truth to it, however. I sympathized with Pa and honestly would not have been surprised if Ma had also wanted to leave. Endless days of piling wood and scrubbing floors and washing clothes and ironing and watching Lil and trying to help Ma in every way I could had worn me to a frazzle. I hated it all, hated it all with a passion I did not dare admit even to myself.

In a fit of frustration one day I had lifted the stove lid over the fire box and thrown the Mothers' Day scroll I'd prepared with so much love straight into the flames. As it burned, I thought, "Good riddance." I was so completely fed up with household chores that I could not, in all honesty, vow to take on any more or, truth be told, continue much longer with what I was doing already. Birth dates be damned, too, I thought irreverently but fervently. I just wanted out. Let someone else worry about what we were going to eat. Let someone else watch people's faces soften with pity when they passed our house or when they offered help.

I even despised having to be grateful.

When Ma sent me to Mr. Spina's butcher shop with our last two hens to offer them against our outstanding bill, he had waved me off, saying we needed them more than he did. "Take them back home with you, girl," he had growled.

Mr. Spina was a great bear of a man, clearly the one Fatso took after. With his heavy beard and hairy arms, he resembled the animals he butchered. He could throw a haunch of venison onto the chopping block with no sign of effort—no thickened blood vessels or grunts or distended muscles. His wife and kids scurried when he yelled. So did the rest of us. I marveled that he allowed the gangs onto his sawdust heap. But then, he treated them as if they were cubs, cuffing them liberally if they needed it, ignoring them completely if they didn't.

I wanted to wring those chicken's necks and drop them in front of him on the counter and march out. Instead I had to say, "Thank you, Mr. Spina" and took them back home, squawking and flapping their stupid wings.

Oh, I hated chickens. They were dirty, smelly, noisy, irksome animals without a shred of brain. When Ma cut off their heads, they didn't even have sense enough to die. They just flapped around the back yard, squirting blood all over. Ish. If I had my way when I grew up, I would live on vegetables.

That was the day I burned the scroll.

A few days later, worn out by Lil's incessant demands for everything we could not afford to buy, ready to scream back even louder than she had ever thought of screaming, I broke the plaque into a million pieces.

Anyone who gets married is crazy, I thought, *and if they have kids, they are stark raving mad.*

In desperation, then, as my last long day and night at home ebbed toward morning, I quit thinking of alternatives. Instead, I got up, went outside, unwound my braids, pumped ice cold water all over my face and my head, and decided there was no sense to quibbling either with Ma or with myself. I simply had to go. Thank goodness that Ma could never stand a squeaking door; ours were well oiled. Thank goodness she had been up during the night, slipping by the davenport, her hands over her mouth, a wraith in white running for the back yard where I heard her retching before she even got to the outhouse; she was now asleep. I had turned toward the wall when she ran by, feigning sleep. It was one small gift that I could willingly give her: she did not have to know that I knew that she was sick. She did not have to have me, too, feeling sorry for her. But my heart ached when I reflected upon how small a hump she made in the bedclothes, barely bigger than Lil.

And—my mind working at blocking it out—there was that business about Lil eating the ashes.

"I must get ready and go," I thought fiercely.

Then I did. First, I worked out the "venial" lie, writing a note saying that I had forgotten before we went to bed to tell her that Mrs. Leinonen from down the block had asked me to come over as early as I could in the morning to take care of the baby while she made a quick trip into Virginia to see her mother, who was ill. She was taking the early morning streetcar, I added. I would be gone all day and most of the evening, perhaps even overnight. "I'm sorry I forgot to tell you, Ma," I concluded, adding to the air of veracity, "but I forgot myself and just remembered." I was sure Ma wanted me to go because Mrs. Leinonen had been so kind to us, sending us something—a loaf of bread or a pie—every time she baked.

Then I wrote a second note. I hoped by the time Ma unearthed that one, it would be too late for her to do anything to stop me. I hid this one under the sprinkling bottle. Since it was Monday, Ma would spend the morning washing clothes and hanging them out, the afternoon freshening the kitchen while she waited for them to dry. It should be late afternoon by the time she took them down and put most of them away, I estimated, possibly even Tuesday morning before she reached for the sprinkling bottle to dampen the starched things. By then, I would be in Ely.

"Dearest Ma," the note said simply, "I am on my way to Ely to find Uncle Charles. Do not worry about me, for I have ample funds for the streetcar fare to Virginia and for the train fare to Ely. As soon as I find him, we will come home. Please have faith in me. I shall not fail. Love, Ilmi Marianna."

Adding an x and an o for Lil, appending another pair for Ma, I dressed in my best school dress, made sailor-style of navy-blue poplin with a white collar piped in red, black stockings and shoes, and tied red ribbons at the ends of my braids. Into my school satchel went my faithful companions, a pencil and a tablet of foolscap paper. Finally, taking a deep breath and one last look at the quiet kitchen, I opened the door, took care not to let it slam behind me, and stepped out into the pink-gray dawn.

For a minute there on the back stoop I quailed. Had I been Amalia Barone, I would have said a rosary. Had I been our Finnish Evangelical Lutheran neighbors, who passed us with pursed lips on Sunday mornings, watching us as we worked, I would have said a prayer.

That would not be a bad idea right now, I thought, and tried. But my lack of church experience—no Sunday School or confirmation classes and precious few Sunday visits—left me at sea. I didn't know the technique.

"Why don't we go to church, Pa?" I had asked one Sunday in Virginia, wishing that like Amalia I could get all dressed up and drink a sip of wine and eat a sweet morsel and eventually go to heaven.

Unfortunately, Amalia's grandmother could not go straight to heaven, Amalia told me in strictest confidence, because her family did not have enough money to get her past purgatory.

Amalia and I, worried that her spirit might haunt us, checked the skies carefully before going out to play. It had been a relief when payday came and the Barones had been able to send her on her way. "Up," said Amalia, pointing toward the sky. "That's where heaven is."

I wished I could be as sure. I knew Pa didn't agree.

"When people die, they don't go to heaven," Pa had informed me one day when I consulted him about the whole situation, hoping grownups knew how to fend off the advances of grandmothers who were still floating around. "And you don't have to go to church to know God," Pa had continued, willing as always to set the ax aside for a few minutes and talk. The wood pile can wait, he always said. "And God? God is . . . all around us."

I had been watching for an early robin, and when I saw it and heard its chirps and warblings and pointed it out to Pa, he chirped and warbled in return and then said in Finnish, "Welcome, small brother." Sometimes when he did that, the birds came to him.

"Why do you call a bird 'brother,' Pa?" I dared ask, since he was smiling.

"Oh," he paused, looked down at me, remembered that I was there, realized I really did want to know the answers to my questions, and sat down on the chopping block. He had thought through this philosophy so carefully that his words came out without a pause: "I believe that we are children of nature: we were born, we died, we were born again. But we don't remember that we ever were here before. When we die and are reborn, some part of us—our spirit—holds within it our past lives."

He glanced down, then, to see if I were following.

I wasn't. Not that it made any difference. Pa was off. I tried to go with him, maybe because it was one of the very few times when his attention had been directed not at Lil but at me, just at me.

"The birds that soar so freely sing of the eternal spirit which permeates and unites us all." He paused, considering, looking far into a distance that my eyes could not see, and added softly, "Their songs arise from that spirit, from the power that flows through them and through us and through all living things, uniting us, making us one."

Looking down at me, he added gravely, "It is a great gift, one of the greatest of God's gifts to creation, that our hearts can share their songs, the beauty and the joy and the meaning. And," he concluded, going back to my first question, "God is that spirit, an eternal spirit that unites us all in the spirit of love, of all that is beautiful and true."

Typically for him, his answer had been broader than my question, but I had never forgotten the essence of what he said, even though I had not at that time completely understood every word.

Those words had been beautiful. I wasn't sure, given the nature of Pa, whether they were true.

While I hesitated there on the stoop, remembering, knowing I had to be on my way yet loathe to leave the security of my familiar world, the birds began to outdo the Kinney Choir, and I realized there was no turning back. Given the nature of Pa, the practical details of survival had best be left to someone else. To me, this time.

Excitement soared, replacing the doubts, as I retrieved the pouch and kerchief from the wood pile, where I had secreted them the afternoon before, and set off—first toward the vacant lot and then out into the great world.

Chapter Ten

"The Duluth and Missabi Main Line Railroad"

"One more stop and I'll be on my way," I promised myself, hurrying across the vacant lot toward the message can hanging from the Good Gang's special tree, the money for my fare tucked safely into my school bag and two identical notes in my hand. I had struggled with the wording because it had seemed necessary that they be phrased in what might approximate legal terminology, even more binding than a normal promise. After many false starts late on Sunday, I had settled on the following draft, two copies of which I placed carefully within the tin can, holding it to prevent the telltale ping.

"On this Sunday, the day after my receipt of the funds that will carry me on my quest, I, Ilmi Marianna Brosi, also to be known as Marion Elmi Brosi, do proclaim that said gift of money, received from Eino Salin" (or, on the other copy, "from Diodado Carmen Joseph Vanucci"), "*et al.* will be repaid in full when and as soon as repayment is humanly possible. To that end I affix this mark in blood" (I had put my thumbprint there.) "as sworn testimony, on penalty of death, with my deepest and most heartfelt gratitude." I had then signed both my names. I hoped it would do.

High above the tin can in a knot hole made larger by Eino's careful carving, a recess had been formed wherein objects too large for the tin can could be secreted. If Eino had meant what he said about allowing me to borrow one of his vocabulary notebooks, it would be there. I could not stretch high enough to see inside even when I climbed to the broadest point of the trunk from which huge branches arched toward the sky. Our Gang had been known to insert snakes and spiders into that recess as preventive mechanisms to keep the spot secure. Thus, reaching in constituted an act of faith, especially for one who, like me, detested snakes and spiders. But reach in I did and felt, to my unutterable relief, the binding and cover of a prized text, identical in form to all of the many carried by upper grade students who studied vocabulary but more highly prized than any of the others because it belonged to the vocabulary king of Kinney School.

I wanted to open the tin can and affix a kiss to the bottom of the note addressed to Eino, but I didn't. No matter that it was no more than a token of my appreciation, it might be misconstrued either by Eino or by the rest of the gang. I compromised by making a small cross out of twigs on the ground right by the tree, a message which, if noticed, was liable to a variety of innocent interpretations.

Then, tucking the notebook into my book bag, I began my journey into the unknown, aware that for the first time in my life, my fate—and in truth my family's fate—lay in my hands, in more than a manner of speaking, for my hands clutched the book bag with a death grip. Brave as I tried to be, firm as my footsteps sounded on the boardwalk, I shivered.

"One step at a time," I told myself fiercely. "One step at a time."

And that was how I did it. One step followed another until I was atop the trestle and in front of the ticket window at the streetcar station, where the agent on the other side of the iron grill barely looked at me before exchanging my nickel for a ticket. One step followed the other as I climbed onto the first streetcar of the day heading east toward Virginia. No one on the car gave me a second glance, workmen and housewives alike half asleep so early was it. I seated myself in the vicinity of a family group, ensconced in the rear of the car, the children munching breakfast bread and sausage and gawking out the window. I gawked too and tried hard to look a part of them. Since they were obviously Italian and I just as dark-haired and dark-skinned, the only one to look askance was the conductor, who expected the mother to hold my ticket as she did the others. He evinced some marginal surprise when I held out my own. But just then the baby started crying, and he escaped to the front of the car while I concentrated on controlling my heartbeats, which were pounding so loudly that I was sure they were audible over the clackety-clack of the streetcar wires attached to electric lines strung high above.

No one gave me a second look when the contents of the car disgorged at the Virginia station. I trailed behind the family until they turned toward "Italia vitsi" and I toward downtown and the imposing brick depot built where Chestnut Street, the main thoroughfare, came to an end.

"One step at a time," I reminded myself, entering the Duluth Missabi & Iron Range railroad depot. My footsteps echoed from the marble floor to the vaulted ceiling, and the walls and woodwork shone with such a gloss of white enamel that I was sure they resonated every sign of fear or hesitation. Passengers awaiting their calls sat in the rows of long, heavy oak pews with curved backs and carved armrests, listening, I was sure.

The sonorous proclamation—"Duluth-and-Missabi-Main-Line-Railroad-Virginia-to-Duluth. FIRST CALL!—ALL ABOARD!"—reverberating throughout the room shook me into quicker action. What if I missed the train?

Reaching the ticket window, I tried to make my voice deep and adult, but it sounded pretty squeaky to me. "A one-way ticket Virginia to Ely, if you please, sir." Leaning over to open my school bag, my cheeks burning, I unearthed the leather pouch and began counting the change into orderly piles of fifty cents apiece.

The ticket master, wearing garters to hold up his shirt-sleeves and a shaded visor cap, reached around orderly circles of tickets, selected two from separate rounds, stapled them together without once looking up, and commented noncommittally, "That'll be seven dollars and twenty-eight cents, please." Without looking at me, for a line had formed, he monotoned, "Next."

The lump that had lain in my stomach moved up to my throat, and I gulped, "S-s-seven d-d-ollars?"

He looked back at me, impatiently. "The total fare from here to Duluth on the Duluth and Missabi plus the fare from Duluth to Ely via the D&IR."

"P-please, sir," I pleaded, the lump trembling just behind my eyes and threatening to break out, "mayn't I just go from here to Ely? I don't wish to go to Duluth."

His look hardened. The line was lengthening. "The Duluth Missabi Railroad doesn't run to Ely," his tone of voice implying that only those of little brain lacked that common knowledge. "The Duluth Missabi Railroad runs Duluth to Virginia or Duluth to Hibbing with stops along the way. The Duluth and Iron Range Railway runs from Duluth to Ely. There is no direct train service from here"—He pronounced the words one at a time as if there were something wrong with my hearing as well as my understanding—"to Ely."

Slinking away from him and from the impatient tappings behind me, I murmured miserably, "I-I-I'm sorry. Th-thank you, anyway," and scraped the coins off the counter back into the leather pouch.

"Next?" Slipping the stapled tickets back into a drawer and frowning, the ticket master addressed the person behind me.

As the one-step-at-a-time philosophy carried me across the room and out the door, I maintained my control over the lump but with great difficulty.

Outside, the glitter of a bright morning sun redoubled on the surface of Silver Lake. It must have been named on a morning like this, I thought, keeping those steps moving until the brick of the depot and the cement of the sidewalk turned into grass, and a wooden bench rose up in front of me near a flower bed filled with small green sprouts. There I sat down, swallowing hard, for the lump lurking behind my eyes had spread to nose and mouth.

All of my plans, so carefully laid, seemingly so easily fulfilled had gone awry. How could I have been so stupid as to take it for granted that the train line ran to Ely? Why had I not inquired before I left Kinney? "What do I do now?" I murmured to myself, my chin and lips quivering with the effort of containing the lump.

"One step at a time," my self answered sternly. "First you have to fight the lump."

In the background the steam locomotive huffed and puffed and hissed and whistled as firemen threw coal into the firebox, preparing for the return trip to Duluth. I had to accept the fact that one option was closed to me. I did not have seven dollars and twenty-eight cents. I could not go to Ely by train.

The lump, though refusing to disappear, eventually lurched back into my chest, where I could live with it without fearing the humiliation of a public overflow. Gradually as my breath and my heartbeat slowed to something approximating normal, my eyes began to focus onto the scene before me. The bench on the grass outside the depot had been built to provide a view not of Chestnut Street and the shops that lined it but of Silver Lake, glinting in the morning sun with a metallic splendor.

The city of Virginia, Queen City of the Iron Range, had been built around two lakes, one for commercial use, the other for recreation. Bailey's

Lake, named for the Bailey family of logging and lumbering fame, was filled with rafts of logs that had been hauled onto the ice during the winter to await summer sawing at Bailey's Mill. It formed an elongated oval between Finntown and "Italia vitsi" on North Side. A wide wooden bridge spanned the narrow isthmus that separated it from Silver Lake. The railroad line ending at the depot followed the nearby shoreline. A white sand beach and full-leafed forest lined the opposite shore.

Hardly seeing the beach or the trees, however, I pondered my options, trying to effect some system on a chaotic maelstrom of questions. How did people who lived in Virginia go to Ely? I knew that they did. Mr. Savolainen, for example, owned a jewelry shop in Ely. Did he have to go there via Duluth?

Pa had left Kinney, heading in all probability toward the St. Croix Lumber Company's central office in Winton, a village just past Ely. I knew very well that he had not had seven dollars and twenty-eight cents to pay for a train ride. Nor could I imagine him voluntarily heading toward Duluth. When he talked about Duluth, he shuddered. He had passed through the city on his way from the boat landing where the steamship packet *America* docked at the end of its voyage in and out and around the curving shoreline and islands of Lake Superior from Fort William and Port Arthur, Canada, where he had embarked, down to the head of the lakes, under the Aerial Bridge, and into the Duluth harbor.

But Pa enjoyed talking about the towns and villages, the ports where the *America* stopped along the way—Belle Isle and Tobins Harbor and Rock Harbor Lodge and Washington Harbor on Isle Royale, Grand Portage, Chicago Bay, Grand Marais, Lutsen, Tofte, Cross River, Little Marais, Baptism River, Beaver Bay, Split Rock, and Two Harbors. I loved to hear him recite the places, as if he had been the boat-master calling out the stops. When he asked me to guess why they were named as they were, I figured out that Tobin and Tofte and Washington were people. Pa had to explain the meaning of "marais"—a marshland—and "belle"—beautiful. It was easy to envision a bay filled with beavers, a rock that was cleft, a notable portage, and harbors divided in twain or lined with rocks. But were people baptized in the river? Was one shaped like a cross? And what did the city of Chicago, Illinois, have to do with Minnesota's North Shore?

Pa had paid $6.80 second class fare for the thirteen-hour ride, too much to be multiplied by four, he had explained once when I had asked why we hadn't been able to go too, even though it would have been half fare for me and no fare at all for Lil. But the cost of the fare did not include meals or a berth. The United States & Dominion Transportation Company charged an extra $2.00 for a lower, $1.50 for an upper berth, which only slept one. And meals cost an exorbitant seventy-five cents for breakfast, $1.00 for supper, and $1.25 for dinner. I agreed. We could not have afforded that.

Nonetheless, when Pa had walked up the midship gangway, my heart had gone after him.

Now my heart wanted to follow him again or at least to trace his path so I could find out how to get to Ely.

I knew Pa would not return voluntarily to the noise and confusion and dirt and busy-ness of the thriving port of Duluth, center of shipping for both iron mining and lumbering industries. But, if not through Duluth, then how?

Moreover, Uncle Charles, too, had managed to get from Ely to Kinney in a direct line, sixty miles perhaps, without heading the ninety or so miles south and east to Duluth then angling back a repeat of sixty miles and more north and west. How ironic that I had never thought to ask how he had come! Since his appearance at our door had the magical quality of a genie's emergence from a bottle, the mundane question of "how-did-you-get-here" had always seemed completely irrelevant.

I sighed deeply, and the lump diminished a bit as rational thought took hold. Of course, there were ways. I just needed to find out what they were. But how?

I could walk down Chestnut Street to Savolainens' Jewelry Shop and ask Mr. Savolainen. But he might well raise awkward questions about how and why I happened to be traveling alone, and there was a powerful likelihood that given his nature and his aura of authority, he might well load me up in his big Buick and deposit me back in Kinney, willynilly.

I closed the door on that option.

Was my four dollars and ninety-six cents enough to allow me to hire a horse and buggy to bring me to Ely? Did any transportation company run a regular route in that direction? For that matter, was there even a road leading to Ely? How could I find out? Worst case, if there were a road, even were there no vehicle, could I simply walk? It might take several days, but I had the time, if neither a map nor food nor drink. Where would I get a map?

As my mind mulled over ways to arrive at answers to those questions, my fingers dug into my school bag for my pencil and paper so that I could make a list of options. The familiar feel of the pencil and paper always had a calming effect on my nerves, and as I began to relax, the lump receding further, my eyes focused on the scenes before me.

There was something . . . my eyes caught something . . . that in those moments of panic my mind had not recorded. I quit monkeying with the strap on my school bag and concentrated on what my far-sighted gaze had glimpsed on the other side of the lake. Movement. Horses. People. Women kneeling by the rocky shore down from the beach, washing clothes, it seemed. Wagons parked under the trees. Colored wagons. The wet clothes being draped on bushes and hung from tree branches to dry were brightly colored.

Gypsies.

My heart stopped. My mouth felt dry.

When we had first moved to Kinney, Lil and I had been playing outside in the vacant lot when Eino Salin raced by on the board sidewalk yelling, "Run! Run! The gypsies are coming!"

Lil and I had stood with our mouths agape as the other kids raced for home. Suddenly Ma had appeared, grabbing each of us, pulling us into the house, slamming and locking the doors, pulling the shades.

"Gypsies," she had told us, gasping for breath. "They steal. Everything in sight. Even children."

Terrified, Lil and I had both screamed, I as loudly as she, until Ma shushed us and whispered, "Be quiet. They don't break into houses. They just take what they can see outside. Shhh."

We shushed.

Ma sat down on the davenport and held Lil against her hard. "They like blond-haired, blue-eyed children."

I relaxed a bit. They'd never want me. Curious, I crept to the front window, pulled back the very corner of the shade, and looked out.

Down the street toward our house rolled a wooden wagon with a curiously carved, brightly painted curved roof. On the seat in front, holding the reins of two tired-looking horses, sat a dark-haired man with long hair and a moustache. Beside him, I glimpsed a woman dressed in red and gold with bracelets and necklaces glinting, long black hair hanging loose, flounces of colorful skirt flowing down the side of the wagon.

I started to jerk back as the wagon passed, but my eyes caught the eyes of someone looking out the wagon's back door, which was hanging ajar. A girl, I thought, seeing curls and color again, blue and green this time. For a fleeting second, as she peeked out, our eyes met.

Then the muted jangle of a tambourine mingled with the creak of the wagon and the plodding of the horses' hoofs, and just that one wagon traversed the silent street. Like ours, every house and every business it passed stood closed and locked. Not until sight and sound had completely disappeared did the citizens of Kinney ooze out again, a few at a time.

Mrs. Salin told Ma that we had been lucky. "Did you hear what happened in Winton last year?" she asked, with a significant glance at Lil and me. We ebbed away, but not beyond earshot. "To George Leppala. Eight years old. Syma Aro's sister's son. He went home from school for lunch one day, and Syma's sister Toini, his mother, told him not to go far because lunch was almost ready, but when she called him in, he didn't come and he didn't answer. The St. Croix Lumber Company even closed the next day so everyone in town including all the men at their boarding house and all the men at the Johnson Boarding House, all the men working in the mill and in the woods during the day, could search. Someone said they thought he had been seen hanging onto the back of a milk wagon about the time he should have been home for lunch, but they weren't sure it was him."

She had looked significantly down the road and back at Ma. "They never found him. Not a sign of him. Not alive . . . or . . .. But," she concluded, too involved in recounting the tragedy to care that we had ebbed closer, "there had been gypsies camped near the creek the day before."

Ma looked around, smiling nervously but with obvious relief when she saw us flickering around the periphery of the grownups. "No one is that cruel," she commented, typically. Ma categorically refused to listen to or to pass on gossip.

Mrs. Salin raised her eyebrows and shook her head, more it seemed in response to Ma's disbelief than in doubt.

The story had gone the rounds. The *Range Facts* carried front-page warnings whenever a gypsy encampment was sighted, and the local constabulary gave the gypsies firm orders to move on whenever they got too close to town, well-chronicled warnings, also on page one.

That is not to say they were always unwelcome. Men who needed horses found them to be excellent horse traders. Women who needed pots and pans, new or used, or who needed theirs mended found them skilled tinkers and peddlers. At carnival time or on Fourth of July, they had been known to tell a fortune or two. But by and large, they traveled along the fringes of a society that was still struggling for its own firm foothold in the wilderness.

It was not that very long ago, Miss Loney told our wide eyes, that even the area around Kinney had been populated only by caribou and Indians, covered with red and white pine forests, threaded by rivers and streams that offered quiet canoe routes between the Indians' wintering places and the spring sugar bush, between their summer fishing holes and autumn hunting grounds.

On the way from Malcolm to Virginia, our train had passed log cabins sitting in naked raw clearings, surrounded by stumps and rocks. The rare Ford Model T or Buick or Chevrolet usually ran only from city street to city street. When drivers like Mr. Ala and Mr. Savolainen tried the county roads, they wore dust coats and goggles and carried saws and axes for clearing brush.

Small towns like our Kinney perched precariously on the verges of lumber mills or ore mines, the frame houses clustered closely together, linked by boardwalk sidewalks set well above livestock droppings and mud. Outhouses sat in back yards. Water was hauled by pail from a central well or from a dug one in the back yard if the water-witch was lucky and the willow branch pointed down.

Wolves still dogged the paths of travelers, for what were called roads often remained paths or parallel ruts meandering through the forest, unsurfaced, unimproved, following routes that originated in days so long ago no one knew where or when or how they began, traversed first by the moose or the bear or the Sioux or the Anishinabe.

Along those fragile inroads into a largely unclaimed land traveled immigrants like us, Miss Loney said, alone or in groups, the Finns, the Italians, the Slovenians, the Cornish miners, the Swedes, the Norwegians, and the gypsies.

Some stopped at some point at some place and roosted for a time, sometimes taking up permanent residence, carving out a home, clearing a garden plot. Others traveled like the native Americans following paths formed by the seasons or seeking the pathless open lands, lured by their dreams.

Miss Loney did not have to explain to me what it meant to want to stop. Because of Ma, I knew. Because of Pa, I also sensed why others wanted to travel on, searching endlessly for something that lay beyond the present place, the present time. Such was the way of the immigrant.

Because of Ma and even more because of Mrs. Salin and her kind, I feared the ways of the wanderers, the gypsies. Because of Pa and even more because of those eyes that had met mine so briefly, I pondered that fear.

Thus, without planning, without any weighing of the consequences of or the reasons for my actions, I found myself pushing the pencil and paper back into my school bag. Getting up from the bench, I looked hard along the shore of Silver Lake, east to the bridge, and on toward the beach and the encampment that lay beyond it.

Gypsies had wagons and horses. Gypsies roamed. Gypsies did not prize children as dark and olive-skinned as their own. Gypsies dealt in things and money. They knew ways.

Taking deep breaths, I drew on Pa's beliefs: "We come from God, who is the source of all life. God is the spirit of all that is true and beautiful."

There had been beauty in that fleeting glimpse of a gypsy caravan. There was beauty in the colorful array on the trees beyond the beach.

"I shall trust in God, the spirit of love and all that is beautiful," I vowed to myself. "And if that trust is misplaced, I will scream and run like hell."

"Sorry, Ma," I appended, and took my first step.

Chapter Eleven

"Mustalainen!"

The locomotive steamed and whooshed and clanked into action, sweeping everything around it—the depot and me—into a centrifuge of sound, a maelstrom of movement, that set a period at the end of one plan and underlined the giant capital letter on my new one.

The gypsies.

I needed more time to regroup, but there was no time. At any moment I might be seen, my solitary self remarked upon, my identity, purpose, and direction questioned. Right or wrong, I had to move. Around me lay danger. Ahead? Surely nothing more serious than what I faced were I to stand still or, worse yet, turn back.

I found myself ill-equipped to do either. I had always dived head first into whatever the day offered, whether sunshine or rain, calm or storm, regardless of Ma's lectures about prudence and caution. She had remarked about my nature daily and daily had striven to correct it. Eino's vocabulary notebook provided her with ammunition, for as I shared new words with Ma while we worked and cleaned, she never hesitated to apply them, and I always came out wanting. Finns were stolid, she admitted. But I was mercurial. Finns were stoic; I, volatile. Finns worked. Like Pa, though I did not wish to admit it, I dreamed. But one Finnish quality I evinced and admitted totally and completely. Others called it stubbornness. I preferred the word "tenacity." I had planned to go to Ely, and to Ely I was going, no matter how.

As the noise of the train receded in one direction, I continued to move slowly off in the other, one step at a time, toward the gypsies.

Everyone I knew hated and feared them. It was true that children hid at any warning of their approach. They were considered culpable of any and every wrongdoing from stealing chickens to kidnapping children.

Yet though Italians considered Finns "dumb" and made fun of us in all of their jokes, I knew that, with the exception of Wilho Field and perhaps even including him, we were not totally lacking in sagacity. Moreover, in a like manner, Finns tended to demean Italians, calling them "dagos" or "wops." Yet Amalia's and Kabe's Italian families had been unfailingly kind to me. Any sense of logic seemed to suggest that in spite of everyone's condemnation of gypsies, everyone might possibly also be wrong about them.

"Well," I said aloud taking a deep breath, "I shall soon find out."

Gypsies: *mustalainen.* In Finnish, the very word sounded like swearing. But as I marched purposefully along the boardwalk toward the bridge between Bailey's Lake and Silver Lake, as I listened to the bridge boards resound even at my light footsteps, as my shoes sank past the buttons up to the high tops in Silver Lake beach sand, I concentrated not on the rumors but on the music Ma and Pa and I had sung on that day not so long ago on the way to Zim. Entitled *"Vanha Mustalainen"*—"The Old Gypsy"—the song offered a sympathetic and poignant picture of a wandering gypsy's life.

My mind recalled another old song Pa played on the fiddle and sang. Reciting the words, I forced myself to take one step per syllable:

> *Mustalaiseks olen syntynyt*
> *Koditonna kuljeskelen nyt*
> *Luonnon lapsi mitä hirolinkaan*
> *Kun vaan vapahana olla saan.*

Mindful of Miss Loney still, I tried next to say the words in English, worrying less about the accuracy of the translation than I did about the beat, though the words were deeply satisfying, too:

> As a gypsy, I was born.
> Without a home, I travel.
> Nature's child, doing what I choose to do:
> freedom makes my life complete.

That wasn't bad. But I liked my poetry to rhyme so I tried again:

> I am an orphan gypsy girl,
> who wanders homeless in this world.
> A child of nature, I'm without a care.
> I have my freedom, wand'ring everywhere.

"Oh, dear," I sighed, "too many 'wanderings.' Maybe 'roaming'?" For a second I was tempted to bring out Eino's notebook to look for another synonym. But no. No stopping allowed. Chin up, my eyes on the colored clothing hanging by the lake and on the outline of the caravans drawn into a semicircle in the woods beyond, I marveled at the similarity between that gypsy girl and me. I too was a low-born waif. I too wandered alone. Like the gypsy girl in the second verse, I sent my harp's song before me, the strings of my voice quivering, seeking a welcome and dreaming of heaven, a golden home where I could know love and joy. So cried the words of her song; thus cried the song of my heart. Her words were mine; mine, hers.

I sang in Finnish and in English, and the words carried me on with hope that the gypsies might accept me and carry me, woes and sorrows and all, away with them.

I had not reckoned on the dogs.

Long before my music reached the ears of the old ones or the women or the children like me, albeit in a gypsy camp, the dogs heard me. They bayed their displeasure at my unfamiliar smell, and their yelps masked my song.

I did not like dogs.

In Malcolm they lived in the barn and herded the cows and barked at me when I got in the way. In Virginia they slunk across back yards in the night, digging for malodorous leavings, howling from the nether regions of the dumps, as wild and vicious as the wolves that Pa said haunted the back roads, lurking on the fringes of society, waiting for the lame, the hungry, the weak, the stragglers, human or animal.

When the dogs smelled me, they knew me for one of the weak ones. They smelled my fear. They sensed my fragility. They heralded their intent.

I froze. The song died on my lips; my heart died within me. Far more than I feared the gypsies, I was terrified of the dogs.

As they raced toward me and surrounded me, yapping and jumping, fangs barred, ruffs bristling, I shrank into myself, clutching my school bag, trying to keep from screaming but screaming all the same, though not a sound came from my throat.

Like That Child in Virginia, I knew again how it felt to be prey. But this time I truly was in jeopardy.

I do not remember much of what happened next. Time lost its forward momentum and swung back and forth like the dogs, in and out of the circle that surrounded me, blurring into a confused impression of fur flying not at me but away, of a huge figure, grizzled and gray. Was it a bear? Was it a man? I saw the bear, brown as the earth, its eyes masked, muzzled with ribbons, ambling toward me on its hind legs. Or was it a man with a woolen coat and a moustache, gray hair curling around a leathery tanned lined forehead, eyes piercing my soul from under heavy gray-black brows?

The barking continued, but it wasn't the dogs. Something growled, but it wasn't the bear.

In English I heard myself scream "Sanctuary!" In Finnish, though the rationale made no sense to me then, nor does it now, I heard myself reciting a lesson I had learned from the *Aapinen*, the beginning reader I had found in Aholas' bookcase and received as a farewell gift from Gramma Ahola when we left Malcolm. During the years while I waited for Ma to enroll me in school, I had memorized it, page by page:

Iso nalle on onneton.
Se etsii lastaan.
Jos osaat,
Niin etsi toinen nalle.
(The big bear is unhappy, sad, forlorn.
It searches.
If it can,
it will see . . . another bear.)

Sobbing, I cried out the words, looking from bear to bear, searching, until the world around me lost form and direction just as time had, and I fell and rose and fell and rose until I heard a roaring around me. Was I tied to the tracks? Was the Duluth and Missabi steam locomotive approaching? Was the scream its whistle? The centrifuge returned as did the maelstrom of movement, and I was lost.

It had been days, weeks perhaps, since I had eaten well. So hunger could have provided an excuse for my disorientation. But looking back, I think it grew naturally from seeds of fear and dread, from the lost images of Uncle Charles and Pa, from the look on Mr. Ala's face when he didn't think I saw him looking at Ma, from Ma's hands trembling in the light of the kerosene lamp, from Lil, who had reached her hand into the firebox of the woodstove one morning to grab a handful of cold ashes and bring them to her mouth and eat them. I had almost been hungry enough to understand, though I had slapped her hands and washed them and cried as I warned her, "Lil, if you ever do that again, I will spank you until you're red and tell Ma."

Never in my darkest nightmare or in my wildest dreams, however, could I have envisioned the scenes to which I awoke later, much later.

When I came to myself again, the combined noises of the dogs and the train had been replaced by the clanking of pots and the jingling of bells; the sunlit morning, by a starlit night. I was lying in a featherbed covered by a downy quilt. But the bed was moving forward slowly, and through the window on the left and above my head, I could see the moon tangled in a woven mesh of tree branches. I wiggled my toes. My shoes were off. I felt my hair. The braids had been undone. Heavy strands lay loosely on the pillow. When I lifted my arms to push back the quilts, I realized I had been garbed with a soft, loose fabric that hung around me as I sat up and draped my feet over the side of the bed and pushed back two bedcurtains, the inner one light as gossamer, the outer heavy as velvet.

On the other side of the curtains, dark eyes met mine as they had for that fleeting second in Kinney. A girl, my size it seemed, was sitting on the stool by my bed. At my movement, she got up, and a shape wrapped in a blanket arose from the floor. A grandmother's wrinkled face surrounded by blanket looked at me, smiled, nodded, and made soothing sounds. The girl reappeared with a bowl of something warm . . . soup . . . which she put into my hands. It was so redolent of chicken and potatoes and herbs that I ignored my manners and gulped down the liquid and spooned the bits of vegetables and meat into my mouth as if I were starving. Perhaps I was. Once empty, the bowl became a flowered china cup of tea, pot-warm, heavy with sugar. I drank that, too, in noisy slurps. The wrinkled hand that took it away returned to smooth my hair and tuck me back under the quilt. Relieved, I drifted on the feathers of night into a sleep so healing that when the wagon stopped and I awoke to a golden morning, I felt reborn.

The window framed a still-life scene, forested, immobile. Slipping out from under the quilt and lifting the curtains, the inner one as golden and fragile as a sunstreak, the outer rich and crimson, I wound myself in the shawl lying on the nearby stool. No one sat beside my bed; no one lay on the floor. Cushions were piled neatly on the other side of a narrow pathway leading from front door to back. Creeping forward, for the wagon leaned that way just the slightest bit, I peeked out through the top of a strange-looking door, which had been cut in half horizontally. The bottom had been left closed, but the top was open, its shutters framing a tiny village of similar wagons and of tents encircling a long, low, broad firepit. Black kettles and an iron cauldron hung from tripods above the flames steaming an aromatic invitation. But no one was there. Even the horses were gone. The clearing in the forest lay before me as if it were enchanted, absolutely still, absolutely quiet.

Then the charm was broken, not, thank goodness, by the barking of the dogs, which lay quiescent under a nearby wagon, ignoring me completely, but by the babbling of small children, six or seven of them at least, Lil's age, running naked toward the circle of the camp, their skin glistening, newly washed. Herding them along, behind them, around them, alongside of them floated a cluster of women bright as meadow flowers. Their flowing upside-down-petals-of-skirts swirled in layers of red and green, purple and gold. I recognized the smallest of the women, the grandmother, who saw me and gestured me down, chirping in a language as quick and sprightly as Ma's Finn when she was happily busy.

Over on the far side of the last caravan, a bear munched breakfast, and a bear of a man unwound himself from a quilt in front of one of the tents, strode over, reached up massive arms, and lifting me down onto a stool by the fire, gestured to one of the women to bring us food.

She did. Hot tea first. Then dinner at breakfast time—fresh fish fried in the black iron pan and unleavened bread the man tore into pieces and shared with me. Vegetables and soup were ladled onto plates and served each of the men and me.

The children, still naked, hunkered down in a circle like small stumps in a clearing, separate from us, waiting to be served by the women. I looked but could not find the girl of the dark eyes.

I was the only female seated with the men and, like them, continued to be served first—tea, fish, vegetables, soup, more tea—until the men, replete, sat back with pipes in their mouths. Too full to move, I sat too, wide eyes watching it all. The women ate, cleaned up, and banked the fire. Then the whole group gathered around my bear-like companion to plan the day, it seemed. Of course, the planning was all done in their language, Rom. But their movements and gestures made the meaning clear. The three younger men were off to do some horsetrading. The three younger women, scarves over their heads, jangling coins flying among the loose strands of hair—"tangled tresses," I amended—held cards for fortunetelling and pushed handwagons of pots and pans and kitchen trifles. Soon only the oldsters, the children, the dogs, the bear, and I were left in camp.

The day passed in a dream. The bear of a man—the grandfather I called him—worked with the bear, teaching him tricks until it grew hot in the middle of the day. Then he perched on a stool, fiddle in hand, and the children danced to his music and played tambourines. All day the children roamed around the encampment, touching and taking whatever caught their eyes, knives even. They played like puppies among the underbrush and the trees, exploring the woods and the meadow, splashing in the swift-running stream, fishing there, scuffling and running to the grandmother for kisses, finally falling into sleepy heaps like the bear under the trees.

The grandmother fed me all day long, little bits at a time but steadily until I could eat no more. In early afternoon, she led me to the nearby stream, where I washed myself well regardless of the cold, and back to the wagon where she tucked me into the featherbed, and I slept away the rest of the day.

A part of my mind knew that I should be concerned about where I was and where the gypsies were going. But all through those long, warm, comforting hours, I neither thought nor planned. Time and place and purpose lay suspended on the other side of that dream world where my body and soul found solace.

When the shadows began to fall and I awoke, the young men and women were returning, each with some contribution to the common weal. One of the women carried a chicken. Laughing, she released it. As it pecked its way across the open center of the camp, she swirled her skirt over and around it, guiding it toward the grandmother, who laughed, too.

I understood at once how and why chickens seemed to disappear when the gypsies passed. That one tasted delicious, roasted to brown crispness on a spit above the fire.

Another of the women lifted a cup of tea and, swirling the liquid, studied the dregs, reenacting her telling of fortunes. Clearly, someone was to be lucky in some ways, but not in all. Another had helped someone who had not helped her. A third had a friend who wasn't a friend. The coins of recompense dropped from the fortune-teller's hand into the lap of the grandmother.

It was evident that the day had been a success. Knives had been ground and pots sold and mended and money amassed. There would be a feast that night.

A feast there was and dancing and fiddle music that made my heart cry. The wives again served their husbands, whose dark eyes looked kindly at them and at me as they ate with knives as sharp as serpents' teeth held in hands that glittered with gold rings.

We ate from china plates flowered with pink and yellow roses.

The gypsies' gestures told me that, though I was a "gorgio," because I had drunk of their water from their glass and eaten of their food, I had become a sister. The men smoked and talked. The horses chomped on hay. Nightbirds sang. Frogs croaked. The bear danced. The dogs slept. Peace lay around us like the mist on the meadow.

And finally in the darkness, his fiddle quiet, the grandfather spoke to a rhythm of clicking tongues and stamping feet and tapping spoons and knuckles rapping on wood, and I felt as if I grasped the essence of the messages, if not the words: "Always help brothers. Never harm brothers. Always pay what you owe, though not necessarily with money. Never be afraid."

I listened, and I was not afraid.

When morning came, rain was pattering on the canvas wagon cover pulled tightly over the curved wooden spokes above me but open in the front. Peeking out, I saw the men tending the horses and arranging sticks on the ground. Were those messages? Money was being dug out from under the cold embers of the camp fire, where it had lain, safer than in any bank.

Seeing me, the grandfather climbed onto the small balcony of the bow-top wagon and asked me in English and in Finnish how he, a brother, could help his sister.

"I must go to Ely," I told him in English and in Finnish.

"That I knew," he said. "We have brought you to Tower. From here, there is a train."

Chapter Twelve

"Arrival"

As the rain let up, a foggy mist continued to weave around the camp, drifting in and out of the trees, so that the caravans, one moment visible, were the next shrouded in ghostly white. How well that suited the ephemeral quality of the gypsies themselves, who could have been dervishes for all I knew, since they seemed capable of instant transformation into any shape, into any identity.

A part of me was not surprised at anything they did or said. Perhaps they divined truth like water witches with a willow wand.

Still, I had been raised to be a skeptic. Thus I had to question the source of the grandfather's knowledge. How had he come to know what I had never divulged? Had it been accident alone that had led them to bring me exactly where I needed to go? Plucking myself off the lip of the wagon, the caravan or vardo as they called it, I gazed at the grandfather wide-eyed.

"Il est très wise," a quiet voice explained in an unfamiliar combination of languages—a bit of English and something else not Rom or Finnish.

There she was, suddenly, the girl whose dark eyes had met mine that day in Kinney, who had kept vigil after I collapsed. She too appeared and disappeared by magic as did her home, the most beautiful of the caravans, which I had not seen before this morning. I could not have failed to remark upon it. Made entirely of wood, every piece was colorfully painted and decorated—the carved fascia board edging the curved roof, a horse figure on the back doorway, the elaborately turned balusters on the front and back balconies. It was to the other wagons what the girl of the dark eyes was to me—infinitely more elegant, richer, more stylized.

"*Je m'appelle Maria,*" the girl said, pointing to herself. "*Et toi?*"

That meaning seemed clear, and I responded instinctively in Finnish, "*Minun nimi on Ilmi Marianna,*" before correcting my language and my appellation: "My name is Marion."

"Bonne," she smiled. "*Vous êtes tres bonne.*"

The accompanying gesture accented what must have been a compliment. A "*kiitos*" slipped out before the "thank you." If it had been a compliment, I could return it with ease, for she was lovely, dressed all in red with a full skirt and loose blouse and red ribbons entwined in her glossy dark hair, damp either from the rain or from an early morning dip in the stream, but hanging nonetheless in ringlets around a creamy olive face. Her eyes were so distinctive—dark brown and limpid—that more than her name they were my key to her identity. To me she was always to be the girl of the dark eyes.

"*Tu ne parles pas français?*" she asked.

"No." I was quite sure she was asking about her language— French? "I speak English, though, and Finnish."

"Ah," she nodded. "Then I shall try to speak in the English." Her voice made music of the words, giving them a lilting quality that turned the interchange into something extraordinary.

I sighed. For two days and nights, her pleasant world had mesmerized me with its extraordinary delights. Hunger and exhaustion were not my only excuse for staying. Here I had found kindness and warmth, and I had allowed myself to sink into them like a featherbed. With searing honesty I forced myself to admit that I did not want to leave. Were I not on a quest, I might have chosen to stay with the gypsies for a time, willingly going wherever their vardos led. A very small part of my mind even considered adopting them as my family or allowing them to adopt me.

That was, I realized, the true danger of the gypsies. It was not that they stole children but that they did not need to. So alluring was their world that, like the rats bewitched by the piper of Hamelin, children willingly followed the gypsies' path. The elders, the grandfathers and grandmothers, offered support and acceptance. Their children and grandchildren experienced an almost total freedom. To travel the world in a beautiful wagon, to laugh at convention and rules, to make games of work, to share the excitement of the chase—how tempting!

With an anguished glance at the girl of the brown eyes, I stood up abruptly, climbed down from my perch, and marched myself over to the grandfather. "I must go to Ely as soon as possible," I explained, my voice tearing a bit with effort. "I must find my uncle. My mother's and my sister's lives depend on it."

Nodding, the grandfather sat down on a stool and drew me onto his lap. "I know, my child," he said, his soothing voice rumbling like the growlings of a friendly, furry bear.

"When you were ill, my child," the grandfather continued, "you spoke to us in both of your languages. You called to us for succor. That we have given. It began, small sister, with that which your body sought regardless of words—food and rest. But there was another need, unvoiced, that of sustenance, nourishment for your soul."

He was right. My soul, too, had lain safely in his embrace.

"Now that you have come back to your self, now that you are whole again, it is another kind of help that you need. That we understand. As you have done, continue to give us your trust. Let us take you by the hand once more. Be not afraid."

Bending my head as if receiving a benizon, I nodded.

The girl of the dark eyes slipped her hand through mine. "Come," she said. "*Ma mère et mon père* shall be of help to you. We must prepare."

Although all of the adults in the gypsy encampment were handsome people, even the grandmother, the girl of the dark eyes led me toward two who were exceptionally attractive. The one I assumed to be her father moved like a gypsy king with the grace of the Arabian stallions he cared for—two chestnut yearlings with arched necks and narrow flanks and legs and feet seemingly fragile yet as strong as dancers. The young woman who served him tea and busied herself with packing low stools and cushions into the glistening green and yellow, blue and red vardo had a white apron over her skirts. But as she moved, yards and yards of softness swirled around her, echoing the wagon's colors. Her ears, her neck, her wrists, her waist were encircled in gold that reflected the glow of the sun and the firelight. Neither of them seemed wholly of this earth.

With the gypsies, anything seemed possible, for theirs was a world in which chickens walked willingly into silken nets, where the future revealed its truths, where even the horses grew young instead of old. One grizzled gray crone had turned overnight into a sprightly prancer with a coat as black as ink or potash.

As the morning advanced, we too were transformed. The girl of the brown eyes and I were both reclothed as gorgios, me in my school dress, nicely brushed and pressed, my shoes polished to a sheen; she in a middy-sailor dress, curls neatened into plaits. So too were her parents transformed—the father by a staid pin-striped suit, celluloid collar, bow tie, cap, suspenders, and watch fob stretching across his flat hard stomach. The mother became a Gibson girl garbed in a traveling suit of gray serge with matching hat and cape, her hair and sleeves pouffed, her waist well-corseted and belted above the bustle. Thus the four of us presented ourselves to the critical gaze of the assembled company about noon that day. By then the sun was peeking at us shyly from between the trees, more familiar with the gypsies than with these gorgios.

The grandfather reviewed the plan in Rom and then in English. The grandmother counted out coins for the trainfare, one-way for me, roundtrip for the three who would make sure I reached my destination safely.

"Farther than that we must not go, for that would be to interfere with and perhaps to change the destiny allotted only to you. Unqualified aide must be given a sister. But we must not change what has been written." Those were the grandfather's last words to me. Then he helped us into a pony trap, which had magically appeared in the camp. The father clicked his teeth, and the well-bred pony pranced off toward the small city of Tower and its Duluth and Iron Range train depot.

Clutching the edge of the seat, I turned back and waved until a bend in the road masked the camp behind a curtain of underbrush and trees, and the gypsies were gone from my sight.

I wished I had kissed him, the grandfather. I wished I had hugged the grandmother harder. I wished I had something of theirs to remind me of their kindness. In truth, however, I have needed no reminder. No matter how time has blurred their images, no matter how our paths have diverged, no matter where I have gone—or where they have traveled, I have never forgotten their kindness.

The girl of the brown eyes reached out one hand to cover mine. We crossed a narrow wooden bridge over a stream that danced toward a lake glinting off in the distance. The pony panted as we traveled up the hill toward the depot. Railroad tracks reaching far into the wilderness roughly paralleled our path.

Concentrating on trying to look forward, with each turn of the wheels I nonetheless tightened my hold on Maria's hand.

The father paid for our tickets. "Only twenty-five cents for our elder daughter because," he explained to the stationmaster, "she is staying in Ely to attend the new high school there. My wife and I and our other daughter must pay the full fifty-cents for a return trip through Tower overland to Embarrass. I have been transferred from the mining office in Soudan to a new office at the junction of a spur track leading north from the Aurora station."

The stationmaster nodded gravely, and he and the father discussed the vagaries of mine superintendents and railroad officers, who assigned clerks and workmen willynilly, uprooting whole families at a whim. The mother nodded with a look of patient forbearance, and the stationmaster offered her a chair, clearly struck by her air of fragile femininity and by her elegant manners, evident though she spoke very little.

His manner made it clear that a woman who combined beauty with virtue was to be honored and not, if she was married, otherwise approached in spite of the fact that such women—outnumbered perhaps four to one—were highly prized. Regret showed in his face.

So we passed the time as we waited for the train, which had left Duluth before eight-thirty that morning bound for Two Harbors, a busy port, and thence across country—empty, desolate country—toward the mines and the logging towns of the Vermilion Range—the small mining towns of Tower and Soudan, the lumbering and milling town of Winton, the metropolis that was Ely with its lighted streets and cement sidewalks, broad thoroughfares, new high school, and two-story turreted hospital. The locomotive pulled one passenger car and two freight cars, both heavily stacked with boxes of equipment and foodstuffs, clothing and store supplies as well as refreshments for the establishments that purveyed beer and spirits. The stationmaster clucked his lips as he and the father discussed those establishments in very low voices, and the mother pretended not to hear. Fifty-two licenses had been sold in Ely alone at the cost of one thousand dollars per license. The father shook his head, and the stationmaster agreed that the world was coming to no good end with such things happening in the midst of young and growing communities.

Finally, the train hissed its way out of the wilderness, clanked up the hill and bustled to a stop with great jarrings and clouds of smoke. A conductor appeared at the entrance to the passenger car, put down some steps, and reached his hand to help the mother up. The girl of the brown eyes and I followed her politely. The father handed the conductor our tickets, and we were ushered toward a set of velvet seats just across from a water spigot and a boxed-in area provided for those who needed to refresh themselves.

The mother and the father and the girl of the brown eyes all seemed to fit very comfortably into this world, and I assumed that it was theirs too in as great a degree as the beautifully colored vardo was theirs. In the camp, they had spoken Rom. To me, the girl had spoken French. At the station and on the train, the father and the mother articulated an unaccented if somewhat melodious English, and the girl of the brown eyes sat attentively, her mouth moving as if she were practicing or memorizing.

The girl and I each sat by a window during that journey past the underground mines of Soudan, along the lake called Vermilion, though it was not red as the ore was red, under forests of virgin white pine soaring as high above us as the clouds, and finally through the areas that had been clear-cut, razed so that nothing but naked stumps and decaying branches and fragile saplings remained. Good blueberry picking there, I thought. Ma always steered us toward those dead places, shorn of trees by fire or ax. Blueberry plants were a part of the rebirth. As those scenes sped past us like the jerky frames of the moving pictures in Boziches' garage, I tried very hard not to think about Ely or about what I would or would not find there. Consequently, I was able to think of little else.

Of a certainty, my new family would dissolve as soon as we reached the Ely train depot, leaving me on my own. That was as it should be. I had already accepted more help than I could ever repay. The father and the mother and the girl of the brown eyes seemed to understand that. When the train clanked through a noisy, jerking series of endless trial-halts before coming to rest beside the depot, though we disembarked together and they accompanied me to the broad porch lining the city-side of the building, there we parted, me to march resolutely one step at a time across a gravel street toward what was obviously Ely's main street, they to wait for the return trip to Tower and parts beyond.

Never in my life had I felt so terribly, achingly, frighteningly alone. Never in my life had I tried so hard to hide my feelings.

"If I manage to appear undaunted," I told myself firmly, "perhaps I can manage to *feel* undaunted."

To that end, I set my eyes and my mind and my footsteps to the fore, leaving the world of the gypsies behind, both the secret world of their encampments and the bridge the father and the mother and the girl of the brown eyes had built between that life and this one.

107

The future I had so anticipated and feared was now the present, and I had to begin the search. But practically speaking, where?

Seating myself on the curb of the cement sidewalk, I took out my pencil and foolscap paper and made a list.

He had money in a bank, so I could look for banks, especially for those that seemed to be used by Finnish people. "Banks," I wrote.

Since I knew he lived in a boarding house, I must ask for the names of Finnish *poikatalos*. "Boarding houses," I wrote.

I knew he worked in a mine. "Mine offices," I wrote.

The act of making a list helped somewhat to allay the questions that rose inside me like the dust dervishes dancing on the street: What if when I found him, he had changed his mind and decided against the move to Zim? Even worse than that, what if I did not find him? What if he had already left Ely? Barely five dollars stood between me and utter destitution. I was not so unfamiliar with city life that I did not know how much food cost . . . or lodgings.

What if the white slavers I read about long ago in Malcolm had taken up residence in Ely? What if they found me as they had found That Child's mother in Virginia? What if they took me away into a life of sin? Could I escape like Pauline?

Shivering, I stopped myself from embroidering further spidery details onto that imaginary web.

First things first, instead. Reaching the corner of Central and Sheridan, I saw across from me the sign "The Savolainen Company" and above the door the number "6." That will be my last resort, I vowed, and turning left, headed up the hill past store fronts with odd-side numbers. It was hard to study store-fronts and signs because I saw so much else.

Just ahead, a Model T Ford swerved around a horsedrawn delivery wagon. One of the horses, spooked by the train whistle that called an eerie farewell to me, reared and pawed the air. A Star touring car with open sides, canvas top, and spare tire by the hood sped by. Pa and I had seen one advertised in the *Range Facts*. And right in the middle of the street a man stood cranking what I thought was an Oakland with gas lights. Crowds of people jostled and pushed me—miners still wearing hard-hats with their candles doused, lumberjacks in plaid shirts and felt hats and boots, children riding bikes, and a mule-skinner who was shouting orders to men loading a wagon marked "St. Croix Lumber Company" and to its tote team of six mules, flapping their tails as they waited impatiently.

Clinging to my schoolbag, I forged ahead until, midway up the steep hill, I almost bypassed a large store, double the size of the others. Above its broad expanse of plate glass windows the words "Finnish Stock Company" had been carved into brownstone. I stepped inside the door, which stood ajar.

When my eyes adjusted, I stood transfixed. It was like Salins' store but doubled. No, tripled. All around the walls, shelves rose floor to ceiling with a walkspace for the clerk between them and the high glassed-in counters framing the customers' walk-areas. No one paid any attention to me at first. Ladies fingered material and matched buttons and thread. Housekeepers ordered cheese or meats or staples and selected cucumber-size pickles from one open brine-filled barrel and crackers from another. A little boy stood with his nose on the glass trying to choose between horehound drops and licorice and other jars of candy, priced five for a penny. A gentleman in a broadcloth suit was holding a box of chocolates, looking at the label, which read twenty cents a pound.

I sniffed the air . . . mmmm . . . and guessed at tobacco, kerosene, molasses, the leathery-scent of new shoes and boots, fresh coffee beans spilling from a huge hand-turned grinder. My mouth watered for the squares of pickled herring and red salt salmon and smaller wedges of cheese ready cut from twenty-five pound wheels visible in cases nearby.

Walking slowly down the center aisle, I tried to keep my stomach from growling and finally reached a long counter in the rear where an impatient masculine voice addressed me in Finnish. "*Mitä haluat, tyttö?*" then repeated in English—"What do you want, girl?"

Oh, how I wanted to give him a sharp-tongued response! I wanted to answer, coolly, haughtily, as if such splendors were commonplace and I was completely unimpressed, "*Ei mitaan.*"—"Not a thing." But the truth was its opposite, "*Kyllä minä haluan kaikkia.*"—"I want it all."

It had been a long time since breakfast.

But I bit back both retorts and addressed my problem directly: "Do you by any chance know Charles Brosi?"

"Ch-a-r-les Bro-si." Wiping his hands on an apron made of mattress ticking, the storekeeper ran the words across his tongue. "Hmmm."

In a spirit of hopeful expectancy, I held my breath.

"Now, where have I heard that name?" he asked in a heavily accented English. "Let me think." Peering at me through small round spectacles, he scratched his chin and smoothed his hands over his hair.

Strands of heavily pomaded waves arched up on each side of a center part. "What is he to you, child?" Although the words were said with a deceptive unconcern, his look was sharp and incisive, as if he could see right through me. Maybe he could. I guessed that men in his position had to understand what people were made of in order to know what they'd want.

Moreover, it was probable that in Ely as in Virginia and even in Kinney, there were men who did not want anyone to know who they were. They did not want any of their Finnish—or American—families, legal or otherwise, to track them down. Some had one family left behind in Finland and another here. Some had made multiple marriages in this country, finding a new woman in every town where they stopped to work. I had not been without ears when the grownups talked while we entertained ourselves with books and games. I had heard stories.

"He is my uncle," I answered, looking the storekeeper right in the eye. Since I had to make him divulge whatever information he knew, without a blush or a blink at the subterfuge—I refused to consider it a lie.—I added, "I have some money to pay him, money my Pa borrowed when he visited us last." There. The storekeeper should not hesitate to help me find one who stood to gain rather than lose by the contact.

He still looked at me sharply. "I will think on it and ask around."

I sighed. Oh, how I wished this Finnish storekeeper were Italian! In Virginia any visit to Parlantis' to buy meat took at least an hour. Mr. Parlanti liked to talk.

As I turned to leave, crestfallen, a woman standing in line nearby suggested, "Try Pertullas' rooming house on Camp Street and the Finnish Boarding House on West Sheridan. Look for an apple tree in the front yard at Pertullas' and a weeping willow by the side door of the Finnish Boarding House. And you might ask around Finn Hill. There are some other smaller places that take boarders."

Grabbing my pencil, I hurriedly scribbled reminders.

Since she had spoken in Finnish, I answered politely, "*Kiitos.*"

Even though the storekeeper's response had been grudging, he also earned a polite "Thank you." I dared not be rude.

He ignored me.

Clearly dismissed, I glimpsed a second man behind a counter way in the back, this one with a cleft in his chin and gray thinning hair. He was looking at me so intently that I wanted to run right out of the store. But when I moved, the direction of his gaze did not, and I realized that he was blind. He traced the edges of the counter with his fingers until he reached the end then sat down at a seat behind a grindstone, set a spigot so water would drip a bit at a time onto the stone, and began to sharpen a set of knives. "Two more places that might be of help," he added, mentioning them casually to the store as a whole instead of to me, "are the Finnish Evangelical Lutheran National Church, D. Ruotsalainen, pastor."

He seemed to see me shake my head.

"Or," and at this one my heart sank, "the Finnish Accident and Sick Benefit Association. West Sheridan Street. Ask for John Porthan. Tell him Jaako sent you."

He nodded at the knives and added, "And if you have no luck, come back here."

It wasn't much, but at least he had given me some additional direction, not only places but names and a reference. "Thank you," I repeated. That time I really did mean it.

Chapter Thirteen

"Finnish Stock"

Once out the door of the Finnish Stock Company, I stood still for a minute trying to get my bearings. I needed to find "West Sheridan Street." The sign at the corner had said "Sheridan." The numbers on the store fronts I had passed, walking east, had run in ascending order. It seemed reasonable, therefore, that to find West Sheridan I had to turn right and that the main street might split into east and west at Central Street, given its name and placement. It ran between the depot and Sheridan and on the other side all the way, I later found out, to the cemetery.

It took all of my self-control not to run, for I might be at that very minute no more than a few blocks from Uncle Charles.

Then the earth shook and the skies screamed, and the world collapsed around me or froze. Even on that busy sidewalk no one moved. On Sheridan Street, cars skidded to a stop. Horses, pulled to an abrupt halt, reared and complained, and wagon brakes squealed.

The shriek screamed on and on and on until it finally assumed the identity of a mine whistle. But mine whistles sounded at specific times—curfew and midday and the ends of the shifts. This was not any of those.

When the earth stilled, people waited for a time. Then the throngs moved again. The wagons, carts, cars, people turned from their preset paths to head either down Sheridan toward the perpendicular Central Street or west where spaces between store buildings allowed passage.

Voices cried out, and all of them spoke the same words: "It's the mine!" "There's been an accident in the mine!"

Only one old man with a cane standing near me, balancing himself with care, continued to stand still. His voice sounded tinny as he recited to no one in particular: "In the Sibley the walls collapsed. Water . . . rocks . . . filled the shaft. Men . . . knocked off ladders . . . buried . . . chest deep . . . in mud. The elevator cage . . . came down. My legs . . . pinned. Never go down in the mine again. Never go down again."

The crowds washed around him, but pulling and shoving and pushing, they carried me with them. Between the buildings we streamed, across the alley, left down Camp Street, past the Ely Bottling Works pop shop with bottles of cream soda and orange and strawberry soda pop stacked in the windows . . . past the depot . . . over the tracks where the High Ball, a freight train, was being loaded for its return trip to Duluth . . . between storage sheds left standing open. Stacked cartons of beer and spirits and coal overflowed onto the gravel near "Daisy Redfield's Honky Tonk." Through a heavily fringed window curtain I glimpsed plush couches lining the walls of a public room.

On we continued *en masse*, though I finally regained control of my feet as the crowd spread out into more open areas past a garden filled with rows of cabbages, past the fence around another garden plot where a small boy stood open-mouthed, a can probably filled with kerosene in one hand, a potato bug in another. No one stopped at the Arcade Saloon but followed instead the street that turned into a trail that led around a pit and on toward a high metal smokestack and toward the scream that also continued.

I tried to cover my ears, but the noise ran through me, pushed against me, melted into me, in much the same way as had the crowd.

The front of the crowd stopped near a high platform, visible from a distance, where a miner stood with a bell in his hand, thus setting the brakes on the rest of us, who ricocheted bit by bit into immobility. When the crowd stopped, the scream stopped. But the silence that fell still held the scream in its grasp, and the silence was hard put to contain it, for it was punctuated by a solemn drum-beat, the tolling of the bell.

"There's the pumpman and the powder monkey!" cried an excited voice near me. Two other men were approaching the front of the platform—one black and red from smoke and blood, bearing the marks of every potentially lethal charge of dynamite that earned him extra pay. Nonetheless it was his support that kept the retching pumpman upright.

"My Pa's the bell ringer!" the voice caroled proudly. "He signals the el-e-va-t'r op-er-a-t'r t' send the cage cars up 'n' down!"

The bell continued tolling steady beats, one after another after another. The crowd swayed to the beat. No one else uttered a word, yet all around I felt the waves of an undertone of sound, a crooning beat, a suppressed moan.

An official dressed like a mine superintendent in a white shirt, black suit and tie came out of a shack near the platform. Holding a hat and a cane in one hand, a piece of paper in the other, he climbed up some makeshift stairs, marched past the pumpman and the powder monkey and the bell ringer, and, adjusting his spectacles, raised the sheet of paper.

The bell stopped. Our breathing stopped. He read in English, his powerful voice resonant as the tolling bell. Translations into Finnish and Italian and Slovenian swirled around me.

I caught most of the words.

" . . . a fall of iron ore on the ninth level . . . crew putting in a raise . . . a considerable mass of ground crushed down a chute . . . remains to be recovered include . . ."

He passed the paper to the pumpman, who must have been Finnish.

Like most everyone else in that crowd, I listened for the sound of one name and one name only. But the bell tolled for all of the others, nonetheless, and the calling of the roll formed a sacred litany I will remember until I die: "Santala, Kaisa . . . Katajmaki, John . . . Looperi, J. . . . Koskimaki, Wilho . . . Nuottinmaki, Kaisa . . . Helpakka, Toija . . . Pyoriasaari, Jacob . . . Hernesmaa, Onni . . . Parsinen, Eino . . ."

No Brosi. No Brosi, Charles.

The pumpman passed the paper to the powder monkey. It shook in his hands. Italian names and Slovenian ones were punctuated by sobs. But by and large with each Finnish name, only the silence had grown louder. Near me, a woman fainted. Down the row another woman's face blanched white, and children turned into her skirts.

The litany stopped. The powder monkey passed the piece of paper back to the official who folded it, put it into his pocket and turned back toward the steps and the shack.

A Finnish voice called out, "Funerals Sunday. Those in the band meet at my place tonight."

Slowly, slowly the crowd dispersed.

Not I. I stood there aghast until I stood there alone. I had not known until then what it meant to work in the mines. I had not known until then what it meant to have a loved one work in the mines. Now I knew.

I knew why Pa had been willing to fight for a union.

I knew why Mr. Wirtanen had preferred other games of chance.

I knew why Uncle Charles had shared our dream and why the farm in Zim had sounded so much like paradise.

And I knew, too, that I now had another reason to find Uncle Charles, a less selfish one. Not only to save Ma and Lil and me, but to save him, too. So that the bell would never toll after the name "Brosi, C."

Back I trekked in what seemed to be the general direction of Sheridan Street, appalled at the extent of my earlier ignorance. I had thought I had known the worst that life could bring. I had been wrong.

Never again would I criticize Pa for quitting the mines.

Never again would I question the need to stop those kinds of accidents, even if it had to be with blood.

Never again would I accept one cent of Uncle Charles' money or one of his generous gifts without full awareness of what he had had to do to earn that money.

As my feet dragged me back toward town, I thought hard about what was important to me. Ma was important. Though I was hard put to admit it, Lil was important. Uncle Charles and Pa were important. Education and knowledge and words were important, for they were the passport out of a world where the bells might otherwise toll for all of us.

I set my teeth together, firmed up my hold on my schoolbag, clenched to my heart every English word I knew, and headed for the newspaper office I had seen on the corner of Central and Sheridan.

Despising the kind of blind searching that left me in tunnels as dark as those that ran beneath me, with every step, I made another vow: "I shall put my faith and trust in what I know is the key to the world around me. Words. I shall put my money on them to succeed where all else might fail. I shall put an ad in the newspaper for Uncle Charles Brosi to read. I shall ask him to meet me as soon as he can in a place owned by people I trust. And in the meantime, I shall get myself a job so that I have food to fuel my body and a place to sleep to rest my mind.

"Never again if I can help it will Uncle Charles Brosi go down into that or any other mine. He will read the message and find me, and together we will set off for home."

"WANTED" read the headline above the ad. "News of Charles Brosi, bachelor. Bring information of his whereabouts to Ilmi Marianna Brosi, care of The Savolainen Company, 6 East Sheridan."

The man in the newspaper office had taken time from what was to be a very busy afternoon to grasp my fifty cents with ink-stained fingers. He also advised me to word the ad in so general a way as to appeal not just to Uncle Charles but to anyone knowing of him. I had concurred. There was only one small problem. The ad would appear in the next issue of the *Ely Miner*—at the end of the week.

A twinge of compunction invaded my other hopeful thoughts: I had already been gone for two full days. If Ma had believed my first note about babysitting for Mrs. Leinonen, she had not had to worry during the first day. But how had she managed after that? I considered sending her a telegram but forbore. I did not dare use any more of the little money I had left. At least she knew where I was and what I was trying to do. She had had a lot of experience with waiting patiently for word from or of Pa. I hoped it stood her in good stead. It behooved me to concern myself with my own problems and leave Ma to hers. But my heart ached when I allowed myself to think of her nonetheless.

Leaving the newspaper office, my leather pouch somewhat depleted, my heart and my feet set resolutely on a course lined with hope and determination, I headed for 6 East Sheridan.

Inside the store, I strode purposefully past glass-fronted mahogany shelves and cases displaying clocks and watches, rings and silverware, past tall racks of fragile Fostoria and Waterford glassware, past tables of dresser sets and cuckoo clocks, along a fine carpet lining the middle of the wood floor, leading toward an imposing man with a pince nez standing, hands behind his back, near an optometry shop in the back of the store.

Stopping right in front of him, I held out my right hand and said firmly, "My name is Ilmi Marianna Brosi, and I am a friend of Mr. and Mrs. Alex Savolainen." That was stretching a point again, but I was getting better at it. Neither a blink nor a blush. "May I please have your name, and will you please help me?"

The pince nez dropped as did his chin, but I give him credit, for his hand reached out to grip mine firmly, and his eyes did not flinch as he answered, "I am Louis Stember, manager of the Savolainen Jewelry Company, Ely branch, and I am happy to meet a friend of Mr. and Mrs. Savolainen. What may I do for you, young miss?"

Before I could complete the answer, I found myself sitting at a small oak table in a back room behind the shop, looking out the back window at a small garden between the store and the alley, drinking the strongest coffee I had ever set to mouth, explaining to Mr. Stember and to his wife, Edith, exactly what I needed and why I was there.

Almost before I knew it again I had been shepherded to their apartment upstairs. My hands and face had been washed and my hair smoothed back. I had been seated at a wide mahogany dining room table set with white linen and silver, glassware and china, and I was eating fresh bread brought from a sweet-smelling kitchen and meeting Mrs. Laitinen, the Stembers' cook and housekeeper, and explaining to them almost all that had happened to me. Downplaying Ma's ignorance of both my plan and my whereabouts, I also left out a good many of the details about the gypsies, notably the bits about the horse that had had a make-over and the chicken we had eaten for supper and any specific description of the site of their encampment. But I did tell of my initial fear and their kindness.

When the words began to run together and my head to nod, I was ushered through a carpeted parlor past ornately carved tables holding fragile, breakable knick-knacks and expensively framed pictures into a cool back bedroom where I was divested of clothing by a clucking Mrs. Laitinen and tucked under the covers and where I slept in total, utter, complete, and blissful peace.

"In the morning," Mrs. Laitinen had assured me, "we will look for your uncle. For now, sleep, little one. Rest."

That was good. For when morning broke, my heart endured its second rending. The question in the ad was answered before the newspaper ran it. But not by Uncle Charles.

The sun was already shining in my east-facing window when Mrs. Laitinen entered, holding a cup of hot strong coffee.

"An important man is in the parlor," she indicated. "One of the most important figures in Ely's Finnish society, a part owner of the Finnish Stock Company, and a member of the board of the Finnish Accident and Sick Benefit Association has come before business hours, at Mr. Stember's request, to grant you an early-morning interview."

My heart sank at the words "accident" and "sick," but I tried to feel suitably impressed and grateful as Mrs. Laitinen patted my hands and took the cup, which I had almost spilled. Assuring me that all would be well, she helped me into my shift and garters, smoothed the dress that, like the grandmother, she had brushed and pressed, buttoned my shoes, and braided my hair as firmly as Ma did, tying the ends with the satin ribbons she had dampened and laid on the window sill to dry flat overnight.

Once she had me looking presentable, she put both hands on my shoulders and brushed a kiss on my cheek. "I'll pray for you, child," she said.

The tears welled up so quickly that I had to blink hard to hold them back. Then she motioned me out the door and toward the parlor.

The man awaiting me was surprisingly young. Surprisingly handsome. I had expected someone elderly, someone like the blind man at the Finnish Stock Company, someone who had known the worst of life and gained from his experiences. Someone like the grandfather, wise with the wisdom of the earth. This one was not that much older than I, not that much taller than I. How, I wondered, could he then be much wiser than I?

We did not, therefore, meet that first time on completely neutral ground. Since he seemed harried, busy, and brusque, I felt all the more more anxious, embarrassingly naive, young, and inexperienced.

I wanted to apologize and run away.

"John," said Mr. Stember, rising from the settee to perform the introductions, "I should like to present Miss Ilmi Marianna Brosie, who has come to Ely on a quest for her uncle. Perhaps you might be of some assistance?"

The word "quest" made me sound like the visionary Sir Galahad or one of the other unworldly knights, out to joust against imaginary dragons. I set my jaw hard.

"Miss Ilmi Marianna," he continued, turning to me with a small bow, "may I present Mr. John Porthan of the Finnish Accident and Sick Benefit Association. Perhaps you might tell him a bit about your uncle."

That suggestion set me at an even greater disadvantage. Miserably, my pride rapidly disintegrating, I admitted, "I know very little about him except that his name is Charles Brosi and that he works in a mine." That was pitifully little. "He promised to take his money out of the bank here and buy a farm in Zim and come to Kinney to get Ma and Pa and Lil and me."

John Porthan sighed. "My dear child," he began, looking down at me as from a lofty vantage, "have you any idea of how many men there are in Ely alone much less in the entire Ely-Winton area? Most of them are bachelors. I expect that is true of your Uncle Charles also?"

I nodded and wished I could sit down.

"Most of them leave no record of themselves during their stay here beyond their names on the payroll of a mining company. Did you know that Ely currently has four mines in operation with hundreds of men on each payroll?"

I shook my head and wished I could go to the bathroom.

He turned to Mr. Stember. "Louis, you must have some idea of the problem here. Many of the names on the mining company payrolls are themselves false, name changes being common for a whole variety of reasons." He ticked them off on his fingers. "Some were changed by the registrar at Ellis Island or whatever the initial point of debarkation. My mother's brother is a classic example. When the official reached him, he was so tired of trying to spell Finnish names that when he was confronted with my uncle's name, Alfred Tervakoski, he asked Alfred, 'What was your father's name?'

"'John,' Alfred answered.

"'Your name is Johnson,' the registrar decreed. So it is to this day that my mother's brother has two names, one Finnish, one American, the second never legally confirmed.

"Some never had names of their own even in Finland, going instead by the name of the house they rented or the owners of the farm where they worked. Some have dropped half their names—the Pyoriasaaris becoming Saaris or the Katajmakis becoming Makis. Some emigrated here to avoid being drafted into the Russian army when Czar Nicholas II decreed that Finns in the Russian Grand-Duchy of Finland could be conscripted into the Russian army. A name change prevented reprisals against the activist's family left in Finland."

Pacing back and forth from one side of the parlor to the other, John Porthan had clearly almost forgotten about me and perhaps even about the source of the question, so involved was he with an issue that obviously hit close to his heart. Suddenly remembering and swinging around, he waved a finger in my face. "Child, have you any idea what a problem this is both for the men themselves, who have lost their home country, their own names, any kind of personal identity?" He ticked those losses off on his hand then rolled it into a fist and shook it at me.

I shrank back, shaking my head. I really had no idea.

"And what about their families, who cannot trace them? How many women in Finland cannot sleep at night for fear that they will never again hear from their husbands, the fathers of their children, who promised to send for them? How many women have been widowed, not by death but by another kind of endless separation? How many more women in this country are married to men who were married already and moreover had no intention of keeping their marriage vows past the point of their own convenience? How many women have been left destitute with children to raise, abandoned by men who moved on without a trace into another identity?"

His pacing had accelerated to a virtual run, and his voice had risen to an orator's harangue.

I shook my head. I truly didn't know, I wanted to say, trying to disappear into the chair.

He didn't pause for an answer but stopped mid-stride to look me full in the eye, "Dear child, do you really think you are the only one searching for a man who has failed to keep his promises?"

Up to that point, I had forced myself to maintain an air of quiet, polite attention in spite of the fact that the lecture, though it obviously involved a source of genuine concern to Mr. Porthan, did not seem relevant to my own problem. But that last question was too much.

Enunciating each syllable with a ferocious clarity, I answered in a voice fully as loud and forceful as his, "I may be the only one searching for a man who keeps his promises. Keeps them, I say!" attempting a roar. "He has not changed his name. The Brosis have been Brosis since Ambrusius went to Finland from Germany in the year 1606. Well, mostly," I amended for the sake of honesty. "And those who did change their names were forced to because of their wife's family's position, not for nefarious reasons." Backing down not one whit, I met him glare for glare. "Charles Brosi he was when he lived in Finland and Charles Brosi he stayed when he came to this country and Charles Brosi he was when he came to us in Kinney and as Charles Brosi he will die!"

I caught my breath and cringed. The word was out, giving voice to my deepest fear. The lurking dread had spilled from my heart, and I could not take it back.

Mr. Stember bit his lip, and even the hieratic John Porthan stilled, sympathy somewhat softening his professorial stance.

"I called on you, John, and asked you to come here with that very concern in mind." Mr. Stember's voice tended to be deep and low, a soothing cello that muted the pizzicato sharpness of the Porthan rhythm. "How long will it take you to determine whether or not a Charles Brosi ever joined your insurance venture and paid premiums to your firm? Can you

remember if either accident or death or sick benefits have been due him
. . . or paid?"

Without realizing I had moved, I found myself standing directly in
front of Mr. Porthan, half of me sheltering in the lea of Mrs. Laitinen's
comforting being, her arm around me.

John Porthan looked from me to Mr. Stember to Mrs. Laitinen and
back again, though it was clear that his eyes were scanning not us but his
office ledgers. "I believe," he enunciated very slowly, mentally running
down the columns of names, "that I have seen that name somewhere. But
I am not sure where," he added quickly as I started, ready to ask. Connect-
ing with my questioning gaze, he responded, much more kindly, "I am
quite sure of one fact, however." He paused.

We waited.

"I am quite sure . . . positive, in fact . . . that no accident, sickness, or
death benefits have been paid to beneficiaries of a man with that name."

My shoulders sagged with relief, and I leaned against Mrs. Laitinen's pillowing form. Mr. Stember patted my shoulder. John Porthan's
finger rose, admonishing the three of us. "That does not mean what you
want it to mean. Not exactly. He may be ill. It is possible that he . . . has
been . . . deceased," he skittered around the word, "and that no beneficiary has stepped forward to claim benefits."

Then he said. "But had our office been notified of an accident, illness,
or death, I would know about it." This was firm. Finger motions emphasized
each word. "That is not to say that it is impossible for it to have happened
without my knowing, given the size of the male population of this area. It simply means that as of this moment, I have not been so informed."

Frustration followed relief. My mind began to work again. "Who
would know to inform you?"

"A doctor, perhaps." Then he shook his head in equal frustration.
"But perhaps not. Dr. Shipley neither speaks nor understands Finnish although he tries to find someone who does when a stranger is brought to
the hospital. It might be helpful to go there."

A sigh escaped from my soul. Mr. Stember echoed it. "Then we
have no definitive answer from you, John, except that to date as far as you
know or can recollect, no benefits have been paid to beneficiaries of said
Charles Brosi."

"That is correct, sir." Suddenly the wind went out of the bellows
of John Porthan's lungs, too, and he sat down on the settee.

So did I, with Mrs. Laitinen beside me, patting my hands.

"Then what do you suggest I do?" I posed the question to the room in general. "Above and beyond what I have already done, which was to place an advertisement in the *Ely Miner* asking anyone who knows of him to contact me here. A man at the Finnish Stock Company suggested that I try the boarding houses. I cannot, simply cannot," I said, "merely sit here waiting. Ought I to pursue that direction, rather than the hospital?"

"I shall check with Dr. Shipley myself this morning, child. He will be coming into the shop to pick up a small gift I ordered for his wife for their anniversary. A moment will arise when such an inquiry will be possible." Mr. Stember moved toward the door. "I shall approach Dr. Shipley."

"Thank you." I smiled at him, the words far more full of appreciation than the brief syllables could carry.

"Mrs. Laitinen, might you help with inquiries to boarding houses?" he requested, pausing at the top of the stairs. It was a rhetorical question, for she was in his employ.

"I shall do what I can, sir," she answered his retreating back. The moment the footsteps descended toward the shop, however, she turned to John Porthan and me with a harassed, faintly embarrassed air. "But that will be very little. Do you know how boarding houses are run, Mr. Porthan?" she asked, obviously hoping he did.

"No, I do not, Mrs. Laitinen. My involvement with business and my living quarters behind our office have neither encouraged nor allowed involvement with the other domiciles available in this fair city."

For such a young man he really is a pompous ass, I thought, then turned my attention to ask Mrs. Laitinen. "How are they run?"

Removing her hands from mine as if distance eased her discomfort, she addressed herself to the porcelain figure of a shepherdess on a nearby table. "Many are run by widowed ladies who have no other means of livelihood. By and large the honorable among them have little contact with their boarders who come and go via outside stairways. Since the miners work twelve-hour shifts, four men rent one bed, two using it at one time while the other two work."

She paused, studying my face. I had caught the phrase "the honorable among them" and so had John Porthan.

"Most of the men pay perhaps twelve dollars a month for the use of their upstairs rooms, sometimes as much as thirty dollars a month if they want meals and other services."

John Porthan's eyebrows rose.

"Like laundry," she hurried on. "Meals are served at the ends of the shifts—breakfast for the men on their way to work, dinner for the men coming home. Sometimes the men pay to have their dinner pails fixed with something to drink at the bottom of the pail and the solid food set on top of a divider. Some of the women agree to do laundry for a price. Some arrange to have the men's laundry sent out, and the men pay them for handling it."

She shook her head then. "The problem is that this is usually just a business."

John Porthan gave me a speaking glance before looking back at Mrs. Laitinen.

"Not that kind of business," she amended hastily, "although of course there are some women who . . ." Her voice trailed off as she looked significantly from me to John Porthan and back again to me with a nod.

Her message was clear. Whatever went on behind the doors of some of those boarding houses, whatever other business was transacted, it was not to be here discussed.

"As far as what is made public, however, by virtue of numbers alone, the men often remain strangers even to their housemates, surely to those who run the boarding houses, especially if they don't take meals." She paused, considering. "Usually the men must accept two basic rules—no drinking allowed in the house and no fighting. However, there have been," she amended, honesty prevailing, "some significant battles between the boarders who work at the Pioneer mine and those who work the Chandler's."

"But there are unwritten rules . . . about privacy . . . and," she struggled to make it clear, "and . . . personal lives. Living like that with no place for themselves, nothing really of their own, most men . . . keep to themselves . . . for a lot of reasons." She raised her hands in defeat, the words failing her. "Can you imagine what it's like to work with and live with and even sleep in the same bed with people you barely know? Not to have a name . . . not to have a family . . .?"

Her arms dropped, rather symbolically, I thought. It did sound awful. "And you can't blame the good people—and most of them are good people—who run the boarding houses. Women who do washing work three days out of the week on that alone. Baking? They've got to make maybe twelve, maybe fifteen loaves of bread three times a week, the men being always hungry and eating more than it's possible to prepare of soup and beets and beans and turnips and rutabaga and potatoes so that unless you have your own garden and can your own vegetables, it costs a lot of money just to buy the food, and then to try to keep up with the dishes . . . well, and if you can't and have to hire a 'tiskari' someone to do the dishes—at nine dollars a month . . ."

Looking each of us straight in the eye, she testified, "I know. I tried it. It's not easy to keep those men fed and their meals made and the house clean and the pantry full and make sure there are three hundred Mason jars of canning in the basement."

Her shoulders sagged. "And that's not really the worst of it." There was a long pause, and I was grateful to John Porthan for his restraint. "Sometimes it's hard to keep them . . . at arm's length. Sometimes they're lonely and sometimes they've had too much to drink . . . and sometimes they're just mean. One of the young teachers who boarded with me kept a small gun in her fur muff. But it was not for protection against wolves and bears, though that is what she said.

"If a woman's married, most of the men treat married women . . . good women . . . real good. I've known boarders to feel so sorry for a wife who's been beaten that they beat the husband twice as bad."

"But," she looked at us fiercely, "because there are so few single women around town, maybe three or four men to every woman, I do not want this child wandering around the boarding houses . . . or even much around town, except for the main streets . . . alone. Not if I can help it."

"I am sorry." John Porthan looked uncomfortable. "I had no idea."

"No idea?" she scoffed. "Well, now you know." With a flourish of her apron and a straight back, she gave up and turned toward the kitchen.

I had never been like me to feel defeat, and I tend to be even less likely to admit the feeling, at that moment I felt totally overwhelmed.

John Porthan seemed to be experiencing much the same reaction. We looked at each other, whether we wanted to or not, with a sense of shared youth and inexperience, more kindred than we wanted to admit.

"I shall double-check our records," he said, rising hastily, seeking retreat, "and get back to you."

"And I," standing up, "am going to seek out the one person who will know absolutely whether Uncle Charles is alive or dead."

"And who might that be?" he asked, surprise mixed with consternation. No such resource had occurred to him.

"The coroner." Throwing the answer at him, I headed for the stairs. Enough of this talk. It was time for me to take action.

Chapter Fourteen

"And so it is with the innocent . . ."

Thus it was that I myself with no help from anyone else, notwithstanding the good intentions of the well-meaning Mr. Stember, my good Mrs. Laitinen, and the impassioned John Porthan, who found out what had happened to Uncle Charles. Surprisingly enough, although the truth dealt me a telling blow, it did not defeat me. In fact, as one door closed, another opened in its place. I went through the new one, spirit undaunted (almost), to piece the past and the future together as it were and try to bend them both to my will. But not right away. Definitely not right away.

It did not take me long at all to find the courthouse. Everyone I asked willingly proffered directions to the brand new building on Chapman Street one block east of Sheridan, a building too imposing to be overlooked even without directions. Once there, I sought out the door with the gold-embossed letters "Coroner's Office," went in, explained my request to the clerk, and set myself down to wait until the coroner himself arrived to answer my questions and release any pertinent records.

The process barely took an hour. It was a matter of public record, I was told with an adult complacency. Officials were pleased with their knowledge of the workings of governmental agencies and with my ignorance. Before the noon whistle, I left the courthouse and set out to find the Finnish Accident and Sick Benefits office with the facts in my hand, my heart so numb from the hard draught of reality that I neither wept nor in truth even felt the pain.

"Charles Brosi . . . hmmm . . . I do not recall . . . Charles Brosi," the coroner had repeated perusing his records. "Is that Brosi with an 'e'?"

I wanted to scream, "What difference does it make? How many men of that name are in Ely with or without the 'e'?" But I knew very well that such demeanor would block accessibility to this adult world. Therefore, like the well-behaved child it behooved me to be, I answered politely, "I am not sure. My Pa, Knute Peter Brosi, sometimes spells our name with an 'e,' but Uncle Charles may or may not have. Family usage varies," I added apologetically, hoping to have covered both bases.

"Hmmm," he hummed, continuing the search, his finger moving backwards up the columns.

I tried to read the ledger upside down and to my despair succeeded. It said "State of Minnesota Division of Vital Statistics."

So, Uncle Charles had been important enough to be noted somewhere. I feared to find out where.

The fears were justified.

"Ah, here he is." The coroner's moving finger paused like the one in Edward Fitzgerald's translation of the *Rubaiyat of Omar Khayyam*. The upper graders at the Kinney School had memorized, "The Moving Finger writes; and having writ, / Moves on: nor all your Piety nor Wit / Shall lure it back to cancel half a Line,/ Nor all your Tears wash out a Word of it."

It had been written.

I held my breath, clinging to some small vestige of hope, though my heart knew immediately where Uncle Charles' life had been recorded, and why. The coroner swung the ledger around so that I could see the subheadings as well as the title of the page:

Registration Book 59. Registration District No. 27N.
CERTIFICATES OF DEATH

I bit my lower lip to hold back the cry, squeezed in my upper lip, too, and held onto the arms of the solid mahogany chair to keep myself from spinning far out of this world into that other world where Uncle Charles was now. For a minute I felt as if he beckoned me, as if I too could slip easily across the narrow border. Then someone set me back onto the chair. I think it was the clerk. Someone held a glass of water to my lips, and I realized there was no escaping this reality.

I knew I did not mistake the note of kindness in the coroner's voice. Big man though he was, his hand under my elbow was gentle as he helped me out of the chair and led me to the high oak counter, where I stood like an automaton while the clerk prepared a sheet of paper perhaps six inches wide and nine or ten inches long, embossed it with a seal, and accepted the $1.00 required as payment.

So small a piece of paper on which to inscribe the death of a dream.

"There is only one small thread to unwind," I thought to myself, "and the skein will be empty."

Minutes later, the Finnish Accident and Sick Benefit office having been clearly visible just across Sheridan, I opened the outside door and, holding the embossed sheet in front of me, walked directly into John Porthan's office and laid it on his desk, my hand shaking so hard that the paper almost fluttered to the floor.

John Porthan got up quickly, set me down in his own chair, leaned over the desk, and read the first few lines aloud. "'PLACE OF DEATH: County—St. Louis—Ely. FULL NAME OF THE DECEASED: Charles Brosi.'"

Without an "e," I thought irrelevantly.

The look of sorrow that crossed his face was so overlaid with pity that my back stiffened, and I motioned brusquely for him to continue.

"'Residence No. Sheridan St. 1st Ward.

"'PERSONAL AND STATISTICAL PARTICULARS: Sex— Male; Color or Race—White; Single, Married, Widowed, or Divorced— Single.

"'OCCUPATION OF DECEASED: (a) Trade, Profession, or particular kind of work—Miner; (b) General nature of industry, business, or establishment in which employed (or employer)—Mining Iron Ore, (c) Name of employer—Oliver Iron Mining Co.

"'BIRTHPLACE—Finland.'

"There is no chance of error, is there?" he interposed, his voice, like my heart, devoid of hope. "This is he?"

"None and yes," I answered flatly.

"'I HEREBY CERTIFY,'" his voice droned on, "'that I attended the deceased from ___ to ___,' Strange. Those are still blank. 'that I last saw h-- alive on __ and that death occurred on the date above at ___.' This is very difficult to read. The handwriting is . . . not clear . . . unsteady . . . but I think it says . . . 'Medical A . . . Found dead 6:00 p.m. May 3.'"

"That was just after he left us, after he visited us in Kinney," I commented, as much to myself as to John Porthan.

"'CAUSE OF DEATH was as follows' . . . barely readable . . . 'Sudden . . . from . . . Heart disease is most probable cause. (signed) Owen W. Pomer, Dep. Coroner.'"

Interspersed with comments about the difficulty of deciphering the words were murmured expressions of sympathy, which I ignored. I did not need sympathy. I needed help. In the wake of shock and sorrow rose anger and questions.

"If 'heart disease' were only a 'probable cause,'" I wondered aloud, "then did the coroner perform an autopsy?" I knew all about autopsies. Amalia Barone's grandmother had had such a performance, and Amalia had recounted the grisly details with some surreptitious pleasure. Grandmother Barone, in addition to being free with the contents of the wine casks in her basement, had not been derelict in the use of the razor strap on the bottoms of recalcitrant grandchildren.

John Porthan's vague murmurings turned sharper as he pointed hard toward two lines confirming 'no autopsy.'"

"Why was there no autopsy," I repeated, "if the cause of death was not confirmed?"

John Porthan shook his head as he continued with the next line numbered "'14: INFORMANT AND ADDRESS.' I assume that refers to whoever contacted the authorities. Does this name mean anything to you? Who is Lillian Brosi?"

I jumped up to look over his shoulder. At the coroner's office I had been too shaken to read the whole document. "She's my sister," I told him fiercely. "She lives with us, not in Virginia, as the certificate states, but in Kinney. And she could not possibly have been the 'informant,' since none of us knew anything at all of what happened to Uncle Charles. Obviously. Or why would I have come here to find out? Moreover," I said emphatically, shaking my head in disbelief, "she is too young to inform anyone of anything. She's nothing but a baby."

Holding his chair out for me and motioning me to sit down again, John Porthan met my gaze squarely, adult to adult. "This looks and sounds suspicious."

"And that is not the least of it," I continued, paying no attention to the chair. "When Uncle Charles left us in Kinney just before this date," I jabbed at it viciously, "he was returning to Ely for two reasons: first, to quit his job, and secondly, to withdraw his life savings from a bank in Ely so that we could buy the farm in Zim." I paused not just for effect but for breath.

We verbalized the same question at precisely the same instant in almost exactly the same words: "What happened, then, to his money?"

John Porthan dropped into the visitor's chair, also breathing hard. I fell into his, exhausted, trying to expel air from a body overburdened by knowledge gained mixed with knowledge still sought.

"What happened to that money?" he repeated. His next words destroyed a vague, faltering hope. "Charles Brosi did not keep his money here. He did not use us as a bank. I checked."

As hope died, the office began to spin, and the body of John Porthan doubled and tripled. I tried the tactic I had used in the coroner's office, holding hard onto the arms of the chair. Then John Porthan too was caught by whirling winds. Sound and motion accelerated then ceased altogether, and I was gone, torn away from that small dark room into a vortex spiraling up, up, up, then down, down, down.

I woke up on the floor with John Porthan bending over me, fanning me with the death certificate, he as white as it. "Poor John Porthan," I murmured as I lay there bemused. "You are ill equipped to handle the exigencies of fate." Then I spun away again.

John Porthan himself admitted the correctness of my perception at the same time as he later explained what had happened next. A man who was far better equipped to deal with the exigencies of fate worked just up the block, and to him at the Finnish Stock Company John Porthan had run, seeking aid.

When I came to, someone was sitting by me on the floor, holding a noxious substance to my nose. The resultant burning sensation as much as the smell, so sharp and pungent it refused to brook my inattention, brought me back to reality far faster than I wished, but I kept my eyes closed regardless. I could be forced to be awake; I could not be forced to admit it.

"I had a dream once." It was a disembodied voice, spectral yet not frightening, ghostly but not ghastly. The word play made me want to smile, but smiles had died, too, with Uncle Charles.

"I had a dream," the voice continued, "that I was a knifemaker, shaping the most beautiful knives in this world, carving handles from ivory or reindeer antlers, engraving them with pictures and symbols, writing my name in script on the blades so that everyone knew who made the knives and as long as those knives lived, so too did I.

"Ladies bought the small knives and used them to cut the threads of their embroidery or hid them in their muffs. Boys of seven dreamed of the knives to be given them when they turned eight, knives that embodied their heritage as they did the skill of the maker.

"My knives cut branches or reindeer bones, their edges so sharp men could shave with them. Fathers handed them to sons and sons to grandsons, and each read my name upon the blade, and my name lived.

"That was my dream."

I lay immobile, but I knew that he knew that I heard. John Porthan breathed deeply from somewhere nearby, and I knew that he too knew I was awake. I was glad he knew, but I could not bear to open my eyes.

"One day when I was ready to be apprenticed to a knife-maker in Finland, I went to the fairgrounds with my friends to see the organ grinder." The voice had deepened, slowed, as if it too were unwilling to awaken.

"But although we watched and listened politely, the crowd around us grew restive and moved against him. Suddenly an egg flew out. The organ grinder moved away, but I did not. The egg hit me in the eye," the voice continued, softly, even more slowly, with pauses as if for breath. But I heard him well. "The egg hit me in the eye," the voice repeated, "And it was rotten."

I almost smelled the stench and gathered myself together, feeling as if it were I who must give comfort. But the voice moved away as did the sense of lingering warmth. "An infection grew and spread. The doctors tried to help me, but there was nothing they could do. I lost that eye. And then the other. And then my dreams.

"Now I sharpen knives on the grindstone and know that my hands could have shaped ones stronger, sharper and far more beautiful. But I am still alive, and my hands still work, and one dream did come true. I came to America." The voice gathered strength at the end and passed some of it to me.

I opened my eyes and reached my hand to him, to Jaako, the blind man from the Finnish Stock Company, but he could not see my hand, of course, and he rose as he concluded, "And so it is with dreams."

John Porthan helped him toward a chair and knelt down to support me as I strove to sit up. The world had stopped spinning, but it still felt suspiciously far away.

"What had the organ grinder done to make someone try to hurt him?" I asked from a distance.

"He had chained the monkey," Jaako said. "Cruelly chained the monkey. Perhaps he deserved the rotten egg, but I got in the way. That happens with fate sometimes," he mused, giving me a significant nod. "The innocent get in the way."

What was the significance, I pondered wordlessly as John Porthan bustled around doing nothing and Jaako waited and the distances shortened and I grew to my own size again.

"Where was Uncle Charles buried?"

It did not seem at all a non-sequitar. I was positive that his body was not floating in purgatory, haunting children. Nor had his soul fallen to the even blacker pit of hell. Ma discouraged any such hypotheses, even the one about a heavenly city of golden, ethereal beauty. I had always had similar doubts. Maps of the world studied in geography class revealed no information about heaven, hell, and purgatory. My memorization of the planets in our solar system included none with such titles.

Amalia had drawn me a picture of the universe once, with heaven on top and hell on the bottom and earth hanging from a thread in the midst of the vast abyss in between. But it did not correlate with Miss Loney's versions, and I far preferred Miss Loney's.

"Nevertheless," said Ma, "there is an afterlife. What we do lives after us, and goodness joined to goodness constitutes a force and a power that can grow and grow until all evil is ultimately consumed, not in the fires of a hell or the glory of a heaven but right here on earth. Therefore, it behooves us to try to be good." At that she always gave me an unblinking, unqualified look, which made it clear whom it most behooved. She need not have bothered, for the lesson had made good sense to me.

Remembering, I mused aloud, "I must honor the grave where his body rests. But . . ." and there I paused, struggling for the words, "Uncle Charles' goodness, joined to and enhanced by the great power of all Goodness, did not die. Out of his life and death can rise a place where peace and rest can dwell, where hope will come that comes to all, and where his dreams can live."

Tears fell unbeknownst as I curled my arms around my knees. "I must honor his dreams," I told Jaako, who nodded. In and of itself, Uncle Charles' money had no meaning. But as a means to a happy ending, to health for Ma and Lil and a home for our family, with or without Pa, it resonated power. All I had to do was find it. And how simple that could be! All I had to do was go to the banks.

I should have remembered Miss Loney's warning that Finns are allowed only five exclamation points to use in their entire lives. I should not have wasted one of mine, but I could not pretend it had not shown itself in my eyes. John Porthan had seen it.

Taking a deep breath, I pulled myself to my feet, blew my nose, reached out a hand to take John Porthan's responding one in a firm grip, and said, "Thank you, Jaako. Thank you, Mr. Porthan. I am sorry for having been such a trial. But I must go now and begin my search. Thank you for the help and for the information."

"But I have not given you the information," John Porthan said, his hand moving me back toward his chair. "Your uncle Charles Brosi did not keep his money here: we are not really a bank though some men do elect to have us hold and invest the money they earn. But we are an insurance company. Do you know what that means?"

I sighed and sat down heavily. John Porthan liked lectures even more than Ma and Miss Loney did. I knew I was about to hear one on insurance companies whether I wanted to or not.

"It is my dream," John Porthan smiled at Jaako, who smiled back in instant communication, "to provide those who work with a means of protecting those whom they work to support should they no longer be able to work. Do you understand?"

I wanted to say, "Not really," but that would simply have extended the lecture.

"That is to say," he continued, disregarding me completely, his eyes on that dream of the future, "a man could pay us a set amount, say a dime out of every one of his checks. Were he to become ill or to have an accident, he could draw on that money and on the capital of the business for financial support until his health improved."

That made sense except that it sounded as if the capital of the business would be at considerable risk, in view of the fact that most of the investors were miners.

"Well, yes, I am aware that mining does have its risks," he admitted to my raised eyebrow. "But it must be remembered that by and large the men who have moved to this community are young, few of them over thirty years of age, and by virtue of the fact that they have already survived a dangerous ocean voyage and a considerable overland trek to get here, most of them are basically very healthy."

My eyebrow dropped. That was definitely true. Although communicable diseases did run rampant at times, by and large those of my parents' generation were survivors.

"Moreover, if a large number of men pay even a small amount weekly or monthly, even if a small percentage of them do get sick or hurt and need to withdraw funds, given investment with interest, the capital will grow of its own accord."

"And in what do you invest?" I asked with some asperity, for it would not be unheard of for a businessman to cast those investments into the form of his own well-being.

"Well," he rocked back and forth on his heels, his eyes focused on the future, "right now we are committing a goodly part of our capital into the future of this city. We have underwritten municipal bonds to help finance a water plant and electric street lights. We have also invested a considerable amount of money in the Shipley Hospital on Third Avenue and Chapman. Have you seen it?"

He did not even wait for a response, though Jaako nodded.

"Fifty by sixty feet in external dimensions, it rises to two stories with an attic that is usable also and a full basement with electricity to run its power plant and hot water and living space for Dr. C.G. Shipman and the associates whom he is bringing in." He was off and running and there was no stopping him. Jaako's smile added encouragement. "Moreover, we are now laying plans for the building of a Detention Center to replace the 'pest house' on Lucky Bay mine road so that those with communicable diseases will have a safe and healthy place to recuperate, thus preventing large-scale quarantines from closing boarding houses, homes, and businesses."

Jaako looked proud. I did not interrupt. I was impressed.

"Finally, we have joined forces with the Finnish Stock Company," one hand waved in that direction and the other gestured toward Jaako, who dipped his head in acceptance, "so that members of the Finnish community can purchase goods at a reasonable price instead of buying from company stores, which will grant endless amounts of credit, of course, but families are never able to pay off the bills and are caught instead in an endless cycle of working to pay debts for food purchased so that the family will have enough energy to keep on working." He paused for breath.

My. I took a fresh look at John Porthan. Young he may be, didactic and hieratic, too, but he certainly was not lacking either in dreams or in the will to make them come true.

"In short . . .," he continued.

In spite of my misery, I swallowed a giggle. Rarely would he ever find himself in that position. At least verbally.

" . . . your uncle Charles Brosi was one of our people." He exuded a fatherly attitude unlikely because of his youth but impressive nonetheless.

I waited patiently to see where he was going.

He finally got there. "You or whoever is his beneficiary is due to receive Charles Brosi's death benefits, which I can pay immediately upon identification of said beneficiary since I have seen a notarized copy of the death certificate."

It was in my best interest not to interrupt him with any questions that might deflect him from the issue at hand. I held my breath.

"Let us check his records and identify his beneficiary right now," he said, pulling out a large flat register filled with names and dates.

"B . . . B-r-o . . . ah, here it is. Brosi, Charles. Insurance paid quarterly. In full. No deductions for illness or accident. Beneficiary listed as Knute Pietari Brosi, brother." He looked at me in triumph.

I wanted to cry. So much for that, I thought. Oh, Uncle Charles, could you not have been more efficient in just this one way?

"Who is Knute Pietari Brosi?" John Porthan could not help but notice my discomfiture, and even Jaako took on a worried look.

"He is my father."

"Then all is well. We simply inform him of your uncle's demise and ask him to come here so that we can verify his identity and award him a check for the full amount. One hundred dollars."

How could I even begin to explain? I wanted to sob noisy sobs. I wanted to scream.

"All that is needed is to find and notify him." John Porthan leaned back on his heels with immense satisfaction then knit his brows as I looked back overwhelmed with despair.

"All that is needed is to find him," I repeated, all of the irony in the world in my voice. Hope, risen, had fallen again and put me right back at the beginning.

Chapter Fifteen

"Great Gulps of Pride"

I had no heart for continuing my quest that day. I felt completely alone in a maze from which I could see no escape.

Miss Loney had shown us a picture once of a castle in England where a princess grew up. Well, not really a princess, but a girl named Anne who became a queen. In the garden of that castle grew row upon row of hedges, some cut and formed by master gardeners into shapes like the markings on a deck of cards, some planted and worked together into walls between which a full-sized person could walk, in which it was possible to be lost forever, were the secret pattern not deciphered, the egress not found.

I felt similarly immured, for just when I had glimpsed an opening, the green hedgerows had closed in around me. All of my faith and hopes had rested upon Uncle Charles. He was gone in circumstances I did not understand, and his insurance money—the death benefits—were as far removed from my touch as he, for heaven only knew where Pa had gone and there was no heaven. It was useless to try to explain the situation to John Porthan: children were not allowed to criticize their elders, most specifically not their parents.

John Porthan and Jaako waited expectantly for some response.

I bit my nails, tried not to think about how Uncle Charles died or where Pa was and concentrated on banks and money.

I had never been in a bank, but I knew quite a bit about them, all bad.

I knew that the gypsies did not trust them. They dug holes under their fire pits and buried their coins there. The heat of the fire stood guard.

I knew that the Barones did not believe in them. Amalia showed me where they kept their money—in a leather bag thrust deep into the hundred-pound tin of flour resting in the corner of the pantry.

I did not think Ma and Pa believed in them. Anyway, I had never heard any talk about putting our extra money into a bank. But then we rarely had any extra.

The notice of St. Louis County Land Sales posted on the wall of Salins' Grocery Store back home had indicated that it was possible to make a downpayment on farm land with the balance to be repaid at four per cent interest over a period of forty years. But Uncle Charles had told us that he had enough money "in the bank" to pay for our farm in full.

Money and banks. Except for investigating Uncle Charles' death, all the rest came down to that.

I knew that John Porthan was looking at me strangely, but I was not able to muster up the energy to care. Sighing deeply, I stood up, mouthed appropriate words of appreciation to him, held Jaako's hand a bit longer than was polite, for I sensed that he knew exactly how I felt, and eased my way out of the Finnish Accident and Sick Benefit Association office.

It was all too much.

My legs led me across the street and up the hill toward Number 6 East Sheridan, through the shop where the Stembers were busily waiting on customers, and up the back stairs. Throwing my school bag onto the floor and collapsing on a kitchen chair, I nibbled the fresh bread Mrs. Laitinen served me with a thick slab of head cheese and a glass of buttermilk. I wanted to tell her about Uncle Charles and the bank, about the insurance money and Pa, but the words refused to come, so I faced other facts instead. I could not continue to presume upon the Stembers' hospitality. The breach between their social position and mine made kindness on their part a matter of extreme condescension and acceptance on my part a source of extreme discomfort.

Ma and Pa did not accept charity. Nor could I.

We worked for what we got.

"Do you know anyone who might hire me as a *'tiskari'* ?" I asked Mrs. Laitinen hopefully, watching as she peeled potatoes and plucked chickens. Inept as I was with other kitchen tasks, I was an expert dishwasher.

Bless her Finnish phlegmatism, her kind forbearance, her inveterate good sense. Without asking me a single question, she answered with a firm nod, "Yes, I do. Me."

While I washed and dried my plate and glass, she wrapped me in one of her voluminous flour sack aprons and explained. "The Stembers are giving a dinner party tonight for Ely's '*kerma kerros*,' the cream of Finnish society. I will be fixing food all afternoon, and I will be grateful to have someone keep up with all of the dishes needed for all of the courses they have planned."

With a deep sigh she waved a hand at the blackboard nailed to the wall by the dining room door. On it Mrs. Stember always wrote the menus for the day. She had had to print with very small letters that morning.

Pointing to the last item, I turned to Mrs. Laitinen with a questioning look. "Angel food cake?" I had never heard of it.

She smiled, but grimly. "Just wait until you get the pan. You'll earn your money today. And," she fixed me with a gimlet eye, "if you know anything at all about serving at table, you can help me with that, too."

Thus was it all arranged. I had a place to stay for another night with the prospect of food to eat and work to do. My self-respect could remain intact, for it was clear that I could truly be of help. Ma would be pleased. I repressed the thought firmly, for Ma was not at that moment pleased with me at all. She was, without a doubt, extremely distressed, and there was nothing I could do about it at that moment.

No matter where my thoughts led, there were problems.

One was resolved during the dinner party that night.

Pastor Ruotsalainen of the Finnish Evangelical Lutheran Church and his lovely young bride were among the guests. I carried food in and plates out as unobtrusively as possible, but I could not help overhearing the conversation, much of which dealt with the mine disaster and its consequences.

"A funeral of magnificent proportions is planned for next Sunday so that all of the Ely citizenry, including the mine workers who survived the explosion, can attend," the pastor informed the other dinner guests. "Once embalmed, the bodies are to be brought to their own homes to lie in state," he explained over the roast chicken with dressing and mashed potatoes, "and a vigil is to be kept until the time of the church services and the funeral procession."

The other guests murmured approval.

I pondered "embalmed" and decided not to taste the chicken.

"After attending each church's individual ceremonies—the Finnish Evangelical Lutheran Church's ceremonies will be held at ten o'clock," he continued with immense satisfaction, "—all will gather and form one single procession. The city band will march first, followed by the flag bearers, and the horse-drawn hearses with their heavy glass windows and rubber-tired wheels and black plumes."

Everyone nodded, aware that only a few miners could afford the hearses; the other coffins would rest on wagons decorated suitably in black.

"Last will come the long lines of mourners dressed in black, walking behind the wagons and hearses."

I almost dropped the gravy boat. There it was. I could join that procession and no one would be the wiser. No one would notice a stranger in that long line of mourners, I thought with great relief. Once at the cemetery, I had merely to look for the mound of an unmarked recent grave, and there was a good chance that there would be a plaque with his name on it, or a cross, much as there was at the Kinney Cemetery for those who died without family.

I had no black dress, but since few children did, that lack would not be noted. I was sure that Mrs. Laitinen would help me find a scrap of black cloth to wrap around my arm, and I would find wild flowers to put on the grave.

My relief at knowing I could give Uncle Charles that modicum of attention and love was so great that for a minute my knees almost gave way. Of all the plans I wove that night as I washed and wiped dishes and scraped the angel food cake pan, that one was the least improbable. Such an act of public grief seemed to me to atone in a small way for the fact that his true interment had gone unremarked in the tumult of life in this busy city. I had never seen so many people in one place at one time. I had never experienced such hustle and bustle. It was no wonder that John Porthan, having come here, had stayed.

But this was also a place where one single man could live and die virtually unnoticed, completely alone. How sad, I thought, wiping away the tears that threatened to re-rinse the dishes. How very, very sad! No wonder Uncle Charles had been happy to find us. To us, he was somebody. To us, he had been important. To us, he had been family. Oh, how I missed him! To his memory, I dedicated two more of my allotted five exclamation points.

While I washed the plates and the cups, I let myself slip into a dream world in which I found out the truth of Uncle Charles' untimely death and punished the perpetrator. As I scraped the walls of the angel food cake pan and the round insert in the middle, I dreamed of accosting the bank president, of demanding and getting the money.

Although not one piece of cake had been left for me to finish off, I devoured every single delicious crumb and planned to make such a cake for Ma when I got home with the money. I had taken my turn with the whipping, working until my arm ached, though Mrs. Laitinen had still done the bulk of the work. I had watched Mrs. Laitinen as she used a long slim knife to detach the cooled cake from the pan, sides, center, and bottom, and marveled at the even softness of the sponge, formed from the whites of a dozen eggs. Frosted with whipped cream and shavings of chocolate, it had been a creation of culinary perfection, almost worth the work of cleaning the pan.

It was hard to balance the showy elegance of that dinner and the dinner guests against the unreality of such daydreams. As I wrapped the silver and put it away in its box, as I set each plate and cup where it belonged, I let myself relive the time I had spent with the gypsies, who had shared all they had with me so willingly and openly.

I had learned quickly about the difference between being a guest and serving as kitchen help, for the Stembers had slipped easily from the role of friends into the role of employers.

It is just as well, I thought, as I washed my hands and face and climbed into bed in the spare back bedroom hours and hundreds of plates and cups and glasses and pieces of silver later, that Ma did not yet know about any of this. For her, the dream and hope remained intact.

I have to admit that I prayed that night before I went to sleep, though I was so tired that every muscle in my body, especially my heart, ached.

I prayed to the image of Jesus that I had seen hanging from the cross above the altar in Amalia's church. I prayed selfish prayers and apologized for them and repeated them again. I prayed to find the bank that had Uncle Charles' money. I prayed for a pathway that led to Pa.

And then I prayed to the gentle figure of Jesus' mother, who stood in a niche nearby, her hands outstretched to all who came to her as supplicants. Jesus' mother's name was Mary, too. I hoped that, because I was praying not just for myself but for my own mother Mary, she might understand and sympathize.

I held her image before me that night as I fell asleep, exhausted, and whether or not she or her son were ever to answer my other prayers, that night she did grant me comfort. I did not feel quite alone.

But the next morning when I got up, it all swept over me again. All through the time that it took me to make my bed neatly, to dress and help Mrs. Laitinen make and serve breakfast to the Stembers, to eat some oatmeal myself, I fought for control. I hated to ask for help, and pride attacked me as I attacked the dishes without being asked. But I had no choice.

Thus, finally, when Mrs. Laitinen finally sat down with her second cup of coffee, I sat down opposite her, folded my hands in my lap, set both feet firmly on the floor, stiffened my spine, and told her about everything that had happened the day before. I shared my suspicions about the death certificate, my despair about Pa's whereabouts, my need to find the money, even the truth about my subterfuge—the fact that I had run away from home, with the best of intentions, I made clear, but run away nonetheless.

Not surprisingly, Mrs. Laitinen refrained from expressions of sympathy and from comment. About halfway through my recitation, she got up to pour two more cups of coffee—a third cup for herself and one for me that for once was more coffee than cream, well-laced with sugar lumps. Managing to keep my voice neutral and my tears contained, largely thanks to her neutral and disinterested air, I completed my story, took a deep breath, drank almost all of the coffee, and then addressed the issues at hand, ticking them off on my fingers one by one. "First, would it be of any use for me to go to Winton to look for Pa? Second, could you tell me where the Ely bank is? Third, do you think the Stembers will allow me to stay here if I continue to help? Fourth, will you promise not to tell them about Uncle Charles . . . not yet, anyway . . . so they won't send me home? And, fifth, how can I find out the truth about what happened to him?"

Typically, Mrs. Laitinen addressed the questions systematically. "'Yes' to finding a bank and staying here and not telling the Stembers about Uncle Charles. 'No' to going to Winton. 'I-have-no-idea-and-it-might-be-better-not-to-try' to finding out the truth about what happened."

"But why not?" I pressed. Surely, someone knew the truth. Surely, Uncle Charles deserved to have the truth divulged. Surely, if I tried, I could solve the mystery.

As she cleaned up our cups and wiped the table, Mrs. Laitinen confided in me, too.

Going to the door to look down the hall and the stairway first, she whispered, "My nephew was given notice that he was fired from his job by a letter delivered to him at the end of a shift saying only that his services were terminated. The spy system had named him a potential union organizer. Someone told. He'll never work in the mines again." She paused to look at me, clearly wondering if I knew how serious that was in a town virtually controlled by the mining companies.

I nodded. "Oh, I do know," I told her.

"Moreover," she continued just as quietly, "ladies in town have been known to sit in swings on their front porches on summer nights and watch who goes by and with whom." There was a pause punctuated by another check of the hall and stairs. "You've got to be careful in this town, who you know and how you handle them," she warned me. "It's not like it used to be when we were all just starting out."

I remembered Jaako and his story and wondered if Uncle Charles had been the only innocent he had been considering and if he had been warning me, too, less directly than Mrs. Laitinen, just in case.

Nor, when I came back to the problem of Pa, did Mrs. Laitinen offer much hope.

"I'm sure he went to work for a lumber company," I insisted.

"Oh, my dear," she sighed, "it is virtually impossible to locate one man from among the thousands who work in and around Winton. The St. Croix Lumber Company does have a record of their own employees, but as many or more men work for other loggers either in the large mills operating full-time in town or out in the woods cutting and hauling. Heaven's above, I sometimes think Winton is even busier than Ely. There's a St. Croix Department Store and seven saloons alone and goodness knows how many boarding houses, one of them—Johnsons' Boarding House—the size of a small hotel. Men are coming and going all the time. Some of the smaller logging companies, the Swallow Hopkins, for instance, have spur lines out to Low Lake, and there are more than I can count."

While she talked, she set a soup stock to simmering on the back burner of the gas stove, chopping celery and onion, leftover chicken and potatoes into a pot of clear, cold water.

Mulling over the situation with regard to Winton, I scrubbed the kitchen floor, found a dust rag, and dusted the living room with great care while Mrs. Laitinen set herself to lunch. In the early afternoon, I accepted a list of groceries and the coinage to pay for them and was directed toward the Finnish Stock Company first and then to Henry Pietala's tailor shop to pick up a vest he had altered for Mr. Stember, and finally toward the Mantel home near the end of East Sheridan where I was to deliver a response to an invitation for a Saturday evening social with cards and perhaps dancing to follow.

All the while, I looked for the banks Mrs. Laitinen had assured me were there and all the while, I must honestly admit, I toyed with the idea of finding the gypsies and going to live with them, turning my back on all else, including being older and responsible. The gypsies had accepted me as one of their own without qualification or reserve. They had housed and fed me, washed and cleaned and dressed me, surrounded me with love and affection, and sent me on my way refreshed and restored. How different they were from the Stembers!

I regretted the exclamation point wasted on the Stembers. After his initial gesture of contact with John Porthan, Mr. Stember seemed to have forgotten me completely, except for a nod now and then as I came and went at Mrs. Laitinen's behest. His wife did not seem to notice me at all.

In a like manner, their friend Mrs. Mantel accepted the note I proffered without thanks or comment, leaving me in the foyer of their luxurious home waiting for a hired girl to show me out. I peeked around the corner at the stained-glass piano window in the living room and at the fireplace niche, so large that the fireplace opening allowed for two full-sized settles, one on each side. Off in the distance, I heard Mrs. Mantel giving directions first to the hired girl and then, it sounded to me, to a dressmaker, whom she was charging with the task of turning an heirloom tablecloth into a party dress before the Saturday evening gathering. The garment was far more important than I.

It was a good thing that the seamstress was not Ma and that Pa was not there. Had Pa heard Ma being addressed in that tone of voice, I knew exactly what he would say because I had heard the words too many times: "Now, you quit, and you tell her 'kiss my ass.'"

Ma was always angry and appalled when he uttered those words, but just then I knew exactly how Pa felt.

It was very clear why and how Uncle Charles had been lost here in Ely even though he was a Brosi, even though he could trace his lineage back to the year 1606. Pa had always been over-proud of that fact, proud that he had been gentry in Finland, son of a landowner from whose properties others took their names, proud of the education he had been given

142

to fit him for the role he had been raised to step into, proud of his knowledge of botany and zoology.

But pride did not help Pa keep a job, and pride did not feed our family, and pride had not kept him from the tender mercies of Russian conscription. Pride had not put food on our table and would not lead to Pa and would not uncover Uncle Charles' bank account. It behooved me to swallow the not inconsiderable residue of pride I had inherited from Pa.

Still, it hurt to be reminded in countless small ways that I was of little or no importance whatsoever. It hurt when Mrs. Laitinen warned me that even if I found the right bank, I could not simply walk up to a bank teller and introduce myself and ask to be given the contents of Uncle Charles' account. It hurt to be a nobody. With that realization one link in the chain of anger I had forged against Pa weakened. He was not in the right. But, a part of me understood how invidious was the nature of the kind of pride I had hoped I had lost on the ladder of Lady Moon.

Given the totality of my own inadequacy and the overwhelming nature of the tasks ahead of me, I desperately needed help, a guardian angel perhaps, to intercede for me, I thought as I trudged back to the Stembers. And against all reason, one appeared.

Chapter Sixteen

"Under an Angel's Wings"

Unbeknownst to me, a lot more had been happening on the home front in Kinney than I ever imagined. I should have known Ma was hardly the type to sit and wait and do nothing. Having found my first note about going to Leinonens to help with the baby, she had waited out that first long day without concern. But by the following morning when I still had not come home and when she finally found the second note, she weighed alternatives just as I had and, also just as I had, accepted help.

Begging streetcar fare from the Salins, Lil in tow, she had left for Virginia next morning (the day I had spent with the gypsies), swallowed her own last vestige of pride, and appealed to the Savolainens.

I think she felt relatively comfortable because it had been made clear by both Alex and Anna that Ma was master, well, mistress, of an art they prized. With her nimble fingers and swift, sharp needle, she created dresses that were catapulting Mrs. Savolainen into the forefront of all the ladies of style, a not inconsiderable number, in that Queen City of the Range. All Mrs. Savolainen had ever lacked was appearance. The culture, the charm, the polish—all of those she had brought with her to the marriage.

But Ma had been able to do the one thing Mrs. Savolainen had never been able to accomplish for herself: Ma made her look the way Mr. Savolainen had always seen her in his heart. Ma designed and cut outfits that made Mrs. Savolainen look not heavy but pleasingly plump. Ma recut and styled her hair from its severe knot into a soft, full, stylish pompadour. In Ma's designs, under Ma's tutelage, Mrs. Savolainen became almost beautiful, and Virginia society, highly critical of its Finnish element but rarely slow on the uptake, approved. Ma had promised her own brand of salvation and fulfilled the promise, in spades. Mr. Savolainen felt himself and his wife redeemed, and his gratitude had known no bounds.

With avuncular good will, therefore, he had offered honest recompense: "I shall find your daughter and bring her home," he promised, "just as soon as I can set my affairs in order and travel to Ely."

And so he had. Of course, neither Ma nor he had believed he had needed to hurry. Ma was certain that I was safe in the care of Uncle Charles. She made it clear that she hoped and believed that asking Mr. Savolainen to follow me was merely a precautionary measure. Yet the niggling sense of worry, brought on Uncle Charles' seeming defection, made it absolutely necessary that she guarantee my safety.

Mr. Savolainen assured her that it was time for him to make a trip to the Ely store anyway, a mere advancement by a week or two of already set plans. Thus, he spent that day (the one in which I myself finally got there) making his preparations, the following day (the one that had brought me to the coroner's office) visiting the Duluth jewelry store, and the morning of my demotion to servant girl traveling by train to Ely.

So it was that at the very same time as I was trudging back down the big hill of Sheridan Street from the Mantels to the Stembers, he was himself marching from the Depot to the corner and up that same hill toward Number 6, the jewelry store.

From the Mantels' front lawn at the apex of the hill, I had been able to see, not so far off in the distance, the pit, the mine buildings, and past them, glistening like angel dust, Shagawa Lake, gold-specked blue surrounded by wilderness, an opal set in jade. I knew the gypsies liked to camp near water, and as I stood there, gravely considering where I was and where I was going, again I yearned to be with them. For all of Mrs. Laitinen's kindness, the work I was doing for the Stembers barely reimbursed them for my room and board: I knew they did not consider me worth additional hard money. And I knew to the penny what was left of the money the gangs had given me: I had started out with $5.01. The streetcar ride to Virginia had cost a nickel, leaving me with $4.96. The gypsies had paid for my train fare, and so far in Ely my only expenses had been the fifty cents paid for the newspaper ad and the dollar paid to the coroner's office for the death certificate. But that left me with only

$3.46. Not nearly enough for the train fare home. Not enough to pay for board and room anywhere else. Not enough for a marker on Uncle Charles' grave, should there be none, and precious little even to buy flowers to lay there.

But by that time my lagging footsteps had brought me within sight of the Finnish Stock Company just across Sheridan, and I thought of Jaako. He had lost one dream but replaced it with another, and I could tell from the unspoken communication that flowed between him and John Porthan that his support figured greatly in John Porthan's fulfilling his own dream. Jaako had not given up.

Every time Pa had left Ma to fend for herself—and us—she had struggled on, always, until now, alone. Yet somehow she had brought us to Malcolm and from there to Virginia and taken care of Lil and me. She had not given up. Whoever was my father—it could be Pa, but I wasn't so naive that I did not suspect other alternatives, too—I was Ma's child. Her strength flowed in my blood, regardless of errors in arithmetic—or in judgment—as revealed in the family records.

I also considered Miss Loney, who, though she was not much taller than I, had taken control even of the big boys like Eino and Kabe and Fatso and the gangs, making them obey her. When she refused to brook dissension in our classroom, all overt dissension ceased.

When children came to school speaking only their home languages, Finnish, Croatian, Serbian, or Italian, Miss Loney did not give up. She taught them to speak and read and write English, and she made them into her teachers so their parents could join the Speak English campaign, too.

Even Lil, once set upon a course, never lacked zeal. When she cried, her whole body cried. When she was angry, her whole body scowled. When she giggled, no one could help but smile. Small as she was, she rarely gave up.

Only Pa gave up. Did I want to pattern my life after his?

I was so intent upon such considerations that I did not see Mr. Alex Savolainen walking up the hill toward me until I almost bumped into him.

When I finally saw him with my mind as well as my eyes, I did not even think of taking evasive action. Instead of running away or trying to hide, I was hard put not to throw myself into his arms and burst into tears.

I think he knew that because, to protect my self-possession, and his own, he simply stood still and waited, bowed as I reached out to him, and, putting my arm through his as if I were a grown-up lady, escorted me into the jewelry store.

Mrs. Stember simpered and Mr. Stember fawned, and Mrs. Laitinen served us all strong coffee with homemade biscuit. When Mr. Savolainen indicated that the Stembers ought to return to minding the shop, they evaporated, leaving us alone at the table.

I wanted to tell Mr. Savolainen all that had happened, and I tried. But something in my throat blocked the words. My chest hurt with the effort of holding back sobs, and no matter how I tried, the tears coursed down my cheeks.

Mrs. Laitinen sent me downstairs to get more butter from the ice-box by the back door, though it seemed to me that the butter plate was full. By the time I got back, I had blown my nose and rubbed my temples and my eyes with a chunk of ice and taken enough deep breaths to clear both chest and throat of obstacles.

During the brief time that I was gone, Mrs. Laitinen had explained the situation insofar as she understood it—that Uncle Charles was dead under suspicious circumstances, that the insurance money could not be paid until we found Pa, that I had not found out which bank held Uncle Charles' money, and that I was "helping out," she said delicately, in lieu of room and board.

That last I heard as I reentered the room without the butter.

Mr. Savolainen cast a steely gaze in my direction, and I started to apologize for not having done more. But the gaze softened immediately, and with remarkably few words he made it clear that he had come not to punish or to hold me in thrall, pending a return to Kinney, but to help.

A halo and wings were completely superfluous. I recognized an angel when I saw one. "First," I begged, pride now being no obstacle, "please, will you help me with the matter of Uncle Charles' money and the bank, and will you help me to find Pa?"

"I will." The affirmation rolled through his whole portly frame and resounded against my heart.

"And Uncle Charles' death . . . can we try to find out what happened?"

"We will." And we did.

But first things first. I did not have to wait until Sunday.

Mr. Savolainen commandeered a carriage, a hack driven by a man from the livery stable, and we traveled along Central up the hill to the cemetery. It was not hard to find Uncle Charles' grave. There were many new "moldering heaps," but only one had been left unmarked by either stone or flowers. While I gathered daisies and laid them on the grave, Mr. Savolainen talked to the driver of the hack, making notes about the location of the plot and the names of those on the cemetery board— who was responsible for markers, for instance, and who took care of the site.

That gave me time to sit quietly by the raw heap of dirt. I didn't know exactly what I was expected to say at a moment like this, but I wanted to tell Uncle Charles that we loved him and that he was not to worry.

"You made a difference in our lives," I said quietly to the spot where he lay. "You were a good man and the best uncle a girl could ever have. Mr. Savolainen is here now, and all will be well," I asserted. "Somehow we are going to make your dreams come true."

I paused, trying hard not to cry.

"We all love you." I repeated the words, keeping them in present tense because the love had not disappeared even though he was no longer of our world.

I told him that Ma had set Lil's watch aside to keep it safe until she was older and more responsible. I didn't mention the fact that Pa had left again. Uncle Charles' spirit deserved peace.

I knew I was imagining it, but I felt his spirit moving around and within me, as if he understood, as if we could both be at peace in this place where butterflies and daisies danced in the wind.

I had not realized that cemeteries could be beautiful. In Virginia, the big kids always said that the cemetery was haunted and that no one should walk through it after dark. But at that moment in that place where "the rude forefathers of the hamlet slept," where tall stands of Norway pines bowed in solemn memory, and the balsam trees lent a sweetness to the air, there was no ugliness.

"Perhaps that's what 'embalmed' means," I said to Mr. Savolainen, who was standing nearby, close enough to lend support, far enough away to give me a private time.

He nodded. "To preserve from oblivion. To imbue with sweet odors, I think the dictionary might say."

"Is there balm in Gilead?" I asked, not quite sure of the meaning of the question, but remembering it from somewhere.

"Yes," he said, looking up at the pines, " there is that which exists to bring comfort from pain. There is a healing time."

As I arose, he took my hand gently, and we stood there for a while grieving—I for Uncle Charles, he for me or perhaps for all of those who grieve.

Mr. Savolainen dismissed the hack at the corner of Sheridan and Central, and the two of us marched across the street to the Finnish Accident and Sick Benefit office—Mr. Savolainen knew of John Porthan —and, with him in tow, up the hill to the Finnish Stock Company—he also knew of Jaako.

We convened, the four of us. While John Porthan, Jaako, Mr. Savolainen, and I discussed what should be done, messengers were sent to find Uncle Charles' bank. Within an hour, we had an appointment at the First State Bank of Ely with none other than the bank president himself. Mr. Savolainen and I went together to his office to root out the facts of Uncle Charles' account.

"Perhaps," I told John Porthan and Jaako, "there's a chance that the money will still be there."

It was a vain hope. Not even Mr. Savolainen's angel dust could conjure up the money.

"Yes, there was an account at this bank in the name of Charles Brosi," Bank President M.K. Niemi confirmed, his fingertips forming a steeple as he leaned back in his chair, "but the funds were withdrawn a month or more ago, as is clearly evidenced by the records." He waved for a clerk to produce them. The money had been withdrawn by Charles Brosi himself, for his signature showed clearly on the withdrawal form.

Mindful of Ma's stringent reminders to curb my tendency toward volatility, I kept my back straight and my face blank. "Restrain yourself," Ma was wont to mutter under her breath, when she sighted warning signs that my feelings of sorrow or joy were seeping past the mask I was expected to keep firmly in place both because I was older and because excessive displays of emotion were considered unseemly. Ma's warnings had been so much a constant part of my day-to-day existence that I had come to hear her words whether she said them or not, whether she was there or not. Thus I bit back the wail rising from my throat into my mouth. If Uncle Charles' money had disappeared with Uncle Charles, then the dreams of what had promised to be a bright new morning were completely shattered.

I could not repress a shiver much like the ones that had told us that Lil, when she was a baby, had lost control once more and needed to be changed. And my eyes were wet. It was easier to repress sobs and wails than to hold back seepage. I tried closing my eyes completely, but even then it was necessary to turn my head toward the plate glass window and concentrate on the traffic outside.

Mr. Savolainen's hands duplicated Bank President M.K. Niemi's prayerful gesture, and the two of them sat very still contemplating the ink well, pen, and blotter centered neatly on the desk. Silence ensued as I tried not to sniffle and they tried not to hear me.

"Do your records list Charles Brosi's address, by any chance?" Mr. Savolainen asked.

"I am certain that we can feel comfortable divulging that information," the bank president indicated, ringing a small bell by his right hand to reconvene the harried-looking clerk.

By the time the clerk returned, his ink-stained fingers holding out a piece of bank stationery with an address written in beautiful script, it was safe for me to open my eyes again.

"The Juola Boarding House on West Sheridan," Mr. Savolainen read aloud.

"It is one of the larger of the Finnish boarding houses," the bank president commented, "and one of the more lucrative," he added dryly in a pointed nonverbal message. "Mr. Juola was killed in a mining accident four or five years ago, and Mrs. Juola's bank account has shown a marked and steady gain ever since."

I opened my mouth to ask why but thought better of it. For a second the looks on the faces of the two men had reminded me uncomfortably of Mr. Ala and thoughts I did not care to pursue.

Mr. Savolainen nodded, put his hat back firmly on his head, picked up his cane, motioned me up, shook the bank president's hand, nodded again to echo my polite "thank you very much, sir," and ushered me out.

"Do not despair, my young friend," he said. "I shall direct my attention to the Juola domicile while you repair to Mrs. Laitinen and pursue the possibility of an early dinner."

Stopping so sharply he almost bumped into me, I demurred. Obviously, a request to accompany him would be refused, so instead of requesting, I asserted, "I am going, too." My jaw was set obstinately, and the last vestige of the flood dried. This time, however, I forbore from restraint. "I must go with you, Mr. Savolainen, please," I begged. "Mrs. Laitinen warned me that I was under no circumstances to go searching around boarding houses alone. But I will be safe with you. No one would dare take advantage of me with you there." It was only partly flattery. For all his abbreviated stature, Mr. Savolainen exuded an air of authority in direct proportion to his not inconsiderable girth.

There was no verbal capitulation, but when he turned west, swinging his cane purposefully ahead of him, I assumed a squire's position just to the rear of his right shoulder, and off we went.

On the other side of Central, the street perpendicular to Sheridan, leading from the depot to the cemetery on the hill, there were neither street signs nor house numbers. But, remembering what Mrs. Laitinen had told John Porthan and me, I had no trouble identifying the houses where miners boarded. Most of them did have outside stairways and doorways leading to the second floor bedrooms where the men slept two to a bed, those working the day shift at night, those on night shift during the day. I looked up. The upstairs shades were drawn.

Rather than going to the door of the first two-story house that looked promising, as I thought of doing, Mr. Savolainen tipped his hat to a passerby, a young man a bit older than I, obviously off on an errand, and asked politely first in English and then, because of the blank look and the shrug, in Finnish: "Please be so kind as to give us directions to the Juola boardinghouse."—"*Ole hyvä ja anna minulle ohjettä löydän Juolaan poikataloon.*"

The lad held out his hand for the coins Mr. Savolainen proferred and pointed toward a white frame house double the size of the nearby homes, the original four-room two-story having been enlarged by an L-shaped addition, two rooms up and two down, built perpendicular to the original, with a broad porch filling the center of the L. Since it lacked the usual outside stairway, I had not deemed it a boarding house.

It did look prosperous, imposing even, with its cornices and balustrades elaborately carved, its white paint fresh, its lawn neatly clipped between the picket fence and the porch. A lady sat there in a double swing making desultory stitches in what looked like a pillowcase pulled taut over a large embroidery hoop. She stood up as Mr. Savolainen opened the gate, no doubt in response to the imposing figure he cut. In his bowler hat, natty suit and tie, pince nez, gold watch chain, and walking cane, he was clearly not a miner.

Nor did she look the way Mrs. Laitinen had depicted the harried owner or proprietor of a boarding house. Instead, she looked like Ma of a Sunday, her hair poofed high, her lawn waist immaculately starched and elaborately embellished with lace inserts at wrist and throat, a gold label watch pinned at her left shoulder.

"Mrs. Juola?" Mr. Savolainen swept off his hat and bowed elegantly.

"Ye-e-s?" It may have been financial security that gave even her thick Finnish accent an air of hauteur. But she was no match for Mr. Savolainen.

As Mrs. Juola stood before us, her back broomstick straight, her eyebrows raised, Mr. Savolainen introduced me as Charles Brosi's niece and asked for information as to the dispersal of his properties after his regrettable demise. Me she would have left to await her pleasure, but Mr. Savolainen, with me in tow, she ushered into the front parlor with courtesy if not enthusiasm.

Seating himself and me on a brand new horsehair sofa, Mr. Savolainen wasted no time on preambles. "May we see his effects, if you please."

"Charles Brosi's effects remain in the trunk which he kept, as most of the other boarders do, in the bedroom in which he slept. After his . . . demise . . ." she obviously had to search for the word, "I had my man-servant and kitchen helper carry it into the attic, where it remains in safe-keeping." Her words implied complete composure; her tone, rather less.

But she was no match for Mr. Savolainen.

"Please to have him bring the trunk here so that Ilmi Marianna Brosi, his niece, may apprise herself of its contents," he requested firmly.

Mrs. Juola opened her mouth to demur but thought better of it, nodded her acquiescence and called the order toward the back of the house.

We sat in silence listening to the sound of heavy footsteps going up one back stairway and then another. Doors opened and closed and then a bump-bump-bump signified that something heavy was being dragged down.

While we waited, Mrs. Juola walked around the room, studying the pattern in the rug that reached almost wall to wall and adjusting the placement of some sheet music on the music stand of a pump organ.

I worked at restraining the lump that threatened to cut off my breath as it had my power of speech. The money might well be on its way to us.

"Must you open the trunk here?" she asked, suggesting that it was inappropriate to clutter so elegant a room with a miner's leavings.

"Yes," said Mr. Savolainen.

She capitulated.

The hired man came in, pulling the trunk behind him. He opened the clasps of the leather binding belts, unsnapped the two front latches, and pressed the center of the lock until it too snapped open.

I held my breath.

I needn't have, for there was very little inside.

The top tray held a shaving mug with a design of pink moss roses around the top, the soap dish still partially filled with the remnants of a round piece of shaving soap. I picked it up. Written on the bottom was the name "Charles Brosi" in a script that looked much like Pa's handwriting.

I swallowed hard.

Near it lay a leather box, perhaps a foot long and six inches wide, two or three inches deep. A narrow leather belt had been glued and fastened to the sides and bottom then run through a leather loop and closed on top just above the word "Records," written in dark ink by the same hand.

Holding my breath, hoping against hope that what we sought would be inside, I handed the box to Mr. Savolainen, who carefully undid the belting and opened the lid, removing the contents one piece of paper at a time:

—a subscription to the *TYOMIES*, with "Charles Brosi" in pencil on the line after "name" written in Finnish—"*NIMI*,"

—a creased and crumpled slip of paper with Registration Number 5263152 written above the name "Charles Brosi,"

—a Registration Certificate with his name and the date above the warning "THE LAW REQUIRES YOU TO HAVE THIS CARD IN YOUR PERSONAL POSSESSION AT ALL TIMES,"

—a light blue card headed "EMPLOYEE'S IDENTIFICA-TION," under the words "Oliver Iron Mining," with the records of his age (thirty-two), weight (160 pounds), height (5'10"), color of hair (brown) and eyes (blue), "no mustache," so smudged as to be barely legible,

—a picture taken at a studio in Fort William, Ontario, of Ma and Pa with Lil on Pa's lap and me between them in earlier, happier days,

—a "thank you" note I had written for her but which Lil had signed "Lillian Brosi" with painstaking care the morning she and I received our watches,

—a side-view photograph of Ma I had never seen before, with her hair undone, hanging in ripples down to her knees.

I swallowed even harder, to less avail.

An "ALIEN REGISTRATION CARD" showed the print of his right index finger on the back, and finally what looked like a birth certificate was written in blue ink in Finnish on fine paper and embossed with the mark of the "DIOECESIS ABOENSIS. Kirkenkirja sivu 789, N:o 437."

Otherwise, the "Records" box was empty. Uncle Charles' money was not there.

I sighed. So did Mr. Savolainen.

So did Mrs. Juola, though her sigh sounded quite different, filled with relief, perhaps, rather than regret.

That was all there was in the trunk, other than the normal accouterments of a man's life—a razor strap and a straight-edge razor, well sharpened, a long thin knife in a leather scabbard, some underclothing for both summer and winter, a dark woolen suit that looked familiar, a dark tie, some shirts.

No money. None at all save a few Finnish coins in a small jewelry box marked "Smith's." The box reminded me of the ones Lil and I had opened to find our watches.

"And there is nothing else?" Mr. Savolainen pierced Mrs. Juola's composure with a gaze so sharp I sat back amazed. "You are certain there was nothing else?"

She met him look for look. "Nothing," she averred firmly.

She did not look at me.

Mr. Savolainen stood up abruptly. "Mrs. Juola," he enunciated slowly and loudly, as if to someone deaf or retarded or foreign, "you may be aware that before Charles Brosi died, he withdrew a considerable sum of money from the First State Bank of Ely."

Her chin rose higher. "I was unaware of that possibility."

"You must also be aware," he continued as if not heeding her words at all, "that his death is under investigation as having occurred in circumstances that are extremely suspect."

I tried hard not to look surprised.

"It is in your best interest, of course," he went on gaining in height and power as he spoke, "to cooperate with his niece in every way possible to further that investigation."

She refused to give him so much as a nod.

"Should that not be the case," he concluded, "I shall not answer for the consequences." The words fairly resonated, as if someone had pulled the knob marked "diapason" on his vocal organs.

"We shall send for the trunk and for its contents, entire." With that final thrust, he maneuvered both of us past Mrs. Juola and out the door.

I was shaking so hard it was all I could do to accompany him. I, who deified words, could find none that approximated my feelings. It was as if we had lost Uncle Charles for a second, this time irrevocably final time, for as his body had been taken from us, so his dreams were gone. And with him and with them went all of our hopes. Once upon a time we had watched the sun rise, and morning had awakened. Now that day had ended in a mass of shattered golden shards, and veils of darkness swirled around us. We were lost, Ma and Lil and I, in a maze from which there was no escape.

I have always hated the last page of a book, the moment when I have to leave the world of imagination for the real world. But this was the real world, and this was "The End." *Finis.*

Mr. Savolainen, his hand under my elbow, thus keeping my body moving forward, surprised me, however. "Now," he said grimly, "we shall begin to fight."

Chapter Seventeen

"Into the Ring"

Mr. Savolainen may have been ready to jump back into the ring. He certainly had pulled no punches with Mrs. Juola. But I was reeling on the ropes, punch-drunk by too many knock-out blows to the heart.

"I do not like that woman," Mr. Savolainen said as, with his hand still firmly under my elbow, he kept me moving forward.

Numbly, I followed, my mind finding it difficult to make connections. Instead of forming a pattern, fragments floated. "Whoever made out the death certificate could have found the name 'Lillian Brosi' on that note in the trunk," I mused.

Mr. Savolainen nodded and forged ahead. But when we came to the city's mid-point at the junction of Central and Sheridan, instead of continuing toward the jewelry store, Mr. Savolainen steered us to the right for a block and then turned left up Chapman Street.

It mattered little to me where we went or for that matter if we went at all, for there was nowhere to go. "If Uncle Charles put the money he withdrew from the bank into the record box in the trunk, anyone could have found it. But how would anyone have known to look for it? How did anyone guess that he had money there? Miners don't have money."

"She knew." Mr. Savolainen's jaw was set grimly. "She didn't even go through the motions of offering condolences, expressing sympathy. The minute she heard who you were, she pulled down the shades."

"She was rude even to you." That had surprised me. Although Mr. Savolainen had accomplished a lot in his lifetime and knew it, instead of being prideful, he was merely confident and competent and unfailingly polite to others. But he expected and usually received a polite response. People listened to him because he knew what he was doing and knew where he was going. If Mrs. Juola wanted to get somewhere herself in this world, it behooved her to befriend men like Mr. Savolainen. Yet, she had been rude.

I was so engrossed in those thoughts that I hardly realized that Mr. Savolainen had finally halted midway up Chapman Street and was opening one of a set of double frosted glass doors, standing back to usher me in.

I hung back, gaping. He wanted me to precede him into the lobby of the Forest Hotel. I knew it was the kind of place where he felt at home. I knew that prideful people like Mrs. Juola—and me—wanted to go there but rarely did for a number of reasons—matters of clothing and etiquette, matters of forks and spoons and tablecloths and farm boots, matters of money and position, matters of old-country dialects and poor English grammar.

Opened a few years earlier to much applause and heraldry, its events carefully documented not only in the *Ely Miner* but in Virginia's *Range Facts*, the Forest Hotel was acclaimed as the most elegantly appointed hostelry in northern Minnesota, with the exception of perhaps the Spaulding Hotel in Duluth. Ma and I had studied the society page pictures of Christmas galas and tea dances, Robert Burns' Day dinners, debutante cotillions, because I loved the descriptions of these elegant celebrations, because she loved the clothes the women wore—gowns and jewels and furs.

Never in my wildest dreams had I presumed to enter that imposing edifice, though I had yearned to see first-hand the carved oak ceilings and wide staircases, the small lift with its iron grill that magically transported guests up to their rooms and suites. But I had fostered no illusions about how far three dollars and forty-six cents went toward a meal there much less toward a night's lodgings.

Thus when Mr. Savolainen stood back, waiting politely for me to enter, I sent him a beseeching glance and prepared to turn and run away down the street. Could he not see my rumpled school dress, badly in need of a washing, my ribbon in need of an ironing, my scuffed shoes, my whole self that could use a sauna? I had not washed my hair. My underwear and stockings had received only nominal attention for days.

But when Mr. Savolainen reached out and took my hand and marched me in, I had no choice but to follow.

Oh, the magnificence! In spite of the fact that the day had just begun to slip into evening, the lobby was dark. Its mahogany wainscoting and ceiling beams were softly illuminated by lamps set on oak tables, which were interspersed among the leather armchairs and sofas lining the walls. On one end of the lobby, a broad staircase led upwards.

Mr. Savolainen ushered me, protesting still, though very discreetly, in the other direction toward a double doorway that opened to an equally elegant section of the hotel, the main dining room. As if he had been waiting, a waiter clad in white shirt, white apron, black tie, and trousers greeted us as soon as we entered. Before I could further demur, he had seated us at a white-clothed table bedecked with napkin, heavy sterling silverware, and crystal glasses so fine that when he poured water and inadvertently tapped the rim, mine rang like a bell.

Seated opposite me, Mr. Savolainen waved the menu aside and told the waiter that we needed quick and hearty sustenance. "What can you bring us rapidly?"

The waiter considered a moment then offered us our choice of three kinds of soup—a turkey vegetable, a beef and barley, and a hearty corn chowder.

Mr. Savolainen looked at me. The waiter looked at me. I whispered, "Turkey-vegetable, if you please."

Mr. Savolainen ordered chowder. "And?" He looked inquiringly at the waiter.

"Perhaps I may suggest a sandwich made of our roasted chicken or roast beef, done to a turn, on fine white bread fresh from the oven."

Mr. Savolainen nodded. "Chicken, please," and smiled at me.

"Beef, if you please." The waiter had to lean forward to decipher my barely audible response. I was feeling much reduced both in form and function.

"Coffee now for the both of us. Buttermilk for me with the meal and a glass of milk for the young lady. Thank you," Mr. Savolainen concluded briskly.

The waiter picked up the menus and backed away as if from an august presence. Returning momentarily with a silver tray holding cups filled with steaming black coffee, a bowl of sugar lumps, and a small pitcher of cream, he served us, me first. I said, "Thank you." Mr. Savolainen nodded his appreciation. The waiter backed away again, and Mr. Savolainen turned my coffee into coffee milk liberally laced with cream and at least four sugar lumps.

"Drink," he ordered, attending to his own cup.

I did with a deep and thankful sigh.

From then until the soup and sandwiches appeared, we simply sat. I studied the room. As the heat of the coffee loosened my tight chest, I gradually regained enough composure to appreciate the gilded carvings on the ceiling, the niches filled with tall vases of fresh flowers, the silk floral wall covering, the chair-rail and the dark wainscoting, the Oriental rug that cushioned our feet.

But oh, the colors! I had studied every page of last year's Sears catalogue, kept in the outhouse for wiping paper. But those pictures were all black and white. I needed Eino's vocabulary notebook to find better words than "red," "blue," "yellow,"and "green" to describe this room. Crimson? Magenta? Vert? Aquamarine? Cerulean? Saffron? Topaz? But his vocabulary notebook had lain untouched at the bottom of my school bag for more days than I cared to count.

When the waiter served us our soup and sandwiches, I sighed deeply, in a quandary again. Where did the napkin go? On my lap or tucked into my neckband? Which of the three spoons was the soup spoon? Did I cut my sandwich and eat it with a knife and fork or take it with my fingers? Perhaps I'd better not eat, I thought, and sat back. But Ma's lessons came to my aid. She had always warned me that if I were ever to find myself in such a situation, I was to look carefully at the actions of others for clues about what to do.

The waiter asked Mr. Savolainen, "Is everything satisfactory, sir?"

Mr. Savolainen nodded and said, "Yes, thank you."

I waited then carefully mimicked every one of Mr. Savolainen's movements, taking the heavy linen napkin from its silver holder and laying it carefully on my lap, picking up the same spoon as he, using the knife to cut the sandwich halves into even smaller pieces. But as soon as I sipped the first spoonful of the richly flavored soup and munched the first bite of sandwich, decorum drowned itself in delight, and I quit worrying about rules of etiquette. I ate and ate and ate to satisfy what I had not recognized to be an absolutely voracious hunger. Spooning every morsel from the soup bowl, I had to remind myself not to lift it to my lips to sip the last of the fragrant broth. I forced myself not to moisten my forefinger to pick up the very last crumbs of the sandwich. I emptied the milk glass three times and shared the last of the coffee, which the waiter replenished generously, with Mr. Savolainen.

Sitting back, finally and utterly replete, I caught Mr. Savolainen's eye and smiled. "I feel much better," I admitted.

"And so you should, my dear child," he answered, smiling back. "You have just experienced a truism that has enabled mankind to survive traumas far more painful even than our visit to the Juolas: it always helps to eat."

I nodded. Such a simple act, yet how satisfying and energizing and . . . restoring it had been.

"The act of breaking bread together," he continued, "creates kinship, camaraderie. It lessens one's isolation."

He looked a bit uncomfortable, perhaps because his words had sounded so elevated, but thinking about them, I realized why Amalia's family set such a store both on their church's act of communion, the sharing of symbolic bits of food and drink, and on their weekly family dinners. I had often been invited to the Barones' on Sunday. I never told Ma and Pa that, like the other kids, I drank my share of watered-down wine. But I did tell them all about the pasta and the sauces and the cheeses and the sausages mixed together. I went home dancing and singing to the melody of *lasagna, tagliatelle, vin santo, agnolotti, bucatini, pecorini,* and *fusilli, rigatoni, orecchiette.*

Of course, that was before I knew I should not enjoy using foreign words but should be sticking to English.

Reaching across the table to pat my hand, Mr. Savolainen knew how to verbalize my feelings though the words had eluded me. "When we share these critical elements of survival with other human beings," he continued, trying hard not to be abstruse, "we form with them a bond, both tangible and intangible, physical and emotional. In eating from the same plate and drinking from the same cup, as it were, we become one."

Had he any idea, I wondered, how true those words were? We were no longer strangers. Tears welled up as I thought of the gypsies. How ironic that they, who were so disparaged, truly lived the meaning of this philosophy!

On both philosophical and practical planes, Mr. Savolainen had provided both of us with what we had desperately needed—the kind of perspective that a full stomach and a time of respite are wont to give.

Our meal complete, we waited until our table had been cleared and brushed of crumbs, responded to the waiter's inquiry about a sweet to complete the meal, and agreed to a piece of hot apple pie fresh out of the oven.

"With vanilla ice cream," Mr. Savolainen amended, to my great delight.

The waiter again disappeared and we were left alone, the dining room, except for us, empty of guests.

"Every war that has ever been fought," Mr. Savolainen began, "has involved not one but a series of skirmishes and battles, each one of which has led in some significant way toward the final end, which is victory. It is victory we seek, is it not?" he asked rhetorically.

I nodded and sat back, waiting. A part of my body sought sleep more than strategem, oblivion rather than action. Unwilling either to disappoint Mr. Savolainen or to disturb our fragile sense of unity, however, I shook off my lethargy and addressed myself to a review of our battle plan, which had been partially developed with John Porthan and Jaako. "I still believe that the only victory possible at this point is one that is achieved in the name of if not in the form of Uncle Charles. His dream and ours of a farm in Zim must be brought to fruition, and that can only be done by our somehow finding the money withdrawn from his savings account."

Mr. Savolainen drew a pencil and a notepad from an inner coat pocket and underscored the words "Find the money." By the words he put a circled number one.

"But remember," I continued, somewhat in the style of John Porthan. "There are two sources of funds. The second is the one-hundred-dollar death benefit owed Uncle Charles' beneficiary by the Finnish Accident and Sick Benefit Association, John Porthan, director. Pa—Knute Pietari Brosi—is named on the form as his beneficiary. To get that money, we must find Pa."

Mr. Savolainen nodded. "No. 2 went down by 'Find Pa.'"

"In order to do that," I observed, "it is probably going to be necessary to go to Winton." I paused. Mr. Savolainen waited. "I am absolutely certain that no mining company will ever again hire Pa because he has been blacklisted."

"Mines" was recorded with a question mark appended and the words "probably no."

"The other major industry in northern Minnesota is lumbering."

Mr. Savolainen kept the pencil poised.

"And the center for the lumbering industry in northern Minnesota is Winton."

He set the pencil tip to paper.

"Ergo"—I liked that word—"it is in the area of Winton that he will most likely be found."

Mr. Savolainen completed the word "Winton" and underlined it.

I sighed deeply. "But Mrs. Laitinen has made it clear that it will do me no good to go there alone. There are too many men, you see, and saloons and all."

He nodded sympathetically.

The waiter appeared, served each of us a large piece of apple pie, and withdrew again in silence.

The pie smelled so good that we both concentrated on eating it as rapidly as good manners would allow, and I on making the ice cream, crust, and apple filling come out even.

Pie plates and coffee cups empty, Mr. Savolainen picked up the conversation as if there had been no intermission. "It seems to me that the most obvious avenue open to us is an identification of those inhabitants of Ely who have enjoyed, since Charles Brosi's demise, an unexpected windfall."

My head snapped up. The Widow Juola's financial success had clearly predated Uncle Charles' demise. Although she had access to his funds, she may not have had great need of them. Therefore, it was likely that someone else figured in either or both acts—what could have been murder, what surely was theft. How clever of Mr. Savolainen, I thought, humbled. It had not occurred to me. "But do you not think," I threw in abruptly, "that whoever took the money might have absconded with it?"

He considered the prospect then shook his head. "No. Whoever took that money either knew Charles Brosi well enough to be aware of his plans or had some connection with the bank from which he withdrew the money. To leave too abruptly would be tantamount to admitting duplicity."

Deeply appreciative of the fact that he was not talking down to me, that he was addressing me as an adult in an adult's vocabulary, I nodded an adult's agreement.

"But who would know of his plans?" Mr. Savolainen continued. "Have you any idea whom he might have been close to here in Ely? A friend from the mines, perhaps, or another boarder at the Juolas?"

That was a difficult one to answer. But this was an extreme situation, and we had broken bread together. I chanced honesty. "There was no one," I murmured, "no one at all . . . in Ely."

Looking deeply into Mr. Savolainen's understanding heart, I explained, "He talked to us sometimes, well, more to Ma and Pa, but I listened, about the way he lived when he was here, the way he had lived for years and years until he found us. He got up to have breakfast, walked to work at the mine, rode the cage into blackness, lighted only by his candle, turned his mind off and dug and braced walls and loaded ore and prayed to have the day end until it did and he rode the cage up, often into blackness again, for the shifts are twelve hours long, and walked to the boarding house and ate supper and had a sauna and went to bed and got up to have breakfast the next day or that night, depending upon what shift he was on. Because he had no family, he never hesitated to work double shifts, overtimes, weekends, and holidays. There was no time left, he always told us, for living. Until he found us, that is."

The tears I had worked so hard to suppress spilled out again and ran down my cheeks, but I did not wipe them away. Uncle Charles deserved those tears, and it was right that they should fall. "And there is this to consider, too." I hoped Mr. Savolainen could follow my thinking because I could never have said this again: "Because we are all he had, it is up to me now to find out what really happened to him if I can and wreak vengeance, if vengeance is needed. It is not enough to find his grave and cover it with flowers and mark it clearly. I vow that I shall not rest until his spirit can rest in peace."

It sounded pretty grandiose coming from me, I knew. But I trusted Mr. Savolainen.

The trust was not ill-founded. Clearing his throat gruffly, Mr. Savolainen drew a line through one word that he had written, obliterating the option of "Friends" and wrote one last word, which he presented to me as if it had been on a silver salver: "retribution."

While I gathered myself together and blew my nose on my grimy handkerchief, he arose and opened a commodious leather pouch, divested a roll of paper money of what seemed to me an inordinate number of bills, passed them with a nod and word of appreciation to the waiter, and collected me.

The waiter bowed us out, holding the already open door even wider and smiling and admonishing us to be sure to come again and to ask for his services whenever we did.

I do not think Mr. Savolainen even heard him, for he set his hat even more firmly on the exact center of his head—as if it were a helmet, grasped the cane as masterfully as if it were a sword, and empowered me to immediate movement with an even firmer elbow hold.

"We are on our way to the First State Bank," he responded to my unasked question.

Two blocks and no more than ten minutes later, we were back in the bank president's office. Fifteen minutes after that, we were out again, a slip of paper in hand. On it had been written the names of the three clerks who had been at work in the bank on the day of the withdrawal, the name of the one who had handled the transaction circled. Mr. Smith.

"He has not been at work these last three days," the clerk had added, apologizing profusely for his inability to conjure up the young man. "He should be at his current domicile, the new Lakeview Hotel on Camp Street, on the same block as the Finnish Evangelical Lutheran Church."

By the time the word "church" came out of the clerk's mouth, we were out the door. This time it was I who was leading, Mr. Savolainen, who was panting somewhat in my wake. We were very near a possible answer, I realized, incredibly and finally close to a key connection.

But not close enough. Young Mr. Smith, the bank clerk, was not, the hotel's proprietress indicated, in his room at this time. He had left for his brother's place of business downtown some time ago and not returned. "The Smith Jewelry Company," she added: Were we familiar with that illustrious emporium? "On the one hundred block of Sheridan?"

We trekked back to Sheridan Street and found it. Closed. We could not see through the windows, which had been papered with signs touting a "Grand Re-opening!" No one answered our knocks.

At that, Mr. Savolainen faded. So did I. We sat down on the stoop and admitted exhaustion then drifted down the hill back toward the jewelry store, agreeing that we had done all we could for that day.

I was hard put not to kiss Mr. Savolainen good-bye, but I contented myself with a heartfelt "thank you very much" as I watched him make his way at an even but reduced pace out the back door of No. 6 Sheridan Street toward the rear entrance to the Forest, where he had booked a suite.

I hoped he'd sleep well.

As I turned to climb the stairs toward my own back room at the Stembers, my feet slowed as his had but for another reason entirely. Words haunted me, pounding against my subconscious mind.

"Smith." I said the name out loud. "Our gift boxes always said 'Smith Jewelry Store.' That Mr. Smith, if there is one, must have known Uncle Charles well . . . and known that he had money to spend. And his brother definitely knew about the money in the bank."

"Grand *re*-opening." That suggested a closure. Why had the shop been closed? Why was it reopening? Because of a windfall . . . a financial windfall? How could I find out when it had closed? How could I find out why it was now reopening?

Perching myself on the top step, I leaned my head against the wall.

Businesses that opened and closed and opened again and the business people who ran them must be newsworthy. Prospective customers must be informed. That information would be transmuted by . . . newspaper?

I shot up and raced for the kitchen. The pendulum on Mrs. Laitinen's maple kitchen wall clock, clicking away the minutes, told me I was "to-o-o - late - to-o-o-o - late."

The clock was right, and I was tired.

Tomorrow, early tomorrow, I told myself, I will hurry to the office of the *Ely Miner*, where I had earlier placed my ad, and inquire about past issues. Were they saved? Could I read them? What had happened to the Smith Jewelry Company between the date of the withdrawal of money and now? Was there any possible connection? How could I find young Mr. Smith, the clerk from the bank, and where?

Suddenly, tomorrow seemed hopeful again—if not of victory, at least of something more than sure defeat.

Chapter Eighteen

"Hypotheses"

The answers to my questions were there, all right, openly inscribed in large print, centered and boxed so that no reader of the weekly April, May, and June editions of the *Ely Miner* could possibly miss them.

Why had the Smith Jewelry Store closed?

The answer appeared in the issue that came out the week Uncle Charles returned to Ely from his visit to Kinney and Zim. The boxed announcement read simply:

Bankrupt Jewelry Store
AUCTION
Sale of Smith Jewelry Company

Just to make sure I understood the situation, I looked to see if the word "bankrupt" appeared under the B's in Eino Salin's notebook. Sure enough: "v. to bring financial ruin upon, impoverish, make destitute, / bankruptcy - n. FAILURE."

How ironic, I thought, that I had to look that one up. I knew exactly what the word "failure" meant.

Scanning every page of the more recent editions, I found a small item on the editorial page within a column of local news. It indicated that Mr. Smith had gone to the Twin Cities. "Smith Jewelry Company," the article continued, "will open shortly with an entirely new stock."

Hmmm, I mused. It had not taken long for financial ruin to be replaced by fiscal solvency. Where had Mr. Smith discovered this windfall? To what—or whom—was this burst of good fortune attributed?

The paragraph concluded with the following personal note: "His friends here are pleased to see him stage a comeback in his accustomed virile manner."

I checked under the V's for "virile" right away. "Masculine, forceful, masterful," Eino's notebook said. The word reminded me uncomfortably of Mr. Ala and the way he had looked at Ma. Of its own volition, my mind flashed to Mrs. Juola, and something within me stirred. I did not like that something. It made me feel . . . I struggled to find the right word . . . revulsion. Shivering, I grouped Mr. Smith and Mrs. Juola into the same category—as enemies, potential or actual.

I was not, of course, the only one in the newspaper office. The man in an ink-stained apron who had answered my early-morning knock on the alley door and given me copies of the old issues was busy setting type, and another man was hunched over a rickety desk, checking the spelling of the names of the men killed in the mining accident, preparatory to the printing of a black-bordered funeral flier, underwritten by the families of the deceased, to be distributed during Sunday's funeral services and processional. But in spite of the flurry of activity going on around me, I felt very isolated and very much alone, as if I had crossed all seven turnings of the river Styx and reached the regions of the dead.

And I had. There it was, a notice so small it was not surprising that no one in Ely seemed to have marked it at all:

> Charles Brosi, an unmarried man about 30 years of age, who has been making his home at the Juola boarding house in this city for several years, died of heart failure this week. He was buried in the Ely Cemetery.

For a long time, I sat looking at those scant four lines, all that had been known of Charles Brosi. My throat tightened and my heart ached, and once again I vowed to avenge his memory, to make his life . . . and his death . . . count, somehow to give public testimony to his word and his worth.

Clenching my hands, I closed my eyes and wished for a knife to seal the vow with blood or a cross to give it what the Barones considered Christian weight.

Scanning the columns to make sure I had not missed any details relevant to my search, I virtuously refused to allow my eyes to light on the new Zane Grey novel, *The Light of Western Stars*, serialized in those issues. In the process, however, honesty forced me to admit that I gleaned enough of the gist of the story to feel terribly guilty.

Vows were only words and thoughts. It was action that was needed now, and information to guide that action. Sighing, I set that paper aside and reached for the May 18th issue.

On the far right hand column of the first page appeared the following news, boxed with a significant headline:

A band of gypsies swooped down on the city Wednesday and were encamped on the Winton Road. The police ordered them to stay away from the city and they made their way south at the earliest Thursday.

What about them was considered so terrible that they needed to be ordered to stay away from a town like Ely? As if this were such a place of safety, I thought, remembering Mrs. Laitinen's and Jaako's warnings and stories.

On an inside page of the most recent issue, just out the day before, I found my own small ad. At least I had tried, I thought. How ironic that not even the newspaperman who had helped me with the ad had pieced together my request for information with an earlier short obituary notice.

But the following announcement, which filled one side of the adjoining page top to bottom, could not be overlooked:

We have just purchased a clean new stock of
Watches
of the highest grade,
Jewelry
in solid gold and filled in the latest patterns
Clocks
of the best makes and designs.
SMITH JEWELRY CO.
Opposite the Elco Theater
Watch for Grand Opening Details.

Tongue in cheek I observed to myself that Mr. Smith's visit to the Twin Cities had obviously been a success.

Thanking the newspapermen, who were too busy to do more than nod in my direction, I wound my way slowly back toward the alley door of the Stembers' Jewelry Store, pondering and piecing, hypothesizing, guessing, wondering how close we were getting to the truth, shaking my head. Where had Mr. Smith the jeweler found the money he had needed to completely restock his store? Had he remembered that Uncle Charles had had enough money to spend on frivolous gifts? Had the other Mr. Smith, his brother, the clerk at the bank, told him that Uncle Charles had withdrawn a considerable sum? Had Mrs. Juola told him that Uncle Charles was dead? Had he then taken the money from Uncle Charles' trunk? Or had it been she herself who had taken the money? Who had made sure that Uncle Charles would never know that the money was gone? And how? Was one of them responsible for his death? Had it in fact been murder?

Only one thing was for sure: even if we were able to trace the money to Mr. Smith, he had very likely spent it all on merchandise for his store. Time at our farm in Zim would have to be measured with a broken watch.

None of the Smiths had any reason to expect officials to investigate either the theft of the money or the circumstances of Uncle Charles' death. It was unlikely he had ever talked about his plans or the money.

Mrs. Juola surely knew Uncle Charles' nature, was aware that he lived a lonely, friendless life. Thus, it was also highly unlikely that he had ever talked about us. The pictures in the trunk offered no clue to identities or addresses, though Lillian's thank-you note did provide a name and a place to affix to the death certificate. Governmental officialdom had not pursued the subject. Mrs. Juola no doubt told the deputy coroner that Mr. Brosi had left nothing at all of any value.

The deputy coroner. Standing stock still for a moment, I remembered reading something. . . . Some part of my subconscious mind had registered a name or, more likely, a title. Racing back to the newspaper office, trying not to slam the door behind me, I expressed my gratitude that the newspapers had not been put away—though from the look of the room nothing ever was. Turning back to the front page of the issue that contained Uncle Charles' obituary, I found the following short item:

> Owen W. Pomer, well-known Deputy Coroner, was hospitalized in Shipman's Hospital early the morning of May 4 from an overdose of laudanum. He is a good coroner and a fine gentleman but a few years ago became addicted to the use of strong drink.

No wonder he had not questioned the scant mention of "Lillian" and "Virginia." No wonder the handwriting on the death certificate had been so difficult to read. No wonder the coroner himself had known none of the details of Uncle Charles' death. Such details as the deputy coroner had provided had no doubt been of Mrs. Juola's making, for who knows in what condition Owen W. Pomer had been when he entered the Juola house or, of a certainty, when he left after making out the death certificate sometime that same night.

Setting the newspapers aside again with an abstract "thank you" to the young men who had allowed me to look through them without purchasing anything, I wandered out of the newspaper office and onto Sheridan Street, dizzy with hunger—I had not taken time for breakfast—and with revelation. The more I thought about all of this, the more it seemed that the nature and character and personalities of these people were the lynchpins on which to hang our hypotheses. Retracing my steps with blind eyes, though the sun was shining and the air smelled sweet and heavy with the last of the spring lilacs, I pecked away at the conundrum.

Our meeting with Mrs. Juola had made it abundantly clear that she harbored no regrets about the loss of one of her boarders. To her, Uncle Charles had no doubt meant nothing more than another face at a table, another source of remuneration. Cash money. He must have seemed like one of a whole generation of lost souls, men without countries, husbands and fathers without families, workers without any future.

But Uncle Charles had not been penniless as Mr. Smith's brother, the clerk at the bank, knew. When I balanced Mrs. Juola's obvious striving toward gentility against (I shuddered) the "virile" jeweler Smith's need for funds, the jigsaw puzzle pieces jibed. The resulting picture was so evident, so plausible, so real that I felt . . . numb.

As they seemed to do almost automatically these days, my feet led me back to the Stembers, through the shop, open for the day, past Mrs. Stember, who nodded and smiled, past Mr. Stember, who looked up from his desk to give me a casual glance, up the back stairway, and into the kitchen, where I plopped myself onto a kitchen chair and reached for a bit of what appeared to be bread dough that Mrs. Laitinen was kneading on the enamel-topped kitchen table.

"Mmm," I murmured, chewing appreciatively. It was not bread dough but *pulla*, my very favorite cardamom biscuit, and her dough tasted every bit as good as Ma's. Like Ma, she slapped at my hand, but playful-

170

ly, adding the motherly admonishment that I would get a tummy ache if I ate too much.

"I did not see you have any breakfast this morning." Pointing at the stove, she indicated a pot of oatmeal simmering in a double boiler.

I filled a large bowl, added a dollup of butter, a generous sprinkling of sugar, and the rest of the cream from the pitcher on the counter, poured Mrs. Laitinen a fresh cup of coffee and one for myself, and settled down first to eat and then to give her an update.

"I think I have solved the mystery," I began once the bowl was empty. The whole story, what I had found, what I had hypothesized, burst out. "I believe that either one or both of the Mr. Smiths decided to get their hands on the money they knew had been withdrawn from the bank. It would have been easy for Mrs. Juola to check the trunk to see if it was there. I believe that they made sure that Uncle Charles would not know what they were doing—I don't suppose we'll ever know exactly what they did—but whether they intended to or not, in the process, they killed him. Mrs. Juola called the deputy coroner and plied him with drink until he barely knew what he was writing on the death certificate. But that ended the matter as far as official action was concerned. And since several weeks passed after that and no one turned up to ask about Uncle Charles, since he had no friends or family in Ely itself, they took it for granted that they were in the clear. Then I turned up with Mr. Savolainen. And we put it all together and that's the end of them! But it's the end of the money, too, unfortunately," I sighed.

Mrs. Laitinen worked as she listened, lifting the mound of dough, pressing it down with the heel of her palm, kneading until it held together and no longer stuck to the table. Then she turned it into a large stoneware bowl, covered it with a damp dish cloth, set it into the warming oven where it would rise the fastest, and scraped the loose bits of leftover dough and flour and butter from the top of the table. For the final cleanup, she used the same technique I had seen Ma use countless times. Mrs. Laitinen ran a wet dish rag over the doughy spot, scraped the edges toward the center with a pancake turner, scrubbed the edges clear, and repeated the process.

Watching her made me feel at home. Her hands could have been Ma's hands. Her bright blue eyes turned from my face to the table and back to my face. She held back comment until I was through and the table had been returned to pristine perfection. After wiping it dry, she unfolded and replaced the starched, embroidered tablecloth, set a spoon-cup and sugar bowl neatly in the exact center, served up a buttered piece of hard cinnamon toast for each one of us, refilled the coffee cups yet again, and sat down with a sigh. "I will take a load off these feet," she said as she did whenever she sat down with her coffee. In truth, those feet did need a rest. I rarely saw her quiet. Like the perpetual motion machines Miss Loney had described to us in science class, Mrs. Laitinen moved constantly, making beds, dusting, sweeping, shaking rugs, scrubbing floors and counters, washing windows, washing clothes, ironing, cooking, and baking. Experiencing a pang of guilt for having skipped out on my morning jobs, I apologized. The Stembers were so very fortunate to have her. I hoped they knew that. I certainly did.

But I did not consider myself quite so fortunate when I heard what she had to say once her feet had been unloaded and my burst of enthusiasm had run out.

"You are setting yourself up for some big trouble, missy," she told me bluntly, "and for some big disappointment."

"How so?" I queried, stirring sugar into my coffee, trying not to look askance at her words. She was, after all, the kindest of elders.

"My dear child," she said, shaking her head and dunking her cinnamon toast into her coffee, "how in heaven's name did you put together such wild ideas, and how could you possibly prove them? And who on earth will believe you?"

The large bowlful of oatmeal I had just consumed landed in my stomach with a thud, turned itself around heavily, and solidified.

"Mr. Savolainen will believe me," I insisted stoutly, and a voice from the door attested to its truth.

"I do believe you, child," Mr. Savolainen affirmed, doffing his hat and cane. Mrs. Laitinen made motions toward serving him at the dining room, but he joined us at the kitchen table, accepting a cup of coffee but waving off the cinnamon toast. "I do believe you," he repeated, adding generous amounts of sugar and some of the fresh cream Mrs. Laitinen made a special trip downstairs to the ice box to get, "but when I awoke this morning, I faced the day with the same mindset that Mrs. Laitinen is preaching to you. I am not sure whether anyone in Ely will believe any of our hypotheses."

I pushed my coffee away, but he drank his with relish, thanking Mrs. Laitinen for the fresh cream, then asserting, "We need proof, child. Absolute proof. Not conjectures. Not hypotheses. Not guesses. Proof."

"What more proof," I maintained stoutly, though my veneer had cracked, "than that Uncle Charles is dead and his money has disappeared?"

Mr. Savolainen's silence spoke volumes.

I tried by sheer repetition to change his mind. "And if it's in the paper, it must be true, mustn't it? They couldn't print lies!"

The silence continued, dousing my enthusiasm like baking soda on a stove fire. Though I hated it, I honored the truth of that silence. "Then we just give up?" My voice broke. "And go home? Empty-handed?"

Mrs. Laitinen got up to begin dinner preparations—*karijalan paisti*, it looked like. Taking lengths of veal and pork from the brown butcher's paper, she began by cutting them into chunks, which she put into a heavy cast iron dutch oven without browning them first. She wielded the sharp knife with the hand of a butcher, swiftly, surely.

I could think of other uses for that knife.

"No, we will not give up." Mr. Savolainen had finished his coffee, and he too was looking at the knife. "But I fear that this victory cannot be won by direct attack. Stealth may be needed. Stealth and . . . strategem. Here is my plan." His last few sentences had been spoken in a whisper.

Mrs. Laitinen and I both leaned forward.

"We need to spook out the guilty parties," he began. "We must make them believe that we know something that will implicate them, that will involve them in those two events, Uncle Charles' death . . ."

"Murder." I said it outright for the first time.

"Probably murder," he agreed for the first time, adding, "and the disappearance of the money."

"Theft." Neither word was strong enough. I tried again. "Grand larceny, perhaps." That sounded a good deal more serious.

"That is step one for today," Mr. Savolainen agreed.

Mrs. Laitinen brandished the knife at us, her eyes as fierce as its sharp point. "Mr. Savolainen, I have no right to speak to you this way, but I do care about this child, and what you are planning is dangerous. The child could be hurt. *You* could be hurt." She looked around the kitchen, tiptoed to the door and checked the stairwell, returned and leaned across the table, her ample bosom heaving. She whispered, "Things have happened in this town, things that people do not want to talk about. There have been babies found . . . dead . . . where they should not be. And three men," she looked around nervously, "at least three men have disappeared. Two from Winton just last winter. The newspapers never wrote about it,

173

but some of us know. The old-timers know. We stick together, and we know."

Mr. Savolainen did not look at all surprised. Setting his coffee cup aside and leaning back with his fingers forming that steeple of contemplation, he looked first at Mrs. Laitinen and then at me, "And so it is all right not to do anything?"

"It is dangerous to do anything!" Mrs. Laitala looked affronted, but afraid. She shivered.

So did I, but I stood up stoutly and placed my hand on Mr. Savolainen's shoulder. "I'm not afraid," I started to say. But honesty prevailed, and I amended the assertion: "Well . . . I am. But I don't have any choice. For Ma's sake and Lil's, for Uncle Charles' sake, for pity's sake, for my own, too," I declaimed, a bit caught up by my own fervor. "I do not have any other choice."

"Hear, hear," Mr. Savolainen responded. "No, we do not have any other choice," he repeated although he did pat Mrs. Laitinen on the shoulder as if granting her understanding if not agreement. "We shall first involve the authorities. After what I said to Mrs. Juola yesterday," he admitted to both of us, "I wondered why we had not done that in the first place. We shall begin with the authorities," he repeated. Taking up his hat and cane, he led the way.

Obviously my position in this household had been changed again — from servant girl to . . . detective? Whatever Mr. Savolainen decreed! Grabbing my schoolbag, I followed him, throwing a kiss back toward Mrs. Laitinen, scrambling down the stairs in my haste not to be left behind, but achieving some measure of decorum as he courteously motioned me to precede him through the store, out the door, and up the street toward the bank.

Mr. M.K. Niemi, the bank president, who condescended to check the records himself without motioning for a clerk, confirmed that the amount of money withdrawn had exceeded one thousand dollars. "$1,256.89, to be exact," he said, writing the sum on a slip of paper.

We brought the slip of paper to Chief of Police Barth Coffey, who listened to our story without comment, largely I was sure, because he was impressed with Mr. Savolainen. But though Mr. Coffey scratched his ear and pulled his nose and owned that there might be something up at that, there was not, he finally decided, an adequate basis for any investigation. "Men come and men go," he affirmed. "They live and they die. Sometimes there's a reason for it. Sometimes not. Sometimes it's better just to leave it alone."

That seemed to be the official stance.

We sighed as we left his office, back on square one, still on our own. Systematically, then, we checked the Smith Jewelry Company. Still closed. We revisited the Lakeview Hotel. Young Mr. Smith, the bank clerk, had not returned. We went back to the Juola Boarding House. Mrs. Juola was out.

When we returned to the Stembers, there was a response to a note Mr. Savolainen had sent to the honorary Dr. G.T. Harris, the mortician who had prepared Uncle Charles' body for burial, inviting him to meet us for luncheon as soon as he had completed his daily tasks. I shuddered to think of what they might be.

In the dining room of the Forest Hotel, Mr. Savolainen had suggested. "Better to get him off of his home turf," Mr. Savolainen explained to me, "and to have him break bread with us and make it clear that I can pay. Puts us at an advantage, you see."

I did.

Mr. Savolainen and I met the honorary Dr. Harris in the lobby, and our friendly waiter ushered us quickly into the dining room and to an empty table. After we ordered, Dr. Harris, apprised of our concerns, owned that he had done no autopsy on Charles Brosi. "No family or friend requested it," he explained. He said that since there had been no previous evidence of heart trouble, the death could have been deemed suspicious had there been any indication of ill use or misconduct. "But there was not," he concluded. "Mr. Brosi died in bed. His heart stopped beating, and he died. It happens," he shrugged, digging into the fresh apple pie our accommodating waiter had provided.

Mr. Savolainen moved sections of pie around on his plate, trying, it seemed, to fit the cut pieces back into a whole. "Could a death be induced by an external cause without marks being left upon the body?" he asked, his tone so neutral as to be completely inoffensive.

"Of course," the honorary Dr. Harris answered with some impatience. "Suffocation, perhaps, or an overdose of laudanum or strong drink such as would cause the systems to depress. Did the man about whom you are inquiring imbibe alcoholic beverages? Was he a user of laudanum?"

Mr. Savolainen looked at me.

"Not at all." I was grateful that this, at least, I knew and knew absolutely. Neither he nor Pa drank. Both had, in fact, voluntarily joined the Vesi Temperance Societies in Ely and Virginia respectively. I figured that would cover laudanum, too.

The good Dr. Harris shrugged again. "Well, it wouldn't be the first death that happened under suspicious circumstances," he commented, "especially in this town. Hmmphf. We've got more saloons than there are school buildings or stores." Leaning toward us, checking to see who was sitting at the nearby tables, he confided, "You would not believe how many knife wounds I have sewn up just during these last few months so that the corpses would be presentable. I have been called upon many, many times to provide significant cosmetic correction before the viewing. The Finns, especially, you know." He glanced around significantly. "They all carry knives."

You digress, I wanted to tell him. *What does a knife wound have to do with Uncle Charles' death at all? You yourself told us there was no evidence of foul play.* But I kept still.

He got the message, nonetheless. "Be that as it may, however," he concluded, standing up abruptly. "I can offer you no further assistance. I was called upon after Mr. Brosi's unfortunate demise to perform the necessary, appropriate, and final act of respects due the body of any deceased personage. I saw no reason to question the deputy coroner's analysis of time or cause of death. Both seemed plausible."

It was of no use to press him. Officialdom's stance remained firm.

Mr. Savolainen's words of appreciation salved the situation as did his suave handling of the check, but another door had clearly closed. We would get no help from that avenue.

"Do not despair, child," Mr. Savolainen said when he returned, the honorary Dr. Harris, mortician, having been ushered out and the bill paid, sitting down at last to eat the pie. "We are making progress."

Progress? I wanted to scoff. *You call this progress? It seems as if we are going around in circles, accomplishing nothing.*

"We are stirring things up, child, stirring things up," he explained to me patiently. "The bees will be buzzing."

"I hope they don't bite," I commented gloomily, pushing the pieces around with my fork.

"Oh, they will. They will. We just have to make sure they bite the right person. Eat now," he admonished.

The nature of his equivocal response escaped me, but I devoured the last pieces of pie with relish nonetheless. At that point, they were the only pieces over which I had any control.

Chapter Nineteen

"Reinforcements"

"The gypsies are coming! The gypsies are coming!"

Through the heavily curtained windows of the dining room of the Forest Hotel, through the double doors standing open to the lobby, we could just barely hear the cries.

Throwing down my napkin and just barely remembering to excuse myself, I raced unceremoniously out to Chapman Street. Sure enough, there were the caravans, the vardos, lumbering down an empty street, as familiar to me as my own home. Most everyone else had cleared away from the adjoining sidewalks, and every child within sight or hearing had been whisked out of sight and hearing so that my single figure standing at attention on the boardwalk running almost a foot above the street—cement sidewalks had been built thus far only on Sheridan—could not possibly have been missed.

Nor was it. By the time I made it outside, the grandfather, leading the horses pulling the first of the vardos, halfway down the hill already, was almost out of earshot. But it seemed to me that he was eyeing the sidewalks with a particular intensity.

The last of the vardos looked like the one I linked to "my" family. Sure enough, sitting on the small back balcony in the opening between the balusters, painted bright green and gold to match the swirls on the horse emblem on the bottom of the door, sat the girl of the brown eyes.

My eyes met hers as the vardo passed, and I recognized her attempts to pass along a message although I had not the background in Rom or in their secret signals to grasp the message easily.

But she was clever, that one. Her hands made a charade of the words so clearly that I understood the "where" if not the "when" of the call. I was to come to the encampment, to follow the vardos if possible. At that I shook my head. If it were not—Her face mirrored my disappointment. —I was to come when I could to . . . the tip . . . to the end . . . to the point. It was one of those words, reinforced with finger touches and arrowed gestures. The point that was . . . I could not understand . . . the point that was—She sifted something through her fingers. It looked like . . . SAND! As I nodded, she laid her head on folded hands suggesting sleep.

Jumping with delight, I nodded my head, mouthed the word "tonight," and mirrored her gestures with ones of my own. I was to go to a sandy point. Even though I had been in Ely less than a week, I had heard of the recreation area maintained by Oliver Iron Mining down the hill from the Pioneer Mine, where groves of trees grew in shady profusion on a peninsula of land extending out into Shagawa Lake. Sandy Point.

The gypsies would not be allowed to stay there long, I knew. The constabulary would roust them out and away as soon as could be. But unwritten law and custom and long-established practice usually prevailed, giving a gypsy band a twenty-four hour bye were they to break no laws and create no disturbances. After all, the services they offered—the horses, the tinkers, even the entertainment—constituted a welcome break in a life that tended to fall if not into outright boredom then certainly into what Eino's notebook called prosaic routine. If the cost included a few missing chickens, some inhabitants of the environs of Ely considered them well lost.

I had a bit of time, then, that afternoon and night, at least, I thought, as Mr. Savolainen took up position behind me in an attitude of unwarranted protection.

"What was all that about?" he asked.

"Help," I answered. "We may have just enlisted reinforcements."

I did not see any of the gypsies again that day. But Mr. Savolainen and I were busy. We made two more fruitless rounds of visits to the Lakeview Hotel and the Smith Jewelry Company and the boarding house, partially to make arrangements to have Uncle Charles' trunk shipped to Ma in Kinney with a note saying that I was fine, not to worry, we were just finishing our business in Ely, partially to look for Mrs. Juola.

But the three members of Ely's citizenry whom we sought—Mrs. Juola and the two Mr. Smiths—had stepped off the board, so to speak, and vanished, although a further visit to the ticket master at the depot confirmed that no passenger tickets had been purchased by buyers of their ilk for any of the return trips to Duluth since Mr. Savolainen arrived.

Ostensibly, then, the three remained still in the area. But where?

Chief of Police Barth Coffey did not seem overly concerned when we revisited him in the late afternoon. "People come and they go," he mused as if it were an original observation on humankind, an aphorism or a time-honored adage, even a commandment perhaps. He liked it so much he said it again: "They come and they go. Why, I've known some to rent boats and canoes and head out on the lakes for the whole summer. Not unusual."

At Mr. Savolainen's generous offer of fiscal assistance to the Policemen's Benefit Program, however, Chief of Police Barth Coffey did agree to a search of the Smith Jewelry Company, one he could justify as "police protection to uninhabited premises," were questions to be raised.

But except for the boxes of new stock, largely unopened, the premises were vacant.

The hired help at the Juola's confirmed Mrs. Juola's continued absence, but, they said, she often spent afternoons and evenings, sometimes days at a time "away." The old man who worked in the kitchen added vaguely, "That is nothing new." Sighing, he talked not to us but to the stew simmering on the wood stove for the evening meal, "*Ei se auttaa.*"—"It doesn't help," then quickly looked around to make sure she had not metamorphosed behind him.

Only the proprietress of the Lakeview Hotel evinced any sign of concern: "Young Mr. Smith did not seem well, did not seem well at all, when last I saw him."

Chief of Police Barth Coffey found nothing suspicious in Young Mr. Smith's room, however, and adamantly refused to grant us permission to join him in his search.

If Mrs. Juola were the queen bee and the Smith brothers the workers, perhaps she had already stung one or both to death, I thought to myself as we headed back toward No. 6 East Sheridan. I rather enjoyed the parallel. Miss Loney had made much of the life cycle of the bee.

With Mr. Savolainen at the Forest Hotel, I ate my dinner in the kitchen. I didn't mind. As time went on, I had found the Stembers' company less and less congenial. Since Mrs. Laitinen was busy serving, I did more finger tapping than eating during the dinner hour, earlier than usual because of the Mantels' party, and I was thinking all the time.

Mr. Savolainen concurred with my opinion of the Stembers, an implicit rather than explicit agreement understood between us but never verbalized. I think he might have severed the connection had the opportunity presented itself. But at the time, he needed the Stembers. He was way too busy to mind the Ely store himself, a fact which I believed he faced with some equanimity. Life in Virginia doubtless also had its prosaic moments. In fact, there had been times when I had sensed that he found this whole experience immensely entertaining. He had thrown himself into the fray with a wholehearted enthusiasm which, in moments when grief ebbed, I wholly shared. Although I shamed to admit it, this detecting business was a lot more fun than housework, even more fun than school. My only regret was the vocabulary notebook, but gradually, as the occasion warranted, I was consulting it again. At any rate, Mr. Savolainen was an able, willing, and supportive companion, more like a friend or an uncle than a Virginia businessman. He made it easy for me to accept help. But I was grateful for those times when it was necessary for him to accept help from me.

He did, most willingly, when, just after dark, the Stembers gone and Mrs. Laitinen busy with the dishes, we headed stealthily past the depot and across the railroad tracks toward the Pioneer Mine and, beyond it, the peninsula called Sandy Point.

Even without street lights, the path circling the iron ore pit leading to the Pioneer Mine was open, clear, easy to follow, worn smooth by the feet of miners coming and going from their homes up Finn Hill or elsewhere in town. The mine area itself was fairly well lighted, and we slunk past, keeping ourselves in the shadows.

Past the mine buildings down the hill toward the lake, however, the situation changed. Although there was a track of sorts, it was blurred by tall stands of pines that laid shadows on the land even at midday. It was hard not to wonder what lurked within those shadows. Moreover, Mr. Savolainen's considerable financial and business acumen did not extend to either husbandry or forestry, and my capacity as a guide met its early demise as we began the descent from the mine site toward Shagawa Lake. He held onto his cane and onto me, and I held onto him, and between us, we found every possible root and rock suitable for tripping and stumbling.

We really had no idea where we were going. The trees were so tall and the underbrush so thick I was gradually losing any sense of direction.

Just as I was about to suggest that discretion might be the better part of valor and perhaps we should turn back, however, we heard a voice coming toward us, singing. Thankfully, the grandfather had anticipated our difficulties and sent us a guide whom I knew and trusted. Just around the first bend in a jog of the trail that ultimately led straight down to the beach, the girl of the brown eyes materialized with pats and assurances, largely unspoken—I sensed she was still working her way into English— but with such clear marks of sincere affection in her hugs and pats that I felt as if I were heading home.

Mopping his brow and wielding his cane like a blindman, Mr. Savolainen did not share my joy. His spectacled eyes did not provide him good night-time vision. But that was not the only problem. From the hesitancy of his step and the many pauses he made ostensibly to get his bearings, I gathered that he believed us to be walking openly and willingly into what he no doubt considered, as all gorgios did, the very heart of an enemy camp. All of our society's popular beliefs and official actions suggested— seemingly proved—that we were in serious jeopardy, he at worst of being killed or ransomed for his not inconsiderable wealth, at the very least of being robbed, I of being captured and taken away to wherever gypsies took children, to be sold into slavery or forced, like Oliver Twist, into a life of theft and degradation.

He didn't say any of this, of course, but every ounce of his being oozed worrisome objections verging on fear. I don't know exactly how I knew this, but I did. To his credit, though he had had to work hard to contain his skepticism when he had listened to my account of the time I spent with the gypsies, he had swallowed his distaste for this venture like a bitter but necessary pill.

I knew it would do no good to reassure him, though I did keep a tight hold of his hand. I too had been the victim of the tales. I too had experienced the trepidation. He could not help but feel singularly out of his league and out of his depth, out of control, and—though he would never have admitted it—frightened.

Thus, I served as protectress. I drew him along, his hand in mine, my arm through his, until we reached the encampment.

The vardos, drawn into the familiar semicircle, were lighted by the central cooking fire, over which hung blackened cauldrons of aromatic stew. The horses had been tethered off in a meadow, and the family was gathered around the fire, waiting. Even the dogs were quiet and contained, for which I was deeply grateful. The grandfather had remembered my fear.

The grandfather greeted me with warmth, Mr. Savolainen with an old-world courtesy that lacked nothing despite its air of authority. One of the daughters seated Mr. Savolainen on a cushion and offered him a cup of something strong to drink, perhaps coffee, perhaps not.

I was grateful that he did not shrink from either the cushion or the cup, accepting both with at least a semblance of pleasure and trust.

It was enough.

He was, in return, first accepted and then ignored.

The grandfather seated me by his side and addressed me instead. "You have found your Uncle Charles."

"Yes." I curled up on a cushion and reached my hands out to the fire. The night was warm, but I needed to feel its heat to reassure myself that I was there. The grandfather poured me a cup of tea with his own hand. I breathed its aroma and sipped, sitting quietly.

The grandfather poured himself some tea and waited. Like the fire, his presence warmed me, comforted me, nurtured me. I had to force myself not to relax completely under the spell of such simple magic. It was . . . alluring. But this was not the time.

I forced words out into the stillness. "I have honored the place where his body rests with my tears and with such offerings as were open to me," I continued slowly, my soul interposing ceremony where it felt the Rom sought it. "I have searched for what he left behind. I believe it his will to have his possessions cherished by those he cherished."

"But you have not found satisfaction in the search." As always, his eyes were keen, though I felt their softness as they studied my face. As always when he spoke, the others were silent.

I answered fully, explaining the circumstances, the actions we had taken, the conclusions we had drawn, the efforts we had made, the bottle-necks we had faced, the despair we had felt, including Mr. Savolainen explicitly in the "we" so as to make our situation completely clear.

The grandfather watched Mr. Savolainen closely as I spoke, weighing and measuring. By the time my tale was told and Mr. Savolainen had seconded its veracity and passed the grandfather's inspection, the grandfather's decision had been made.

"We shall accept the stranger into our camp and give help to our sister," he announced to the family.

The family did not respond with words. None were needed, for the grandfather's decisions were law. But I could feel a drawing together of that circle, with Mr. Savolainen included within its bond as was I, and some of the weight of the world lifted from my shoulders.

"First, we shall send a vardo to Winton in search of your father. Do you seek to accompany its people? You may do so in safety." The assurance was absolute.

"I do," I replied firmly, my response also absolute.

"We do," Mr. Savolainen amended.

"That should be done now. Immediately. For should you return to Ely at this time, you may yourselves be at risk."

Mr. Savolainen looked keenly at the grandfather, and the look was returned, but no further explanation was offered, and Mr. Savolainen had better sense than to ask for one.

The grandfather motioned to the parents of the girl of the brown eyes, and immediately they set to work, he to hitch the horses, she to pack their share of food and utensils and cushions. The girl of the brown eyes reached out her hand to me, and I clasped it, fighting back tears. It was good to be the child once more. It was good to be told what to do.

Mr. Savolainen stood up, shook the grandfather's hand, expressed a "thank you" that clearly came from the heart, and like me awaited further instructions.

By the time the moon had fully risen, he and I and the girl of the brown eyes had been tucked into the vardo, wrapped in quilts laid upon cushions, and encouraged to rest. "By the time you awaken," we were told simply, "we shall be in Winton, and there we shall execute the grandfather's plan."

That we did not know the details of the plan was insignificant at that moment. It was enough for us to believe.

When we awoke from our rest, the vardo having lurched to a stop, the sun had, in fact, arisen. The father was already dressed in his gorgio business suit. As he explained the plan, the mother offered toilet articles to Mr. Savolainen so that he could wash and shave and comb his hair.

"We must breach the ramparts of the St. Croix Lumber Company's general offices," the father began, standing at attention, his hands behind his back. The mother brushed Mr. Savolainen's coat. We paid close attention.

"In the guise of attorneys come from Duluth, we will tell them that we are newly arrived on the morning train in search of the beneficiary of a not inconsiderable sum of money, recently bequeathed him and sent him from Finland. It will be in the best interest of the lumber company offices, we shall indicate, to facilitate the financial transaction since the beneficiary, Knute Pietari Brosi, who may perhaps be one of their workmen, might well be interested in investing some percent of his inheritance in the lumbering industry."

The father could almost outdo Mr. Savolainen with his air of aristocratic and totally natural hauteur. It did not hurt, either, that he could speak fluent Finnish, French and, I gathered, Italian and Slovenian as well as English either with or without a slightly British accent. "But not Croatian," the mother admitted apologetically, when I commented on that fact.

"And I?" asked the mother.

"Ought the saloons be checked?" the father asked me.

I discounted the possibility of Pa's being in or living above any of the seven saloons. He abhorred the noise and the smoke and shunned the libations.

Thus, the father said, my "mother" should direct herself to the boarding houses in the guise of a leading figure in the Minnesota Christian Temperance Movement seeking support for the establishment of a chapter in Winton, separate from the one in Ely. The pitch was likely to earn her both approbation and information.

The girl of the brown eyes and I were assigned to the schoolhouse.

When we were ready to go, we stood for inspection. "'*Bien*'— good," said the father, studying the four of us. Mr. Savolainen looked as if he had stepped out of a haberdashery. The mother and daughter and I could have posed for the Chicago Mail Order Catalog. From somewhere, new school outfits had been unearthed, and though I still wanted a bath and a shampoo, at least on the surface I looked presentable. We weren't overdressed, of course. But our wash dresses were made of good gingham, mine blue, hers red. In spite of our dark stockings and shoes, I felt elegant, for the yoke had three insertions of embroidery and there was a wide ruffle over our shoulders with embroidered insertions and edges, and the ribbon bow for our hair matched the trimming at our neck, waistband, and cuffs. The mother was more severely dressed, as befitted her role, in a black ladies' Canton Sailor Hat, a black silk Eton jacket over a black and white stripe percale waist trimmed in white embroidery, and a black street skirt interlined at the bottom with crinoline. Only the tips of her black kid dress boots showed as she walked. In all, she looked the very epitome of the Christian Temperance movement.

Leaving the vardo well secreted in the woods, we approached Winton on foot, arriving at the depot at the same time as the morning train from Ely. We joined the passengers who disembarked, some on vacation heading into the woods, some returning from various business ventures, some coming to seek employment. Mr. Savolainen and I followed the family's lead, and somehow they managed to integrate all of us into the group just as if we had been in the train all along.

The girl of the brown eyes and I kept our eyes open for children—it was time for the school day to start—and followed the little ones and big ones who were all trekking in the same direction. Although we caught a few sideways glances, strangers tended to come and go so frequently, families moving in and out, that no one remarked us especially, and we looked pretty much like everyone else.

Presenting ourselves at the principal's office, we curtsied and applied for admission, explaining that our parents had just come to the Ely-Winton area seeking work and, not wishing us to miss any more days of school, begged that we be enrolled as interim students until they could accompany us to make formal application.

"We know it is close to the end of the school year," I added. "We are hoping to get the summer's assignments so that we do not fall behind."

The girl of the brown eyes stood silently by while I did the talking. But her eyes spoke volumes about her concern for learning, and her straight back and folded hands, when seated, marked clearly her cognizance of correct decorum.

It is strange, I thought, as the principal ushered us down the hall to the first-through-fourth grade room, how easily adults can be manipulated by children who know how to speak correctly and behave nicely. How strange that so few children have learned that lesson! How few ever grasp its relevancy to the accomplishment of desired goals!

Before the morning had advanced past opening exercises, we were seated side by side, two to a desk. By the end of the morning recess, we had established connections with the most effective chain of informational dissemination known to man—eavesdropping children.

By lunchtime, when we joined the other children heading "home" for lunch, we knew that Knute Pietari Brosi was not rooming with any of the families in Winton whose children were in the first-through-fourth grades. When we rejoined the mother and the father and Mr. Savolainen outside of the Finnish Temperance Hall at the top of the hill, a spot so obvious that none of us could possibly have missed it or lost our way, the mother further established that Knute Pietari Brosi had not moved into Johnsons' Boarding House on River Street, the largest of the many open in town. The men had also eliminated the St. Croix Lumber Company as a possible employer. But they did have a lead. Swallow & Hopkins had recently run a spur railroad to a small saw mill operated by two Finnish brothers who did their own hiring and logging in the farming community of Embarrass, and a man fitting the description of Knute Pietari Brosi had been seen working at that mill.

Picnicking on the bread and cheese and soda pop Mr. Savolainen had purchased from the River Street Saloon, we first compared notes and then agreed that before we left, we needed to make at least two additional stops. The girl of the brown hair and I were to go to the Post Office and leave a letter for Pa just in case the business office had been wrong and he was in the employ of the St. Croix Lumber Company but out on the lakes or in the woods rather than in Winton. Both the father and Mr. Savolainen asserted that such was unlikely, since the spring thaw had long since opened up the lakes for the winter's produce of harvested white pine to float or be guided toward the huge mill, the biggest they had ever seen. But it was unwise to leave even that small stone unturned.

The father and Mr. Savolainen planned to stop at the fire station down by the river and at the two-story sauna building across from Johnsons' Boarding House; the mother, to visit all of the smaller Finnish boarding houses, presenting herself still under the aegis of the Temperance Society.

"We shall meet again," the father directed, "at 4:32 when the afternoon train departs for Ely, appear to board it, and slip away to the vardo."

It was agreed.

I worked hard at the wording of my note, for I felt that my experiences in Ely had helped me to understand Pa at least a little, to consider his decisions with somewhat less asperity, to recognize his good intentions, and to come to some terms somewhat with his inability to effect them. He loved Ma, but he could not live with her. He loved Lil and me, but it was not in him to take care of us. His overweening pride, his unutterable frustration, the lure of his own dream worlds always in the end turned him away. But I sensed he meant well, and I trusted that, given the strength of our need, he might at least for a time do the right thing. Thus, I wrote the following:

Dear Pa,

Uncle Charles is dead, and his money has disappeared. Ma and Lil and I are destitute.

Since you have been named Uncle Charles Brosi's beneficiary, the sum of one hundred dollars will be paid to you by John Porthan at the office of the Finnish Accident and Sick Benefit Association in Ely upon your arrival there in person. Please go there as quickly as ever you can and then come home with the money, or there will be neither home nor family left.

Sincerely, your loving daughter,
Ilmi Marianna Brosi

The signature gave me pause. Should I, I wondered, use the name "Marion"? Perhaps not, a small voice within me answered. Perhaps it would be better to remind him that I was not yet an adult, that I was still a child. It might remind him that he was still a father.

We met as prescribed at 4:32. No one at the fire station, no one at the sauna building, and no one in the other boarding houses had ever heard of Knute Pietari Brosi. Thus any hope of making a Winton connection rapidly dissipated, though there remained the possibility of an Embarrass link.

As the vardo carried us back toward Ely that night, our hearts were heavy, but given the nature of the gypsies and the fact that we were together, Mr. Savolainen and I no longer alone, hope remained alive.

Chapter Twenty

"Truth and Consequences"

Meanwhile, in Ely, the grandfather too had been at work. Thanks to the very nature of the gypsy way of life, at least one member of The Family had been able to make contact with virtually every household within the city limits and with virtually every business person. How this could have been done I did not question, nor did I question the results of the survey. Thanks to the grandfather and The Family, Young Mr. Smith had been found.

That was the good news.

The bad news was where he had been found. As the proprietress of the Lakeview Hotel had feared, he was ill. But he was not in the Shipman Hospital, which could have made our access to his bedside fairly simple. He was in the pest house, the precursor to the planned detention hospital, under strict quarantine. His illness was the dreaded Spanish influenza.

The elder Mr. Smith and the redoubtable Mrs. Juola had not yet surfaced. The grandfather believed them to be together at a cabin or a campsite on Burntside Lake, just south of Ely. A boat had been rented in the elder Mr. Smith's name and not returned. Thus, the grandfather hypothesized, they were either celebrating their victory or making themselves scarce pending my departure from the Ely area or both. They could be justifiably certain that neither Mr. Savolainen nor I could continue our quest indefinitely. They were also, no doubt, living in hope that their being out of sight would also put them out of mind. They had run to hole like foxes under pursuit. Mr. Savolainen admitted to the grandfather that his loud baying the day we visited the Juola Boardinghouse may well have been as much the cause of their making themselves scarce as any desire they may share for—he looked at me, paused, then finished, delicately—co-habitation.

I rolled my eyes at that one. How could adults be so simple as to think that the larger and more general the term the more limited our understanding? No wonder I had chosen to study vocabulary! How short-sighted were students who did not!

"I know how I can get into the pesthouse," I commented to the group in general, for the grownups were making hard work of that one.

The grandfather's tendency was to look askance at a child's intercession into adult discussion, but as always he treated me differently as if I were an exception. "Yes, my child?"

"I shall develop the influenza."

They looked at me blankly.

"Or, at least, I shall develop its symptoms."

It took the rest of the night and most of the morning to convince them all that I was right, but reason finally prevailed, as it is wont to do, or perhaps it was just my perseverance.

Mr. Savolainen said it should be he. So did the grandfather and the other adults in The Family. But my decision was absolute, my resolution adamantine. My family had been violated; I must effect revenge.

Eventually the grandfather agreed. "This girl is a gypsy to the soul," he said. He and Mr. Savolainen also agreed to my suggestion that both the minister of the Finnish Evangelical Lutheran Church, D. Ruotsalainen, and Chief of Police Barth Coffey be invited to appear at the pest house when we got through to Young Mr. Smith to make sure that whatever he said was given moral and ethical and legal validation.

"Officialdom," I thought ruthlessly, "will have to be represented. When they hear the confession first hand, they cannot refuse to act."

By afternoon of that same day, having been carefully dosed with a variety of medicinal herbs calculated to create symptoms similar to those exhibited by sufferers of the real influenza—the grandmother knew exactly what to give me and how much—I was deposited back at Stembers. Mrs. Laitinen was informed of developments, and I proceeded to become very ill.

My head ached as if it were exploding. My bowels and my stomach loosened so rapidly and so fully that I could not reach the outhouse in the alley in time but had to rely upon the night-pot for one end of me and a bucket and series of towels for the other. I was alternately so hot that I could not stand covers then so cold my teeth chattered.

Dr. Shipley was sent for, of course, and the Stembers maintained a resolute vigil well away from the sickroom. Thank goodness we had included Mrs. Laitinen in the plan. She was of immeasurable help, maintaining a calm demeanor no matter the mess. But she looked very worried anyway, and Mr. Savolainen did not need to make a pretense of his wringing of hands and pacing of floors.

At any rate, I really was sick, so sick, in fact, that I cannot remember to this day how I got to the pest house or what it looked like or who brought me there. But deep within myself I knew that I had managed to be admitted. I told myself over and over again that the symptoms would abate and vowed that, as soon as ever they did, my charge was to find and interrogate the Young Mr. Smith.

Influenza cases not having reached epidemic proportions, at least thus far, there were only a few patients in the pest house. One case of scarlet fever, isolated from all others, was visited only by nurses gowned and scrubbed and masked. A room full of children, all from one family, down with the chicken pox, cried and itched and cried some more. A baby wailed endlessly somewhere in the rear of the building, dying, the word was, from putrid sore throat, diphtheria. The Young Mr. Smith and I, the only two suffering, it seemed, with influenza, were kept in adjoining beds.

Poor Mr. Smith, I thought, as my symptoms gradually abated and I began to recover my wits sometime during the night. I blessed the grandmother, who had assured me that although the herbal infusion made the onset of illness extremely rapid and the symptoms very uncomfortable, its duration was definitely limited.

"But Mr. Smith still feels as sick as I did," I thought with some sympathy, "and since the only cure for influenza is survival, he will keep on being sick until he gets well of his own accord or dies."

During the moments when his moaning ceased and his breathing indicated that he was awake, I tried for a lucid connection.

"Mr. Smith," I whispered, "can you hear me?"

He groaned a hoarse "Yes."

"I presume that you do not wish to die with murder and theft on your conscience," I continued, coming straight to the point. It was no time to beat around the bush. He might at that very moment be dying.

"Wh-wh-what are you s-s-saying?" The stutter was not an affectation. I could tell I had shaken him to the core. "Wh-wh-o-o are y-you?"

His bed was surrounded by curtains, hung floor to ceiling, and so was mine. I could have been a ghost for all he knew.

It was tempting to try out that role. I could use a spectral voice and frighten him into a confession, threatening purgatory and hell should he withhold information. But that felt like a cheap trick, and I opted for honesty. "My name is Ilmi Marianna Brosi. My uncle, Charles Brosi, is the man you killed, and it is his money that you stole, and this situation must be rectified before you die, or you will burn in hell for all eternity." That last phrase was a bit extreme, I admitted to myself, but I was desperate enough to try anything. After all, he might be a Lutheran or a Catholic and believe it.

To tell the truth, I hoped he was and I hoped he did and I hoped he would.

"But I-I d-d-did not kill him!" He tried to scream the words, but his parched throat restricted him to a cracked croak.

"Someone did," I avowed. "He's dead, and his money is gone."

Silence followed that assertion. But I could hear his hands plucking at the sheets and his body thrashing back and forth under the covers. "P-p-please."

In spite of my anger, I remembered all too clearly how I had felt just hours before, and I could not completely withhold sympathy. "Look," I began in a less argumentative tone. "I loved my uncle. Ma and Lil and I are desperate. We need that money for food. Lil is eating ashes from the stove, for God's sake!" I did not usually allow myself the expletive. But needs must.

"P-p-please believe me," he repeated, separating the words for emphasis and trying to reach the curtain to pull it back, "I did not kill him."

"Then your brother did. Or Mrs. Juola."

"No, neither of them. Not my brother. Not *her* either."

I caught the sardonic inflection of the "her" and sympathized wholly.

"Nooo," he repeated, the sigh turning into a moan before it ceased. "It was the kitchen man, the hired help, and he did not mean to do it."

Silence thudded down. I shook with the force of the aftershock. My God, I wondered, and it was more prayer than curse, what is the truth of this?

191

I heard the nurse coming on rounds to administer laudanum to Mr. Smith and subsided. It did feel good to lie back on the pillow. My heart was thudding so that my chest hurt, and my stomach was cramping again. Opening my curtains next and taking a good look at me, she must have considered me improved, however, for she merely offered me a glass of water and went out again. I could have used the laudanum.

There was no sense in pursuing my questions. Mr. Smith fell asleep before she was out the door.

By the next time he awoke up, I was almost myself, out of bed, dressed and ready. Dr. Shipley had been apprised of the situation and had concurred with our plan, though reluctantly. Mr. Savolainen had known just how to move him: the Shipley Hospital needed more beds. Chief of Police Coffey and D. Ruotsalainen, pastor, also sat in high-backed chairs arranged around Mr. Smith's white iron bed.

When the young Mr. Smith awoke and saw us sitting like a jury or St. Peter's adjutant angels on Judgment Day, he blanched even whiter than the sheets, grayer than the sky on that dark and cloudy day. But he accepted the inevitable. Very slowly, with many interspersed groans and coughs, none of them faked—he really was very, very ill—he volunteered the whole of the story or as much of it as he knew, at least. Chief of Police Coffey opened an official looking pad and took notes. D. Ruotsalainen got up now and then to wipe Mr. Smith's face and pat his hands. Mr. Savolainen sat with both hands on his cane, and I . . . I hate to admit it, but I eventually curled back onto the bed I had been so quick to leave, wrapped myself in the blanket, and fought to contain moments of intense anger or dizziness or nausea interspersed with a kind of numbing pain and with unwilling, but perfidious sweeping waves of sympathy.

"We . . . they . . . had no idea . . . about the money, that is," he began, faltering. Taking a deep breath, he forged on, "My brother remembered that a man called . . . Charles Brosi . . . had bought some gifts from the jewelry store. He spent enough money there so that my brother made note of his name. 'A good customer' my brother called him. I'm sure he mentioned him to Mrs. Juola." Young Mr. Smith glanced at D. Ruotsalainen apologetically. "He told her most everything."

D. Ruotsalainen nodded. It was neither a unique nor an unfamiliar circumstance.

"Then that Tuesday . . . he—your uncle, Charles Brosi," he tried to look past the curtains to get to me, "he—did not go down to breakfast prepared to work his normal shift. Instead, he had on his Sunday suit. Mrs. Juola wondered . . . so she watched him when he left the boarding house long enough to see him go past Central . . . up the hill on Sheridan. She knew . . . something was up. When he got back much later that day, he took his trunk down from the attic, told her that he would be leaving the next day, ate his supper, and went to bed.

"That much Mrs. Juola told . . . my brother . . . when they . . . met . . . that night.

"I . . . I'm . . . not sure . . . exactly what happened then at the boarding house. But according to his bedmate . . . sometime during the night . . . your uncle . . . must have had some kind of a bad dream . . . or a seizure maybe?"

Dr. Shipley had joined us, standing a little apart, leaning on the door jam. Young Mr. Smith directed his question at him, and Dr. Shipley nodded. Such things were not unknown.

"The bedmate said he went . . . to Mrs. Juola's room . . . to ask her to get a doctor. Mrs. Juola wasn't there, of course. . . . She was gone . . . for the night . . . ." He paused for a while, perhaps recollecting where she had gone for the night, then gathered himself together and continued, "So the bedmate said he went down to the kitchen to ask the hired man to get the doctor . . . I am sorry . . . I don't know their names. . . . They're some unpronounceable Finnish garble."

My sympathy for him lessened.

"Anyway," he sighed again, "the bedmate told us later—or at any rate told my brother and Mrs. Juola—that the hired man had been drunk as usual, not passed out, but drunk. The two did go upstairs—according to . . . the bedmate—and hauled Mr. Brosi down. I figure they took his arms and legs and just kind of bumped him down the steps. That couldn't have been good for him, could it?" Again he looked at Dr. Shipley.

Again, Dr. Shipley nodded and shook his head.

"Then, according to what the bedmate said, he went back to bed to sleep . . . because he had the early shift next day. . . ."

Young Mr. Smith paused, struggling. Partly because of the facts, the words he had to say, partly because of the energy it was costing him to say them. More, perhaps, because of what they meant . . . to Uncle Charles, to me.

"Anyway . . . it seems that the hired man did try dragging him and got as far as the back door . . . but then the hired man did pass out. When

Mrs. Juola found the two of them late that night . . . in the early morning actually . . . she said, the hired man was still out cold, and Charles Brosi was still breathing but barely.

"She said she did call . . . she said she did call . . . for . . . she said it was the doctor . . . or did she say the coroner? I'm not clear on that," he insisted fervently, breathing harder, trying to hold his head up from the pillow so that he could make us believe him. "Maybe he had already stopped breathing and then she . . . well, anyway, someone did come . . . and he stayed for a long time. But it was too late by then. His breathing had already stopped."

By that time the pronoun reference had become impossibly jumbled, but we had no doubt about which "he" was which. Moreover, all of us around that bed knew that what the young Mr. Smith was telling us had to be the truth, insofar as he knew it. His words rang true, despite their raggedness, despite the difficulty we had sometimes hearing him and deciphering what he was desperately trying to say.

Then he struggled to sit up, pulled himself, in fact, by hanging onto the curtains, and gasped, "But please, please, believe me. I did not kill him!" The effort took everything out of him, and he sank back so exhausted we barely heard him breathe.

The doctor stepped in then, of course, took his pulse, shook his head at us, and motioned us out of the room.

A mumbled litany ran on and on from a barely audible voice: "Ask Mr. Brosi's bedmate. . . . Ask the hired man . . . or Mrs. Juola, even. . . . I didn't . . . I didn't . . . I'm innocent . . . of that wrongdoing . . ."

The doctor took a bottle of laudanum from his pocket and measured many drops of it into a glass before filling it with water and holding Mr. Smith's head up so he could drink. Mr. Smith quieted.

Although the men did get up, they only went as far as the door. I lay back, even when the doctor firmly motioned me out.

Instead I whispered, "I believe you" to the curtains he was pulling around young Mr. Smith. Then I did get up, eluded the doctor's grasp, approached the bed instead, and tried to make Mr. Smith meet my eyes. "But the money. What happened to the money? Is that the wrongdoing you are guilty of? Did you steal it?"

I know what I did seems cruel. When I look back on that moment, I am not even proud of it myself. But I had to know. I owed it to Uncle Charles, to Ma and Lil and Pa, and, yes, even to me. "What happened to the money?" I spaced the words out syllable by syllable and repeated them as loudly as I dared, given the fact that this was a place of illness.

It was all I could do not to lean over the bed and grab him and shake him.

All of his energy had dissipated, both from his voice and from his body. I could barely hear his reply.

"The money?" he asked. "What does it matter? He's dead."

Had I not, before, believed him to be innocent, at that moment I knew he was. He had not killed Uncle Charles, and he had not stolen the money. Yet he had been implicated in both actions. It was not just the influenza from which he was suffering. His illness was compounded by an insidious mixture of grief and guilt. Tears coursed weakly down his cheeks, like rain on parchment paper.

I wondered, cruelly, why the tears? Why the regret? He had not known Uncle Charles. Why did he grieve?

A small voice deep inside of me answered, "It is himself he mourns for." Not just because of his illness, not just because of Uncle Charles' death, the voice continued, but for another reason. Of what had he been culpable? What had been the extent of his own duplicity? If he had borne no responsibility for Uncle Charles' death, why the guilt?

Ignoring the whispers from the hall and the increasingly assertive motions of Dr. Shipley, urging me to leave, I plopped myself back on the chair, thinking as hard as I have ever thought in my life, feeling myself so close to the truth that nothing could have torn me from that room. Of what was the young Mr. Smith guilty, if it were not Uncle Charles' death? An idea flashed by, and I grabbed it. Did he consider himself guilty not because of anything he had done to Uncle Charles but because of something he had said to his brother and Mrs. Juola? Mr. Savolainen and I had established when we were at the bank that the young Mr. Smith had known about the withdrawal of the money.

The truth lay somewhere there. It must have been he who told his brother and Mrs. Juola. How else could they possibly have known?

And if she knew about the money when she returned home late that night or early morning, whichever, and found Uncle Charles gravely ill, then might she not have considered the benefits of allowing him to die? Whether by a sin of commission—what she did—or a sin of omission—what she did not do—she made sure that Uncle Charles did not survive the night. Moreover, instead of calling the doctor, she had called the deputy coroner, then filled him so full of alcohol that he later had to be hospitalized.

Uncle Charles had died not because of an overdose of alcohol or laudanum or because of suffocation or because of whatever seizure or illness had overtaken him that night but because of neglect. He had been hauled downstairs out of a warm bed onto the cold kitchen floor and left there to die. And Mrs. Juola had watched it happen and waited and made sure he got no help, no help at all, from anyone. She was a murderess in everything but deed. My hands clenched, and my face twisted with fury. I wanted to tear her limb from limb.

To what extent poor young Mr. Smith was, in fact, culpable I did not know. But there was no doubt that he considered himself guilty, whatever he had or had not done.

I stood vigil by his side all through that long day as the coma into which he slipped deepened imperceptibly, not just in case he awoke again, not just to ask him more questions, but because I refused to let another human being die alone as Uncle Charles had. I stood vigil by him as I had not stood vigil by Uncle Charles, and the tears I cried were for both of them, victims of someone else's greed. By afternoon even I knew that the young Mr. Smith would never lose the brief appellation that had differentiated him from his brother. By nightfall, there was only one Mr. Smith left in Ely, and it was from him that we must ultimately wrest the whole of the story.

I tried not to keep crying for the young Mr. Smith when we all left the pest house finally. I tried not to keep crying for Uncle Charles.

But all that seemed left was the grief—grief for all that Uncle Charles had lost, for he had deserved to experience the paradise of Zim—grief that he never knew happiness. Vagrant lines from the older kids' memorization of John Milton's *Paradise Lost* flitted through my mind. I mulled over the torments of lost happiness and lasting pain. I trusted that for Uncle Charles the pain had not been lasting. My grief was for his paradise, lost. Even though of all people he most deserved heaven, I could not find the faith within me to believe him there. He was dead. For eternity. To the world. To us.

And it was also for us that I grieved. Since he had come into our lives not all that long ago, months only, he had been the constant upon which all of our dreams had rested, the rock underlying their foundation, the hope for a kind of fundamental security that, given the nature of Pa, our family had sought in vain, and thus always lacked. It was not that Ma did not try. But she could not do everything. She could not provide us with the security of a paycheck and a home. Except for sewing, she had few saleable skills. And none of us was willing to have her market her other desirable qualities.

It came down, as far as Ma's financial support of us was concerned, to the fact that she had no education upon which to build any kind of financial security. Small wonder that school was all-in-all to me. Grimly I faced the fact that my love for learning, apart from the joy it had given me in and of itself, had a far less altruistic and far more practical and mundane base. Were I able to teach, I could support my family. Teaching salaries, although not large, were steady. And if I could earn not only a normal school degree but somehow someday a true college degree, other worlds would open to me.

Those were my thoughts as we trudged back to Stembers, for Mr. Savolainen had waited with me, sharing the vigil. Some of my concerns I spoke out loud, and he responded with a quotation from a poem he had read and memorized when he was in school. He said it had been written by Thomas Gray and was called "An Elegy Written in a Country Churchyard." He knew and liked country churchyards, he told me, and had learned the whole of the poem. Holding me, sometimes by the hand, sometimes by the waist, for I was feeling very weak, he quoted some of the stanzas to me. Tears ran down my face again as I heard about the "short and simple annals of the poor" who lived "Far from the madding crowd's ignoble strife, . . . Along the cool sequestered vale of life."

That was Uncle Charles in a way, I said. He loved the "cool, sequestered vale of life."

"And money isn't everything," Mr. Savolainen reminded me: "The boast of heraldry, the pomp of power, / And all that beauty, all that wealth e'er gave / Awaits alike the inevitable hour. / The paths of glory lead but to the grave."

"In Ma's case, unless I get an education," I answered him bluntly, "the path is leading there right now, not only for her but for Lil."

"I had no idea," he told me with deep regret.

And then when I could go no farther, we sat down on the edge of the boardwalk, and he held my hand while I told him everything. Not only about how little there was at home to eat but everything. For weeks I had set the question of those two misaligned dates—March 19 and May 4—resolutely out of my mind. Perhaps I had used my concern about Uncle Charles' whereabouts, or, in a larger sense, his fate, as an excuse to set my own questions and fears in abeyance.

"I don't know what I want," I sobbed to Mr. Savolainen as he patted my shoulder and listened. "Part of me wants . . . not Pa but another father. Maybe the difference between those dates means that what Pa is . . . is not in me. If my real father worked instead of dreaming, faced responsibilities rather than hiding from them, set goals and achieved them, if he gave those qualities to me, I can someday earn an education which will lead to security, not merely day-to-day survival for all of us, Ma and Lil and me. If . . ." I paused, heartbroken because for all of his frailties I could not completely disavow Pa.

"But I don't want to be accountable for those things in me which I fear came from him. If he is my father, the only answer is to separate myself from him forever. But I don't want to!" I sobbed. "I just want to accept him as he is and will always be . . . without caring. Without . . ." this was the hardest part, "wishing that he loved me."

This all came out in such a gush of words and tears that at the end I felt limp.

Mr. Savolainen looked as wretched as I. "For now, dear child," he finally said, helping me to stand, "may I ask you to try to file the dates and their meanings away into some dark corner of your mind where you need not think of them and let them rest?"

"I'll try," I sniffed. "But I can't completely disavow the feelings that creep in whether I want to give them names or not: Hurt. For all the love I've never felt free to give. Anger. For all the pain that has grown around that love and for all I have missed. Sorrow. For all that Pa and Ma and Lil and I—our family—could have been but are not and now will never be."

It was incredibly painful to attach words to feelings that had lain hidden within me for as long as I could remember. I had wrenched them out of some deep place where they had lived in darkness.

"I've tried to lock them in, but no matter how I try to keep the dark dungeon closed, the drawbridge flings itself open when I least expect it. It opened . . . during this long day's vigil. I'm sorry, Mr. Savolainen," I repeated over and over again as we walked in the back door of the Stembers and started up the stairs. "I'm sorry."

Then, in spite of his warm and comforting presence, the knowledge of it all—the loss of Uncle Charles, the mist surrounding my identity, the doubts about the future—all began to whirl around and around me like paper pieces flying in the wind. I tried to catch them, but they went too fast, and then I was whirling with them, around and around and around and down.

The doctor who came to recheck me did not think it was a recurrence of the "influenza." Mrs. Laitinen knew it was not. Mr. Savolainen knew too much and went back to wringing his hands and pacing. The Stembers stayed downstairs although they did allow me to be brought back up to their spare room.

The grandfather might have known without being told, but he and The Family were busy with other pursuits.

Once it was clear that the wringing of hands and the pacing were serving no useful purpose, Mr. Savolainen too became very busy, a part of my mind registered, with other pursuits.

But Mrs. Laitinen never left me. As I faded in and out of consciousness during the next hours . . . it may have been days . . . she was always there, holding my hand, bathing my face, murmuring soothing nonsensical sounds, singing old Finnish songs in a quiet monotone.

In my delirium, I felt the grandfather hold me as I cried. I heard him assure me that family comes first. I heard him promise to keep me safe.

In my dreams, Mr. Savolainen patted me on the shoulder and told me he could not be prouder of me if I were his own daughter.

Over and over again, as Mrs. Laitinen held me to her warm and ample bosom until her housedress was as wet and wrinkled as the schooldress I wanted to burn, she told me that I had done what I had to do, that I was a good, brave girl, that she loved me.

Even the Stembers condescended to utter words of condolence, from a distance, of course, both upon the death of Uncle Charles, informing them having been long delayed, and on this present suffering.

But I knew why I was ill. I knew within myself that I had been cruel, cruel to one who was suffering. I had shared his suffering, albeit for a brief time, and was sharing it again of my own volition. I had been cruel to one who had also put family first, who had lost himself in the doing.

I lost my self in the doing for a while, too, and too weak to care, left the rest of it to officialdom and to the adults who worked under the umbrella of justice.

Chapter Twenty-one

"Homecomings"

Later, I pieced together a summary of how the grandfather and
The Family had filled the hours and days of my illness. Their allotted time
having clearly elapsed, Chief of Police Barth Coffey and his men had
reminded them firmly to leave, which they did. But the vardos traveled no
farther south than Burntside Lake where, using the same kind of door-to-
door, campsite-to-campsite scouring done in Ely, The Family unearthed
Mr. Smith and Mrs. Juola.

At least, I believe they did, though the fact of the matter remains
a mystery to almost everyone.

The only absolute fact is that Mr. Smith and Mrs. Juola simply
appeared of a morning in the boat the elder Mr. Smith had rented. It was
tied to the dock of one of the boathouses in the cove down from Finn Hill.
As the boat was fastened to the dock so they were fastened to the seats of
the boat, securely fastened. With rope.

Chief of Police Barth Coffey collected them after receiving a brief
note, hand-delivered by a small boy from Finn Hill who could not identify its sender other than that he was tall and dark and spoke Finnish with
an unusual accent:

To Chief of Police Barth Coffey:
  Mr. Smith and Mrs. Juola have been returned to
Ely and can be found near one of the Finnish boathouses.

They have confessed in writing to the theft and use of the money Charles Brosi withdrew from the First State Bank and have offered, in lieu of imprisonment, to make restitution. Their confession is appended; leniency, suggested, since the money has been spent on stock for the Smith Jewelry Company and can be repaid only upon that company's reopening. Careful evaluation must guarantee the repayment of that which is owed to the estate of Charles Brosi.

There was no signature on the note, but the confession had been written, dated, and . . . unbelievably . . . even notarized by none other than John Porthan, who refused all attempts to elicit a detailed explanation of how, when, and where that occurred.

He only said that he felt that he owed something to members of The Family, who had saved two people he cared about, and that this was his way of repaying the debt.

Chief of Police Barth Coffey took the matter under advisement and gave his verbal assent to the option of restitution rather than imprisonment when the matter was brought before the judge, who also concurred. Thus, the Smith Jewelry Company did reopen rapidly during the time that I took up residence in another world, bounded by the four walls of the Stembers' back bedroom. Mr. Savolainen refused to hear of my being brought to the pest house, no matter what the Stembers said.

Outside, the wheels of the adult world continued to turn. During the hearing held in the judge's chambers, Mrs. Juola's hired man was called upon to give testimony about happenings the night of Uncle Charles' death. But even after much prompting—including verbal admonishings from the judge and liquid appeals from Mr. Savolainen—he never could remember exactly what had happened the night Uncle Charles died.

Oh, how I wish I had been sitting in the judge's chambers when the court turned to Mr. Smith and Mrs. Juola! Mr. Savolainen was there, of course, and he tried to give me a first-hand account of it all, but since he was neither a colorful nor a painstaking storyteller, he could not embellish the facts with details even had I been open to hearing them.

Most of the time I knew when he was sitting by my bed, and I grasped the intent of his monologue, which was designed both to allay my concerns and to retain my contact with reality. But he had to repeat it all for me later, because at the time I was no more capable of retaining the information than I was of sitting through the testimony. It all refused to connect. I refused to connect, even though Mr. Savolainen insisted afterward that he had laid the facts before me, such as they were.

It seemed that young Mr. Smith, having handled the withdrawal of Uncle Charles' money, had mentioned the transaction to his brother that same night, with some surprise that a miner could, even over a period of ten years, have amassed so large a sum in his savings account. It was a casual mention, mere dinnertime conversation, he must have thought. Of course, the young Mr. Smith had been warned when he took the job at the bank that information to which he was privy was to remain within the confines of the bank's walls, never to be discussed with the public. As an oath of secrecy, it ranked right up there, according to the Bank President M.K. Niemi, with the Catholic confessional. The bank's depositors must be able to trust their transactions to remain the kind of private knowledge shared in other circumstances with a doctor or a lawyer or a priest but never elsewhere.

Young Mr. Smith had obviously not considered his private conversations with his brother more than a slight bending of the rules.

His tragedy was that he did not, until it was too late, know his brother. Even less did he understand the extent of his brother's involvement with the shadowy Mrs. Juola.

The senior Mr. Smith had passed the information along to her, of course, as he did most everything during their evening trysts. Thus, she was well aware of the existence of that large sum of money when she returned to the boarding house the following morning to find two men on her kitchen floor—the hired man, passed out from drink, and Uncle Charles, comatose.

That the hired man tended to drink too much was common knowledge. But since he otherwise was a good worker and since his binges occurred at infrequent if regular intervals, Mrs. Juola had allowed him to remain in her employ. She had other more important concerns than mundane household chores.

It was an irony of fate that one of his drinking bouts coincided with Uncle Charles' illness.

At any rate, Mrs. Juola found them both when she got home early in the morning after a night spent with Mr. Smith, who had filed for bankruptcy because of his inefficient business practices and who was desperately struggling to find investors willing to set him up for a second go-around with the jewelry business. So far, there had been no takers, not even Mrs. Juola, who shared her favors much more willingly than she did her bank account.

No one else either at the boarding house or at the mine had known of Uncle Charles' plans. No one at the boarding house or at the mine had known about the money.

Mrs. Juola testified under oath that she had inquired at the mine office about survivors. She admitted she had found the name "Lillian" in his trunk and the name of a photographer in Virginia on one of the pictures. She had shared both pieces of information with the deputy coroner that sad morning. He had drunk deeply of the brandy preferred one who endured so difficult a job, had heaved a deep sigh about the unfortunate lonely nature of a bachelor's life, had made out and signed the death certificate, and had proceeded to continue to drink brandy until he forgot everything, including the unfortunate demise of Charles Brosi.

And why should he remember, I am sure he and Chief of Police Barth Coffey asked the court the morning of their appearance. Men died all the time in Ely. They came and they went. Some were buried in their mine clothes in unmarked graves because there was no one to care for their bodies or to mourn. It was the way it was, they attested, solemnly. There had been no reason for them to investigate.

"Mr. Smith and I assumed responsibility for his funeral," Mrs. Juola told the judge with some complacency before the court got into the matter of the money.

The judge praised them for their kindness.

Then the attorney hired by Mr. Savolainen got into the question of the money. The bank president testified to the amount, its existence and its withdrawal.

Mrs. Juola blanched.

D. Ruotsalainen, pastor, and Chief of Police Barth Coffey both submitted sworn statements summarizing the words of the departed young Mr. Smith.

Mrs. Juola stood up and tried to leave.

The hired man asserted that the trunk had never left the Juola boarding house, that it had been brought from Charles Brosi's room up to the attic, where it had stayed until Mr. Savolainen and Miss Brosi appeared. Mr. Savolainen's attorney helped him with the wording.

Chief of Police Barth Coffey seated himself next to Mrs. Juola and stayed there until she returned to the witness stand.

Mrs. Juola declared under oath that given the nature of Charles Brosi's solitary life, she had no idea that he had family.

"Probable perjury," Mr. Savolainen's lawyer whispered, "since Mr. Smith, the jeweler, knew of the purchases made for relatives in Kinney."

Question raised, she suggested that many men purchase jewelry and gifts for persons other than family.

She certainly knew that to be true.

Moreover, she insisted, if there were no family to inherit the money, if there were no family to notify, then the dispersal of the money had seemed open to a variety of options, one of which she admitted suggesting to Mr. Smith or, informed of the situation, he to her. Neither was quite sure, even under oath, who had thought of it first. And, in fact, it was unimportant that the court determine who it was who actually removed the money from Uncle Charles' trunk or from his person.

What was important was that the young Mr. Smith had not agreed with any part of his brother's decision making. When the elder Mr. Smith returned from a late-night visit to the Juola household, jubilant that the opportunity was now availing itself for him to restock and reopen the store, the young Mr. Smith had decried the whole plan and insisted that he was going to the authorities. His brother and Mrs. Juola had spent days trying to convince him that what they had done and were intending to do was fair and honest. The young Mr. Smith never was convinced.

The elder Mr. Smith had loved his brother. In his memory, he had testified honestly.

Although doctors give little credence to the probability that physical illness can result from emotional distress, in the young Mr. Smith's case, the knowledge that his indiscretion had led at the least to theft, at the worst to murder surely could have been a factor. So could whatever treatment he did or did not receive in the company of his brother and Mrs. Juola during the days between their taking of the money and his falling ill.

Frankly, I did not put anything at all past her.

Some small part of my mind must have heard Mr. Savolainen's story whether the whole of me wanted to or not, for during the dark days of my delirium, Mrs. Juola took form in my mind as the epitome of evil and the central figure in nightmares that left me drenched with sweat and screaming.

In my mind's eye, I saw her bending over Uncle Charles' body. I saw him reach out to her for help. I saw her hold a pillow to his head when he was too weak to push her away. I saw her dig a key from his pocket and run upstairs to open the trunk. I saw her count the money. I saw her face. I heard her laugh. I watched her dance to the ecstasy of Mr. Smith's appreciation.

And I had watched the young Mr. Smith die.

I wanted to see his brother and Mrs. Juola die, too. I wanted to see them ride the tumbrils to the guillotine. I wanted to sit by Madame Defarge and watch the knife fall and cut off their heads.

I saw the blood spurt, and I screamed again, this time with joy. It was revenge, pure and simple, that I sought. Never a pallid restitution.

Then I submerged into a black blankness, and even that bleak imaginary world disappeared.

So did Mr. Savolainen. No matter how ill I was during those days when the wheels of justice made their turns, the small part of my rational mind that continued to function wondered why and where he had gone, but the larger part of my mind that refused to function at all simply put him too in abeyance.

Mrs. Laitinen's hands tried to keep me from moving too far away, but my thoughts pulled me off somewhere into a misty sky where I lived alone, separate from that other girl who had traveled with the gypsies and come to Ely and unraveled a skein of lies. Not the same one who had closed the couch on Wilho Field and sung "Lady Moon," who had wanted to win first prize in spelling and vocabulary and be triple-promoted, who had planned to cross the line between Finntown and the future, whose name was Marion, not Ilmi Marianna.

I could not find either girl in the mist that continued to swirl around me, ebbing and flowing, opening into patches where I saw blood-suckers and wood piles and Mr. Ala's face so clearly that I screamed until blissfully the fog moved in again. It moved in on little cat feet and rubbed against my legs and purred. For a while I held it to myself, but then the fog and I separated, and I found myself in the back bedroom of the Stembers' apartment singing,

> One misty, moisty morning when cloudy was the weather,
> I chanced to meet an old man clothed all in leather,
> clothed all in leather from his heels up to his chin,
> but where did he go and where did he go and where did
> he go again?

I sang the question, and I knew the answer. He had gone far away to the cemetery on the hill, far, far away in his caravan, far, far away to a spot I could not see although the white pine grew there, taller and taller and taller until they reached the sky and I reached the sky and fell again.

Mrs. Laitinen's hand caught me before I fell too far.

So did the sound of the fiddle.

It sounded like Pa's fiddle, but the bow squawked just a little when it touched the strings. Rosin, I thought. It needs rosin.

Then I fell asleep.

When I awoke, someone was holding my hand, but I knew it was not Mrs. Laitinen.

I wanted it to be Ma, but the hand was too big, too calloused, too hairy. Without opening my eyes, I felt its palm. There were indentations on the fingers that touched the strings. I knew that it was Pa's hand, Pa sitting there beside me.

The hand withdrew and was replaced with a narrow piece of paper.

Curiosity opened my eyes whether I wanted to or not, and I drew the paper up so that I could see it through the mist. Benjamin Franklin stared up at me with 100s on the corners. "Thank you, John Porthan," I said dreamily, closing my eyes again.

"How about a *kiitos* for Pa?" a deep voice asked.

"*Kiitos*," I repeated obediently.

"Will you bring that back to Ma?"

"Yes, with all my heart. Will you come too?" Even I heard the pain in my voice. Even I winced.

"*Sattuu*. Perhaps," came the answer. "If she will have me."

At that, the fog and the pain congealed around me, and I cried, "Have you? She doesn't have a choice! WE NEED YOU! March always needs May."

It did not make any sense at all, but it did. Pa had many faults, but lack of mental acuity was not one of them. "You read the family record book."

Mrs. Laitinen appeared. Mr. Savolainen appeared. They bumped into each other in their attempts to urge Pa out and soothe me.

"I did." Pushing away the fog with both hands, then holding my chest to keep the pain from overflowing, I struggled to sit up, twisting sideways and using my elbows for support. I almost strangled on the next words, but they forced their way out: "Are you my Pa?"

Mrs. Laitinen and Mr. Savolainen froze. So did Pa, halfway up, halfway down.

"Yes."

I could not mistake the answer. It was unequivocal.

"I just did not . . ."

Since he never did, there was no need to finish the sentence. That he did not was a fact of life, had always been a fact of life, would probably always be a fact of life, typical of Pa.

I sank back, accepting that final reality, wishing the fog and mist would return. But they did not. Nor typically did Pa. It was Mr. Savolainen who took me home to Ma. He who broke the hundred dollar bill into smaller sums that we could handle more easily. He, of course, who had located Pa in the lumber camp in Embarrass in the first place and brought him to Ely to collect Uncle Charles' death benefits from John Porthan and the Finnish Accident and Sick Benefit Association.

Before we left Ely forever with a first installment of funds in hand, Mr. Savolainen said that he wanted me to call him "Uncle Alex," but old habits die hard, and it took years of practice before I could do it without consciously thinking of him as "Mr. Savolainen" first.

We made the train ride from Ely to Duluth and Duluth to Virginia in two stages, with Mrs. Laitinen along to observe the proprieties and to do for me all of the small things I was too weak to do myself.

When we finally pulled into the station in Virginia, Mr. Savolainen's car was waiting for us. Mrs. Savolainen—I could never call her "Aunt Anna"—wanted us to stay at their house overnight. But I was so anxious to see Ma and, I hated to admit it, even Lil, that Mr. Savolainen capitulated, wrapping me in a blanket and settling me into the back seat. Mrs. Laitinen sat with me, my head on her lap, and Mrs. Savolainen climbed in, for the ride she said, but I saw her holding Mr. Savolainen's hand over the floor shift gears.

By the time we got to Kinney, I was too tired to get out of the car by myself, and that made Ma cry. When I saw Ma cry, I cried, too, and so did Lil, and for a time there things were pretty watery. Mrs. Laitinen bustled into the kitchen and started supper while we sat on the couch, holding each other's hands, and getting our words all mixed up as we asked and answered questions that we had to repeat all over again the next day.

I was too tired to sit at the table so Mr. Savolainen carried me onto Ma's bed, and she and Mrs. Laitinen undressed me and Ma fed me *puuroa* just as if I were the littler one and Lil the older. Lil held the bowl and patted my head and rubbed my cheeks until I fell asleep in the middle of the meal.

Next morning, summer came. The shade was pulled up, and the sun was shining on the blankets, and the bed made shadows on the floor, but I didn't fall into them. I sat up and called for Ma and got up all by myself and ate at the table. Thin Finnish pancakes with crisp bacon and lots of butter and maple syrup.

Mr. and Mrs. Savolainen had made sure the larder was well stocked before they left the night before, and although Mr. Savolainen had convinced Mrs. Laitinen to leave Ely and move to Virginia to "do for" them, they left her with us for a time, "just for a while," Mr. Savolainen insisted when Ma demurred. She did not argue back.

Ma insisted that I use the night-time pee pot instead of trying to walk to the outside toilet, and though I felt better, I allowed myself that luxury.

It seems impossible, but I am quite sure that Lil emptied the pot.

Except for having my face washed and my hair well brushed and rebraided, we did nothing that whole day but talk. And eat. I ate and ate and ate bits and pieces of treats that Ma kept on a tray by the couch.

Lil did not even ask for her own.

We cried some. For Uncle Charles and for the dreams that had died with him. Ma said we would still buy a farm, but it would have to be a small one because, she admitted with honest directness, we could not count on Pa. We cried some about that, too. But, Ma said, the farm had to be big enough to support four people.

"Four?" I asked, with some trepidation. Had Mr. Ala returned and had Ma succumbed?

"No," Ma laughed, reading my mind. "But we will have another mouth to feed next spring." She patted her tummy.

She had gained some weight while I was gone. Mrs. Savolainen must have taken good care of Ma and Lil just as Mr. Savolainen had of me, I thought. Then I thought again.

Ma smiled a little self-consciously and nodded. "Yes," she said. "I think you and Lil will have a brother. Or a sister. But I think it will be a brother." She did not seem at all unhappy about it, and Lil was grinning.

I grinned, too. If it were a brother, we would finally and for sure have a man around the house.

Late that afternoon, there was a knock at the door. It was Eino Salin, looking for his vocabulary notebook, I thought.

But he said, "No. You can keep that one. I have a copy, and I have got some new words in a new notebook, too."

He brought them over next day, and I tried to get right to work. So did Ma and Mrs. Laitinen. It was a Wednesday, baking day, and Eino stayed for a piece of fresh *pulla*.

Chapter Twenty-two

"First Things First"

But no matter how hard I tried, and I did try hard over the next few weeks, I could not manage the return to normal for which I knew Ma and Mrs. Laitinen and Mr. and Mrs. Savolainen, even Lil, were waiting and hoping. Somehow I found it easier to stay in bed, simpler to nibble bits of meals from a tray than to eat at table, more comforting to look out the window at the clouds than to read. Even Eino Salin's notebook, though it sat on the bedside table waiting patiently, failed to tempt me.

Mr. Savolainen went so far as to bring Dr. Raihala from Virginia ostensibly to visit Ma and make sure she and the baby were progressing satisfactorily. But the doctor spent more time with me than he did with Ma, and I knew that I was the real reason he had come.

I answered his questions. Beyond that I could find little to say. Words had flown from my mind like the hummingbirds in a silent spring.

Eino often appeared, offering to help me with the lessons Miss Loney had given Ma for me to do over the summer. Strong in her belief that when I returned all would be well, we found, when the final report cards were sent home after Memorial Day, that Miss Loney had not only double but triple promoted me. I knew I should be grateful for her faith in me and assiduous in my commitment to the lessons. But I was so tired, so very tired, that even when Ma propped pillows behind my back and laid a board across my lap for me to use as a desk, I found myself holding the pencil and turning the pages of the books listlessly, unable to form any relationship with the words.

Lil perched on the end of my bed one morning and asked me, "Ilmi Marianna, are you there?"

"No," I answered haltingly, "I am not really anywhere. I am somewhere else instead."

"Please come back," she pleaded, and I knew that she meant it.

But I could not garner up the energy.

Late one night Ma came in in her nightgown holding a kerosene lamp high with its wick turned down to a candle glow. When she bent down, however, she could see that my eyes were open rather than closed, that I was not asleep though I had been lying there quietly since early evening.

"What's wrong, Ilmi Marianna?" she asked, setting the kerosene lamp on the bedside table and smoothing my hair with her cool hand.

I did not know how to answer her. There were no words for how I felt, even in Eino Salin's new vocabulary notebook. So I turned my back and looked out the window at the moon shining on the vacant lot next door. It reflected off the tin plate hanging behind the can we used to send messages in the old days so very long ago. I sighed for those days. Had I turned toward her, Ma might have seen my eyes glistening. I closed them tightly and pretended to fall asleep, and soon she left, taking the lamp and a lot of the light I was living by with her.

Ironically, though a part of me wanted to be alone, another part of me wanted to cling to her and to Lil every minute of every day. I did not want to go outside. I did not want to see anyone else, though I hesitated to hurt Mrs. Laitinen by withdrawing from her ministrations or Mr. Savolainen by refusing to accept his. Otherwise, I turned myself into a turtle, pulling myself into a shell, retracting my appendages and my head completely, coming out only when I knew it was completely safe—when I was alone or when only Ma or Lil was there.

Mrs. Laitinen reminded me of Ely. Every time I saw her the nightmare returned, even during the day. Mrs. Juola was holding a pillow over Uncle Charles' face, then counting the money she had taken from the trunk, throwing it up into the air so that she and Mr. Smith could dance in the rain of bills that floated around them.

Mr. Savolainen reminded me of restitution. He and Mr. Porthan had been named "executors" by the judge, and sure enough Mr. Savolainen appeared regularly—weekly, in fact—with cash money, enough for us to live on and a bit to spare, to set aside for the farm in Zim, Ma said, thankfully. I did not want to think of the farm in Zim. I did not want to see the money, nor did I want to see Mr. Savolainen though I knew that it was not his fault that the judge had chosen restitution rather than revenge.

I wanted revenge. Thus, when I thought of Ely and of Mrs. Juola, other thoughts inevitably followed, and they were not nice. I was not nice for thinking them, and I was ashamed. But I thought them nonetheless.

Sometimes I envisioned tumbrils and the guillotine and blood spurting from severed necks as their heads were cut off, hers and Mr. Smith's.

Sometimes I locked both of them into the pest house in a room filled with people who were dying of influenza, and they knew they had to get it and they knew they were dying and they anticipated the agonies to come and the horror of their deaths, and I smiled.

Sometimes I tied them back onto the boat they had taken to Burntside Lake, and I took them out into the middle of Shagawa Lake or to the dropoff past Sandy Point where the gypsies had camped, and I drilled a hole in the bottom of the boat, just a small hole, so the water would run in slowly, very slowly, and they would know that the boat would fill and that it would sink and that they would die, and I was glad.

Sometimes I gave them both to the gypsies and told the grandfather to dress them in bear suits and make them wear them forever and do tricks and eat only leavings. But that did not work because the grandfather's dark eyes looked ashamed when I suggested it, and I knew I should be ashamed for thinking it, and whatever I had eaten that day came back up again, and I knew I deserved to be sick because I was a horrible person, far worse than the worst of the images of gypsies. Thoughts "Both of lost happiness and lasting pain" tormented me, and I viewed the future as Satin did hell, as "a dungeon horrible," filled with "darkness visible, . . . where peace / And rest can never dwell, hope never comes / That comes to all; but torture without end / Still urges."

So the days of summer slipped by, and I slowly slipped away too into a place where no one could find me or hear what I was thinking or know what I was plotting, even though I knew it could never come true.

Or could it? Could those dark dreams turn into the kind of prayers the lost Archangel Satan answered, his power having been second only to God's when he was in heaven? Could he answer my prayers not from there but from hell? There he reigned supreme. Moreover, according to John Milton, he could escape at will, since God's ministers of vengeance and pursuit had been withdrawn. Such was God's ruling—the ultimate punishment he wreaked upon Satan—"That with reiterated crimes he (Satan) might / Heap on himself damnation, while he sought evil to others."

I too sought evil to others. Yet never even during my darkest hours was I a fool. I knew full well in my heart that in my acts of vengeance, damning Mr. Smith and Mrs. Juola to ugly and horrible deaths, as their executioner, I was in a sense damning myself.

The only book I cared to read during those dark days was the library copy of *Paradise Lost*. I asked Eino to check it out for me, and I memorized enough of the lines so that when it had to be returned, it lived within me. Of course, no matter how I took John Milton's words into my self, I never accepted Milton's assumption that through the creation of hell God would eventually save mankind. It seemed to me that God himself needed to do undergo some stringent self-evaluation if He truly believed that his creation of evil was the best way to make the world become good again. In spite of my joy in the incredible power of the armies of words John Milton commanded, I could never buy that basic premise.

If Satan deserved punishment for daring to set himself above God in heaven, then God also needed a lesson in humility and a stern lecture about the insidious nature of pride. A God who was all good should have found a kinder, gentler, more loving way to discipline and teach a lesson to Satan, his closest friend, an archangel of great beauty and exceptional powers, who was worthy of being saved. If God had to rely on the fires of hell to effect change in Satan, He must not be very persuasive.

In short, I thought God needed to look just as hard at His own objectives and methodology as He did at Satan's. Ma had told me over and over again when my pride and my sharp tongue got the best of me that love works far better than hate and that I could catch many more flies with honey than I ever could with vinegar. Why else had I been punished if not for exacting revenge on Wilho Field? Such were the lessons Ma had always taught.

But during the long hours and days I spent trying not to remember all that had happened in Ely and, of course, thinking of little else, my soul rebelled with force and fury from Ma's lessons of love and patience and kindness and humility. I wanted the power to build a hell where Mr. Smith and Mrs. Juola would burn forever.

Ma's lessons had been too well ingrained, however, and the more I dwelt upon hatred and revenge, the hotter the fires of hell burned not only for Mr. Smith and Mrs. Juola, but for me. I knew that what I thought and planned and desired was as evil as what Mr. Smith and Mrs. Juola had thought and planned and desired.

So the forces warred within me until I could neither eat nor sleep nor read nor study . . . until sometimes I wondered whether I could, in fact, continue even to live.

What would have happened to me had events not taken an unusual and striking turn I do not to this day know. But they did, and soon enough so that I was able at length and at last to find salvation and peace.

It all began with pebbles on the window glass deep in the dark of a long and lonely night. Ma and Lil and Mrs. Laitinen had all fallen asleep long before, and I had doubled the pillows up behind me so that I could look outside at the moon and the stars, wishing I knew a witch's incantation to carry me over the miles in the moonglow to Ely, though whether to visit Uncle Charles' grave or to dig ones for Mrs. Juola and Mr. Smith had not been determined.

"Dit-dit-dit-dit!" A cascade of small rocks clinked on the window panes then hit the sill with small thudding sounds, too soft to awaken anyone asleep but loud enough to catch the attention of anyone who was not.

I crawled to the end of the bed, pushed up the bottom of the double-hung window, and peeked outside.

Crouched right under the window were three dark bodies, each one holding a lighted candle so that their faces were illumined. Eino Salin. Kabe—Diodado Carmen Joseph Vanucci. And Fatso Spina. When they saw me, they gestured for quiet, fingers to lips, but motioned emphatically for me to crawl out the window and join them.

Ma's bedroom, where I had been ensconced since I got home, was, like the rest of our small apartment, easy to access from outside since the house had no real cellar but sat on a low foundation of stone.

I whispered, "I can't."

"Yes, you can," Eino hissed back. "You don't have to walk. We'll carry you. There's a meeting."

I sighed.

When Eino called a meeting, the members of the Good Gang always tried to attend. But when Eino and Kabe and Fatso convened the entire membership of both gangs, there was no gainsaying the call. All members who were told to attend did. That was that.

I had no choice. "Just a minute. I have to get some clothes on."

"No. We won't look at your nightgown." Fatso rarely spoke emphatically, for his role was usually that of negotiator. Thus, when he gave an order, we listened.

"Promise?" I asked anyway.

"Promise." The word was repeated three times in three different voices. I could not help but accede.

"I have to have stockings on at least." Finding them would give me a minute to weigh my options.

"No. It's really warm out. You should've had the window open. It's a nice night." Kabe's voice ran on like honey or molasses. He never used one word if he could think of two or two if he could come up with four.

Eino handed his candle to Kabe and reached up to grab my arms. Fatso and Kabe closed their eyes until I was on the ground, clutching the nightgown primly to my chest, making sure it hung all the way down. Then Eino took all three candles, and Fatso and Kabe made a chair of their arms and nodded me onto it. I sat. They lifted. We were off.

Only once did I voice any displeasure, for it was, in fact, a smooth and easy ride. But when I realized we were heading toward the chicken wire fencing and the edge of the mine pit, I started to shake. "No," I whispered fiercely. "I will not go down into the cave. Not the cave."

"You haven't got a choice," Eino answered grimly. "If we have to, we'll blindfold you. But with us you will come. Period."

No one ever argued with Eino either when he used that tone of voice, not even me.

In days gone by Fatso and Kabe had used to pretend to huff and puff when they carried me anywhere on their "arm-chair," but I had lost so much weight that they did not even make a pretense of teasing, even when I grabbed their necks in a strangle-hold as we neared the verge of the pit.

"Close your eyes if you have to. We're almost there," Eino said from ahead of us as he disappeared down a path that seemed to drop straight into the bottom of the world.

It didn't. Surprisingly, it slanted slowly, and it was plenty wide enough for the three of us. I opened my eyes just a bit to check and closed them again when I saw that there was no railing on the edge. Then we turned in toward what seemed like a solid wall of rock. It wasn't. We went right through an almost invisible opening. Kabe and Fatso ducked, lowering their arms, and then set me down on a firm, hard surface.

Eino relighted all three candles, gave Fatso and Kabe theirs, and hunkered down. Everyone I knew from the Good Gang was there. So were all the kids from the Bad Gang, I realized, as the candlelight illuminated rows and rows of faces.

Unbelievably, a joint meeting had been convened on this most disputed of all premises, the highly prized, secret mine cave, once the scene of a suspected dynamite plot to destroy the Good Gang. And everyone was there.

I felt like a victim approaching an altar. Why had I been brought there? What was my punishment to be? Had the kids managed to read my mind? Were they going to deal with me as society must always deal with the evil monster Frankenstein? Did they fear me and loathe me and seek to destroy me for my horrible thoughts?

I turned to run, but Eino and Kabe blocked the door, and Fatso grabbed my arms and set me down in the center of the circle.

"What's wrong?" he asked. "We have to know. Are you dying?"

All eyes were on me. I shook my head.

"Then what?" Eino and Kabe assumed positions on either side of me, but they did not look mad at all. They looked kind of . . . scared. And concerned. "Why are you staying in bed and why aren't you studying and why have you quit caring even about vocabulary words?"

Murmurs rose from all around me, echoes and variations of those same questions.

I started to cry. "I don't know!" I repeated it over and over again. "I don't know what's wrong! I just know . . ." The words trailed off.

Fatso waved everyone else to silence, took my hand in his, and addressed his words directly to my eyes and to my heart, using his very best diction, for Fatso knew the right way to talk when he cared to do it. "Something bad has happened. You know something that you do not want to know. Is that right?"

I nodded, still crying.

Eino reached over to offer me a large and very dirty handkerchief. I said "thank you" and blew my nose with my free hand.

"It is something that happened while you were gone," Fatso continued. His voice was very kind, very soft, his hand very warm.

Kabe's hand patted me on one shoulder and Eino's the other. The ice within me melted a bit.

"Just say 'yes' or 'no.' That's easy, right?" Fatso asked.

It was. I tried, and the "yes" came out just fine.

"It's something that happened . . . to your Uncle Charles?" Eino prompted.

Fatso waved him quiet and firmed his grip on my hand and waited while I bit my lip and the tears welled out again. There was nothing else to do but try again. "Yes," I whispered.

"He died." Fatso said it so matter-of-factly that I caught no hint of pity.

I nodded.

"That's why you are so sad," he continued in a kind of flat monotone, no inflections, no expression. As if he were not asking a question at all, just stating a fact.

There was not a sound from the circle, but Eino and Kabe kept patting, awkwardly, of course, yet it was . . . soothing. So was Fatso's voice.

"Yes." I paused. "And no. It is not just that . . . he is . . . dead." I was not sure where the words were coming from, but they flickered like the candle flames.

I concentrated on the flames and on Fatso's voice: "It's that . . ." he prompted.

"It is that I . . ."

There was no response, just patience, waiting.

Then the floodgates broke: "It is that . . . I think they killed him, Mr. Smith and Mrs. Juola, and then they ran away and when they came back the judge said they were to make . . . restitution." The last word dripped with venomous secretions of anger, sarcasm, and nightmarish dreams.

"Restitution," Fatso repeated, trying to understand. "They had to apologize?"

"No. They just have to . . ." I was really struggling with this part.

"They just have to . . ." He helped me again.

"They just have to pay back the money as if that will do anybody any good . . . well it will do Ma and Lil some good and we will get to buy that farm in Zim but it won't do Uncle Charles any good because he's dead and they used his money to restock the jewelry store and now all they have to do is repay the money because the judge said so and then they're safe and free and clear and then they'll get rich because they've been able to use Uncle Charles' money to make the business go and what do they care that they have to pay us some of it and what did they care that the young Mr. Smith died and what do they care that Uncle Charles is dead? They wanted him dead . . . all they wanted was his money and he's dead and they're alive and no one cares and they got off scot free well not scot free because they will have to pay the money but free still and no matter what they did and no matter what she said I don't believe she sent for the doctor. I think she just let him die or made him die and I hate her I hate her I HATE HER!" The last words screamed like the mine whistle in Ely after the cave-in. They screamed on and on until there was no one to pull the whistle any more.

When I woke up, I was no longer in the cave. Nor was there a crowd around me. Just Eino and Kabe and Fatso were there, and I was lying in the swing on the Vanucci's front porch and Mrs. Vanucci was patting the blanket covering me and Eino and Kabe and Fatso were leaning on the balusters and watching me with frightened eyes that gradually relaxed as I did when Mrs. Vanucci held a glass to my lips and told me to drink it down. I coughed, but she refused to let me stop drinking until the glass was empty. It tasted like grape juice but richer, more intense, much stronger.

I could certainly understand why Mr. Vanucci went to sleep soon after supper. The more I drank, the more the edges of reality blurred, and when the glass was empty, Mrs. Vanucci laid me back on the pillows and told the boys that that was enough for one day.

But Fatso, who usually knew far better than to contradict adults, said, most politely but very assertively, too, "Please let us talk to her for one more minute, Mrs. Vanucci, and then we will bring her home."

"You may have one more minute," she capitulated, but admonished him with her finger, "just one, and then I will bring her home."

She shook that finger at us and went back inside the house. The other three converged around the swing.

"You are not alone," Fatso whispered. "We will be your knights. We accept the fallen glove and make your quest ours. We refuse to accept guerdon and ask for no token of victory but only seek to fulfill our vow." He held out his right hand, flat. Kabe and Eino did the same, laying theirs over his. Fatso took my right hand and laid theirs atop it and said, his eyes intent upon ours, "Repeat after me."

There was a pause as he considered. Then he continued: "With the touch of my hand, I make this sacred and solemn vow. Repeat it!" he reminded us impatiently.

"With the touch of my hand, I make this sacred and solemn vow." We each replicated not only the words but Fatso's exact tone of voice, not together but one after another so there could be no denying that we had all said it.

"That we will wreak vengeance upon Mrs. Juola." .

"And Mr. Smith," I added quickly.

"That we will wreak vengeance upon Mrs. Juola . . . and Mr. Smith." Three repeats.

"And that we will begin . . ." continued Fatso.

"And that we will begin . . ." the rest of us agreed.

". . . when . . ." Fatso provided with a stern look at me.

". . . when . . ." we echoed, trustingly.

" . . . when Ilmi Marianna Brosi is herself, truly well again."

Eino concurred with undue emphasis, I thought. So, severely restricting himself to Fatso's exact words, did Kabe.

Then they waited.

I thought about it, but there did not seem to be any other choice.

"When I am truly well again," I finished, hesitantly, I must admit, but the words came out.

Eino and Fatso and Kabe must have been holding in their collective breaths because when they exhaled, the force of it actually shook the swing.

Chapter Twenty-three

"Restoration"

During the next few days our house turned into the center for gang activity in Kinney. At least one member of either the Good Gang or the Bad Gang danced attendance on me from morning until night.

When Sara Salin came over to play dolls with Lil before breakfast, she sat like a toad staring at me until I got out of bed, dressed, sat down at table, and forced down a whole bowl of *puuroa*, laced with at least a quarter of a pound of butter and a half cup of brown sugar. Then, setting good manners even further aside, she arbitrarily reached for two slices of *pulla*, ladled on enough butter and raspberry jam to make even Lil gag, and thrust it at me. She did not even blink until I had finished off every crumb.

At the exact minute that she left off monitoring my consumption of breakfast and turned to Lil, someone knocked on the door. It was Eino, his hair and face soaking wet from a dousing under the back-yard pump. Ma settled me onto the infamous davenport, but Eino made sure I had two notebooks in hand, one to fill, one to use as reference, with an assignment due upon his return from the Andersons' wood lot and a morning of helping his Uncle Onnie cut pulp.

The Salins must have drawn the straw for morning duty because between then and noon, one or the other—and there were seven in all— perched by turns on a kitchen chair to make sure I didn't lollygaggle.

Eino actually had the audacity to beg lunch from Mrs. Laitinen as he grilled me, reading definitions and waiting impatiently until I recited back the matching vocabulary word, spelling it correctly.

The afternoon must have been assigned to the Vanuccis. Armando watched me eat. Celia went with me to the outhouse. Kabe read aloud from the upper grade leisure reading assignment for summer, Sir Walter Scott's *Ivanhoe*. Much as I loved stories, I had to admit that the first chapter with its deadly background of old English history bored even me into a long deep afternoon nap. Baldo, who was sitting by the bed when I woke up, stuck to me like a burr through two cups of well-sugared milk-coffee and two well-buttered pieces of cinnamon-sugar *korppu*. And so it went until I threw up my hands—and almost my dinner—and cried "Enough already!" to the mathematics lesson.

By then I had gone through all of the older Vanuccis and been relegated to Sabatino, the youngest, who listened to my recitation of every single one of the times tables through the 9's with his thumb in his mouth and his blanket stuck into his nose. It was a marvel that he found space for breath.

There was no end to it. Eventually every child in town under the age of fifteen (by which time kids usually had graduated from eighth grade and all formal education into adulthood) took a turn until Eino, Kabe, and Fatso agreed to a shake-down and granted me some respite.

Ma, Lil, and Mrs. Laitinen were still, however, assigned supervision of my bowel and bladder movements and my sleeping and eating patterns. Only over my vehement and stringent objections did my three male witches forbear from making out a chart so my family could keep a written record for them to check.

During the days that followed, Fatso took over mathematics study; Eino, vocabulary—lists, memorization, and sentence or paragraph writing; Kabe of the golden voice, reading and literature.

Social studies and science were covered on a revolving basis by sixth, seventh, and eighth graders. Penmanship by the hated Wilho Field because his was uncontrovertibly the most elegant, though he was admitted to my presence with grave reservations, especially from Ma and Lil. No one really needed to do spelling because I seemed to learn it effortlessly, as if by osmosis, but on Friday nights for the duration of the summer, a spelling bee was held at our house. Kids numbered off "one-two-one-two" then lined up on each side of the kitchen if it rained or on the board sidewalk in front of the house—our front yard was too small—if it

220

were sunny and competed. Sighs of relief were expelled audibly when, finally, things returned to normal, and I won every time.

Any lapse from perfection on my part, either in attitude or quality of work, was met with grave looks and frowns. I had to write every error of any kind one hundred times correctly under the strict supervision of Eino, who brooked no more dissent than had Miss Loney.

The only part of the whole process which gave every one of us unalloyed pleasure was Kabe's oral reading of *Ivanhoe*. Although many of us were capable of battling our own way through Scott's elaborate sentences, long paragraphs, and abstruse vocabulary, we never admitted it, individually or collectively. We unanimously preferred listening to Kabe reading it aloud in his sweet tenor, "doing voices," as Lil said, a different one for each major character. So successful did his reading become that the audience, which had initially consisted of me and Lil then Fatso and Eino, then whatever Vanucci or Salin or Spina happened by, grew with each chapter. By the time Gurth kissed the pilgrim's hand and the pilgrim, Ivanhoe, in disguise, of course, left his home, Rotherwood, for the tournament at Ashby, the mass of listeners had grown to above twenty, and there it stayed solidly through the rest of the book.

At first, after supper, as the summer evenings muted to a golden dusk, we sat around our kitchen table. But as the number of listeners and my strength increased, we gravitated first to our front steps and then to the school steps, which, facing west, offered us the longest possible light and a sort of a stage for Kabe. Eino and Fatso set a chair for me at the bottom of the steps, where Miss Beck had stood with her school bell at the beginning of each school day. Then I was moved to the bottom step ensconced in blankets under, in back of, and around me until even my guardians could see that they were superfluous. Around me ranged the others, Good Gang on one side, Bad Gang on the other, a yard or so of neutral territory safely in between.

As superfluous as my blankets were the evening "come-home-calls" that echoed around town at bedtime from each of our mothers: "Il-mi-Ma-ri-anna!" Ma yelled. "*Lil!*"

Mrs. Spina rang their dinner bell, an appropriate call for "Fatso." I wondered if she realized that.

Mrs. Salin mainly had to get the attention of "Eino-and-Sarrrr-aaa!" They took charge of shepherding the rest of the family home.

Mrs. Vanucci tended to run some variant of her children's names all together, depending upon whom she remembered at the time:

"Sabatino-Dominic-Celia-Alcide-Baldo-and Kaaaaa-bbee!" They usually ignored her completely until she concentrated on her eldest: "Diodado-Carmen-Joseph-Vanucci-right-here-right-now!"

Usually, then, they went.

But when the Black Knight (King Richard in disguise) and Wamba the Saxon clown, and Robin Hood and his merry men stormed the evil Norman Reginald Front-de-Boeuf's castle Torquilstone, our parents should have been warned to beware and be patient. Not one single child went home to nestle snugly in bed until the outer rampart of the castle had been breached. Mothers who came to collect their broods wound up listening, too.

The audience swelled as the siege progressed. When Wamba entered the Norman stronghold in disguise and covered Cedric the Saxon (Ivanhoe's father) with his cloak, thus allowing him to escape, we held our breaths until Cedric was well out of danger and cheered when he threw a gold coin at a treasonous priest.

And there was no stopping Kabe the night when the battle was concluded, even after the sun set. A kerosene lamp appeared miraculously, the mothers didn't even bother to call but sidled in around the edges of the group, and we all swatted mosquitoes and held our collective breaths, more in medieval England than in Kinney, as DeBracy released the touchstone that fell almost hitting the Black Knight. Even a few of the fathers wandered over to hear Ulrica-Urfried cry her death song as flames consumed her and the evil Norman knight Front-de-Boeuf and his castle of Torquilstone. Kabe's voice finally gave out about the time when Brian de Bois-Guilbert saved but abducted the beautiful, courageous Jewish healer Rebecca, who had made sure that the wounded Ivanhoe, whom she loved, was saved from the flames.

Eino declared a hiatus then, not just for the night but, when we got together the next night, expecting Kabe to continue, for the book too. Kabe had laryngitis anyway, which should have been no surprise. But we were too excited just to let those chapters lie. I'm not sure who had the idea, but someone must have said it would be fun to act them out, and that was all it took. Assigning parts or opening them up to volunteers, Eino laid the groundwork for a reenactment of a series of scenes that we ultimately decided to stage the weekend of the Fourth of July for the entertainment and edification of the public. The small price of one penny per person admission with children under the age of five allowed in free would replenish both clubs' treasuries.

I disagreed about the stipulation. "We should charge double for children under the age of five," I argued, remembering all too well how Lil had acted at that stage. But I was overruled.

Kabe was Ivanhoe, of course. We didn't mind at all that his hair was black instead of Saxon gold. Eino agreed to take the part of the infamous villain and Ivanhoe's nemesis, the Norman Knight Templar (a soldier-monk), Brian de Bois-Guilbert. Fatso was big enough to be the Black Knight, whom some of us already knew was really King Richard in disguise.

I, of course, was Rebecca, daughter of the wealthy Isaac of York, the center of the love triangle. Her feelings for Ivanhoe were reflected in Brian de Bois-Guilbert's illicit attraction to her, for he was bound by the monk's rules of chastity as well as poverty and obedience.

To Wilho Field was given the part of the evil Reginald Front-de-Boeuf, and his cousin Helmi took the part of the Saxon Ulrica-Urfried, who avenged herself on both the father and the son of the Front-de-Boeuf family, burning Reginald alive and, as the towers collapsed, throwing herself to be consumed by the flames.

That was the only really difficult scene to stage because we knew we could not light a fire in the hall. Fatso painted red flames on the biggest cardboard boxes his pa and Mr. Salin could unearth, a conflagration so vivid those of us close to it actually felt warm.

Even Mr. and Mrs. Savolainen appeared for the performance. Mrs. Laitinen, too.

Eino and I got a standing ovation when, defying Brian's dastardly advances, I—Rebecca—threatened to jump from the parapet rather than succumb to his offer to make me his handmaiden. Eino's words of explanation and repentance were so moving that I almost capitulated. But when he approached, ready to take what she was not willing to give, Rebecca climbed to the open parapet and cried, "I spit at thee, and I defy thee," from a perch far more precarious than Lady Moon's ladder.

Kabe and Fatso took turns standing guard over this one, but Wilho Field did not repeat his own dastardly deed. He was finding too much pleasure in playing the villainous owner of the castle, Reginald Front-de-Boeuf, who threatened to grill the well-oiled body of Isaac of York on a charcoal burner if he refused to pay the required ransom and give up his daughter Rebecca to Front-de-Boeuf's evil hands.

We imported David Schibel's son Mark to add authenticity to the scene and play the part of Isaac. Mr. Schibel, owner and proprietor of the

Palace Clothing Company, a men's store on Chestnut Street in Virginia, was considered an honorary Finn because he spoke the language so well. Helsinki Finn at that, though he was familiar with the regional dialects, too. Of course he had a large number of Finnish customers both because he was such a good talker and because his prices were always open to suggestion and debate. Anyway, Mark actually memorized all of his lines and earned applause as he—Isaac—courageously refused to turn his daughter Rebecca—me—over to Front-de-Boeuf regardless of the cost to his pocketbook or his skin, no matter the threat of torture. His fervor at one point raised resounding cheers, as Front-de-Boeuf, Wilho Field, twirled a mean moustache and loomed menacingly above the bound body of Isaac.

Except for that confrontation and the scene between Eino and me, the loudest applause followed the final stage of the battle and its aftermath when Ivanhoe's litter was carried from the burning castle and he rescued, unharmed, and when the Saxon princess and Ivanhoe's love Rowena's would-be suitor Athelstane was "killed." Fatso's younger brother Butch's head was tough enough to withstand an overly realistic whack.

Fatso got the biggest laugh of the day when, doubling as Friar Tuck, he staggered up from the dungeon. Everyone recognized the bottle in his hand as some of Vanuccis' wine.

The final scene—when Eino Salin—Brian—actually carried me—Rebecca—out of the hall, abducting me from the ruins of the castle on one of Mr. Nylund's horses—also earned a standing ovation.

We promised and eventually delivered a follow-up depiction of the final section of the book, which took place at the Preceptory of Templestowe, English headquarters for the perfidious Knights Templars, where Brian—Eino—brought Rebecca and where Rebecca—I—was convicted of witchcraft and sentenced to being burned alive. But that did not occur in Kinney, and it did not, to our great regret, include Kabe. All of the parts were played instead by the Finn kids, though we included every single one of the pupils in the small school in Zim, which had opened in the Salins' back room for the families who had bought land and made a mass exodus into the country that fall.

But though my lessons and Kabe's reading continued after the July performance, that afternoon constituted the turning point for the gangs' evaluation of the state of my health. I was, by all and sundry, including Ma and Lil and Mrs. Laitinen, Eino, Fatso, and Kabe, even Mr. and Mrs. Savolainen, pronounced and declared to be well and truly well, and Mr.

Savolainen treated us all to ice cream as soon as we had changed out of our costumes to celebrate both the play and my recovery.

After that our focus shifted somewhat—at least Kabe's, Eino's, Fatso's and mine did—back to our ultimate goal and the topic and aim of our oath. Revenge. It was time to save the real Rebecca, me, from the evil machinations of her torturers. After she was discovered hidden at Templestowe, the home base and Preceptory of the Knights Templar, where Brian threatened to keep her until she agreed to become his mistress, Rebecca was accused and convicted of witchcraft and threatened with death by fire should a champion not arrive to fight for her.

In our minds, Mr. Smith took on the guise of her accuser, the vile Preceptor-General of the Knights Templar, Lucas de Beaumanoir; and we stretched the book's contents to allow for an illicit connection between him and a Norman harlot, Mrs. Juola.

We knew that it was too late to rescue Uncle Charles from death in the dungeons as had been done with the concussed but surviving Athelstane. But Eino and Kabe and Fatso had sworn to take up arms on my behalf, and had I really been on trial for witchcraft, every one of my three knights would have stepped forward to take up the gauntlet I threw down in my plea for a champion, no matter how it happened in the book.

The novel ended with a fight to the finish, one final joust between the two opposing forces—between the noble Saxon knight Ivanhoe and the villainous Brian of the Knights Templar. Of course, the good guy won. We vowed an equivalent ending to the battle we envisioned between the evildoers in Ely and our Good Gang. That a confrontation would occur was not in question. The questions were how and when and where; our only concern was the strategem.

Addressing that concern took us most of the rest of the summer and eventually involved the enlisting of a prominent, powerful, and surprisingly willing set of accomplices. We knew from the outset that we were bound by certain constraints. No matter how much I desired it, I could not have Mr. Smith's and Mrs. Juola's heads stuck on a pike near the Kinney city limits. No matter how I hated to admit it, John Porthan and the grandfather and Alex Savolainen and the judge were right. Ma and Lil and I could not survive without the restitution money so we could neither dynamite not burn the store that provided it. We would never dance on the rubble of that Torquilstone, nor would we sing a death song as it collapsed into itself in a holocaust of cleansing fire.

In Medieval England, under Prince John, of course, such battles and conflagrations really did occur. John, who acted as regent while King Richard fought in the Crusades, was a false and faithless ruler. It was a lawless time. Fortunately—but perhaps unfortunately for us, northern Minnesota's legal and judicial systems operated with strict adherence to society's rules. Looking at the total picture, Fatso, Eino, Kabe, and I glumly admitted even to ourselves that we did not have many options.

But there were a few, and those we examined microscopically, searching for one that was even potentially viable. We wrestled with details for weeks, it seemed, raising questions and concerns, taking turns playing devil's advocate, struggling with loopholes. Ultimately, every plan we proposed as a possibility was thrown upon the rubbish heap.

But the talking did help because the more we considered alternative plans, the more we sharpened our awareness of what we were aiming. Moreover, our reading of *Ivanhoe*, which continued nightly until we finished the book, also served a purpose above and beyond our enjoyment of the story and eventually the creation of a new vocabulary notebook composed entirely of words from the book. It offered us an insight into what we truly sought.

"It is retribution we seek, not really revenge," I said to the others one night just before the final recall home and to bed. It had taken awhile for me to amend my own thinking. I had read the dictionary and weighed meanings carefully before this attempt to put the thoughts into words:

"Revenge implies almost an equivalent evil and a vindictive spirit, meaning somehow that the people getting vengeance are themselves small and mean. Retribution, on the other hand, suggests a just, fair, and merited requital. Like Brian de Bois Guilbert's death, which was the inevitable consequence of the kind of life he led."

It didn't take long for the others to concur.

Thus, finally we were able to identify exactly what it was that we needed and wanted to accomplish. First, our act of retribution upon Mr. Smith and Mrs. Juola must be, like Brian's death, the inevitable consequence of the kind of life they led. Secondly, it must not in any way affect the value or worth of the jewelry store. Instead, it must strike Mr. Smith and Mrs. Juola where it would hurt the most.

"And where is that?" I asked, rhetorically.

Fatso hit his fist in his palm and laughed as he said, "Smack dab in the middle of their pretensions!"

Eino rubbed his hands together. "We needed to knock the ladder out from under them just like Wilho Field did!" Then, looking abashed, he glanced over at me.

I grinned. In retrospect, it had been funny.

"And," continued Kabe, along the same lines of thought but in his own inimitable wording, "the punishment must be incurred with the same stunning sense of incredulity that greeted the return of Athelstane seemingly from the dead. Neither Mr. Smith nor Mrs. Juola must be able to anticipate its coming. They must remain completely oblivious until it is too late for them to move off center stage. Then, they will be revealed as the villains they are."

"Hear! Hear!" I applauded. Kabe really did have a way with words when he wanted.

But how could we engineer such a "just, fair, and merited requital"?

The question haunted our every waking moment, and every night when it got so dark that Kabe had to quit reading, we pretended we did not hear the summonses and gravitated to our front porch, the four of us.

In our wake trailed the new girl.

Mary Peterson's niece, the new girl had been shipped off from somewhere far away called Evanston, Illinois, to spend the summer with her aunt. When there were no other takers, she had volunteered to play the part of Rowena in our play.

I considered it extremely ironic that Rowena was always considered the heroine of *Ivanhoe* just because in the end, we found out, she married him. Of course, we should not have looked at the last chapters before we got to them, but it was humanly impossible not to do so. Anyway, the new girl seemed to fit the role of Rowena just fine. At first she too gave the appearance of being something of a nonentity . . . partly because she was tiny, even smaller for her age than I . . . partly because—since she had been born in Finland— she spoke English with an almost indecipherably thick Finnish brogue, far worse than the rest of ours . . . partly because, like Rowena, she seemed elegant, aristocratic, well-bred, and totally ineffectual.

I was hard put to forgive her for the fact that, like Rowena's, her hair was long and thick and blond and curly. She lisped and tended to mispronounce words—"aminal" instead of "animal," for instance. And to make matters worse, she didn't even have a decent name. Her aunt called her—the kids laughed when they heard it—"Java." Where that came from none of us ever were to figure out, not even she, but there it was.

In consequence of those deficiencies we all considerably underestimated the acuteness of her brain. Because Rowena was a wimp who dissolved in tears when confronted even with the chivalrous advances of the well-mannered Maurice de Bracy, the part played by Kabe, of course, who had no trouble with dual roles, we assumed that Java was wimpy, too.

Oh, were we wrong!

It was rude, however, whatever our estimation of her character, to forbid her to follow us. Once at our house, Ma refused to allow us to send her home and insisted she had a right to a spot on our steps just as much as Eino and Kabe and Fatso did.

Not that Ma knew. Most nights by the time we got to our house, she was sound asleep—now back in her own bed, for I was well enough to share the davenport again. She tired increasingly easily though she was barely into her fourth month, as Mrs. Laitinen delicately put it.

Because of our dearth of beds, Mrs. Laitinen too eventually left by evening. Mr. and Mrs. Savolainen paid for her streetcar fare so she could spend nights at their large home in Virginia and mornings there doing for them, then come to Kinney for an afternoon of helping Ma. It was a lot to ask of her, but Mrs. Laitinen, imperturbable and indefatigable, took it all in stride.

At any rate, though I suspected but never proved that Lil eavesdropped every chance she got, we held those nightly work and planning sessions at least nominally in secret. Kabe was always the first to be called home. We all knew that when Mrs. Vanucci went from yelling for her whole family to yelling "Kabe!" to repeating the full "Diodado Carmen Joseph Vanucci!" many times in succession, he had better be on his way. When Mrs. Vanucci had to come after him, she hauled him home by the ear.

But Salins lived right next door so Eino could hang around until the last minute, and since Mary Peterson's bar was open all night, she and Java slept all day anyway, and Mr. Spina had long since given up trying to outdistance Fatso, who pretty much did what he pleased. Thus, the four of us at least talked on and on through those long, sweet, sultry summer nights until either mosquitoes or sheer exhaustion did us in. Sometimes we were so tired by the time we had to give up on one more possible plan that we were tempted to camp out on the steps. But given the fact that in the end there were always two boys and two girls, we were both too young and too old to find that alternative anything but wanting.

Some nights we spent talking about what I really wanted to do to the Smiths.

After I had shared the dreams of the tumbrils and the guillotine and the rowboat with a hole, Fatso and Eino and Java took their turns. By the time we were through brainstorming, the Smiths had eventually been . . . staked to an ant hill and left to be eaten alive . . . tied to the tracks of the Duluth and Iron Range Railroad at the base of the hill leading up to the Tower Depot where a train heading down could never have stopped . . . French-fried like Isaac in the dungeons of the jewelry store then fed to Mr. Stina's pigs, who threw them up . . . tied to a stake and burned alive as the Knights-Templar planned to do to Rebecca. I applied the torch to the faggots around them.

By the time we had fully embroidered the first three alternatives, acting them out with great enthusiasm, we had the giggles. When we acted out the building of the brush fire with Java as a repentant Mrs. Juola, screaming soundlessly as we burned her alive with Eino pretending to be Satan welcoming her to hell with vivid descriptions of the heat of eternal damnation, we were laughing so hard we almost rolled off the steps.

Who could ever have guessed that laughter could be so healing? My guilt at the blackness of my thoughts was whitewashed almost completely by the time we finally called a halt to those extremities. Later, all any one of us had to say was the word "faggot," and we broke each other up. Ironically, the more we stoked the fires of revenge, the more the hatred within me was doused. I felt almost as if I had been born again, as if I could now accept " Marion Elmi." Almost, but not quite.

We spent other nights examining our fiscal resources with great care. No plan could be brought to fruition without money. Our performance of *Ivanhoe* at the hall had helped. And I had with great ceremony returned the amount of money the gangs had loaned me in full view of the entire membership soon after Ma received our August payment from Mr. Smith, which left our family with enough and to spare so I felt myself able and free to pay my debts. But we knew all too well that we had very little room for maneuvering. And it was getting closer and closer to the end of summer, to the witching hour of our planned exodus to Zim, to the start of a new school year, and to Java's scheduled departure for Evanston.

Still, every single plot had to be rejected. To be successful the plan had to have panache. It had to radiate a beauty from its own simplicity, and it had to prove its worth by the inevitability of its result. It had to work.

Creative though we all were, we thought and planned and hoped and tried and failed.

229

Chapter Twenty-four

"Restitution"

Then, one night late in August, while Eino and Kabe and Fatso and I sat glumly staring at each other, in despair but half-laughing at Java's lisping, "Cur-th-eth, foiled again," she suddenly waved us to silence.

Snapping her fingers, she firmed her slouch of defeat into the straight back of resolve. "I have it. It's all here." She pointed to her head and chuckled and pulled Fatso up and dragged him down the stairs and pranced all the way to Salins' store and back, though heaven knows she could barely maintain any semblance of rhythm. Usually she sat on the sidelines when the rest of us waltzed and polka-ed at the hall on Saturday nights. Truly she was cursed with two left feet. But that night she bounced along as true to the imaginary beat as Fatso, and a rare picture the two of them made, he with enough bulk to make two of her.

Kabe had sneaked out the window to join us, his mask of obedience having slipped in indirect proportion to the level of intensity. He and Eino and I stood up and watched them and waited and cursed Java when they got back because she refused to divulge her plan. We begged and pleaded and threatened her with bodily harm, but she remained adamant.

"Tomorrow night will be better. Let it be then. Tomorrow night," she murmured abstractedly. "I need to think it through." Off she went toward Mary's Bar at a wandering pace, as if she were not quite there, leaving us behind too frustrated to sleep. We could have strangled her.

The next night was even worse. She still refused to tell us, insisting we figure it all out for ourselves as she led us step by step through her own thought processes.

"What does the virile Mr. Smith want of life?" she asked.

We knew the answer but hesitated to put it bluntly. Eino equivocated. "Success in his business, of course, and," he paused before adding delicately, "in his relationships."

"Right. Which of those must remain completely sacrosanct?" she asked, rhetorically.

We answered in unison. "The business."

"Ergo," said Java,— She sometimes told me I was contagious—"it is clear how we are to punish Mr. Smith."

Our eyebrows rose; our hopes fell. That was nothing new. We had always known we would stick it to Mr. Smith by sticking it to Mrs. Juola, to put it indelicately. The question had only been how.

"So, we study the motivations of Mrs. Juola," Java continued. "What does she want most out of life?"

None of us even bothered to answer. We had played that tune, too, many times before. Every aspect of Mrs. Juola's demeanor had indicated her desire to rise above herself.

Java persisted. "By whom could her goals be granted? Who has the power to give her what she wants . . . other than Mr. Smith."

I threw out the answer scornfully. "People like the Mantels and the Stembers. Ely's own upper class *kerma kerros*. That's obvious." After a day of waiting for this moment, it was turning out like my chocolate cakes always did. Flat.

"And whom do we know well who are the real *kerma kerros*?"

Eino was the first to look hard at Java. A glimmer of light had peeked through. "The Savolainens, for sure."

"Then let us just hypothesize here for a moment. What if we were to enlist the aid of the Savolainens? Suppose they were to give a really big and very exclusive party to which they invite all of the really important people in the towns where they have stores, Virginia, Duluth, and Ely." Java looked at Fatso and Kabe and me expectantly.

My head snapped up.

"Why might they give such a party?" she continued and answered her own question. "Why, to celebrate the sale of one of their stores to someone else, say . . ."

I caught the ball. "The Ely store to the Stembers. That's really going to happen. Mr. Savolainen's talked about it with Mrs. Savolainen and with Mrs. Laitinen. I've heard him say he does not want any part of that business any more."

My words were beginning to fall over each other so Java raised one hand in a slow-down signal.

Fatso took over, grinning from ear to ear. "Might Mr. and Mrs. Savolainen consent to underwriting a party on the occasion of that sale, a well-publicized celebration?"

I nodded and shook my head at the same time. "Of course they would." My mind was racing. "And suppose the party were publicized in a way that meant that everyone who was anybody heard about it, but everyone who was anybody kept it quiet because it was planned as a surprise for . . . say . . ."

Fatso picked it up, "the Stembers . . . to honor the . . . the transfer of ownership. And suppose everyone who was anybody was directed very clearly, but not told, you get the drift, to brush up the tux and buy a new dress and check out the contents of the jewel box for the party to end all parties to be held . . ." He paused.

"In Ely at the Forest Hotel," I threw in. "And everyone who wants and expects to be invited makes reservations to stay at a hotel there, perhaps even to ride an especially chartered railroad coach done up for the occasion, but hired secretly since no one wants the news to get out or the surprise for the Stembers ruined."

Kabe joined the fray. "And Mrs. Savolainen really does extend invitations but only by phone, by word of mouth, to the people who will really come to a real party."

"Including Mrs. Juola and Mr. Smith," said Java with emphasis.

"Of course including them," we repeated with infinite joy.

"But just before the party, when Mrs. Juola has already put on her new dress and new jewelry and has her hair done and Mr. Smith has ordered her a corsage and they are all dressed and ready to go as the other guests are, the Savolainens throw in the clinker." Java sat back and smiled. "Mrs. Savolainen sends out, by special messengers, dressed and hired for this occasion, the engraved formal invitations by which guests will gain admittance to the beautifully decorated private dining room at the Forest Hotel . . ."

Fatso smiled, looking as satisfied as he did at the last bite of roast turkey with all the trimmings.

232

". . . where a sumptuous dinner has been prepared and a string ensemble is already playing." Java laughed. "Can't you just hear it?"

Eino leaned back until his head hit the topmost step and grinned and grinned and grinned. "But Mr. Smith and Mrs. Juola don't know about the engraved invitations. Right?"

Java nodded approvingly. "Right. No messenger comes to their door, or doors as it may be, as one does to the homes of Ely guests or to the hotel rooms of the visitors."

Eino took up the tale, looking at the sky and at the infinite possibilities. "And when the Smiths get to the Forest Hotel and approach the entrance to the dining room, they all dressed up and ready to go in, somebody hired for the evening asks for the invitation they can't produce."

"And they are refused admission," I concluded wonderingly.

"And of course instead of simply leaving quietly and unobtrusively, Mr. Smith loses his temper with the maître d' and calls even more attention to them as the other guests pass by, presenting their invitations and entering the dining room." Kabe's golden voice trumpeted the ending.

The rest of us sat in silence, honoring Java's brilliance.

She added, slowly, "I almost feel sorry for them."

Even though I did not want to admit it, I knew what she meant.

"Will Mr. and Mrs. Savolainen go along with it?" Kabe asked. "That is the question."

"After all Ilmi Marianna and her family have been through, can you imagine them not?"

All of us hoped Eino was right.

None of us knew exactly how right he was.

For when we approached Mr. Savolainen and presented our plan one evening while Mrs. Savolainen and Ma were inside drinking coffee and discussing patterns and Mrs. Laitinen was reading to Lil, he stroked his chin and scratched his forehead, took off his glasses and polished them, and finally sat down on the front porch stairs where the rest of us always perched, considering.

We waited, holding our breaths.

"There is something that Ilmi Marianna does not know which affects my feeling about your plan." Clearly trying to decide whether or not to tell us what I did not know, he reached out a hand and took hold of mine. Kabe and Eino and Fatso leaned forward protectively. Java put her arm around me. We sensed something bad

233

It was.

"The reason John Porthan acted so willingly as emissary for the gypsies in the handling of Mr. Smith and Mrs. Juola," Mr. Savolainen began slowly, "is something the grandfather told him the night they brought the two back to Ely and left them in the rowboat by the boathouses. They did not really just leave a note, as was the implication. One of The Family sought out John Porthan, told him . . . the whole story . . . and enlisted his aid."

"The whole story?" I queried. I thought we knew the whole story.

Mr. Savolainen stopped for a while, looking down on my hand and patting it gently. "We left out one part. For many reasons, it did not seem . . . as if it would be of any help . . . in resolving the situation but would only create more . . . ill will. But perhaps," he shook his head, "perhaps John Porthan and I were wrong. Perhaps you have a right to know."

He looked at me with such compassion that I almost said he need not tell me after all. But I didn't. Instead I turned my hand so I was holding his in my clasp as I had been held in his. It seemed to help.

"What I—we—did not want you to know . . . what the grandfather told us . . . was that Mr. Smith and Mrs. Juola had made contact with the gypsies themselves . . . before and after the young Mr. Smith died . . . before the gypsies came back to Ely and again while you were ill." He stopped, wiped his forehead with a fresh white handkerchief, released my hand, then changed his mind and drew me close in a fatherly half-embrace. "Mr. Smith and Mrs. Juola wanted the gypsies . . . offered them money to . . ."

He did not have to continue.

The words poured out from Kabe and Fatso and Eino: "They wanted the gypsies to take her away?"

Mr. Savolainen nodded.

"To hurt her?"

He nodded again. "And eventually, me, too."

All five looked at me, torn. It was clear that they wanted to enact vengeance—swords or knives swam visibly in their eyes—and at the same time to give me . . . what was it? Consolation? Support?

At the thought of Mr. Savolainen's being hurt, I at first had turned white. But suddenly I remembered the whole situation, and at that moment I knew that I really was well and truly well. Instead of crying or collapsing, I actually grinned. "So they made contact with the gypsies to see if the gypsies could get rid of us? of me? The gypsies! How droll!"

I laughed.

Mr. Savolainen looked at me in astonishment for a moment and then grinned back at me, enormously, immensely relieved, and finally he laughed, too, and we sat there, the two of us, chortling until tears ran down our cheeks, and we collapsed completely against the stairs and each other. My tears were a weird mixture of pleasure and pain. "The gypsies? How droll!" I repeated.

Then, of course, we had to tell Eino and Kabe and Fatso and Java the whole story of the gypsies' help and kindness. While I talked, Mr. Savolainen loaded us into his big car without even asking permission and drove us to Virginia and treated us to double-decker chocolate ice cream cones.

His only concern was his wife's kindness. "Even given the full story, will she agree?" he wondered aloud as we drove back.

Ice cream cones in hand, all six of us approached her. The proposal did give her pause, and we could see her mind reflecting upon all of its ramifications. But in the end, given the full story, she capitulated.

And so it was that Mr. and Mrs. Savolainen sold their store in Ely to the Stembers and planned the party of the century to be held at the Forest Hotel in Ely less than one month from the night Java hatched the plan. Mr. and Mrs. Savolainen added only one condition. We were to attend the party. All of us. Ma and Lil and I and Eino and Kabe and Fatso and Java.

When Ma heard the whole story, at first she cried and then, taking a deep breath, she threw herself into her contribution to the plan—the making of new dresses for Mrs. Savolainen and Mrs. Laitinen and herself, for Lil and me, and for Java, who was given special permission to extend her stay in honor of the occasion.

Mr. Vanucci and Mr. Spina and Mr. Salin vied with each other to see whose son would be decked out most elegantly, and David Schibel of Virginia's Palace Clothing Store did them all proud.

The Savolainens insisted on paying for the material for our dresses and for the necessary accouterments and for our train fare and the hotel expenses, although it took awhile to convince Ma. Finally she agreed but only, she insisted, if she could provide Mrs. Savolainen's dress without cost. It was to be a masterpiece of simplicity, made of an elegant black satin so rich and lustrous my fingers ached just to touch the material. Even before the dress was cut and sewn, the fabric, draped becomingly around Mrs. Savolainen, made her look as willowy and slender and aristocratic as any queen.

Mr. Savolainen decreed pearls for the dress and ordered her a full set—matching choker, broach, ring, bracelet, and earbobs set in antique silver.

Although Ma had initially planned to wear black, for she considered us still in mourning, all of us begged her to agree to half-mourning. Mrs. Savolainen found a bolt of gray chiffon that floated around Ma in a heavenly haze. Once she saw it, her arguments ceased.

Java and Lil and I were, of course, relegated to the usual white lawn. But Ma made much of our dresses, too, dropping the hems to tea length and curving the necklines down just enough to show off the gold chains with heart lockets which Mr. Savolainen afterward insisted we keep as momentoes, though initially he had suggested only that we borrow them for the evening.

Mrs. Savolainen, bless her kind heart, bought all of us silk hose, Ma's like a spider's web of gray, ours white, of course, but filmy soft. And all three of us were fitted for black patent leather Mary Jane's, early Christmas gifts, Ma said and smiled a bit tearfully, in Uncle Charles' memory.

Even Mrs. Laitinen consented to wear the elegant creation Ma designed for her—a heavy maroon taffeta with high, tight neck, long fitted sleeves, a close lowered waist, and a skirt that fell smoothly in front but extended into a small train as she walked. And oh, my, walk she did, up and down the kitchen, admiring the train every time Ma did a fitting.

The sewing, the planning, the packing, and the traveling—in the first class coach of the train—consumed our every waking moment with consultations held daily as the Savolainens executed their share, the major share, of the steps toward the ultimate denouement.

They made me feel as if the entire plan suited them to perfection, as if the decision to spend what seemed like a king's ransom on a party meant nothing at all, as if the selling of the store and the giving of the party constituted mere stage dressing for our joint and unified ultimate objective. Restitution. Mrs. Savolainen defined it as "the final restoration of all things and persons into harmony with God's will." She could never do anything cruel.

"But," she told us as the plans progressed, "after much reflection upon the accounts Mr. Savolainen has given of the events that transpired in Ely, I do believe that both Mrs. Juola and Mr. Smith have lost contact with God's will. Moreover," she mused, "it was the sins of pride and greed that caused the archangel Lucifer to fall from God's grace. It is the charge of all Christian people to learn from Lucifer's misjudgments."

There was a long pause. We waited. Mrs. Savolainen rarely addressed us, and when she did, we listened.

"Of course, it is not for us to presume upon God's ultimate judgment of Mrs. Juola's and Mr. Smith's wrongdoing. Still . . . there is such a thing as an earthly atonement. And," she concluded with a hopeful smile, "who knows? They may find that this experience causes them to evaluate their personal lives so that they grow again into harmony with the divine."

"Fat chance," whispered Fatso. But he made sure she didn't hear.

Settled into a suite at the Forest Hotel well in advance of the hour of the party, with ample time allowed for Ma to rest, Fatso and Kabe and Java and I—and Mr. Savolainen—took one last, far more pragmatic, look at our plan, reviewing the sequence of events one last time.

The messengers and the engraved invitations were at the ready.

We were urged to eat, but the food stuck in our throats. We were ordered to bathe, and that we did with a sumptuous lack of concern for amounts of hot water. And finally, we were dressed, all of us as elegantly as any of the gentlemen and ladies on the pages of Sears & Roebuck or even the Chicago Mail Order Catalog. I wished the girl of the brown eyes and the mother and father could have seen us.

Ma managed to create soft, high pompadours for all three of the ladies, allowing some tendrils of curls around their faces, even her own. For once, Java's curls were allowed to bounce free, though a satin bow held the front and sides high on her head. Lil's golden fuzz refused to hold a bow, but Ma brushed it until it glowed. And my thick black mane had been set, wet, into rag curls, which were kept on for a full day, ugly as they were, no matter the teasing I received, until the curls were set so firmly that no amount of excitement could release them, except for the ones that escaped from my own big white satin bow, which sat like a bridal crown on my head.

Truly, when evening finally arrived, we felt as refined and magnificent as royal consorts, worthy of holding a scepter rather than a sword.

Mr. Savolainen had even tried to convince Pa to come from the lumber camp to escort Ma. Of course that part of the plan didn't fly. Otherwise everything fell into place just as Java had said it would, with one and only one major revision in the course of events, thanks to the nature of Mrs. Juola.

Thus we took our places that night in mid-September in the flower bedecked lobby of the Forest Hotel in Ely, Ma and the three of us girls seated primly in a row of straight-backed chairs positioned along the wall on the lobby side of the double doors leading into the dining room.

From there emanated the melodies of a string ensemble, members of the Duluth Symphony Orchestra, hired to provide dinner music and accompany the dancing. From there emanated the scents not only of hothouse flowers, for the rooms were filled with roses, but the tempting smells of turkey and ham and freshly baked bread and all kinds of incredible treats for which we did not know the names. But we would, oh, we would, as soon as this drama played itself out.

I had never doubted that it would, never, that is, until Ma and Java and Lil and I were seated on those mahogany chairs with their soft maroon leather cushions, the boys ranged behind us, one to a chair, in positions of attention, standing straight, their hands clasped behind their backs.

Then, I panicked. Around us swirled the perfumed scents and rustling movements of silks and satins and taffetas and chiffons. The fiery highlights of jewels—rubies and diamonds and emeralds and pearls—flashed like colored fireflies in the soft candlelight. Although the Forest Hotel managers were proud of their new electric lighting system, Mrs. Savolainen had insisted upon candles. Candelabra banked every table, serpentine stands lined the walls, tapers framed the flower arrangements.

Studying the men, bowing and escorting their wives with a hand on the elbow or supporting them on crooked arms, I understood for the first time why the evening dance club in Virginia was called the Penguin Club, though that mundane animal was hardly adequate to epitomize the glory and the power emanating from this white on black masculinity.

Even Fatso and Eino and Kabe were transformed, I had to admit, though Java had been warned by Mrs. Spina to remind Fatso not to stick his finger between his neck and his collar and Eino's normal florid complexion had blanched absolutely white so worried was he that he would do something wrong. Kabe, standing behind Lil and teasing her unmercifully until we warned him not to get her too riled up, looked absolutely natural and comfortable, of course, the rented tuxedo fitting him as if it had been tailor-made, his curly hair rising in a Byronic wave, wearing even his white gloves as if to the manner born.

To a casual spectator, to the guests flowing by, we no doubt looked as if we too belonged, as if we too considered all of this splendor simply mundane, another of those evening events to be taken in stride.

Ma praised us, her voice barely audible.

I blanched. "What if the same thing is true of our enemies? What if, instead of reacting as we think they will, Mr. Smith and Mrs. Juola rise to the occasion just as we are rising to the occasion and behave like a true gentleman and lady? What if instead of our serving as avenging angels, "messengers of vengeance and pursuit," so to speak, as Milton put it, we become willynilly the keepers of the golden key, having opened as it were the door to paradise? What if after tonight the two find themselves accepted by the others here, the very ones whose world they have sought to enter?" Of course, the questions never raised themselves quite that lucidly, but those were the thoughts in my mind.

"Or . . . what if they somehow heard about the invitations . . . and decided not to take a chance on coming? Or . . . worst of all . . . what if somehow they were able to get their hands on an invitation and we have to watch them breeze past us and into the dining room leaving us to watch their triumph?" To tell the truth, I put nothing past their skill with machinations. They had, I knew, just narrowly escaped success in the commission of not just two but three, perhaps four, major felonies—not only some degree of murder and grand larceny but also kidnapping, perhaps with intent to kill.

I twisted my dance program until it curled, shedding all of its glitter on my gloves and my skirt.

Then Java stopped breathing. Lil froze into a small white corpse. The three bodies behind me poised absolutely motionless. And Ma's breath drew in with a gasping muted sound, for Mr. Smith and Mrs. Juola had entered through the Chapman Street doors, just a bit late, of course, but fashionably so.

Some of the other guests were already passing into the dining room. Because the receiving line was making slow headway past the Savolainens and the Stembers, however, the majority of the guests were still sipping champagne and making polite conversation and smiling and greeting each other in the lobby.

Mr. Smith and Mrs. Juola got as far as the middle of the room before we saw them stop and focus their attention upon the gold-rimmed creamy embossed invitations held prominently in the gentlemen's hands. The invitations had been for couples—either Mr. and Mrs. or Someone and Guest. They were mere paper, of course, but paper as valuable as the gems with which the women were bedecked, for those pieces of paper symbolized inclusion, acceptance, position, and prominence. Like golden keys, they epitomized and underscored each person's position in the social milieu of northern Minnesota society, particularly northern Minnesota Finnish society. Like the rich layer rising atop the milk, these people were the *kerma kerros*, the *crème de la crème*, the best, and they knew it.

Mr. Smith and Mrs. Juola were too quick not to respond immediately. We saw them turn to each other, Mrs. Juola's eyebrows raised, her glance pointedly marking the men's gloved hands and what they held.

At first, we were sure we had failed, for they seemed to handle the situation well. Mrs. Juola slipped back as if looking for the ladies' room to leave her light wrap and refresh herself. Mr. Smith approached the maître d'hotel with an air of confidence.

"Where are we to pick up our invitations?" he asked. We could see his lips form the question.

The maître d', well and truly instructed and notified of his role in the proceedings, looked appropriately blank, shook his head, waved Mr. Smith off firmly but gently, accepted an invitation proffered by another guest, noted the inscribed names, turned, and read them aloud to the massed group in the dining room as the couple paused at the doorway to be introduced and then continued their forward movement toward the receiving line.

It was done elegantly. The maître d', imported from Duluth's Spaulding Hotel and even more aware of his power and circumstance than the gentlemen guests, as elegantly garbed as they, contributed an appropriate air of hauteur to his task. No gentleman's gentleman, no royal butler, no major domo could have announced the names with more respectful emphasis. He even managed a hint of a British accent.

Each couple he introduced stood between the open double doors to the dining room in full view of the attentive assemblage. The lady curtsied gracefully, the gentleman bowed, they moved forward, and another couple took their place.

Mr. Smith quickly backed away and hurried toward the other end of the lobby, where he shook his head at Mrs. Juola, looking suddenly not at all powerful and confident but very ill at ease.

Mrs. Juola could have saved the situation, then, by simply bowing out with good grace. She could have made a pretense of a tear in her dress or a fit of weakness or the remembrance of an important item which caused them to leave unobtrusively.

Instead, she lost it.

Mr. Smith had drawn some attention merely by the speed of his passing, for he had jostled some couples in his hurry. But it was she who brought to life the essential difference between what it means to be a lady and what it means to be a lady of the night.

When she turned away from Mr. Smith toward us, I think she may have guessed or at least caught a glimmer of the reality of the situation. The look on her face suggested that she definitely recognized me. For all her faults, she was not lacking in intelligence. The expression on my face may have made it very clear that this public potential for humiliation had not occurred accidentally.

Good manners and grace could still have prevailed. They did not.

Perhaps she was too angry, perhaps too disappointed to contain herself. Perhaps . . . I studied the high color on her face, the slight waver in her step . . . there may have been another contributing cause. Or perhaps she really was intrinsically a tramp.

Ma always preached to Lil and me that each time we committed an act of cruelty or evil or wrongdoing, no matter how small, we destroyed a part of that which was good in us just as each time we did something kind or good, we increased that part of us which was good.

Every single time we did something wrong, she warned us to beware: "It all happens little bit by little bit," she said, "but the bits eventually grow together so that we ourselves create during our lifetimes, through our actions and our conscious and unconscious decisions, what we ultimately are as human beings." I could recite the lecture verbatim. She always ended it the same way: "Like Marley's ghost, during our lives, we form our own chains."

Mrs. Juola's chains pulled her down. She threw her gold beaded evening bag onto the carpeted floor and pulled off her corsage and threw it down, too. It was impossible not to notice because at the same time, she began swearing. Finnish words. But no one had to be Finnish to understand their meaning. And since there aren't an awful lot of ways to swear in Finnish, she pretty quickly ran the full gamut before switching to English.

"*Saatana . . . saatana . . . .* God damn upper class shits" was the general tone. "Think you're too God damn good for ordinary people like us. Think you can jerk us around and invite us and then uninvite us. Well, I'll show you!" She headed off toward the dining room, obviously bent upon wreaking havoc with the Savolainens, with Mr. Smith behind her trying to remonstrate and stop her at the same time.

Even though Ma and Lil and Java and I stood up, at first it was a little hard to see because the milling crowd shifted like a beehive disturbed. Then a path opened down the center of the lobby, and the boys stepped forward to make way for us to move to the edge of that path.

By the time Mrs. Juola passed us, she had pulled off her jewelry—her rings and a necklace, a bracelet, even a tiara, for she had done herself up to the nine's—and she was throwing them back toward Mr. Smith and swearing at him to leave her alone. Then she saw me and swore at me and at my phalanx of family or supporters, and she shook her fist and yelled that she'd get me if it was the last thing she'd ever do.

Eino told me later in confidence that he thought she had fortified herself pretty strongly with liquid spirits, maybe trying to build herself up for the second when they entered the lobby or maybe to celebrate this moment of what she had expected to be their ascension into society.

Whatever the cause, those actions were the last things she ever did, as far as society was concerned. Not that the *kerma kerros* did not know what it was like to lose their tempers. Not that they did not know people who had had too much to drink.

But That Woman had stepped beyond the pale, for she had done both not only in public but at a time and in a place where such actions were universally condemned. Mr. and Mrs. Savolainen were held in high repute not only by ordinary people like us but by everyone with whom they came in contact, high and low alike. It was not only we who had enjoyed their kindness and generosity or who had received their gifts of friendship and warmth. Had they been poor, they would still have been popular. Because they were rich, they were revered. No one ever said or did anything to besmirch their reputations. They were considered, not only then but for as long as they lived, completely above reproach.

In vilifying them, Mrs. Juola had condemned herself forever to the outside of a closed and locked door. Never need she expect to be invited by anyone who mattered at all to any event that mattered at all.

I am sure that none of the society people ever dreamed that the events of that night were anything but an unfortunate and embarrassing accident, a contre-temps. But that night the Savolainens too were human. They too, at least that one time, stood flat on the firm surface of Mother Earth rather than on the rarified regions of heavenly beatitude. They had sought and attained retribution.

Mrs. Juola got her just deserts, for it was against her coarseness rather than against the lack of an invitation that the Finnish high society of Duluth and Virginia and Ely erected an impassible barrier, joining together to isolate her as if she had not been there.

The maître d' hardly paused in his pronouncements. The receiving line continued. The music played. The guests reformed their groups.

Mr. Smith dragged Mrs. Juola out by her arm.

Had she been the lady she professed herself to be, the whole incident could have worked against us. She could have foiled our plan. Latent sympathy had lain inchoate there, ready to flower into apology and admission and inclusion.

Even I, for a brief second, had felt the sympathy that had emanated toward the invitation-less couple. But, as Ma reminded me later when I felt some qualms of conscience, in the end Mrs. Juola had brought about her own downfall. It takes more than money and clothes and jewelry to make a lady, Ma often said. That night she was once again proved right.

When the lobby door closed behind them, there was only a brief pause in the evening's activities. Mr. and Mrs. Savolainen excused themselves from the receiving line as if nothing of note had occurred—for how could they have known, the other guests obviously surmised, when they were in the dining room—and came themselves to usher us in. Mrs. Savolainen took Eino's arm; Mr. Savolainen took mine. Fatso escorted Java on one arm and Lil on the other. Kabe bowed before Ma and kissed her hand as if she were a queen.

In front of the most important people in northern Minnesota society, we were personally escorted to the doorway of the dining room, where the maître d' introduced us by name and in order: Miss Lillian Lydia Brosi and Miss Sieva Linden escorted by Mr. Charlemagne Caesar Spina (No wonder he lets us call him Fatso, I thought.). Mrs. Knute Pietari Brosi escorted by Mr. Diodado Carmen Joseph Vanucci. Mrs. Alexander Savolainen escorted by Mr. Eino Walfred Salin. And finally, when the room was completely quiet, even the string ensemble having stilled, "Miss Marion Elmi Brosi escorted by Mr. Alexander Savolainen."

Suddenly, perhaps at an imperceptible signal I had not caught, everyone began to clap.

Mr. Savolainen led me to the center of the receiving line where, with him on one side and Mrs. Savolainen on the other, I was further introduced to everyone as their sometime ward, their dear and special friend.

243

I curtsied and smiled and curtsied some more. Ma's lessons in deportment stood me in good stead that night. But I tried hard to keep at least one foot firmly on the floor every minute. Instead of pride, I honestly experienced only a kind of humbling sense of gratitude and relief. I had not done any of this alone. Had it not been for the kids in Kinney and the kindness of the gypsies and John Porthan and Jaako and the Savolainens and Mrs. Laitinen and yes, even the Stembers, none of this could ever have come about.

It had taken many months and much pain, but as that night passed by in a dream with us eating and dancing and making polite conversation, I finally and at last grasped the meaning of Lady Moon's message.

"Whom are you loving?" the people of the world had asked.

"All who love me" was the heartfelt response. It had been hers; it now was mine.

I looked around me that night, and I counted my blessings. Ma and Lil. Mr. and Mrs. Savolainen. Mrs. Laitinen. Kabe and Eino and Fatso and Java. John Porthan, who asked me to dance the first waltz. Jaako, who toasted me with wise, unseeing eyes.

And, though they had been the only ones to refuse the invitation, "with regret," they said, in my heart were the grandfather and my "mother" and "father" and the girl of the brown eyes.

And Uncle Charles, too.

For once, my vocabulary failed me. There were no words to say how much I owed them. How much I loved them.

"And they love me," I knew it to be true. "And they love me."

Epilogue

Looking back, I wish I could say that the days and weeks and years to follow were lived happily ever after, but they were not.

We did move to Zim that fall, although not to the paradise Uncle Charles had chosen. We bought what Ma felt we could afford with the monthly restitution money, a two-room shack we called "Happy Corner," not far from the other families who moved there from their rented homes in Kinney. It was big enough for the three of us, Ma and Lil and me.

Baby Teddy—born too soon—lived each night in our prayers.

Pa came back once in a while, though he never did settle down until Mesaba Park hired him as caretaker. There he remained until his death with his poetry and his fiddle and his chipmunks and his dog Baby, much happier than he had ever been with us.

Even though I had started school three years late, I finished eighth grade with my class, the top student yet. Mr. George Baccalyer, deputy superintendent of the St. Louis County School System, spoke at our graduation. "Marion Elmi" Brosi gave the valedictory address entitled "The Importance of a Rural Education." Not even Ma attended the graduation. I walked three miles home in the dark that night alone, tore up my speech and dropped the pieces into the creek.

I never saw any of the gypsies again. They were, in fact, made so unwelcome in northern Minnesota that their vardos, finding smoother trails to follow, disappeared not only from the winter encampments in the meadows but from the roadsides and the fields and the towns. But, since they were able to cross the bridge between the world of the Rom and the world of the gorgios with ease, I have never ceased looking for them.

I wish I could say that I now practice humility, but I still fall down sometimes when pride saws off the ladder.

I also have to work hard every day of my life to balance my dreams with reality, for Pa still lives within me. So does Ma. The good that was in them will live forever as will Baby Teddy and Uncle Charles and Mr. and Mrs. Savolainen and the grandfather, always and forever in my prayers.

I still grieve some for young Mr. Smith, who will never grow old. When he died, with him died some part of my own youth, and I entered that strange and nebulous world of adulthood considerably before I was ready for it or it for me.

In spite of all the pain, however, I gained immeasureably during those months of my eleventh year. During the summer that I lived the tale of my two cities, Kinney and Ely, Minnesota, I found that strength of will and purpose, when combined with honesty and honor and love, can accomplish almost any end.

It was a powerful and frightening lesson.